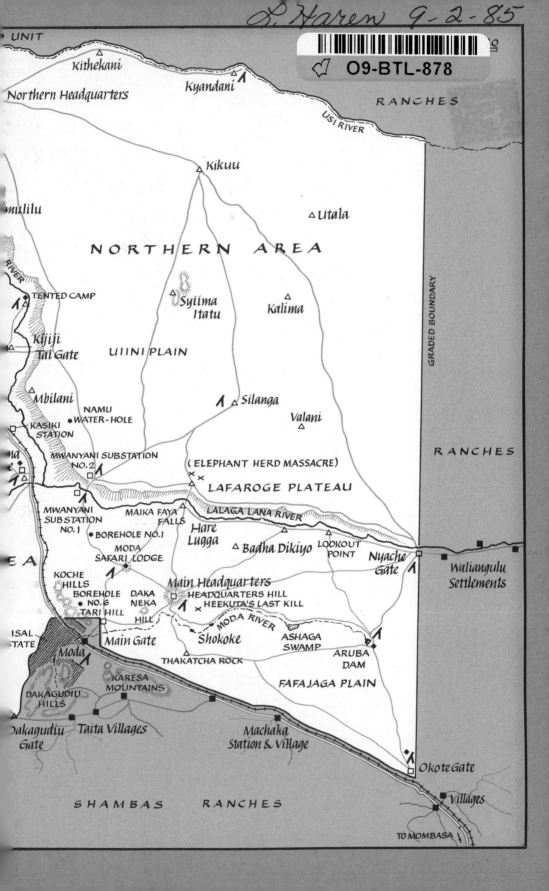

KEEPERS
OF
THE
KINGDOM

A Novel by
Glennita Miller

SIMON AND SCHUSTER
NEW YORK

This novel is a work of fiction. Names, characters, places, and incidents are either the product of the author's imagination or used fictitiously. Any resemblance to actual events or locales or persons, living or dead, is entirely coincidental.

COPYRIGHT © 1982 BY GLENNITA MILLER
ALL RIGHTS RESERVED
INCLUDING THE RIGHT OF REPRODUCTION
IN WHOLE OR IN PART IN ANY FORM
PUBLISHED BY SIMON AND SCHUSTER
A DIVISION OF GULF & WESTERN CORPORATION
SIMON & SCHUSTER BUILDING
ROCKEFELLER CENTER
1230 AVENUE OF THE AMERICAS
NEW YORK, NEW YORK 10020
SIMON AND SCHUSTER AND COLOPHON ARE TRADEMARKS OF
SIMON & SCHUSTER

DESIGNED BY GWEN TOWNSEND
MANUFACTURED IN THE UNITED STATES OF AMERICA

1 3 5 7 9 10 8 6 4 2

LIBRARY OF CONGRESS CATALOGING IN PUBLICATION DATA

MILLER, GLENNITA, DATE.
KEEPERS OF THE KINGDOM.

I. TITLE.
PS3563.I3784K4   1982   813'.54   82–16788
ISBN 0–671–42523–4

The excerpt in Chapter 14 is from A NEW EARTH *by Elspeth Huxley. Reprinted by permission.*

To my son, Jonathan,
who fell in love with
Africa, her people, and
her animals.

And for my father, Glenn,
who would have if he
had lived.

CONTENTS

CONTENTS

VII · SATURDAY

VIII · SUNDAY

KEEPERS
OF
THE
KINGDOM

I · PROLOGUE

CHAPTER ONE

Sunday Night

S HE WAS TIRED. The sun had finally gone down, and the evening breeze had risen, to ease her agony as she continued to plod along the well-beaten trail toward the water that still lay far ahead.

It was dry, very dry, and the flat land stretched for miles on either side of the track she followed. A few bushes and trees stood scattered over the land in defiance of the failure of the rains, and as she passed they reached out with dry bony branches to scrape and rattle over her hide.

She glanced down at the small son who stumbled along beside her and reached out to caress his head with her trunk. He was nearly exhausted, and instinctively she slowed her pace to enable him to keep up with her own longer stride which had been forcing him to run along beside her, with a tripping, tumbling gait that now threatened to succumb to the effects of hunger, thirst and weariness.

Stopping for a moment to allow him a brief rest, she gathered him to her, to feel his labored panting against her body, while she glanced over his head to study the moonlit landscape in search of movement. The dried-out branches of the nearby trees clattered in the wind, and she heard the low chuckling churr of a nocturnal bird.

Tonight the moon would be high and full, and so the danger was great, but there was no choice for her: she had to have water. They both had to have water. They'd had none for two days now, and her mouth and throat were parched with want.

Wearily she stepped out again and felt her calf obediently fall into place beside and slightly behind her. On they moved through the bush toward one of the few water holes that retained the remnants of moisture, collected many months ago before the rains had failed.

The moon was climbing now, and bright enough to cast her shadow in sharp relief on the ground beside her. She knew this well-beaten track; she'd been coming to this place with her family throughout her life, as had the generations before her, because it was known and remembered as one of the few watering places that would not dry out when the rains didn't come. But if she knew of this, then so did the predators. So she continued to move slowly and watch carefully.

It wasn't far now; just to the top of that rise and then down the other side to where the small shriveled pool lay nestled against the rocks of a kopje. She dragged herself up the incline with a weariness she'd not felt before. But then, the first time had been when she was the age of the little one who now trudged beside her. It had been long ago when she had first followed blindly beside her own mother in search of water in a land that knew great droughts repeatedly in the course of a lifetime. She herself had known many such times during her nearly fifty years of life, and as she had grown older, and finally old, she had led her growing family here often when the need arose. Now she had led him here, the last in a succession of offspring and all that remained of the large family she'd once had.

Reaching the top of the rise, she stopped in the concealing shadow of an acacia tree and studied the area before her. To the side lay the small spring-fed pool, now shrunken to a pitiful remnant of itself and containing the last muddy dregs of water surrounded by the cracked scabs of mud which indicated its former size. Nothing moved, and no sound was heard except the shrill chirrup of the insects of the night. She waited and watched for any sign of an enemy.

Suddenly the little one made a soft plaintive sound deep in his throat and lurched forward. He'd roused himself from his exhaustion and had become aware of the water below. Instantly she moved out after him, down the small hill and across the dried and fractured mud to the thick, scummy water, where she stopped and stood a moment beside the youngster, who had waded knee-deep to gulp and guzzle.

Everything remained quiet and motionless. Reassured, she stepped forward and felt the warm water cover her tough, callused feet, but as she began to lower her head, she sensed, rather than consciously heard, the faint thrum of the flying projectile, just before she felt it bury itself deep in her side.

With a high, harsh scream of pain and terror she spun about.

Blindly and without reason she began to run; her instincts shrilled their demand for distance, for her to flee.

As she crashed through the bush, her first conscious thought stabbed at her brain: her little one. She halted, turned, and saw him behind, struggling through the thornbush, trying to keep up. Gaining her side, he whimpered in fear, and she reached out again to draw him to her for a moment before turning to plunge on, with him close beside her. Her thirst was momentarily forgotten in her desire to place distance between herself and the attacker.

A frantic bewilderment flickered across her consciousness. Who? Where was he hidden? Why? The wonder died without having been answered. There were no answers. It just was.

The moon continued its climb into the star-flecked sky as they moved rapidly away from the water into the trackless dry bush country. She soon became aware of her thirst again, her hunger, and now something else: it was becoming difficult to breathe.

Her panic controlled now, she slowed to a walk and felt the pain low on her left side, just below the ribs. Stopping for a moment, she felt at her side; nothing was there but a hole that ran blood. Turning back to face in the direction from which they'd run, she searched, but nothing followed. Straining all her senses, she waited and watched. The light breeze moved silently, the dry bush trembled, the insects buzzed softly, and several bats glided sound-lessly past. The little one beside her sagged against her legs and slowly slipped down to huddle at her feet. Still she stood and waited. Her breath continued to come in quick shallow jerks, and an acute feeling of sickness washed over her and left a stabbing pain in her stomach to join the hurt in her side. Still nothing followed.

Turning to her offspring, she pulled him up, gathered him to her, and held him against her strong legs. That last pounding run had taken what little remained of his strength. She stood holding him for several long minutes as she made low, soft sounds in her throat to comfort him while she rocked him against her. She felt his strength returning, and she took a step forward, then another. He wobbled unsteadily along beside her. Moving again, but now slowly, she realized that the parched feeling had gone. Her mouth and tongue felt wet; she swallowed once and then again; the saliva washed down her dried throat to soothe the rasping thirst. The warm wet collected at the corners of her mouth and ran over her lower lip; she swallowed again thirstily.

The moon was risen high now, and their shadows had finally disappeared. A lion roared distantly, and ahead a solitary giraffe bull watched their approach without interest as they plodded on by.

Her heart was beating slowly now, but strongly loud in her ears as her breath came light and fast. And the pain high in her stomach remained and grew in intensity.

She stopped again; she felt lightheaded, and the moonlit landscape reeled about her for a moment before winding to a stop. She lurched forward as the first cramp clutched at her lower stomach and then settled into a series of twisting contractions. Slowly she drove herself on through the thick tangle of bush, penetrating it with greater difficulty now as she became aware of a growing weakness. The little one plodded at her side, head down and unaware of her deterioration. Occasionally he lurched against her, unknowingly smearing her blood across his shoulder.

The realization came slowly, a steadily growing awareness of danger as she felt, rather than saw or heard, a presence near her. She stopped and turned. Straining to focus and direct her failing senses, she tipped back her head and studied each tree and clump of dried bush. Her blurring eyes swept the area as her ears strained to hear the slightest sound of a displaced rock, a broken twig, the rasp of a body pushing through the thornbush. She struggled to sense the presence of one who might be following, and as she did so she felt the prickling creep of fear steal over her.

She heard nothing, saw nothing, smelled nothing, but something was there. Something was coming after them, coming near. The fear grew in intensity and crept up along her back and neck before rushing in a cold tingle over her head and face. She whirled about and propelled her failing legs on. The little one followed closely without a sound, without question. She tried again to break into a run, but the effort resulted only in a tottering shuffle that brought her heartbeat pounding in her ears. She stumbled and fell to her knees, where she remained, dazed and confused. With great effort she shook her head to clear it. Her son stood uncertainly before her; he became two and then wavered, and as she watched, he slid sharply into focus and was one again. He reached out and touched her face, and her fear returned. She had to get him away. It was coming closer.

She regained her feet and stood weak and trembling for a moment with him gathered close to her churning stomach. Taking a tottering step, she swayed and forced herself on as the twisting and writhing in her bowels continued, now accompanied by the excrement that began to run unheeded down her legs.

Her steps wavered as she wound slowly and without reason or direction through the bush, leaving behind a noxious trail. Staggering on blindly, she felt and heard nothing but the drumming of her heartbeat. It thrummed once, then paused a moment; gave three rapid beats; then paused for a longer moment before beating twice slowly, in marked contrast to her quick, panting breath. Her mouth was dry again; sticky, gummy dry, and her swallow caught in her throat as the first sharp pain exploded in her chest.

She stood stunned; her trembling legs began to buckle beneath her, and she sank to her knees, where she remained a moment before slipping down onto her side on the warm earth. She lay silent, conscious only of the fluttering in her chest and the searing pain that hovered near it. Her breath was beginning to slow now; the dreadful panting was over. She lay unmoving and concentrated on the pain that continued to stab at the fluttering in her chest. Dimly she became aware of her offspring as he crept close to nuzzle at her. His presence recalled the fear, but the fear of what was lost to her now.

Still she knew she had to go, had to get her little one away. Her head came up. With incredible determination she forced herself into a sitting position and tried desperately to get to her feet. Willing her legs to function, she dug her feet into the soft soil and heaved upward until she began to rise. The trembling increased to a quivering palsy that shook every limb until she collapsed under her own weight. Her feet scrabbled at the earth as she tried again; legs bent, feet dug in, she heaved and twisted to pull herself up beside her youngster. The name of her fear returned to flicker across her consciousness as she dimly sensed that it was coming closer, and her terror for her son gave her the strength for one last attempt that brought her to her knees, and finally, with a jerk, to her feet, where she stood shaking for one triumphant moment. Then, inevitably, finally, she crashed to the ground.

She lay on her side, unaware of the quivering spasms that shook her entire body. There was no sound except for her agonized gasps for air. After a time she became aware of the little one who stood beside her, but her glazed eyes couldn't see him very well. She was unaware of the dark, slender figure that crept soundlessly from the bush toward her.

She heard nothing, felt nothing. Her eyes sought her son and fixed themselves on him, and the moon beyond his head. She felt cold, very cold, but she didn't feel the last voiding of her bladder and bowels. All she saw was her son's head outlined against the stars beside the moon as the periphery of her vision began to close in and become smaller. The sky began to shrink, and blackness gradually filled the outer edges of her sight. Smaller and smaller the world she saw became, until only the outline of her son's head and the moon remained.

17

Slowly and relentlessly her peripheral vision crept over her son, and the darkness advanced to obliterate him, until only the bright cold moon remained, to steadily become smaller and smaller until it was only a bright pinprick. She didn't see the tall figure advancing to stand over her, or hear her son's first shrill screams of terror. All she knew was that the twinkling yellow point of light winked out, leaving nothing but the dark.

II · MONDAY

CHAPTER TWO

Midmorning

I<small>T WAS ALREADY HOT</small>: ten thirty in the morning, and the sun had been up for five hours. Now it hung there, almost overhead, while the dry earth threw back a retained heat of its own. Parched, red laterine soil that hadn't tasted rain for months stretched away into infinity, broken only periodically by gray scrub. A few trees stood scattered about as if placed there as an afterthought; their barren limbs stretched leafless branches toward the sun in supplication as if to say, "Enough!"

The trees were not entirely without life, however. The birds crowded together there and waited with the patience of their species: huge, dark brown birds with long wings and small naked heads, armed with massive and efficient beaks well suited to their sinister occupation in life.

Warden David Karanja sat hunkered down on his heels and inhaled deeply on a cigarette while he grimly studied the lifeless carcass in front of him. The elephant was lying crumpled on her right side, her left foreleg bent and lying in a scuffled depression, as if, having fallen, she'd tried repeatedly to rise again. Her massive head lay surrounded by a halo of dark coagulating blood, while her one visible brown eye stared without sight at the sky through its thick fringe of three-inch-long black lashes. The front of her head had been grossly mutilated in the poacher's struggle to remove her ivory; the alveolar sockets were crushed and splintered. Her trunk had been hacked from her face and lay nearby with the remains of the long, slender tusk pulp, or nerve.

She appeared to be a senior adult cow and had probably been the matriarch of a herd; her huge, fanlike ears were tattered from years spent moving through thick bush, and the accumulating wrinkles around her mouth, eye, and neck were a sign of advanced age. After examining her lower mandible, he estimated her age at forty-five or fifty years. He shook his head sadly, sickened by the mindless waste caused by greed. What had been last night a magnificent and intelligent animal was this morning just ten thousand pounds of rotting flesh—and all for fifty pounds of ivory.

Poaching had reached epidemic proportions, and he could almost understand how a man could be tempted to go after one of the big bull elephants with their heavy ivory. But a cow? Whose tusks would be only a fourth the weight and value of those of a bull? A cow who had a yet-to-be-weaned calf at her side? Disgust set his mouth in a hard line. He had a personal vendetta against all poachers, but this one would be special. Very damn special.

As he watched his assistant warden cut the arrowhead free from under the cow's wrinkled gray hide, just below the rib cage on her left side, his thoughts were abruptly interrupted by a piercing squeal. As he glanced beyond the elephant cow's carcass, his face creased into a reluctant smile as he watched five of his Field Force Rangers scramble about and stumble into one another in the thick thornbush in their attempts to surround and subdue the small survivor—a tiny male elephant calf. He'd been found this morning standing bewildered and alone by the body of his mother when Unit 3 of the Field Force came to investigate the circling of the vultures overhead.

The calf had apparently been driven away from the side of the cow when the poacher caught up with them in the early hours of the morning, but after the removal of the cow's ivory and the departure of the poacher, he'd crept back to the only security he knew and had been found standing by his mother's head, patiently waiting for her to get up. David's smile faded as he reflected that he would have stoically stood there beside the carcass until death came from thirst; unless lions or possibly hyenas, drawn by the scent of the kill, got him first.

David took a moment to study the little calf who was now standing with his short, stocky legs braced in the circle of rangers, his tail tensely extended behind him. Slowly weaving his head from side to side with his ears outstretched in agitation, the youngster closely followed the movements of his would-be saviors with wide frightened eyes that stared suspiciously and fearfully out of the small face, whose ridiculously stubby little trunk was now curled under and back. David saw that he was a borderline case—three feet or so tall, about one year old; any smaller, any younger, and they were impossible to raise. Young elephants were extremely delicate and usually unable to tolerate anything except elephant's milk, but if they had begun to browse then there was a chance. Just.

David sighed and, after stubbing out the head of his cigarette on a nearby rock, stood up. He was a tall and lean man; his height belied his Gikuyu surname and offered proof of the Masai mother from whom he'd inherited his long, lanky frame, finely molded features and dark brown skin, not quite dark enough to be called black.

"Warden Karanja?" The voice behind him interrupted his thoughts, and he turned to see Assistant Warden Mohamed Agaran, extending the recovered six-inch-long arrowhead with its wooden shaft wrapped in a tuft of dried grass. He carefully took hold of the covered end and examined it with a feeling of unease; almost an intuition. There was no mistaking the distinctive old-fashioned workmanship; only one tribe used to make arrowheads like this—the Waliangulu, sometimes called the "Elephant People," who, as a hunting tribe existing solely on the wildlife, were the only people who'd been living in the area when it had been gazetted as Aruba National Park thirty years before.

Beneath the drying blood David recognized the black tarlike poison which had been applied to the arrowhead's foreshaft just prior to the hunt. There were several methods used by different tribes to extract the poisonous properties of various toxic trees and shrubs for the production of poison, but the hunting tribes in this part of Kenya invariably used one of three species of *Acocanthera* tree to produce an intensely toxic cardiac glycoside called *ouabain* which, when introduced into the bloodstream on the end of the arrowhead, caused death by overwhelming the muscular contractions of the heart, producing heart failure.

When fresh, the poison implanted by one well-placed arrowhead could kill an adult elephant within two hours. David glanced up at the elephant cow before him now and knew that she had been such a case. But the toxic properties of the poison diminished if it was not protected from the elements, or with age, and the potency deteriorated; if used then, the poison would fail to kill quickly. Death might not come until months later, due to the presence of the arrowhead in the flesh, starting infection and creating suppurating wounds which would leave the animal virtually rotting on its feet. This was even worse, and he knew he'd never be able to overcome the swift rush of murderous rage when he discovered yet another crippled and suffering elephant or rhino still clinging tenaciously to life as it decomposed in agony under the hot sun.

Still holding the grass-wrapped arrowhead, he turned to a nearby Field Force Ranger and said, *"Nipe kisu chako."*

The ranger immediately reached to his hip, and after slipping the requested knife from its sheath handed it handle first to the warden.

Murmuring *"Asante,"* David took the knife and carefully began to scrape away what little was left of the original thick coating of black poison from the thin four-inch-long wooden foreshaft below the barbed metal head until he exposed the delicate pattern carved into the wood. Two opposing spiral patterns had been carved down the length of the shaft, and each time the spirals crossed they formed an X.

The pattern seemed ominously familiar, and the premonition of trouble grew as something nagged at the back of his mind: a half-remembered conversation with his predecessor, the ailing Warden Nichols, whom he had replaced two years before. He knew he'd either seen or heard of this particular identification mark before, but he couldn't recall what it was. Turning to his assistant warden, he extended the shaft so that the crossed spiral pattern was visible. "What does this tell you?" he asked speculatively.

Mohamed looked up from his examination of the dead elephant. His instant recognition of the clan signature was significant. "The Woruwayu." He frowned as his eyes met David's, and he added, "The clan of *wayu*—the people of patience."

The words triggered David's memory, and he recalled Warden Nichols' long and frustrated account of an elusive Waliangulu hunter of the same clan who'd poached in the area on and off since its gazetting. In spite of Nichols' dogged determination to capture him, he'd been taken just once, only to escape immediately.

Turning to the arrow's head and using the point of the knife, David scraped away the blood and remnants of tissue until he revealed the X, centered between two slash marks filed into the metal head. After a moment's somber study of the hunter's signature, he knew his intuition had been right. He'd been shown an arrowhead like this two years ago. "He's back again," he said in a voice tinged with bitter resignation. Here was another problem to worsen the already critical conditions at Aruba.

The assistant warden responded with a string of obscenities in Turkana. Ten years of his career had been spent at Aruba. Ten years spent trying to take this one poacher. He'd never succeeded.

"Tell me what you know about him," David said, in the hope that

Mohamed's firsthand knowledge would prove more informative than his own memories of Nichols' conversation.

"We know very little," Mohamed replied regretfully. "His name is Heekuta Neko. In Waliangulu it means 'one born in the middle of the night,' the son of Neko—'the lion.' His name, his clan, and his personal identification marks on his arrowheads are about all we know, or ever knew, except for the fact that he always hunts alone, and he always takes the left side." Seeing David's puzzled expression, he explained, "The best Waliangulu hunters had a preferred side of the animal. Some men shot their prey on the right side, some took the left.

"Four or five times a year," Mohamed continued, "we'd find several elephant carcasses, all killed within a few days, and all with his arrowheads left behind. Then nothing for a couple of months before he'd suddenly return for a few more before disappearing again."

"But it's been two years since he was here last," David objected.

Mohamed shook his head mutely. He had no explanation for the inconsistency. Nor did he have any more information.

As David considered the few facts known about the Waliangulu, one thing became important: he'd been poaching at Aruba since its gazetting. Thirty years. He must have been close to twenty when he started, in order to have acquired the strength to draw the massive "big bow" of the Waliangulu elephant hunters. So he had to be around fifty now, old for one of his people. Glancing up at Mohamed, he said thoughtfully, "He's an *mzee* now. He must be slowing down. What do you think our chances are of getting him this time?"

Mohamed studied the warden's face; he knew what David wanted to hear, and it did not agree with the only answer he could give. He shook his head. "Not good," he answered carefully.

"Why not?"

"Because he doesn't make mistakes," Mohamed replied deliberately. "This isn't a *shamba* farmer. He isn't an out-of-work *kijana* from Nairobi who wants to make some fast money in ivory. He might have fifty years," he conceded, "but that's fifty years of experience and knowledge of the bush. He's the best hunter of a hunting tribe, and he's living as his people have always lived—by hunting elephants. As before, we'll find one of his kills, and even though we'll be right behind him . . ." He shook his head, glanced away, and concluded reflectively, "No, I don't think we'll get him. He won't let it happen. He never has."

David studied Mohamed's profile, disbelieving what he'd heard.

As head of the park's paramilitary anti-poaching Field Force, the Turkana assistant warden was the best man David had. He'd never known him to suggest that a thing couldn't be done; that any man couldn't be taken. What's going on here? he wondered.

Mohamed's dark eyes came up to meet David's probing study. Their gaze held, and David sensed the presence of something indefinable in the assistant warden's black eyes, just before they fell, shutting him out.

"He was within twenty to twenty-five feet of her when he placed that arrow," Mohamed said in an effort to explain a feeling he hadn't known he'd had until asked. "By moonlight," he added with a small smile as he wondered defensively: How many men, including Wardens, would approach within twenty feet of an elephant at night, even with a high-powered rifle? There would be only enough time to get off one round before the charging animal was on them; and if that one bullet missed the difficult brain shot that could drop an elephant like a stone? No, there would be few who would want to try. How many then, he asked himself, would try with a bow and arrow?

"He didn't take an easy shot," he continued, "like just hitting her in the stomach, where the poison would be diluted by the food until it took her forever to die. No, he avoided the belly and took a difficult spleen shot around the side of the stomach. She would have gone down within two hours, and he would have been moving along just behind her all the way. He axed out her tusks and was on his way, hours before dawn." The implication was clear. The man was a professional. Even packing the ivory, he could be forty miles away by now, and Unit 3 of the Field Force had started tracking him just thirty minutes earlier. Unless he made the mistake he never made, he was gone again.

David stared out over the thick tangle of gray scrub in the direction taken by Unit 3 and the departed poacher. His expression was grim. He'd heard what Mohamed had said, and he understood, to a degree. The Waliangulu would be difficult to take; but he disagreed with the idea that it couldn't be done. But there was something else he thought of.

"There's one thing about this man that's bothered me ever since I first heard about him," he said thoughtfully. "Why does he continue to use his identification mark on his arrowheads? And why leave them in the carcass?"

Mohamed frowned. The question had apparently never occurred to him before. He shook his head. "I don't know."

Karanja studied the arrowhead he held and wondered: What was the purpose of this one poacher's continuing to use a signature on his arrowheads? Was it to advertise his contempt for the laws prohibiting hunting and his determination to exist as his people had existed in the past—as hunters? And why did he leave the arrowhead in the carcass? When accessible, the arrowhead was removed after it had served its purpose and taken away to be used again. Even in the old days, when all the Waliangulu arrowheads carried the hunter's personal inscription, the identification mark was valuable only when an elephant might possibly wander for miles before dying. If the carcass was located by another hunting party, the inscription on the arrowhead provided proof of ownership of the elephant. Very rarely did anyone make an attempt to appropriate the tusks from another hunter's kill. There were few rules among hunters, but none tried to break this particular unwritten law, because the penalty, if you were caught, was high, and there were pleasanter ways to die. So after the tusks were removed, every effort was made to recover the arrowhead. Why leave it for the authorities to find and identify? Why leave it and have to forge another? No one continued to use his personal inscription anymore; the risks were too great. Besides, no one followed the old ways anymore. No one except this one man. But again, why?

Why did he make his kills in the heavily patrolled and traveled Southern Area of the park, close to Headquarters or ranger substations, rather than in the park's obscure corners where the carcasses would be undetected? It had to be because he wanted them found. He wanted them to know it was him again. What was it, Karanja wondered—contemptuous defiance? The thought stung. He turned back to Mohamed, who stood silently waiting.

"I want him," Karanja said flatly. There was no room for disagreement. "He's poached hundreds of elephant in Aruba, and each time he's made sure we know who's responsible. It's a challenge, and in thirty years no one's taken it up." He was angry. The man's success galled him. "I want to know who's going to do it now?" He waited, his expression an unyielding demand.

"I will," Mohamed replied simply. There was nothing else he could say.

David searched his face, then nodded. He didn't know the reason behind Mohamed's pessimistic attitude, but he didn't care. He couldn't personally accept the idea of defeat, and he wouldn't let one of his men do it either. "Good enough," he said, satisfied. "Take what you need. But get him."

* * *

SERGEANT LEMBOKO FELT the sweat pouring down his face and under his woolen shirt as he strained and grunted *"Sasa"* through clenched teeth. At the command of "Now," the other rangers gave one last heave, and the calf was up and onto the wooden floor of the Bedford lorry. Swiftly they replaced the slatted wooden tailgate, and the calf was confined and ready to be transported back to Headquarters and the orphanage. It had taken five of them to hoist the struggling baby elephant almost four feet off the ground and onto the rear of the lorry. Now the calf stood there, tensely flapping his ears and feeling the wooden sides of his enclosure with the tip of his trunk while four rangers crawled up over the sides and into the back to help brace the youngster during the ride back.

Just then the calf lashed up and out with his trunk and made a determined charge at Corporal Lugumba, hurling him against the wooden slats. The Orma tribesman grunted as the breath was knocked out of him and shoved back while his fellow rangers shouted and pushed the calf away. The frightened and bewildered calf backed into a corner and stood flapping his ears while the rangers moved in quickly to pin him up against the sides of the lorry as it slowly began to move.

Sergeant Lemboko took a seat beside the driver of Unit 1's Land Cruiser and proceeded to follow the lorry out of the bush. He was smiling because he knew that for those four rangers, the ride back to Headquarters would more than pay them back for the chuckles they'd enjoyed at his expense earlier when he'd gone butt-first into the thornbush while trying to help capture the calf. He bent down and pulled out a sharp two-inch-long gray thorn from where it had stuck in his woolen sock and then worked down under the puttee above his boot top. Flinging it out the window, he regarded the small rips and tears in his khaki shorts and shirt with annoyance. One of his wives was quite clever with a needle, but even after mending the tears would still show.

Sergeant Lemboko was proud of his uniform. Most of it was still influenced by the designs and fabrics originally introduced by the British during the colonial days, and whoever had decreed angora wool shirt fabric for a ranger force operating all day under the hot East African sun had obviously not been a person who was likely to have to wear those uniforms under the same sun. Nevertheless, he was proud of it, and his wives kept both pairs of heavy, wide-legged shorts spotless and well enough starched to stand up by themselves.

Just ahead, Lemboko saw the lorry lurch sideways, its left wheels rising and falling abruptly as they passed over a fallen tree trunk. His eyes lit in expectancy as he watched the calf lose its footing and sag against the Rangers. Two men went down, and a howl was heard over the sound of the engine. His grin changed to a gleeful chuckle of satisfaction.

DAVID KARANJA CLIMBED into the intense heat of his Land-Rover and reached for the packet of cigarettes lying on the seat. After reflecting momentarily on his decision to quit smoking, or at least cut down to one pack a day, he lit up and started the engine. He sat there a moment and then opened the dash vents before closing the door. It was unbearably hot inside the vehicle; outside, there was usually a breeze to cool the effect of the sun, but inside a metal vehicle the heat intensified. Running his hand across his perspiring forehead and back over the top of his head, he felt the dampness of his hair, cropped short to the scalp, leaving just a close-fitting cap of crisp black. He wondered briefly how hot it would be today. During the dry season, the Research Center's meteorological station could report a soil surface temperature of over 160 degrees Fahrenheit at 1500 hours. Too hot—and it had been going on too long without the respite brought by rain.

He noticed that Agaran was leaving, and soon he would be alone in the bush. Good. He had to go by the park's Research Center, but first he felt like driving slowly back to Headquarters Hill by himself and taking the opportunity to look around. There were too many days when he was caught up in the administrative problems of supervising a national park of over five million acres, an area considerably larger than the country of Israel. It seemed as if he rarely got the chance to get out of the office and really see it, particularly since he was without his plane. It was as if he'd somehow lost his sight.

He shifted the gears and let out the clutch before circling around to the tracks they'd made coming in from the road. Driving slowly over the rough ground, he looked at the area around him; the red earth showed here and there between clumps of barren gray scrub and leafless trees, and what grass there was left was now scanty and dried out.

Perfect weather for poaching, David reflected grimly. Denuded vegetation allowed poachers to spot their quarry easily from any elevated ground in the area or by merely climbing a tree. Not that the whereabouts of the trophy animals was difficult to ascertain. The rhino and elephant, along with most of the other species in the park, were congregated at, and dependent upon, the few sources of permanent water, and so the poachers knew precisely where they could be found. Not only did they know their exact whereabouts, they also knew that the trophy animals were in an extremely weakened condition. A year of erratic and below-average rainfall had taken its toll on the rhinos and the herds of elephants. It was all they could do to survive the critical conditions imposed by a harsh climate; they had nothing left with which to resist an additional threat.

David stopped the Land-Rover on the circuit road which meandered along the Moda River Valley. A couple of hundred meters away he saw the park's small herd of big orphans browsing on the leaves of the *Cordia goetzei* trees while one of the two herdsmen, who were their constant companions, peeled off strips of the trees' dry, brittle bark.

Through his binoculars David watched the eldest cow, Sarah, as she reached out and up to the Samburu tribesman seated on a branch above her. As he offered her the handful of bark strips, she tipped back her head and extended her long, dexterous trunk to take the offering; curling her trunk under, she clasped the bark and in one fluid motion lifted it back and into her mouth. Immediately, her long gray trunk snaked up and out again to reach for more.

It was interesting, David mused, that the *Wazungu*—the Europeans—thought of the elephant's trunk as a "nose" while East Africans referred to the trunk as *mkono*—the arm, particularly the lower arm and the hand. It was a more fitting name somehow.

He couldn't remember exactly when it was that his fascination with the elephant had begun. It must have been early in his childhood when he was growing up in the mission compound within sight of Mount Kenya—or *Kirinyaga*, as his father's people called it: "the mountain of brightness." The animal stories told him by the missionaries who'd raised him had played their part, as had the long walks in the nearby forest with the missionaries' longtime friend, the local game warden, Frazer Kent. Those early stories of animals with human characteristics had started it, and he smiled as he remembered Pooh, Br'er Fox, and Bagheera. The walks with the game warden, who enjoyed describing the behavior and habits of every baboon, bushbuck, and buffalo, made the creatures real, but it was always the elephants who held his rapt attention the longest. Before he was ten he'd heard and memorized everything Frazer Kent knew of the forest elephants; he knew about their complicated social structure and family life, their feeding habits, and their behavior patterns; he understood their tremendous strength, their uncanny intelligence, their gentleness. He'd spent hours and walked miles just to watch them, and by the time he turned twelve and was given a huge, brightly colored book about the elephant for his birthday, he was committed for life. He still had both the book and the feeling.

Some boys outgrew their childhood interests, some didn't. He'd finished mission school and gone on to university; accepted his first postings as assistant warden, and later warden; and here he was: warden of Kenya's biggest and finest national park, containing one of the world's largest elephant populations. He should be happy, or at least satisfied; but the circumstances made it impossible.

His gaze drifted away from the orphan herd and focused on the Fafajaga Plain which stretched for miles beyond. The metallic blue sky held a few large white clouds, which moved slowly ahead of the wind to send dark blue shadows creeping over the red earth below. It was unbelievably barren. It was hot and it was dry, and most of all, it was endless. Eighty-five hundred square miles of bush that he couldn't even patrol properly because his light plane was smashed up truly became endless when seen a small piece at a time from a Land-Rover; a nearly total failure of two successive rains in a dry country became a seemingly endless drought. And the men willing to hunt elephants were too large a number to count, because inflation had driven so many people to withdraw their money from falling pounds and dollars to invest it in the rare and valuable like gold, silver, precious gems, and ivory. As the world market price of ivory went up, so did the price per kilo paid to the native poacher. The number of poachers rose accordingly, until now his rangers were outnumbered by perhaps as many as thirty to one, and all of them were scattered over one of the biggest national parks in the world. No, he knew he had no hope of controlling the poachers. There were too many, the stakes were too high, and he didn't have enough men to catch the bastards. The scene back at the cow's carcass returned to mind and he thought grimly: And now the best of the lot has taken up his bow again. He closed his eyes in weary frustration.

Conversations, overheard years ago, came back to him. The missionaries had often recalled the numbers of rhinos and elephants sighted when they'd first come to Kenya thirty years before—and how many fewer were seen each and every succeeding year. He thought of Warden Kent, shaking his shaggy head sadly and muttering gruffly, "Someday they'll all be gone."

As a child he hadn't listened. It hadn't seemed possible. But now it was happening.

Resolutely shaking his head, he reminded himself that he didn't have time to spend dawdling in the bush ruminating over his problems. There were things he had to do, and first among them was to warn Research that there was another orphan on its way in.

THIRTY-FOUR KILOMETERS AWAY, Unit 8 of the Field Force pushed on through the thick gray thornbush, following the trail of three poachers whose tracks they'd discovered just after dawn. It had been just half an hour since they'd found where the poachers' tracks had crossed those of a solitary rhino near Namu water hole, and there the rangers had found two shell casings and the spatter of dried blood. The corporal in charge had urged his men into a steady lope, which had helped to close the distance between the rangers and the poachers who were following the wounded rhino, but the relentless pace under the merciless sun was grueling.

As he momentarily slowed his men to a walk, the corporal's eyes darted from the tracks and the occasional dark globbet of blood on the ground to the thick clumps of bush ahead. Just then his lance corporal nudged his arm and pointed. The corporal glanced up from the trail to see the six vultures circling ahead. One by one they began to drop earthward. He barked, *"Twende haraka,"* and his men fanned out beside him, running. But they were too late.

HEEKUTA NEKO SAT on his haunches and watched the pot of water begin to boil on the charcoal fire glowing brightly between the three flat cooking stones. He reached for a can of dried milk and the packet of tea, added some of each, then sat back to wait till the tea leaves had steeped the milky mixture to a rich brown.

He was tired. He was getting old—too old to stay up all night hunting and trekking long distances. It had never bothered him before, but it had been a while since he'd hunted. He was pleased that his aim was still so sure, his skill undiminished, but he was not pleased when he remembered how hard it had been for him to get his breath as he'd struggled to pack the tusks out of the park, and they were the tusks of a cow as well—much smaller than those of a bull.

Even after the few hours' sleep he'd allowed himself, he still felt the crippling fatigue of the previous night, and he remembered how once he could have run all day and all night with twice fifty pounds on his back. He frowned as he recalled how he'd left the carcass hours before dawn and struggled south to reach the tarmac of the main road in order to lose the rangers who would later follow his trail; how after reaching it, he'd continued for more than two kilometers before cutting back into the park area and turning toward the village.

He'd meant to conceal the tusks near the road, but by then his legs had begun to tremble with fatigue, and dawn was fast approaching. He'd made it here to the old *shamba* house just as the sky was lightening. He'd buried the tusk in the clearing outside, and he

32

didn't like to do that. It wasn't good to have the evidence of his poaching so close, and besides, it meant that he would have to return this evening to remove them and secrete them somewhere else before he went to contact the Arab buyer. He didn't want the man to connect him with this house.

Leaning forward, he tipped the lid of the pot to see that the *chai* was ready. Picking up the old folded pieces of milk carton that served as pot holders, he removed the tea and slowly poured it through the bright orange plastic tea strainer that rested over his chipped enamel cup. Setting aside the remainder of the tea to keep warm on the hot stones, he stirred four spoonfuls of coarse sugar into the cup and leaned back against the mud wall while his mind returned once more to the days when he could have run for miles.

He saw the *aruba*—the elephants—as they used to be; the huge bulls with their heavy ivory dirty with the red soil, and smudged with green from tusking the big trees and prying off the thick patches of living bark. He remembered the ivory of those days; ivory like that taken by his father, Neko, the ivory of six arms' length* that had gone to Nairobi for the *Wazungu* to come and stare at; the big ivory that he himself had brought home after days spent hunting in the bush.

He remembered the pair of tusks with which he had bought his wife, Diramu. They had been very big; big because her father had demanded large ivory for this daughter; demanded it because she was worth much ivory. She was gone now, and the big ivory had gone as well.

As he sipped his tea, he glanced around the dark windowless house, whose corners flickered with shadows in the orange light of the fire. It was small and rectangular, its walls a latticework of poles caulked and covered with mud, and roofed with old flattened petrol cans nailed to wooden rafters. It was nothing like the huts of his people as they had been in his youth. Nothing like the first hut he and Diramu had built together at Shokoke with the help of their friends in the week after their marriage many, many years ago. He thought back to that week and remembered how the women had cut the poles and stripped their branches, and he and his friends had set them into the ground in a circle five and a half arms across, and bent them inward to tie together high in the center. More poles had been lashed horizontally to the domelike framework while the women cut grass and tied off the neat bundles that were used to

* One arm equals the distance between elbow and fingertip; approximately eighteen inches. Six arms would be approximately nine feet.

thatch the walls and roof. It had been a large hut; large enough to hold three beds for himself and Diramu, and for the children who would come, besides the cooking area with the same three flat stones over which had hung a rack which served as a storage area for food, clothes and belongings. It was true that the things kept there smelled of the smoke from the fire below, but for that very reason they were safe from the mice and insects.

That home was gone now. It had been destroyed by the *askari* who had come to tell them that they had to go; that the land was no longer the land of the Waliangulu, or, as they referred to themselves, the *Wata*. It was to be the land of the national park. The *askari* had destroyed the few rows of maize the women were just learning to grow, and the lorries had come to take them away against their will. And when the Waliangulu were gone, the *askari* had come back and burned down the round grass-thatched huts, and soon the village at Shokoke, which had been home to generations of Waliangulu, had disappeared.

They had been taken in the lorry to a place near Shimba Hills, at the coast, he and Diramu and the four children, and they had taken their few belongings in the woven *kikapu,* and had carried their cooking stones with them, because home was where a woman knelt to cook at her hearth, and that hearth was home.

In the land of the Giriama he had built another hut, but it had been small, and the poles did not go deep, and the thatch was not made thick, because he knew that hut would not know them long.

After a few months he had returned home to hunt, because the shillings were gone and the small *shamba* Diramu had planted had not yet brought food, and the Giriama still paid well for ivory as they had always done. When he came back he found his village gone and it was as if it had never been, but he found that his people were returning. They came quietly and in small family groups, and the people settled on the land that no one wanted. They built their huts near to, but away from the village of Moda that had grown up beside the sisal plantation, or they went north and east and settled near the Lalaga Lana River just outside the park.

They returned, one family at a time, and their small *shambas,* each with its thatched dwelling, huddled close to the boundary line that separated them from their land. They came as close as they could to *Lafawata*—the country of the *Wata*—but they could come no closer.

He had returned to his family on the coast then, with the money received from the ivory of the one *aruba* he'd taken east of the park, and again they took up their cooking stones, and they returned to settle outside the boundary just ten kilometers from their old home. He had built this house then, but instead of building in the old way, he'd constructed a mud house like those being built by the other displaced tribesmen in the nearby village. Diramu had planted her maize and beans outside the door, which faced the east, and the cooking stones were once more placed below the storage rack.

The months passed, and the first small crop withered and died because the rains failed, and the shillings were gone again, and his wife and children were hungry, so he had gone out to hunt once more. But where he once strode boldly out of his village with the other men of his family, after having consulted the *abamuruati* and ascertained that the signs were good and that the hunt would be successful, he now slipped away by himself in the darkness without knowing of the disasters that might befall him, without the help of his ancestors or family, alone.

He had taken his weapons from their hiding place in the roof and left with his quiver of poisoned arrows, each wrapped in dik-dik skin, his bow, and his knife. He'd slipped away before the moon rose, and returned to the old deserted village where his people had lived for generations. He'd sought and found the huge and ancient *yaka,* the tree the Wazungu called baobab, and there he'd knelt beside the grave of his father. He had buried him many years before, digging a hole deep with sharp pointed sticks and laying his father in it on his right side with his face toward the north, for the Wata had come from the north, and his head pointing east, because the rivers ran that way to the sea, and after covering his father with the red soil, he'd carefully laid the old man's bow and quiver of arrows on the mound.

This was where he had returned that night, years later, to seek the help of his father's spirit, the father who had been known as the most famous hunter of his generation. He had set out his offerings and he had prayed to the *ona* of his father, and he recalled him to his side from Waka, the universal god, to whom his father had gone upon his passing from earth. He'd known that the handful of maize and small bit of tobacco twisted into a corn husk was a poor offering, but he'd known too that his father would understand that it was all he had: the last of the maize and the last of the tobacco; and because it was everything, the gift became great.

He'd knelt beneath the old tree and prayed for his father's *ona* to return to him, and as he prayed, his earlier confusion melted away to become anger. He grew angry because the land was no longer his, because the villages were gone, because his people were scattered. And as he became angry, he felt the spirit of his father come to stand beside him, and he knew that this would not be the last time he would return to his people's land to hunt.

He had left the tree with his father beside him then, and together they'd crept close to the new Park Headquarters, and he and his father's spirit had taken a fine old bull with ivory of five arms' length. He had packed the ivory out, and as he'd left his people's land he'd felt his father's spirit slip away. He had buried the ivory far from his home, and the buyer had come and he had taken the shillings the ivory brought. Every few months he would return to the park, and each time he returned to the tree with better offerings and he prayed, but the spirit of his father never came again. Still, Heekuta knew that he watched, and that his father knew he would not let the *Wazungu* forget that this was not their land.

Each time he returned, he would take five or ten elephants, depending on the volume of his hate at the time and the need of his people, and he would take them from close under the white noses. They had caught him only once, years ago, in the small hut east of the park which he'd built to use when he hunted north of the Lalaga Lana, but they hadn't been seeking him, they hadn't known of him then, and they hadn't kept him, either. Since then he'd become even more secretive. He'd never returned to the hut where he'd been captured, while those who had known him in his youth had drifted away or had died years ago; now even his name was forgotten.

Diramu had died almost twenty years ago, and the children had gone soon after. One daughter had married a Giriama and had left for the coast, and so she and her children were lost to her people. The other daughter had become the wife of the town and had drifted away to lie with any man. His elder son had died of the malaria, and the younger had become a drunk who was later crippled by a big bull and lived far north on the charity of his neighbors and what little his woman could provide from a small *shamba.* That was the way of things when a people were lost without the land, and without the old ways that had held them together and made them proud.

His village was gone and his people were gone, along with his wife and children, and he was alone. Even his father's *ona* had failed to return. Yet Heekuta knew that the spirit of Neko would come one more time, when it would be time for Heekuta to join his *ekra,* the ancestors of his clan.

As he finished the last of his tea, he leaned forward to scratch in the dirt at his feet with the tip of his knife. His mother had told him that he had been learning to walk when the first war between the Waingereza and the Wagermani began; laboriously subtracting 1914 from 1977 and adding one year, he nodded to himself. Yes, he was an old man now, and it would not be long before his father's spirit came once more, for the last time.

He poured the rest of the tea through the bright plastic strainer from the Indian's *duka* and looked around the house again. It was empty of all but the old cooking stones, a pot, and his cup, because he rarely came here. There was no reason to come. He came only to recover his weapons before he hunted, and once more afterward when he would replace them in the roof that was slowly rusting away. He nodded sadly to himself. Yes, even the old ways of building a home were gone.

Getting up, he crossed the room to the corner where a large clay cooking pot sat and closely inspected the contents. Seven days ago he had brought a huge hunk of wood that he'd hacked from the trunk of the *makahadah,* the tree of poison, and he had chopped the wood into slivers the size of his smallest finger. After placing the wood in the pot, he'd added the mummified body of an elephant shrew, and then poured in the rainwater that he'd collected and saved in gourd calabashes months ago. During the past week the water had slowly darkened as it drew the poison from the soaking wood, and it was now the dark color of very strong tea and therefore ready.

Tomorrow he would return and would remove the wood slivers and the small bones of the rodent-like shrew, whose body had now transferred its desirable behavior characteristics along with its flesh to the steeping poison. Desirable because it was known that the elephant shrew would not, and could not, cross a road or path used by people—it would drop dead beside this insurmountable obstacle; and therefore, the poison would transfer this habit to the elephant who was to be the target for the poisoned arrowheads, and he too would fall at the side of any pathway he attempted to cross.

Following the removal of the wood and small bones, he would boil the blackened water over a charcoal fire throughout the day until the resulting condensed poison was the consistency of gummy porridge, and it would then be set aside to thicken further as it cooled. The result would be a toxin that could kill an antelope before it could travel fifty meters, or an elephant within an hour or two.

Returning to the hearth, he took a pinch of snuff from a tiny stoppered gourd that hung suspended on a leather thong around his neck; then he rinsed his cup and pot in a gourd of water, doused the flickering fire, and returned his few possessions to their hiding place in the cracked mud wall above the cooking stones. Turning,

37

he glanced over the interior of the house, apparently empty with the exception of the clay cooking pot and three flat stones. There was nothing here left to steal and, therefore, no reason for anyone to break in. Stepping outside, he closed the door and fastened the latch with an old rusted padlock.

Pausing for a moment in the slender shade of the house, he looked over the *shamba* and his memory brought back the time when the small cultivated plot had rustled with green growing maize and the sounds of his children's laughter and his wife's singing were to be heard. There had been the quickening of life and living here then, but now the sun glared down on a dead, deserted house that was beginning to buckle and fall, and a parched garden which was returning to rank bush, and all that had been was gone.

Slipping his hands into the pockets of his old khaki jacket, he stepped out into the heat and crossed the quiet clearing. After pushing himself through the thornbush thicket that surrounded and concealed the house and its abandoned garden, he rearranged the prickly branches to cover his passing and began the long, hot walk to the place he now called home.

CHAPTER THREE

Noon

D<small>R. JEFF FORBES STOOD</small> at the open doorway of the Research Center's main building and studied the bushland below him as it sloped down from Headquarters Hill. As he evaluated the vegetation, his sunburned forehead wrinkled in a frown.

"What in the world are you scowling at?" The soft, questioning voice startled him. He glanced up and grinned as his wife, Audrey, came up the steps and onto the wide veranda, accompanied by her friend Halima Abdi.

"I'm not scowling," he protested. "That was an intense scientific study you ladies interrupted."

"For?" Audrey asked as her husband's arm found its accustomed place around her waist.

"A paper I'm writing, or rather, a paper I'm trying to write. Some of the foreign institutions and foundations that help support the Research Center want a report on the drought conditions here and how it's affecting the wildlife."

"Is that all?" Halima inquired. "It sounds like one of those little reports that seem a snap to do at first, but later prove difficult."

Jeff chuckled in appreciation. Halima was an African; a woman. But not an African woman of yesterday. Young, single, and attractive, she was also educated, intelligent, and quietly assured, one among the new generation of African women who saw an alternative to immediate marriage and children. She, like the others, had goals for herself, her people, and her country, and was committed to them. She'd been transferred to Aruba three months before as the Education Center's new director, and very soon she and Audrey had become friends. The two women were much alike, but from widely dissimilar backgrounds—like travelers who'd reached the same destination, only by different routes.

"That's exactly what's happened," he agreed. "But I have a feeling you didn't stop by to discuss my efforts at creative writing."

"No, I didn't," she conceded. "I wanted to return this." She handed him a small glass-covered tray containing mounted specimens of some of Aruba's more spectacular butterflies. "They were a huge success. Thank you. The children enjoyed them enormously. I don't think they ever really looked at butterflies before."

She hesitated, conscious of Jeff's knowing smile. "I thought that while I was here . . . I'd ask about the displays you thought you might have time to do for the Education Center."

As Jeff began to chuckle, Audrey poked him in the ribs and said, "You're a dreadful tease." She turned to Halima. "The glass arrived last week, and they're almost done with the dung beetle display, including the cross-section of the underground egg chamber, and —"

"And," Jeff interrupted, "we'll have the termite nest finished later this week, as well as a nice selection of exotics, including butterflies and moths, by the end of next."

Halima's smile was immediate and infectious. "Thank you. I can't tell you how much I appreciate your help—"

Jeff waved away her gratitude. "Our pleasure." And it was. The purported purpose of the park's Education Center was to instill in Kenya's young an appreciation of their country's natural habitat and wildlife, but before Halima's arrival it had only gone through the motions. She had brought to the Center the vital spark of the enthusiastic teacher; the life cycle and role of every insect, reptile, bird, and mammal within the ecosystem, and their interdependence on the soil, vegetation, and weather were to her an exciting story, and she was able to infect her students with the same fascination, not only for the few days they spent at the Center, but for long after they left. In consequence, there wasn't a scientist at Research who didn't gladly offer his services when Halima needed volunteers to lecture on their specific subjects.

"At the risk of being repetitious I'll say it again: thank you. And now," she added in amused response to an impatient toot from the Education Center *kombi* parked in front of Research, "I've got to get back." With another smile and a brief wave she ran down the steps to the *kombi*, where she called out to Audrey, "See you later," before climbing in beside the driver.

After watching the vehicle pull away onto the dusty road below,

Audrey glanced up at her husband. "Tell me about the paper you're writing. What's the problem?"

His attention abruptly returned to his report. "It's just hard to find the right words to describe a situation and environment so alien to anything people in Europe or North America know." He nodded in the direction of the dry bushland. "I'm trying to describe Aruba and what's happening here so they'll be able to see it— *really* see it. Then perhaps they'll understand what we're up against." He shook his head as he continued, "It's bloody hard." He smiled. "I'll read it to you later."

"I knew it had to be something important or you wouldn't have decided to work through lunch," Audrey said, her brown eyes alive with amusement. "That's why I brought you this." She held up a small woven basket, and as his face lit with appreciation, she marveled again at this man of hers. Left to himself, he'd forget to eat or to change his socks until he was a walking skeleton with rags in his shoes. So she packed him lunches when he went into the field, or like today, brought them to Research when he failed to arrive home, and each evening she stole his discarded clothes while he showered and replaced them with fresh.

The reward was always the same—a look of pleased surprise, which ended in a funny lopsided grin of gratitude. Nothing was ever expected, nothing was taken for granted; it was why she never left off performing the small kindnesses of early marriage—only enlarged on them.

His smile widened. "Thank you, love. It's the only time I have here when it's quiet enough to write."

As they passed into Jeff's office, Audrey asked, "How was your morning?"

"Fine." He sat down at his desk and began to unwrap a sandwich, adding glumly, "If you don't count the fact that the meteorological station was broken into and badly trampled by an elephant during the night."

"Oh, no!" Audrey exclaimed. It could take weeks, if not months, to replace all the station's instruments.

As David walked in the back door, he heard Audrey's exclamation of concern and immediately responded. "If it's another problem then I don't want to hear it." His half-smile indicated that he was teasing, but not completely; a man's jokes often revealed what was on his mind.

Jeff grinned. David was one of his closest friends, but even though the Research Center and Main Headquarters were only half a kilometer apart, they'd seen little of each other lately. Steadily increasing work loads had seen to that.

"Nothing for you to concern yourself with," Jeff bantered as he noted the stress and fatigue on David's face. "It's just one of the Center's daily crises. Nothing that can't be handled."

"Excuse me, Doctor?" The deferential voice hesitantly interrupted.

Forbes looked up to see the cheerful face at the doorway. James Mugalu, his research assistant, was a young man of the Taita tribe with a fascinated interest in botany.

"Yes, James?" Forbes prompted. He had been waiting for this report.

"It's not as bad as I thought, sir," James said with a respectful nod at Warden Karanja. "The chain-link fence was down, with two fence poles broken, but the *fundi* is fixing that now. The top of the rain-gauge canister was bent. I think it was stepped on."

"Can it be fixed?"

"Yes, sir. I bent it back; it's only soft tin, and now you can't even tell it was damaged. The dry bulb and the wet bulb for the humidity readings are all right, and so is the sunshine recorder. The wind-directional instrument was knocked down, but we set it up again and it seems to be working—I compared the readings with the Main Headquarters airfield by radio."

"What else is damaged?"

"The anemometer is smashed, so we can't register wind speed, and two soil-temperature thermometers are broken, for the surface and two-inch-depth readings." He held up two huge soil thermometers. "But I can replace the broken ones in time for the fifteen-hundred-hours readings. Everything else is fine."

Jeff smiled with obvious relief. "Thank you, James. You've taken care of it well."

"Thank you, sir." The young man's face was radiant with the praise as he disappeared out the door.

Reaching for his current THINGS TO REORDER list, Forbes added at the bottom of the page: *1 anemometer*. He scowled as he wondered how much that would cost; probably too much.

"How in the world," he muttered to Audrey and David, "do they expect a man to stay inside a tight budget when elephant come racing through his met station?" Thinking for a moment, he took up the list again and added: *soil thermometers—2 spares*.

"Stop fussing," Audrey admonished him gently. "You're awfully lucky it wasn't worse."

"I know," he said. "I only fuss because you take such pains to jolly me out of it." He smiled up at her, then turned back to David.

"Now that that's taken care of, to what do we owe the pleasure of your company?"

"As a matter of fact, I came to see Audrey," David replied. "I went by the house, and your *shamba* man told me the *Memsaab* was here." He smiled at Audrey's grimace. She hated being called *"Memsaab,"* had always hated it. But their gardener was an old man, an *mzee,* and for him it was unthinkable to call her anything else. What was for her an archaic reminder of a colonial past in which she had played no part was for him what had been the proper address for European women in his youth, and so was still correct. He would not, and could not, change, and she'd finally given up.

"I'm afraid your family is about to be enlarged," David added, and was thankful for the bright look of expectation his remark brought to Audrey's face. The reaction of most women would be considerably different.

"What have we got now?" Jeff asked in amusement.

"Another elephant calf."

"How old?" Audrey inquired hopefully. It was the little ones she was fondest of.

"A year at most. He's about three feet or so." Seeing her pleased expression, he added, "He should be arriving any minute."

"Now?" she exclaimed. "And I haven't any formula ready. I've got to go." She headed for the door.

"I'll give her a hand," David said as he followed her out. "I suppose it's the least I can do," he added ruefully. Between the drought and the poaching, it was a rare week that didn't see him on Audrey's doorstep with another of the park's animal orphans.

"Don't worry," Forbes called out as David climbed into his Land-Rover. "She loves it."

Jeff grinned as he watched Audrey through the window while she ran along the short path between the Center and their home next door, and he thought of the young lady she'd been when they had met, ten years before, at the University Vet Hop in Dublin, and how he had quickly married her and whisked her off to a new and very different life in Kenya before she could have second thoughts. He'd returned home with a fistful of diplomas and degrees, and this statuesque redheaded wife. He was fond of saying he didn't know which of the two accomplishments he was prouder of.

The local people called her *"Mama Wanyama,"* and Animal Mother suited her very well. She would mother anything and anybody. Perhaps if they could have had children of their own she might not have developed such a love for the animal orphans, but they'd both recovered from that disappointment long ago, and now it was never even thought of except with a feeling of relief.

As he finished the last bite of his sandwich, he wadded up the napkin it had been wrapped in and discovered the unfinished report glaring at him from the desk top. Grumbling to himself, he picked up his pen and got back to work.

Soon his earlier question returned to plague him, and his bushy brows knitted together as his forehead wrinkled into its habitual frown of concentration. "How," he muttered intently to himself, "can I make them see what's happening here? Really see it. And understand."

"IS THERE ANYTHING I can do to help?" David asked, feeling a little out of his element.

Audrey looked up from where she knelt beside the elephant calf, still holding the huge rubber-nippled formula bottle with which she'd been trying to coax him. With a definite shake of her red head, she replied genially, "No. Thank you." It was her firm belief that men had no business trying to raise young animals. They just didn't have the necessary patience; and besides, what man was going to heed the hungry whimpers of an infant animal at two in the morning? He'd roll right over and continue snoring. "We're doing just fine," she added with a wry expression before lifting the bottle again to poke it into the calf's mouth.

"It doesn't look like it," David observed as the calf resisted and the milk began trickling down Audrey's arm, to drip off her elbow into a puddle on her aproned lap.

"Blast it," she muttered. She clambered to her knees and gripped the calf's lower lip firmly in her left hand. David moved forward and stood behind the calf to prevent him from backing away. As he wedged the little elephant's backside between his knees, he chuckled. The battle was on again, but he didn't doubt the outcome. The calf was going to finish that bottle; he just didn't know it yet.

Glancing beyond Audrey, David nodded at Corporal Lugumba, who was sitting with the rest of his men nearby on the lawn while they watched Audrey and drank the hot tea and ate the biscuits she provided whenever the rangers brought in another orphan. Watching his men observing Audrey so intently brought to mind the difference in the attitudes of the European and the African toward animals, particularly in regard to the wildlife, and he remembered an incident that had occurred years before when Nichols had been Warden.

It seemed that Nichols had spotted an impala ram hobbling about with a broken leg and had ordered one of the units to find and destroy the animal, adding that the meat could be taken home to the men's families, as was usual. The rangers had found the ram, but rather than shoot it, they'd tied its legs together and thrown it into the back of the Toyota. Later, Nichols had arrived on patrol and while talking with their corporal had noticed the impala lying in the bed of the pickup; at that moment the animal had thrashed about, and when Nichols saw it was still alive, he'd flown into a rage.

He'd bellowed for someone to kill the animal, and then he'd yelled and sworn at the men in English, and none of them had understood why he was angry. The men had reasoned that of course it was still alive—it kept better alive. What difference did it make? It was going to die anyway.

Nichols had said that if they had to destroy an injured animal, they were to kill the animal quickly and not let it suffer. If the meat went bad, then they could do without, but the animal was not to be left to live in pain. The rangers wondered at this, because they knew that suffering was part of life. Besides, they didn't really think that animals could feel pain. But even if they did, as the *Mzungu* Nichols said, then what difference did it make?

As David watched his men, he considered the ambiguity and the conflict within himself. Born of one race and raised in the culture of another, he saw and acknowledged the viewpoint of each.

To most Africans, an animal was only an animal. While there were two kinds, man's animals and the bush animals, they had one thing in common: they represented wealth, because food is wealth; and therefore, animals had value. But to the *Wazungu,* animals were often companions and more, to be talked to, bathed, petted, and fed; and this latter chore often fell to a *Wazungu* family's African cook, who was responsible for cutting up and serving more meat to the family dogs each week than he and his wife and children ate in a month. To many Africans, David thought, it must seem that Europeans treated animals better than they did people. Particularly their people.

Neither point of view was right, of course. As usual, the ideal attitude lay somewhere in the middle and was, therefore, difficult to find. Nevertheless, he followed that path as best he could. The capture and arrest of a man who'd poached a protected trophy animal for its ivory or horn was clear-cut and satisfying, but there were other times—times that he tried not to remember, times when he'd looked into the eyes of a thin, ragged man who'd been caught taking an impala or a bushbuck and he'd seen the reality of the hungry women and children waiting for his return on a drought-stricken *shamba* just outside the park boundary. On more than one occasion he'd looked away and let the man disappear into

45

the bush. But he'd done so with his guts in knots, and he'd damned them for their hunger and their need.

David glanced up to see the unit's corporal placing his cup on the tray beside Audrey as he murmured shyly, *"Asante, Mama."*

Audrey smiled as she took his hand. *"Asante sana, Lugumba."* She was always pleased by a new *mtoto wa mnyama.* The rangers liked her because she always gave them tea and biscuits; and more important, somehow—she always remembered their names.

As he walked around the house to his Land-Rover, David reflected that even though his rangers of today, who had been yesterday's hunters, failed to feel as Europeans did toward animals, they did understand that the wildlife must not be poached because foreigners came from everywhere to see it, and they brought money, and this money made jobs for their people. If all the wildlife disappeared, the *wageni* wouldn't come, and few would have work. Yes, this made sense to them.

So at home they protected their cows and goats against predators and the *shifta*—the guerrilla bandits in the north; and here they protected the elephants and rhinos against the poachers, not for the sake of the animals, but because they belonged to them. It was their job to hunt the poachers down, and if necessary, they killed them, for they were thieves who would steal what was theirs. And for that there was no mercy in them.

HALIMA STOOD AT the window of her office and watched without seeing as the crowd of children noisily scrambled out of the Center's aged bus after their morning game drive to Thacatcha Rock. Giggling and shouting to one another, they dashed toward the dining room for their hot lunch of *ugali* and *mchuzi,* and soon the grassy area in front of the Center was empty, except for the half-dozen guinea fowl who hopefully scratched about for the remnants of the children's morning handout of maize. Still Halima stood unseeing; the pleased expression with which she'd returned from Research had faded, to leave her face sadly pensive, with traces of a remembered hurt in her large dark eyes.

She glanced down at the letter she held—the only personal letter in the morning mail for the director of the Education Center. She took a deep, ragged breath as her even white teeth caught her lower lip. Turning away from the window, she crossed the small room to her desk. She laid the blue envelope before her on the desk pad and studied the handwriting she knew so well while two words repeated themselves in her mind: It's come.

How long had she waited? How long had it been since she had finally given up any semblance of hope? As the writing blurred before her, she tore her eyes away from the letter and stared hard at the white clouds moving slowly past her window. I will not cry, she promised herself, and instead she remembered.

She'd met him a few months after her graduation from the university, and their attraction for each other had been immediate and intense. He'd been a biologist with the Department of Wildlife when she accepted the position of Assistant Director of the Nairobi Park Education Center. He was tall and slender, as she was, and while he wasn't classically handsome, his features had a proud, finely sculpted regularity that was attractive. They'd made an ideal couple and complemented each other in many ways. They were of the same tribe, the same general background and education, and since their jobs were related, they had kindred interests. She'd appreciated his quick intelligence, his sometimes pensive moods, his boyish humor when amused. There was never enough time when they were together talking nonsense or making love.

It hadn't been absolutely perfect, of course. Nothing was. There were times when she knew he didn't take her work or her opinions seriously; occasions when he failed to introduce passing acquaintances to her, leaving her standing by, a faceless, nameless appendage; days when, preoccupied, he didn't call or come to her, but when he did he expected her to be there, without question or remonstrance. In this and in other small ways he illustrated some of the problems encountered in a culture that was rapidly changing. He was a man, she a woman; but their places in society—their roles—were changing, and they had to find their way; first alone, then together. She'd never doubted that they would or that their relationship would progress to its obvious conclusion.

She'd waited a year, then two, then three years and still he never mentioned marriage. It wasn't that she wanted to rush into such a commitment in the near future; it was just that the total absence of any word regarding the subject bothered her. Finally she brought it up in a natural way, as if it were understood that it might be one day. Anxiously she hoped it would be accepted as such, but it wasn't. His initial blank expression, followed by a clumsy attempt at recovery and his guarded evasions, had brought her to her feet when he caught her.

"I love you," he'd whispered hopelessly. "You know that I do, but . . ." He'd faltered and stared hard into her eyes, searching out the understanding he needed. "I thought you knew . . ."

"Knew what?" she'd asked, forcing her voice level, expressionless.

47

"That when I married I would have to take a traditional wife," he said, before adding an explanation that failed to explain. "My family would never accept anything else."

She'd stood there as he turned away to light a cigarette with hands whose unsteadiness revealed the turmoil inside him, while the word "traditional" reverberated through her mind. What was "traditional"? she wondered numbly.

"I'm afraid," she said hesitantly, "that I don't know what you mean by that."

He'd glanced up at her, incredulous, before dropping his eyes. His acute embarrassment was palpable.

She didn't relent; she couldn't. "I asked you what you meant by 'traditional,'" she'd repeated. "You can't mean that your family would object to a wife who would walk beside you wearing high heels and a dress, rather than trailing behind you in bare feet and leather apron with a jug of water on her head." She'd nearly laughed. It was too preposterous. A distraught chuckle had begun to well up in her throat, only to evaporate at his words.

"It wouldn't hurt if you were more like that," he'd said defensively, "but besides that, it's because . . ." And here he'd had the grace to falter before adding quietly, reasonably, "you're not circumcised, Halima."

It was several seconds before she even took a breath. Then she silently gathered her handbag, her wrap and, putting his hands away from her, walked out the door into the dark.

She'd walked the three kilometers home through quiet streets and thought: He's a biologist, a scientist. How could he? Desperately she tried to assuage her hurt in derision: An educated man, a modern man of the twentieth century, demanding a mutilated bride from the Dark Ages. My God. It's not possible.

But it was. The faces of some, not all, but some—of the girls she'd known at the university returned to her. She heard their pleased, laughing voices as they gleefully compared their bride prices—the bride prices being paid for them by young lawyers, doctors, engineers. All of them educated, all of them enlightened, but yet still clinging to some of the old ways, the old values, because of a deeply felt lack of new ones.

She'd arrived at her apartment to hear the phone ringing. Silently she'd undressed and gone to bed, where the intermittent ringing of the unanswered phone came muffled from the next room to punctuate her thoughts. She remembered her childhood and the knowledge she'd had that one day, at puberty, she would pass through the rites which would enable her to join the tribe as an adult. Exactly what those ceremonies entailed was not known by the young, but pain and confinement were fearfully whispered about as being part of the mystery.

When the time had drawn near, her father's mother had come to discuss the arrangement with her son and his wife, and she had been sent outside. Soon loud voices from inside the house had prompted her to creep near and peek in the window of the small bungalow allotted her father as a rapidly rising civil servant. Her grandmother, in the tribal dress the old still wore in those days, had been standing in the middle of the room shrieking imprecations in Orma at her son. Most of what she said was lost on Halima because of the rapidity of the vitriolic diatribe delivered in the tribal dialect, but she knew it concerned herself. Her mother had bowed her head, stricken dumb by the old woman's verbal attack, but her father merely sat quietly listening, blinking periodically through his thick glasses. That picture of her father had remained with her always, because everything he seemed to be as a man was reflected there at that moment: he'd sat erect with his feet flat on the floor, his forearms lying easily along the arms of his chair, and his long, narrow hands motionless. With his thin face upturned and his expression almost studious in his respectful concentration on his mother's words, he'd listened silently to all she had to say, weighed it deliberately against his own carefully thought-out convictions, nodded his head, and in clear, definite English said, "No."

Before her grandmother could say a word, he repeated himself in Orma, "No. My daughters will not be circumcised. First, because it's being discouraged, as it should be, and secondly, because this is a thing of the past, and the past is where it belongs. Halima and Fatuma are for the future."

"No decent man would have such a woman!" her grandmother shrieked, spittle running down her chin.

To which her father quietly replied, "I would." Her mother's head had jerked up to stare in bitter shock at her husband.

So she and her sister, along with a number of others, had escaped what was even then a dying custom. It wasn't till years later, after they'd both been sent by their father to secondary boarding school in Nairobi, that they'd learned exactly what it was they had escaped. When she understood the implications of a radical clitoridectomy, and the subsequent sexual mutilation, she'd recalled with a certain horror that those who fought so keenly for the retention of female circumcision were the mothers and grandmothers of the tribe. It was as if they could not bear for their daughters and granddaughters to escape what for them had been inescapable.

The next morning she'd taken the phone off the hook and sat drinking innumerable cups of tea. She had no way of knowing if

49

his, or his family's, objection to her uncircumcised state was sincere or if it was merely an excuse to avoid marriage. It would do no good to argue or plead in the face of such archaic attitudes, real or pretended. They were beyond reason. The ugly truth was that she was, for him, a desirable mistress, but not quite good enough to be wife and mother. Her ability to enjoy the former state had disqualified her for the latter.

She'd written him a letter then, a reasonable and sincere explanation of what she felt that morning. She'd written that she loved him, but that she could not, and would not, now or ever, apologize for what she was: a whole woman. That he had to either accept her totally as that, or not at all. That there was nothing for them to discuss, so she didn't want to hear from him unless, or until, he felt that he could love her without reservation.

He never called again. Days went by, weeks. She stopped looking for him at Headquarters, ceased to wait expectantly for the mail. Soon the phone's ringing failed to bring her heart up into her throat with hope. Months had passed now, over a year, and the sharp empty pain of waiting and hoping was only a memory.

She found that she could study the envelope without the threat of tears. She traced the letters of his name above the return address with her fingertip as she wondered what he looked like now. Had he changed much in the last year? Had she? Would it be as good as it had been before between them? Was it ever possible to go back to what "used to be"?

She remembered the feel of him lying beside her in his bed, felt again his hand running down over her hip, her thigh, her knee before turning to slip up the inner curve of her leg . . . suddenly her thighs tightened together involuntarily. Her eyes closed and she shook her head. The past would always be there, between them. Like the scars she didn't have.

Sadly, but with a sense of irretrievability of what had been, she picked up her pen and wrote across the envelope, *Refused. Return to Sender,* and once more the words blurred before her eyes.

LEAVING THE FORBESES' HOUSE, David followed the dirt road around the base of Headquarters Hill and turned up the track that led through the garage and workshop areas. Pulling in behind the Main Headquarters building, he parked and jumped out.

"Karanja!"

Checked in his progress toward the Radio Room, David turned to see his Assistant Warden–Works, Bruce McKinney, hurrying across from the garage with a sheaf of papers fluttering in his hand.

McKinney was a small, slightly built Scots/English mixture who had come to Kenya after World War II. As a factory-trained mechanical engineer, he had been sent out by the manufacturer of an English-made four-wheel-drive to service the growing number of the company's vehicles in Kenya. Quickly tiring of Nairobi two years after his arrival, he'd accepted the position of Assistant Warden–Works instead of renewing his contract with the car manufacturer. He was in his mid-fifties now and would be retiring soon, and David was already aware of the problems that would cause. There was no question of replacing Bruce McKinney with someone of equal value; that was an impossibility and David knew it.

As McKinney reached him, David could see that he was disturbed about something. "I'd planned to send my Works Report over yesterday," McKinney said in the soft burr that had never left him as he handed David the typed pages, "but when I came back from lunch I found one of the new Land Cruisers waiting for me. The driver said, 'It just wouldn't go.' "

He paused to dig into one of the voluminous pockets in his grease-spattered coveralls until he found a battered packet of cigarettes. Offering one to David, he added, "I took one look and decided to break it down to make sure of my suspicions before I brought over the Works Report. I thought you might like to in-clude the latest casualty." His eyes telegraphed his repressed anger as he lit his cigarette and added through a cloud of smoke, "The engine had seized up. I asked the driver if he'd been putting oil in regularly. After a blank stare, he swore up and down that it got plenty of oil. 'Yes, Bwana, every day,' he said."

David interjected, "Who's the driver?"

"He's a new man from Amboseli. Joseph Ngah."

David nodded, and Bruce continued: "I tore the engine down, and there wasn't enough oil in her to lubricate a squeaking door hinge. What with one thing and another coming up to interrupt me, I didn't finish until late. By then you'd left—and," he added pointedly, "so had our Joseph Ngah."

"Has he shown up?"

McKinney silently shook his head. "I sent a man over to staff quarters early this morning and again at lunch. He's not been seen since yesterday morning."

David thought for a moment and then asked, "Does his family live here?"

Again McKinney shook his head. "The wife and children stay on the *shamba* somewhere in the Machakos area."

David knew that the driver had realized the vehicle was seriously damaged and that McKinney knew he was to blame, so rather than stick around, he had obeyed his first impulse to run off. It wasn't an uncommon occurrence. Maybe he'd be back, maybe not. Meanwhile, all David could do would be note that he was absent from his duties and give it a week or so to see what developed; that, and see to it that the vehicle was repaired.

"What's the damage, and how much to fix it?" he muttered.

"The engine is gone. It's going to need reboring, new pistons, bearings, and a crankshaft." McKinney shrugged. "I'd estimate fifteen thousand shillings for parts and eighty man-hours' labor."

David was disgusted. This kind of problem was absolutely unnecessary. Enough situations arose that were outside the control of man, like a drought, or an infestation of army worms or locusts in the vegetation; but unwillingness to make the effort to perform a job as directed and explained was inexcusable. He had been doing everything he possibly could to put an end to lethargy and incompetence at Aruba, but it was hard going. Kenya's people were just coming into the technological age, and some of them were moving a little slowly. This was the second time a vehicle had been crippled because some fool had forgotten to put oil in it.

Returning his thoughts to the question of the Land Cruiser, David said, "Do the best you can to get it moving as quickly as possible. We need it."

"I will," replied McKinney dourly. "And don't worry yourself. It'll not be happening again."

David watched McKinney thread his way back across to his office through the lorries and graders moving out for the afternoon's work details, then turned to McKinney's Vehicle Workshop Report, which was to be incorporated into his own larger Warden's Report. It was all there: the condition and status of every one of the hundreds of machines and vehicles in use at Headquarters, Research, and Education; plus the date and extent of every repair done and the total quarterly expenditure in labor, parts, petrol and oil, right down to the last nut, bolt, and liter.

David respected and relied on McKinney; the man was experienced and efficient. He was one of a small handful he could count on to make their departments work and work well without constant supervision; but that was one of the problems of being Warden: having to concern yourself with the simplest of questions and details, and being ultimately responsible for everything.

He knew that if his typist, Margaret, opened the last box of a dozen pencils, she would never think to mention the fact to the accountant, who requisitioned supplies, so that they could be ordered in time to arrive before the remaining pencils were used up. She would wait until the very last pencil was down to a three-inch stub before gravely announcing to the Warden, *"Kalamu zime-kwisha."*

At that point, having been told the pencils were all finished, he would have to see that someone else was made responsible for obtaining pencils from one of the *dukas* in the village, and would also have to remind Margaret to see the accountant about ordering more. If he was really on top of it and could remember the incident with everything else on his mind, then after a day or so he'd check up and would probably find that someone had bought a box of ball-point pens in town, and the accountant had ordered a dozen erasers. That would be another of the rare days when he'd wonder why the hell he'd wanted to become a warden.

Shaking his head, he turned and entered the Park Headquarters building and headed for the Radio Room. He had a message to send to Department Headquarters. A particularly unpleasant message.

MAIN HEADQUARTERS RADIO OPERATOR Ranger Komora Duba listened with half an ear to the HF radio transmission picked up on the Redifon's Channel 1 from the Department of Wildlife Conservation and Management Headquarters in Langata, outside Nairobi. With only two HF frequencies to service all the national parks in Kenya, a schedule of three daily call-up times had been assigned to maintain some order and to help keep the channels clear of a constant babble of messages transmitted and received all over the country. He glanced at the clock; it was nearly noon, and the next call-up was now in progress.

In a moment Langata Headquarters would be calling this station; at that time any messages relating to this park would be transmitted from Headquarters, and any outgoing messages would be received and passed along. The system worked well and made it possible to communicate instantly with Headquarters and all other Department of Wildlife stations in a country whose telephone system was in its infancy. Besides, many of the people and places requiring the ability to communicate were scattered over Kenya, in areas miles from telephone lines. Ranger Duba had heard that in America there was a city called New York where there were so many telephones in use that it required a stack of directories almost as tall as he was just to list all the numbers. If it weren't for the fact that it had been Warden Karanja who'd told him such a thing, Ranger Duba would have dismissed the story as ridiculous. His glance found the Kenya Telephone Directory sitting on the shelf next to the files kept of Field Force and Gate radio reports. The telephone directory listed all the phones in use in Kenya, and it was less than one inch thick.

At that moment the door was flung open and the warden walked in. Duba jumped to his feet and saluted before reaching for the pile of messages that had accumulated for Karanja that morning.

David acknowledged the salute and murmured his thanks as he took them. Reaching across the table, he found a pen and a pad of radio-message forms and, still standing, began to write out a message for transmission.

Duba silently watched him, noting the tension in Karanja's shoulders as he leaned over his desk. He knew the contents of the warden's message. He'd known since dawn.

"Six-oh-three . . . six-oh-one calling. Six-oh-three, six-oh-one calling. Do you read me?" The voice of the radio operator at Langata recalled his attention to the transmission being received from Department Headquarters.

Duba instinctively turned up the volume control, and instantly the static and the voice increased as he heard his call sign repeated loudly, followed by the call sign of the transmitting station.

Depressing the switch on the hand-held microphone, he acknowledged his presence: "Six-oh-one, six-oh-three reading you. Go ahead."

Langata answered, "There is a message for you."

Duba picked up a pencil and, reaching for a pad of paper, prepared to take the communication.

"Message from Acting Director of Department of Wildlife to Warden Karanja, I repeat, message from Acting Director to Warden Karanja—do you read?"

Duba finished writing the information and acknowledged, then glanced up to see Karanja watching him and listening, "I'm reading you—go ahead."

"Australian television film company arriving Aruba National Park on fifth November. I repeat . . ."

As the operator repeated the message, Duba finished writing down the last few words, and when the Langata operator inquired, "Did you copy?" Duba replied, "Affirmative—go ahead."

"With letter of introduction and authorization . . ." As the transmission was repeated, Duba finished writing and acknowledged, "Affirmative—go ahead."

The Langata radio operator continued, "We request your cooperation and assistance in their filming . . . I repeat . . ."

Duba waited for the operator to finish the repeat, noting the Warden's sour expression over the incoming information.

Langata continued: ". . . the evidence of increased poaching activity. I repeat . . . the evidence of increased poaching activity. Did you copy?"

Duba completed the message and replied, "Roger, message taken correctly—thank you. I have a message. I repeat. I have a message. Do you read?" He reached out for Karanja's completed message.

Langata affirmed, "Roger—go ahead."

Duba noticed that the static was increasing and muttered under his breath as he glanced over the form. This was going to be a difficult message, delivered simultaneously to three different stations, and he wanted decent transmission and reception. "Message from Warden Karanja to Director, Department of Wildlife; with repeat to Permanent Secretary, Ministry of Tourism and Wildlife; with repeat to Senior Warden, Coast Province. I repeat . . ." Ranger Duba continued the repetition of the persons to whom the message was directed. Receiving permission to raise the other stations involved, he began, "Five-oh-two, six-oh-three calling . . ."

As he waited for the acknowledgments, Ranger Duba quickly scanned the message he was about to transmit; mentally he blocked the message into short pieces for easier transmission and reception. "Field Force Ranger Daniel Wambogo," break, "was shot to death last night," break, "when his unit was ambushed," break, "by a band of Somali poachers." Break. "Full report will be forwarded to you." Break.

Duba clucked his tongue sadly. He'd had to transmit this kind of message with increasing frequency lately, and it made it harder that he'd known this man well, since Wambogo and his family had lived next door. Duba tried not to recall the anguished screams of Wambogo's woman when she'd been told after the patrol returned at dawn, but it was hard; they were too fresh in his memory.

AS DAVID LEFT the Radio Room, he thought grimly that the last piece of news he needed was of another film crew or journalist, or anyone else, coming here to "cover" the poaching situation. The park had always welcomed a number of newspeople who came yearly, because Kenya was proud of her wildlife and wanted the tourist trade that publicity would bring. But it was unbelievable how the stream of journalists swelled into a flood when anything unfortunate was there to report. Then they came out of the ground like beetles in a rainstorm, and scurried here and there trying to outdo one another in capturing on film an animal slaughtered by poachers, or dead from some freak climatic condition.

Headquarters had requested that he cooperate and give any assistance required to the journalists, in the hope that the public would understand the difficulties involved in the management of huge wildlife refuges and in the conservation of the vast numbers of animals, but somehow their successes rarely came across to the public; only when there was a disaster beyond anyone's control did people sit up and pay attention, and that was when newspeople developed a condescending attitude and enjoyed picturing Government officials or the warden in the worst possible light.

David knew one thing: the next time some cameraman asked to take a picture of him standing next to an elephant calf dead from starvation or poaching, that cameraman was going to find a singular lack of cooperation.

"What he will find," he muttered to himself, "is this warden's boot up his insensitive ass."

As he approached his office, he noticed the Indian waiting patiently beside the door, and he recognized the man as the foreman of the nearby sisal plantation.

Glancing up, the man saw him and hurried forward with an apologetic expression. "Mr. Shelby asked me to deliver this to you, Warden," he said as he offered him the letter he carried.

David groaned inwardly when he saw the envelope. He nodded and thanked the departing Indian, sure already that it would be bad news from a nice man.

Duncan Shelby was manager and major owner of the Kenya Sisal Company, Ltd. Many of the sisal estate's twenty thousand acres bordered on the irregular southern boundary of Aruba National Park, both above and below the village of Moda, and one-fifth of the estate's acreage had been abandoned as far as crops were concerned because of the depredations by wild elephants.

Shelby was a reserved but extremely polite gentleman of the old school, and as usual, his letter conveyed the personality of the man:

I regret to have to inform you that a large herd of some hundred elephants have again invaded our crop west of Tari Hill and north of the Mombasa/Nairobi road. I have met with Game Warden Maimbo in Moda and he promised to come out this afternoon with thunder-flashes to try to move them back into the national park.

I'm afraid that this tactic will prove fruitless. I understand completely the dire straits in which the animals find themselves as a result of the drought, but I should like to point out that we too are suffering, and I shall count myself fortunate if I can harvest a fraction of my crops this year.

I would certainly appreciate your assistance in this matter, and will look forward to meeting with you at your convenience to discuss the situation.

Very sincerely yours,
D. Shelby

As David walked into his office, he decided that he'd wait to see the result of this afternoon's operation with the thunder-flashes. He too doubted that they would prove effective. If not, then either he'd send Agaran or he'd go himself with Maimbo at dawn tomorrow morning, and they would have to shoot a couple of the larger animals in order to panic the rest back inside. Dismally he wondered what good it would do. The elephants were hungry and the sisal plants were right over the park boundary. And what animal ever paid attention to man's invisible property lines? They'd be right back in a week, if not the next day. He hated the idea of having to shoot an elephant, unless, of course, it was seriously maimed or a rogue—usually one and the same. But understanding the reason behind the elephants' feeding in the estate crops failed to justify the results, and he knew that he might be forced to put down one or two, rather than allow them to wander over the area destroying crops that were desperately needed.

Several plantations and estates now bordered many of the country's national parks and reserves, and since the game refuges weren't fenced, the animals came and went as they pleased; plant any crop near the boundary and you were asking for visits from the wildlife, particularly during the dry season or a drought, when their own food sources dwindled. Fences didn't do much good. There were few barriers that would stop a herd of elephants.

Still, he had to do something. Shelby's plantation dated back to the early part of the century, fifty years before the colonial government had decided to establish a national park on his doorstep, and Duncan Shelby had always been a cooperative friend of the park in the past. David knew he'd have to do what he could to return the favor. He sat down at his desk, took up a red pen, inked a checkmark onto the right-hand corner and dropped the letter into the folder labeled IMPORTANT MATTERS PENDING before turning back to the messages that had accumulated during his absence.

Quickly disposing of several miscellaneous items, he soon reached the bottom of the pile and smiled when he found the short note from one of his favorite people. Vera Batey was definitely unique. She was an elderly, warmhearted, but salty and razor-tongued missionary nurse in the nearby village.

David had met her shortly after his posting to Aruba when she'd treated him one evening for a scorpion bite. The meeting was like a trip home to childhood. Vera's brisk ministrations and tart scolding had stripped away the years and left him a barefoot boy in ragged shorts with the runny nose that presaged a bad cold because he'd gone out to play in the chill evening mist without a jacket, instead of a thirty-five-year-old warden whose habit of going barefoot in the house had earned him a savage sting from the irate scorpion he'd inadvertently stepped on. But the old warm, fussed-over feeling was the same, and he'd begun to chuckle. She'd glanced up from the hot tea she was making, which accompanied every emergency, and her sharp gray eyes had met his dark ones; in that moment she'd known she'd been seen through. After a minute she'd smiled a soft, self-conscious smile and patted his hand as she said, "You drink that tea while it's hot, now . . . and eat all your biscuits."

Sunday dinner two or three times a month at Vera's had become a habit, and both of them looked forward to the visits. Perhaps the note was an invitation.

He opened it and scanned the contents. It was something else entirely.

Dear David:

Another rabid dog came into the village this morning. This time six people were attacked and bitten. Please come as soon as you can. Something has to be done.

V.

He was alarmed. This was the third incident involving a rabid dog within the past fortnight, but the first two attacks had resulted in only a single victim each time. Now there was a total of eight victims.

Dropping the note on the table, he walked over to the huge map on the wall which illustrated the vastness of Aruba and the immediate surrounding areas, including the village nearby. The whole area was a rabies control zone, and rabid animals were not unknown, but this was beginning to sound suspiciously like an epidemic. Studying the map, he picked out the locations of the recent attacks. He would have to get in touch with the District Health Officer and get all the information available relating to recent incidents of rabid animals and see if a pattern emerged that would indicate the specific area of the outbreak. Perhaps it could be contained. It had to be.

He jotted down a letter of inquiry to the Health Officer and dropped it into his OUT box for his typist, Margaret, to find when she returned from lunch, before catching up his beret and heading out the door for the village.

MARGARET GITHU WAS NOT taking her lunch today. It was the end of October, and Warden Karanja was just finishing the Warden's Quarterly Report for the months of July, August, and September. Margaret was nervous. She had come here only three months ago to replace the Warden's previous typist, who had married and left, and Margaret wasn't sure if the Warden was pleased with her or not. She didn't think so. Dismally she comforted herself with the knowledge that she really did try hard; in fact, she had never worked so hard ever, anywhere, and she wanted very much to stay. Not only was it a good job with better-than-average hours and pay, but there was a Gate Ranger whom she'd been seeing a lot of in the staff quarters. Thinking about the handsome young ranger at the park's Main Gate brought a small, secret smile to her thin face before she forced her mind to return to her work.

Ordinarily the Warden was very nice; it was just that he insisted on an absence of spelling errors, and her knowledge of English was not as good as his. But then, how could it be? He had been educated at a university in America, and she had just a fourth-form education in her village, with a few months' training at typing school in Nairobi.

The Warden wrote out the drafts of his correspondence and reports, and then she typed them up for his approval and signature. Sometimes it was hard to tell from his handwriting just what word it was he wanted, and her efforts were returned marked heavily in red ink, necessitating a complete retyping of the offending letter or report.

Getting out her well-thumbed and grubby English dictionary, she began to check her report for errors in spelling and to see if some of the more obscure words made sense in their context. Reading and checking against the Warden's draft, she made light pencil notations and held her breath tensely. In the section on the Field Force and Anti-Poaching Operations, she found that "The Field Force was required to preceed on foot . . ." should have read, ". . . required to *proceed* on foot . . ." and "Three Wakamba arived with bows and poisoned arrows" must really mean "Three Wakamba *armed* with bows and poisoned arrows."

Margaret was almost in tears as she quickly began to correct the errors, hoping that for once, she could realign the machine perfectly so that the new words would slip into place at just the right height and space position, and the original mistakes wouldn't be noticed. She had to get the report finished today. The Warden had impatiently inquired about it early this morning. Her fingers trembled, smearing the white correction fluid, and she moaned softly.

GATE RANGER WAMBUA MULOLO was pleased when he saw the two tourist-filled *kombi* vans from one of the large tour companies pull off the road from Moda village to stop before the park's Main Gate. It looked as if it were going to be a very profitable day.

The first thing he'd learned after leaving Ranger School at Embakazi, two years before, was how to supplement his meager salary of 525 shillings a month. Perhaps meager wasn't the right word; actually the salary was more than he could make in most of the other situations available to a man with his limited education and skills. And it was also true that the other rangers managed to get along on the same salary very well, even those with two wives and numbers of children. But still, another man's idea of what was sufficient was not likely to meet Mulolo's requirements. "Sufficient" would never be enough anyway.

He watched while the two drivers parked their minibuses, and as they walked toward the ticket office where he stood, he counted the heads of the tourists left behind to wait. There were six in one *kombi* and seven in the other, a total of thirteen visitors at 20 shillings each; plus 20 for each of the drivers and the same for each of the vehicles. He mentally added it up: 340 shillings.

"Habari gani?" Mulolo asked of the drivers, with whom he'd done business before.

"Safi tu," replied the taller of the two men as they shook hands. They were pleased to see him on duty, instead of another ranger with whom they did not have an understanding.

Mulolo smiled and turned to ring up the tickets: two vehicles with one passenger each—80 shillings.

"Eighty shillings," he said in Swahili, and taking the notes, he dropped them into the slot at the top of the safe that was emptied by the accountant each day.

That left 260 shillings to be divided between them: half for Mulolo and half to be split between the two drivers. Mulolo slipped his share into the sweatband of his uniform hat, and after a few minutes of conversation the drivers returned to their *kombis* to drive their bleary-eyed and dusty charges to their waiting rooms at the Safari Lodge. They were on one of the "milk runs"—six parks in eight days—and an enterprising driver could make a tidy sum of money if he was able to come to an agreement with enough of the rotating Gate Rangers in the various parks.

Mulolo closed the gates behind the departing *kombi* vans and stepped back into the cool of the ticket office. He smiled again in satisfaction. A clever man such as himself could always find a way to make a little extra.

There were several ways to fiddle the gate receipts, but it wasn't smart to use any one of them too often; it only increased the chances of being caught. He'd seen too many less-than-smart rangers who had learned one fiddle and then proceeded to use it like a dog with one trick until they ended up wearing a coarse white prison uniform.

No, the prison uniform wasn't for him. He liked the one he had on now; it provided him with many opportunities, including the Warden's typist, who knew everything that went on at Head-quarters, since she either read it, typed it up, or overheard it. He'd been understandably annoyed when the last typist had been sum-moned home to participate in the wedding her parents had arranged for her, but as soon as he saw Margaret's timid face, he knew it wouldn't be long before he'd be in her bed and doing business as usual.

It was amazing, he thought, how women on their backs could talk; it was as if the effort of opening their legs opened their mouths as well. The endearing thing about Margaret was that she didn't know the meaning of discretion. He was her man as far as she was concerned, and there wasn't anything that she could, or should, keep from him. There were already none-too-subtle hints from her about the *shamba* field that was to be hers, and how much money she sent home monthly for her mother to invest in goats for when she married and went home to raise a family.

"Goats!" Mulolo giggled to himself derisively.

He shouldn't complain, though; she'd believed him when he told her he was going to volunteer the next time a new Field Force Unit was to be organized and trained. The Field Force Rangers were highly thought of, and Margaret was pleased that he would soon join the more heroic field units; and when he asked about the movements of the Field Force, she understood that it was because he was anxious to join them and so he wanted to know everything about where they went, and what they did. What she didn't know was that he didn't give a damn beyond the fact that there were people who paid very well to know where the Field Force Units were deployed each day, people who made considerable sums of money in poached and smuggled ivory and horn, and who had no time to spend bailing their employed hunters out of jail and coming to the attention of the authorities through arrests and charge sheets. Such people didn't make mistakes and paid well for valuable services rendered by others who were smart enough not to make mistakes either.

Mulolo knew very well where he fitted in. He was smart; he didn't make mistakes; and he was very valuable because, through Margaret, he had access to information that no one else had except the Warden.

Once a week the Warden assigned the patrol duties for each unit for the next seven days, and these regular but rotating patrols were typed up by Margaret. Every morning the designated patrol for that day was taken from the safe and given to the corporal in charge of each unit. If the unit was bivouacked in the bush, its patrol directions were sent by VHF radio. Occasionally there were changes, but Margaret usually knew these the night before, and it was a simple matter for Mulolo to flag down the beat-up old Volkswagen that came through the gate early each morning with the Nairobi newspapers, and slip a folded note with the 1 shilling and 20 cents into the driver's hand in return for the English newspaper he couldn't read.

Abruptly he jumped; a car horn had sounded just outside the ticket office. Grumbling at the interruption to his thoughts, he stepped out the door to see that Warden Karanja had stopped behind the gates and was drumming his fingers on the steering wheel. Mulolo snapped to his smartest salute and ran quickly to the gate. Throwing it open, he jerked ostentatiously to attention and again saluted rigidly as Karanja nodded in acknowledgment and drove through on his way to the village. As soon as the vehicle was gone, Mulolo's expression relaxed into a self-satisfied smirk.

CHAPTER FOUR

Early Afternoon

V ERA BATEY's Mercy Mission Dispensary in the village of Moda was the only source of medical aid within a radius of seventy-five kilometers. Vera was a tall, gaunt woman, who could have been anywhere between fifty and sixty-five years of age, with a husky contralto voice which, heard over the telephone or from another room, conjured up visions of someone young and provocative. Actually meeting the lady was a shock; she was within an inch or so of six feet, and "angular" would be a polite way to describe her bony frame. White, wiry hair, snatched into a bun on the top of her head, framed a thin face where old-fashioned rimless spectacles were impaled on high prominent cheekbones. The generous but slenderly sculpted nose was topped by a pair of pale gray eyes that always wore a slightly surprised expression, although it had been years since anything, or anybody, had had the originality to amaze her. She knew and understood the human condition; and she'd run out of patience with the whole thing years ago.

Not quite a doctor, yet much more than a nurse, Vera attended to the illnesses and injuries of every man, woman, and child in the vast area. She dressed burns, dewormed the children, patched up the losers of the *pombe*-club brawls, treated malaria, pulled rotten teeth, and all for 5 shillings a visit, including injections and take-home medicine. Return visits for the re-dressing of wounds or checkups of bad chests and such were free, but the treatment of venereal disase and the delivery of babies was increased to 40 shillings. It was suspected that the higher fee was meant to act as a deterrent to repeat offenders, but it didn't seem to accomplish its objective.

She was called *"Mama Mkali"* by the local people, and "Sharp Mama" was what she was to them; they were scared to death of her, and with good reason. She'd spent her life nursing and scolding the poor in developing countries, and she'd discovered that by raising her husky voice, she produced an awe-inspiring bellow that, coupled with threats, usually achieved the results she wanted. While it was true that the people feared her intimidating manner, it was she to whom they turned when they were sick or hurt. They trusted her. They came from as far away as a hundred miles, passing up other dispensaries, infirmaries, Government hospitals; they came by bus or *matatu,* or they walked, because they knew that this tall, skinny woman with a voice like the rumbles heard during the rains would always help them.

They walked down the dusty, deeply rutted dirt road till they came to the mission veranda, partially shaded by a few pawpaw trees, and took their places on crude unpainted benches. Occasionally a woman would comfort the fretful, whimpering baby she carried on her back, wrapped in a cotton *khanga,* or the feverish child who stood at her knee and whose small face wore the tracks of tears. Men sat with crossed legs, or if the benches were full, squatted on their heels on the cement floor, and smoked or took snuff while they waited with a dirty, bloodied cloth wrapped around an injury.

They sat quietly, making little conversation, waiting for the sound of the small school bell which signaled that the line would now be one person shorter, and as the next patient stepped into the little office, all slid forward one place, so that one more could take a seat at the end. Today was a typical Monday. As Vera turned away from her examination of the young Kamba, she glanced at her watch: it was a quarter past two. Just fifteen minutes since they'd opened after lunch, and they were already swamped.

After washing her hands at the chipped enamel basin, and making an impatient wipe-and-dab motion with the thin cotton towel that hung from a rusty nail beside the old-fashioned iron washstand, Vera left the young man to the ministrations of Adam, her assistant, and walked out of the small examining room adjoining her office.

Stepping down into the long, narrow ward containing six iron beds, she crossed to the first bed and bent down to pull the heavy woolen blanket aside to inspect the middle-aged wife of one of the park sergeants. She'd been the first patient seen after the lunch break, and the moment she'd stepped into her office, Vera had known that the woman had malaria, and a severe attack at that.

Thirty-odd years of experience gained in the examination and treatment of as many as two hundred sick human beings each day, on six of every seven days of the week, enabled her most often to tell at a glance what the problem was and how bad.

Putting her hand to the wet forehead of the woman, she felt with satisfaction that the raging fever had dropped. But had it dropped enough? After inserting a thermometer into the woman's mouth, Vera turned and walked over to the window to look out onto the veranda where the afternoon's allotment of sick and injured waited.

Leaning against the cool stone wall beside the window, she realized how tired she was. There were dozens left to see—too many to finish with by closing. She'd be working late again. She briefly thought of closing the doors at five thirty, after telling them all to go away and to return in the morning; it was an idea she had considered many times before, but never carried out. Vera avoided the veranda; seen one at a time in her office they were bearable, but to have to be confronted with the supplicating stares of so many pairs of eyes all at once made her want to scream wildly that they were too many, wanting too much. They needed doctors, hospitals, laboratories, and she had none of these. But she said nothing because she knew she was all they had.

As she turned from the window and prepared to return to the woman, she noticed that the last bed in the row of six was still occupied. It stood against the wall farthest from the office and examining room, protected from view by a tattered folding screen. With a feeling of guilt, Vera realized that she'd forgotten all about little Mutisia Milili; she'd supposed his parents had returned for him, but they hadn't. They were probably finding it difficult, if not impossible, to arrange for transportation home; most tribes were repelled by death and no one would willingly offer a ride to a parent carrying a dead child.

Vera uncovered the small head and looked again at the handsome face of the three-year-old. He was only the latest victim of ignorance. There would be more this afternoon, and again tomorrow, and each and every successive day. By the time his distraught parents had rushed in with him this morning, there was nothing Vera or anyone else could do. He'd been sick for many days, his parents said, but they thought he was getting better, only this morning they couldn't rouse him. In their efforts to help the child, they'd poured warm milk into his mouth, but he had remained very still, and in their fear they brought him to her.

She'd known then it was too late, but still she tried. Hurriedly she had slipped a tube into the milk-filled lungs and sucked and sucked and spat the bubbly milk onto the floor, where it had splattered over her legs. She had applied artificial respiration while she prayed soundlessly, her only conscious thought: Too long, it's been too long. He's gone.

Finally she had sat back, still on the floor beside the bed, her hands covering the child's small chest. Turning to the parents, who crouched beside her, she'd said, *"Amekwenda sasa. Amekufa."*

They understood. He was gone now. Dead. The father nodded and looked away; the mother sat and stared at her only child as the first tears slipped down her face. They said nothing. Sickness and death were part of life; they accepted that; expected and endured it with a stoic fatalism that in its turn caused death.

For years Vera had fought this attitude; the blind acceptance which caused the sick to be kept at home in the dirt-floored and mud-walled *shamba* huts until it was too late. She'd reproached and berated them, condemned them for trying to treat the very ill with bush medicine, love, and the inevitable witch doctor or faith healer. It was true that she had made some headway, but it was a desperately slow process. When she was young it had seemed she had all the time in the world to teach and to bring understanding; but nearly forty years had passed, and she knew that she had little time left and still far to go.

With an effort she'd resisted her impulse to accuse the parents of having killed the child, because by not seeking medical help they'd allowed the illness to reach a critical stage, and then they'd poured milk into the mouth of a child unable to swallow, and he had drowned. Instead she quietly explained that the sick must be brought to her early; that food or liquid must never be given to anyone who was not completely awake and aware that he must swallow. Dumbly she saw that not all was understood, that they failed to comprehend the implications of what she said. They didn't realize that they were responsible. Perhaps tomorrow a glimmer of the truth would be suspected, wondered at; perhaps their next child would be brought in time. Perhaps not.

Vera sighed, and covered again the face of the child before stepping from behind the screen to return to the woman. Checking the thermometer, she saw with satisfaction that the chloroquine injection had taken effect and her temperature had fallen to just below 101 degrees. The fever had broken; the woman could go home. Helping her to her feet, Vera told her to dress, and after giving her a small packet of tablets, she accepted the 5-shilling note the woman produced from a clean knotted handkerchief hidden in her bra.

After cleaning up the vacated bed and folding the heavy wool blankets used to sweat out the woman's fever, Vera returned to the small examining room to see how Adam was getting on. As she glanced over her assistant's shoulder, she caught sight of Muthoka's pain-contorted features, and she pitied the boy. She saw that Adam had finished incising and draining the deep inguinal abscess in his groin, a complication of venereal disease, and was now packing the cavity with eight inches of the half-inch gauze wick which would continue the drainage as it was withdrawn, a half-inch each day, until the wound healed from the inside.

As she prepared the penicillin injection, the young man cried out sharply, then subsided into strangled sobs. Vera thought dourly that he certainly didn't sound like the same boy who'd strutted in an hour ago in the secondhand platform shoes and tight pants which had probably cost him two months' wages. "Oh, yes," he'd said proudly as he'd given his best imitation of the *towni* boys he'd seen at the village bus stop. He liked to go to the Diamond Pombe Club in the evenings. Yes, sometimes he went every night. "And," he'd added boastfully and not a little defiantly, sometimes he "stayed all night." The last part, she'd supposed, was for the express purpose of shocking the old missionary nurse. "As if he could," she muttered to herself sadly.

Vera hadn't needed to hear anything he'd said once he mentioned the Diamond Pombe Club. She knew it well; that and a couple of other popular beer bars were heard from often here. An average of four to six cases weekly of VD at Mercy had been an effective advertisement of a questionable nature.

After administering the injection and reminding Muthoka to return the following day, and to bring his young pregnant wife for treatment, Vera washed her hands again and left the examining room to return to her office. She found David Karanja patiently waiting.

Her tired face lit with a smile as he stood to take both her hands in his. "I was beginning to think you weren't coming."

"I'm sorry. I didn't get your note until just now."

"Well, come in the back, and we'll have a bit of lunch while we talk."

As they passed through the small ward, David glanced at the empty beds. "They're gone already?" he asked—referring to the attack victims, who he knew would require hospitalization at the Government hospital at Mombasa, over a hundred miles away.

Vera nodded as she opened the door to her small living quarters adjoining the dispensary. "Two ambulances from Mombasa came and took them just before noon."

Passing through her small parlor and into the kitchen, Vera

67

added, "But we'll have something to eat first and then discuss it."
Studying his lean frame, she said, "Late or not, I don't suppose
you've eaten any lunch." Speculating further, she peered over the
tops of her spectacles and added pointedly, "Or breakfast either."

His guilty look confirmed her guess. Fetching a covered dish from
the refrigerator, she began to scold him furiously. "I don't think
that old man who works for you ever bothers to get you a meal. If
you were any thinner, David, a strong gust of wind would blow you
right out of your park."

"Bubu is a good cook, as a matter of fact," he protested. "Not as
good as you, but still good. It's not his fault that I don't get home
for regular meals."

"At the risk of sounding like a nattering old woman, I'll say it
again," Vera replied tartly. "It's time you found yourself a nice
young lady and got married." Her gray eyes were direct as she added,
"It's a woman you need at home, to look after you and see that you
get a warm meal at whatever hour you get in."

Looking sideways at the elderly missionary nurse, David said
mischievously, "Whenever you're ready, I'll deliver the bride price.
Three cows is considered sufficient"; he pondered, then decided,
"but since you're educated, I'll give four for you."

The dumbfounded expression on her face made his joke a huge
success. He dissolved in laughter as Vera flung her dish towel over
his head.

"Shame on you," she said, chuckling, as she heated the chicken
curry on the stove. "I said, a *young* woman."

As usual, Vera's cooking made the lunch that followed a special
treat. After finishing the huge plate of spiced curry and rice which
brought tears to his eyes, David pushed back from the table and
wished for a cigarette; a meal like that needed one to finish with.

"You can smoke if you have to," Vera said indulgently before
adding a prickly afterthought: "But go get the ashtray out of the
parlor. Don't you be putting your nasty ashes in my dishes."

As David left the table, he knew the pleasant hour's reprieve from
the park's problems was over. Returning to the kitchen with the
seashell that did duty as Vera's only ashtray, he said, "Tell me about
the rabies attacks."

"Well, the first attack was, let me see . . ." She thought a moment.
". . . two weeks ago. A young man was badly mauled by a neighbor's
dog when he fell asleep under a tree while he was tending the family
goats near the village. From his description of the animal, it sounded
as if it were rabid."

She picked up the dishes she'd been stacking, and carried them to the sink. "The dog disappeared into the bush and hasn't been seen since. The next attack was last week. A woman heard her *mtoto* start screaming in terror outside their hut, and she ran out to see a strange dog advancing on the toddler; she snatched up the child and dashed inside again. Her husband came running and managed to kill the dog with a *panga*, but not before the dog bit him on the leg. When I treated the man he said he was sure the animal had *'ugonjwa wa wazimu'*—the disease of madness.''

Wiping off the plastic tablecloth, she added, "Then this morning one of the village dogs reappeared after an absence of several days and attacked a number of people in the *soko*. I was summoned immediately, but by the time I got there, six people, including three children, had been attacked, and one child was badly mauled. I'd been told it was a mad dog, so I'd armed myself with a *panga* and I rounded up all the men in the marketplace. They grabbed everything from rocks to knives and long sticks, and we took after the animal, which had wandered off in the direction of the national park. We were right behind him when he broke into a stumbling run toward the thick bush on the other side of the park boundary, but when we got into the dense thornbush I had to tell the men to discontinue. In the underbrush, the animal could dash out and attack and then retreat before the men could manage to kill him.

"We returned to the village, and I administered first aid to the victims." She shook her head sadly and added, "It's amazing how much damage that animal inflicted. No one had the sense to try to kill it; they just ran around getting in one another's way and made no attempt to fight back. But then, Africans are usually terrified of big dogs."

"A big dog?" David asked in surprise. "Who had a big dog? Most village dogs are quite small."

"Yes, I know—those little yellow things with curled-up tails. No, it wasn't one of those. It was a big black animal—an Alsatian mix of some kind. It belonged to a villager here whose son brought it back from Nairobi a couple of years ago. It was a handsome dog, and well cared for, too—one of the few dogs or cats here that were. Most of them live on what they can catch or they go hungry." Vera shook her head; the way pets were cared for, or rather, not cared for, was a sore point with her.

"That's why," she continued, "he was able to do so much damage. He was known by everyone, and the people were afraid of him. When he went mad and started savaging anything in sight, everyone panicked and tried to get out of the way."

"You said that he ran back into the park?"

"That's right," she said as she poured the tea.

"Has he been seen since?"

She shook her head as she offered him cream and sugar.

David stirred his tea slowly. "You know that rabies is endemic here. Many of the wildlife have it; they can carry it, so to speak, without actually suffering from it. I suppose it's because they're exposed to it in small doses, if that's the right way to put it, throughout their lives. An animal can live its life out and die at a ripe old age without ever experiencing the symptoms, or appearing to be rabid. But," he said, "it can bite another animal and *that* animal can become rabid."

"Like our village dogs?" she asked as she picked up the half-worked rug she was hooking. Her hands were never idle.

"That's right. I doubt if your domesticated village cats and dogs have any natural immunity or resistance at all."

"But why now, David? I've been here for more years than I want to admit to, and it's never happened before."

He considered one of the ideas that had occurred to him earlier before saying, "I really don't know for sure, but I'm going to try to find out. I think I'll radio Dr. Yakub at Research Headquarters in Nairobi and see if he has any information, and I'll talk with Jeff Forbes in the morning. I have a suspicion or two."

"What is it? Can you put an end to it?"

"No. If I'm right, then we'll know why it's happening, but I can't stop it." He frowned in concentration. "I've heard that if an animal carries rabies—that is to say, he has rabies but doesn't act like it or get sick with it—he can be made to suffer from it if he's put under severe stress. It's been done in laboratories. With a wild animal, it's usually enough just to cage them; that alone creates a sufficient stress factor to cause the animal to develop the disease symptoms. Or food or water can be withheld for a limited time. An animal who doesn't have a 'sleeping' case of rabies would just be uncomfortable, but a potentially rabid animal would begin to sicken."

Vera looked up from drawing a strip of wool through the rug's coarse burlap backing. "Like a person who's in a run-down condition catching a cold when the rest of the family doesn't?"

"I guess that's the way it works." He smiled. "You're the nurse; you tell me."

She chuckled slyly. "That's what I keep doing. I've said it before and I'll say it again: what you really need is a pretty young—"

He interrupted: "Five cows."

She shook her head. "I give up."

For a moment neither spoke; nothing was heard but the soft, rhythmic plopping sound of Vera working her rug, and the occasional muted squeak of the bats overhead. A few days before, they'd somehow got back into the space between the roof and the ceiling boards, but Vera had been so busy lately that she hadn't taken the time to organize a bat-removal, find-the-hole-and-plug-it-up exercise. Still, she'd have to do it soon. A frown appeared on her face as she concentrated on the rabies problem. "You said a stress factor?"

David nodded.

"And withholding food?"

He nodded again.

"And water?" she continued. She looked up as she lowered her work to her lap. "The drought," she exclaimed.

He nodded again. "Yes, I think it's more than possible."

She considered the idea carefully and then said, "There's always an occasional rabies incident in any area where there is a large wildlife population, so what you're thinking is that because of a severe climatic stress factor, the incidence of rabies is rising in the wildlife. Possibly drastically."

"I think so, but I'm not a veterinarian. I'll have to check with the men who do know."

"If you're right, what can we do?"

"Not much, I'm afraid," he said. "Tomorrow I'll pull Units One and Four off their regular patrol and send them into those areas of the park which border on the village. For the next few days I'll rotate the five units in the Southern Area so that one unit is always working the thick bush near the settled areas. Their instructions will be to shoot on sight any domesticated dogs or cats that have gone wild, and any sick-looking predators; that includes the big cats, plus the hyena, hunting dog, and jackal, as well as the small predators— anything that eats meat, in fact, including the baboons. Damn!" he exclaimed in sudden irritation without thinking. "What a mess!"

Vera glanced up in offended surprise, a sharp retort ready. She didn't condone swearing and had never known David to do so in her presence. Then she saw the tension in his face, and her expression softened in sympathy.

"I'd like you to do something for me," he said, controlled now. "Speak to the chief and subchiefs in the morning, and tell them to have their people confine all their dogs and cats. I'll speak with Warden Maimbo in the village tomorrow and get his cooperation." He looked up. "I'm sorry, but every stray dog that isn't tied up will be shot. It's the stray animals that are usually responsible for these outbreaks, because they contract the disease from the wildlife. Family dogs and cats will have to be vaccinated immediately; all others will be destroyed."

"I'll see the chiefs early tomorrow," Vera promised. "When will the strays in the village be shot?"

David thought a moment. "I'll have to check with Maimbo, but probably the day after tomorrow. Any strays inside the park will be put down starting tomorrow. I'll be seeing the Senior Warden for the Coast Province in the morning. I'll ask him to send a veterinarian up Wednesday to vaccinate the village pets who have homes. In two days every dog and cat in the area will be either vaccinated or put down."

Later, as Vera walked with him to the Land-Rover, he said, "I'm going to send Bubu to you in the morning. I want him to help your *shamba* man remove the bats from above the ceiling, and seal any openings so they can't take up residence again."

"You don't need to do that," Vera began. "I can get to it in a week or so, and—"

"Tomorrow," he interrupted. Climbing into the Land-Rover, he added, to forestall any further disagreement, "I've heard that bats can carry rabies. Besides," he teased, "I want to protect my investment of four cows."

He started the vehicle and waved goodbye; then Vera's voice called out over the sound of the engine. He glanced back.

"You said *five*." Her face was triumphant with the parting shot.

WHEN SET ASIDE as a game refuge in the late 1940s, the area that was to become Aruba National Park had consisted of thousands of miles of trackless bushland that no one wanted, because the rainfall was insufficient for agriculture, while the dense bush harbored the tsetse fly, which infected man's domesticated animals with trypanosomiasis —sleeping sickness. Consequently, only one tribe had lived in the area: the Waliangulu, a hunting tribe living solely off the wildlife, particularly the elephants. After the gazetting, it had been necessary to remove them for relocation in areas outside the Park's boundaries, so they had been taken to settlement areas on the coast. Their weapons—their knives, arrows, and famous "big bows"—had been taken from them and replaced with seed, farm implements, and goats. But the Waliangulu were hunters—not agriculturalists like the Taita, and not pastoralists like the Masai. So they ate the seed corn, slaughtered the goats, and began the long trek home. They'd returned in ones and twos and in small family groups, and they'd built their huts close to the park boundaries that tried to keep them out of their hunting grounds. The hunters had gone into the bush and returned with the long, supple tree limbs from which they'd fashioned their bows and arrows, and their life had gone on as before; only now it had another name: poaching.

By the late fifties, the poaching situation had become critical, and the continued existence of all wildlife in the Coast Province was threatened. It hadn't been just the Waliangulu—they were just the best of the hunters. The poaching at Aruba was practiced by every tribe in southeast Kenya and beyond, and it brought about the necessity of creating a paramilitary Field Force to protect the wildlife in the national parks.

By this time, though, most of Kenya's tribes had adapted themselves to the changes brought by the Europeans, and in settling into the twentieth century they had forgotten many of the old ways of their individual tribes. But not so the proud and independent nomadic people of the dry lands and deserts of northern Kenya. They had resisted change, and had continued to teach their children how to survive in the harsh conditions of their homeland. Consequently, the colonial wardens had turned to the north to recruit the men of the Turkana, Boran, Samburu, Orma, and Somali tribes because they were the ideal choice for a Field Force that was to operate exclusively in the inhospitable bush country they were accustomed to. When Mohamed Agaran had come from the Turkana tribal land to begin training for the first Field Force Unit, he, like the rest of the recruits, was coated with red ocher and wore only a brief loincloth. The tribal markings of his people showed in the ritualistic scarring of his abdomen, in his perforated and distended earlobes, and in the gaps where two teeth had been pulled from the front of his lower jaw when he was seven years old.

Few would have believed it possible to turn such a man into a qualified Field Force Ranger. However, what he'd required in the way of training was not as important or vital as what he'd already known: he knew the bushland and could survive there with only his spear to provide for food and protection; he knew the use of every bush, tree, herb, and creeper, whether for food, medicine, poison, or utensil; he could track down and kill or trap anything or anybody, and he understood the ways and habits of everything that lived in the bush. He also had one other qualification which gave him a tremendous advantage over his fellow recruits: thanks to a few years of mission schooling, he was able to read and write.

The grueling demands of the Field Force had appealed to him, and his natural instinct to lead rather than follow had led to a swift rise through the ranks to sergeant. Then the Kenya Government had offered to further the education of a few selected men who lacked advanced schooling, but whose demonstrated ability deserved a chance at the education required for further promotion. Mohamed had been sent to Mweka College in Tanzania for two years to absorb the principles of range and wildlife management and park administration.

But it hadn't been easy for a man approaching his thirties to settle down to the classroom routine of lectures and lessons. Taken out of the bush and off patrol, he'd had to struggle to absorb the education that was being poured into him in the alien environment of a modern campus. He'd attended his classes and returned to his quarters to study, and every day had had its period of helpless frustration that grew until he had been tempted to quit. But something had made him stay on for one more week, then another, and slowly it had all begun to make a little more sense.

He'd known at the time that what he was doing would prove to be the hardest thing he would ever do and it was probably this knowledge that kept him at it until he graduated. Then, after being posted to two other national parks for a period of three years each, he'd been sent back to Aruba, where his career had begun almost eighteen years before. But where he had once been a raw and primitive recruit dressed in loincloth and ostrich feathers, he'd returned as a smartly dressed and well-educated assistant warden. It was difficult to reconcile the difference, even to himself.

As he sat on the edge of his desk and stared out the window to the Moda River Valley below, Mohamed looked back over the years in the hope of finding the answer to a problem that plagued him today. Instead, he found that it was as if the young man he'd been were someone he'd known well a long time ago, but who was now left behind and almost forgotten. The thought was oddly disturbing.

He'd spent the last two hours going through old file cabinets, searching for any information regarding the Waliangulu poacher, and the logical place to start had been in the records kept of the massive three-year-long anti-poaching campaign that had begun the year after he was recruited. The operation had required the combined efforts of the then Colonial Army, Police, Game Department, and National Parks and had covered the entire Coast Province and part of Central Province. When it was over, so was poaching, and almost every able-bodied Waliangulu male was in jail. But not this one.

He glanced down at the faded, termite-riddled folder in his hand

and was disappointed. The previous wardens had kept excellent records of every operation, raid, and arrest, but there was little useful information on the pages labeled HEEKUTA NEKO: the man picked up only once—accidentally.

It stated only that during a series of night raids on Waliangulu villages just outside the park boundaries, a man had been taken after ivory had been found buried in his hut, but during the walk back to the vehicles the prisoner had managed to slip his hands out of the handcuffs and disappear into the bush. Mohamed's jaw clenched in disgust. They hadn't even held him long enough to get him back to Headquarters, so there was no photograph, no record of interrogation, no information. Nothing.

The arresting rangers' description of a man seen only briefly by torchlight was worthless: average height, average build, and traditional tribal markings. A "young man," they said, and Mohamed swore softly: that could mean anything between boyhood and middle age. The prisoner had refused to answer questions, and so his name had not been learned until days later, when a Giriama informer identified the signature on the man's confiscated arrows and bow. Shortly after, two notations had been added: *appears to hunt alone,* and *takes left side.* And then, the beginning of the record of his kills for the next two decades. The number of these notations stunned him. They were in the hundreds. Higher during the sixties, tapering off during the seventies, until two years before, when they suddenly ceased.

"Why?" he murmured, his forehead creased in perplexity. It was as if he'd suddenly died. What had happened two years ago? Had he been injured? His eyes narrowed in speculation.

Perhaps Karanja was right. The man had to be fifty, maybe older. The skill of the Waliangulu hunters lay not only in their ability to creep close enough to an elephant to drive the poison-covered foreshaft through the tough skin and deep into its flesh to guarantee maximum absorption of the poison, but also in their successful escape from the enraged animal's trumpeting, screaming charge after being hit. Few who had not seen such a charge could believe the agility and speed of an angry elephant; and few could hope to evade the six tons of fury that pursued at twenty-five miles an hour. He nodded. It was possible. Perhaps the man had not been quick enough, one time, two years before.

Then he sighed, and throwing the folder down on the desk, he walked to the window to glare out at the dry bushland.

It was wishful thinking, no more. He'd seen the man's tracks that morning, and they were not the tracks of a cripple. Further, there

75

was no way a Field Force Unit following an eight-to-ten-hours-old trail could be compared to the immediate charge of a wounded elephant. He was beginning to grasp at straws. The frustrated feeling he'd experienced years ago came back.

The reason they'd never taken the man before had nothing to do with how fast he was, but how cunning. There was nothing the man didn't know about bushcraft. He came and went as he chose. By the time they knew he was operating in the park, he was gone. They would find and follow his trail until it disappeared, but they'd never even glimpsed him. They'd never come close enough; perhaps they never would.

His bafflement grew. He'd been on many of those trails himself, and he knew how it was to see the man's tracks disappear into rocks, at a river, on the lava beds. There was an infuriating feeling of having been outwitted, outmaneuvered. He felt it now.

Years ago, he'd sensed that Warden Nichols failed to understand the Waliangulu because Nichols was a white man, an *Mzungu,* and by not understanding him, by underestimating him, Nichols had never been able to catch him in spite of his relentless pursuit. This morning he'd felt the same about David Karanja, because Karanja was from another place, another tribe, a different background; too different from the man he wanted to capture. But I've never felt *I* didn't understand him, he thought. So when Karanja asked me this morning, why did I say that he couldn't be taken? When did I make that decision? The confusion mounted.

"I've always understood him," he muttered desperately in an attempt to make some sense out of his thoughts, and then an idea flickered across his consciousness: Perhaps it's that I understand him too well. Perhaps I know him as I knew the young man I was, the one I've left behind and almost forgotten. His eyes had turned inward, searching; his breathing was shallow, almost nonexistent. He felt the first dim shadow of self-doubt.

He'd spent the first eighteen years of his life existing as the Turkana had always existed, and no man had known more about the bush than he did. It was all he knew, or had ever known; it was home. But then had come one promotion after another, and he'd been in the office, or in meetings or seminars, and less time each day had been spent in the bush, until now . . . ?

The unthought-out, unspoken realization came slowly, but relentlessly: he knew that the youth he'd been could have taken the Waliangulu, but not the man he'd become. The reason he'd felt the Waliangulu couldn't be captured was not that he thought the man was better; it was that he himself had become less. He had sensed, or feared, that by reaching out for the future, he had let go of something vital, and that was the strength of the past.

His dark hand came up to pull at his earlobe in a nervous, unconscious gesture, and he was suddenly aware of the perforation for the first time in years. How long had it been since the ivory earplugs had been removed? He glanced down the opened neck of his shirt and saw the top of the neat rows of raised scars which had been incised over his chest and down his belly during his youth, and it was as if he were seeing them for the first time. Then his eyes traveled down the once-bare legs, now covered in sharply creased khaki uniform trousers, and on to the highly polished leather boots, crossed negligently at the ankles. He became aware of a rushing windlike sound in his ears, and as it grew into a piercing keen he asked himself: What have I become? Who am I?

He knew now that he had to find the Waliangulu. Not for Karanja; not for the park; but for himself.

CHAPTER FIVE
Late Afternoon

DAVID ENTERED THE Headquarters building, and as he acknowledged the greetings and salutes of the rangers who were going about their business, he passed into the Radio Room to check in as usual after an absence.

Finding nothing for him, he continued on to his office, where he saw the neatly typed Quarterly Report displayed prominently in the center of his desk. He would have to proof that and get it off immediately. He made a point of being as punctual as possible with his Warden's Reports, in spite of the fact that he hated paperwork and it seemed that the volume doubled or trebled each year; particularly since the former National Parks and the Game Department had been merged together into the all-encompassing Department of Wildlife Conservation and Management some two years before.

There was no doubt of it; since the National Parks had become a government body, the number of forms, documents, and reports that had to be filled out, filed, sent, received, and digested had swelled into a blizzard of paperwork. Still, the Warden's Reports were a vital source of information for Department Headquarters, and besides, they were an important reference for him if memory failed and he wanted to know the details of something that had happened last year or the year before.

After making sure his ashtray and red pen were close at hand, he settled comfortably in his leather chair, put his feet up on the corner of his desk and began to read:

KENYA NATIONAL PARKS

Aruba National Park

Warden's Quarterly Report
1st July—30th September, 1977

STAFF:
Senior Staff:

On 1st August, Miss Halima Abdi was transferred from Nairobi to take over as the Director—Education Center, replacing Mr. Henry Peterson of the Peace Corps.

Assistant Warden Francis Matasa was promoted to Warden and transferred to Shimba Hills National Park on 15th August.

Junior Staff:

In July, Assistant Accountant Samuel Mwasi discovered that Gate Ranger Walter Musobo had fiddled the gate receipts at the Okote Gate in the amount of 9,500 shillings. He was later convicted at the District Court at Moda and was sentenced to 2 years' imprisonment with 8 strokes of the cane. The money was not recovered.

On 1st July, Field Force Cpl. Ida Godana was shot in the left shoulder in an exchange of fire when his unit flushed a group of 4 poachers operating in the area of Dakadiko. He spent 3 days in hospital and is now returned to light duty. Two Somali poachers were killed, 1 was captured alive and 1 escaped with wounds into the bush.

Field Force Ranger Molu Jadan, while in an intoxicated state on 4th August, started a fight with and caused grievous bodily harm to another ranger in the staff quarters near Main Gate. The C.I.D. in Moda took up the case and referred it to the District Court, where Ranger Jadan was convicted.

Owing to the epidemic in Tanzania, all staff and their families were inoculated as a precaution against cholera on 18th August by Vera Batey from the village dispensary.

On 22nd September, Driver K. Mongoi and Field Assistant David Cira escaped serious injury when their Land-Rover GK495 went out of control and crashed into a baobab tree when the driver attempted to avoid a herd of zebras that had dashed into the road.

It is with the deepest regret that I have to report the following deaths:

Field Force Ranger Ezra Kimari was killed on 20th July during our efforts to remove a wire snare embedded in the foreleg of an elephant calf. While he was attempting to separate the elephant cow from her injured offspring, the cow attacked Ranger Kimari and tusked him. He was rushed to the local dispensary, and later flown by the Flying Doctor Service to Nairobi, where he died soon after his arrival in hospital.

Field Force Ranger Joseph Ogutu died of multiple chest wounds on 9th August while en route to hospital in Mombasa, and Ranger Dida was killed instantly when shot in the head on 14th September. Both deaths were the result of confrontations with Somali poachers in the Kalima area.

THERE WAS A light tap at David's door. Radio Operator Komora Duba stood just inside the door saluting smartly.

"Yes, what is it?" inquired David wearily. His Warden's Reports were beginning to read like obituary columns.

"Unit Three Field Force reporting on VHF, sir."

David's interest was caught immediately. "Go ahead."

"Corporal in charge reports that the Waliangulu poacher was tracked in a south-southwesterly direction, and at no time did the rangers sight the man. His tracks were lost at the Mombasa/Nairobi road when the poacher reached the tarmac. Corporal requests to know . . . Excuse me, I mean he . . ." Here Duba stumbled verbally as he groped unsuccessfully for the right word while he translated the message he'd taken down in Swahili into the English that was required on radio and when addressing the Warden and Assistant Wardens.

"Yes, the corporal wants to know . . . ?" David said patiently.

"Yes, sir. He wants to know if they should continue the search and cover the sides of the road to pick up his trail."

David glanced at the large wall clock: fifteen minutes till four. They'd been tracking the poacher for six hours now and had never glimpsed him. Heekuta had several hours' head start on them. He must have reached the road while it was still dark, and he could have gone east or west from there. He could have buried the ivory anywhere, and he might have got a lift from a passing vehicle and disappeared in any village along the road. Or he could have walked along the tarmac toward the nearby village, and his tracks would now be lost in the maze of prints left by herds of goats, cattle, and villagers. It was no use. They'd never find his point of departure from the road. He was gone, again.

"No, bring them in."

"Yes, sir." Ranger Duba saluted and withdrew.

David leaned back and wondered grimly if there would be only one kill this time, or was it the beginning of a series? Probably just the first of several, since he hadn't been operating for two years. It was damn odd that he hadn't been heard from for such a long time; it seemed his previous appearances had always occurred at two-to-three-month intervals. David recalled how, after Nichols left, he'd anticipated the poacher's next return, but months had gone by, and then years, and he'd finally decided that the park had probably heard the last of the man. Wishful thinking.

Turning back to the Warden's Report, he quickly began to scan the sections covered under the heading WORK CARRIED OUT. It was remarkable, he thought as he read the individual projects listed, how little tourists really saw or understood of the national parks they visited.

They came to see the wildlife, so that was what they looked for and that was all they saw. They drove in at one gate, traversed anywhere from fifty to two hundred kilometers of park roads, and exited at another gate. If asked to speculate on the number of personnel required to operate the park, the visitor from overseas might struggle to remember how many rangers he had actually noted: perhaps two at the gate where he entered. And then he'd multiply that by the number of gates he knew of—maybe three or four—and come up with the number eight. Doubling that for good measure, he would most likely guess that the park employed fewer than twenty souls. When reminded that the figure should include all those required for maintenance work, your average tourist would blink, glance blankly about at the miles of bushland, and say, "Maintenance? What maintenance? A national park is just land set aside to preserve its natural state. There is no maintenance."

David shook his head. There were 560 people employed at Aruba National Park, and he was understaffed; in some areas, critically. He had Gate Rangers and Field Force Rangers, artisans and laborers, drivers and mechanics, clerks and typists, and that figure didn't include the teaching and administrative staff at the Education Center, or the numbers of scientists and their assistants in the Research Center.

He continued to read through the pages reporting on the construction and maintenance of the projects in progress and their cost in supplies, equipment, and man-hours, remembering with a smile that when Aruba had been set aside and gazetted thirty years earlier, the park had consisted of thousands of kilometers of bush, one warden and his assistant, six scouts, and one old lorry. Times had certainly changed.

His thoughts were interrupted again by Sergeant Lemboko's voice at the door. "Warden Karanja. Game Warden Maimbo is here to see you."

"Fine. Send him in." Game Warden, Park Warden—they're one and the same now, David thought glumly. A warden is a warden, period. There used to be a difference, but not anymore.

He glanced up as Warden Jombo Maimbo came in. He was a large man, as tall as David, but where David was lean in build, Jombo was thick and stocky, and his burnished black skin was as glossy as the plumage of a Cape rook.

Without preamble Jombo stuck out a big hand and remarked jocularly, "I thought you'd like to know that once again I've done your work for you."

David shook the proffered hand and said, "And as usual, you've come right over to congratulate yourself." He smiled in wry amusement at Maimbo's conceited banter.

Pulling a chair around to the side of David's desk, Jombo continued, "Shelby said he'd written you a note explaining about the elephants in his sisal, so I'll just add that they were there as he said, and now they're gone."

"How?"

"My last thunder-flash, which didn't do any good, and four rounds of number five shot delivered by a four-ten, which did."

David nodded. "Good. I was afraid we'd have to put down a couple to get them out."

"So did I," agreed Maimbo.

"But then," David queried thoughtfully, more to himself than to Maimbo, "how long will it be before they're back?"

"Tonight, tomorrow, next week," speculated Maimbo, shrugging. "Shelby thinks he has an idea about preventing recurrences."

"What is it?"

"I don't know. He didn't say, but I think he's planning to discuss it with you."

"Good. I'll welcome any suggestion. Besides Shelby's plantation, what else is the Game Department up to?"

"Things don't change much, with or without amalgamation. In the old days, you took care of the wildlife inside the park boundaries and I took care of the wildlife outside the park. It's still just about the same."

"I heard about a buffalo shot in town. What happened?" David's voice had hardened almost imperceptibly.

Maimbo's reply came immediately. "One of your smaller herds decided to visit the township schools last week, and about thirty-five wandered into the primary school and out again while the children were in the classrooms. Then they invaded the secondary school while a soccer game was going on. All the running about with the ball and yelling must have excited the buffs, because they began running after the ballplayers. We got there about that time and had to shoot one young bull. The others circled around that small hill behind the school and headed for the park." He paused and then added laconically, "I brought you a hindquarter of the meat and left it with the *mzee* who works for you. Didn't he tell you?"

"I got the meat, and I guessed that it must have come from you." David didn't add that it was Bubu's pantomime of the huge, stalking Jombo that had identified the Game Warden as the sender of the gift. "You know he's mute," he added.

"Is he? I didn't notice. I just told him to give it to you. I don't remember if he spoke or not."

"He's called Bubu," David explained. At first it had bothered him that the man was known by the Swahili word for his affliction, and so he'd asked the old man what his real name was, but Bubu had just shrugged his shoulders. Perhaps he'd never known his real name.

Remembering the rabies problem in the village, David changed the subject. "I'm glad you came by. I was planning to come in to see you tomorrow."

After explaining about the rabies attacks and the necessity of eliminating the stray animals responsible for bringing the disease into the village, he asked, "Can you get started the day after tomorrow?"

Maimbo nodded. "We'll begin Wednesday. By the end of the week we'll have got them all."

"Have your men deliver the carcasses to Research. They'll be sent up to Nairobi for autopsy. Then we'll know if the problem was where we thought it was."

After a few moments of conversation, Jombo stood and said, "I've got to get back to my office for a meeting. I'm late now, but I wanted you to know that the elephants are out of Shelby's crops."

David nodded, and as Maimbo left the office, his eyes followed him; it was surprising how quickly the man moved, considering his size. He had an unusual and distinctive way of walking—a rapidly prowling, yet heavy-footed gait which made David think of something big, caged.

There was something about him that made David stand back and watch. An unsureness, almost a dislike. He suspected it was no more than the mild antipathy between National Parks and the Game Department.

In the past, the two agencies had shared the responsibility of conservation: National Parks in the park, and the Game Department dealing with the wildlife outside the park boundaries in the areas of game control and licensed hunting. The National Parks had been a tightly run and well-supervised organization governed by a board of trustees, while the Game Department was a sprawling branch of civil service, answerable to a Government ministry. As with all organizations, there were good people and bad in both groups, but whereas in the smaller, more personal institution of Parks the bad apples were usually quickly spotted and expelled from the community barrel, the same could not be said with regard to the Game Department.

Consequently, there had been ugly rumors of widespread corruption within the Game Department and enough arrests and convictions to lend the rumors credence. When amalgamation came and the two organizations merged, it was generally accepted as being badly done, with the Game Department personnel receiving preferential treatment. The Park's staff hadn't forgotten.

He hoped that his attitude toward Maimbo wasn't just a result of the bad taste left by a political decision made by others two years before in Nairobi. Maimbo wasn't responsible for either the merger or the way it had been carried out.

Then Frazer Kent crossed David's mind, and he smiled. There was a good man. Completely honest, and one of the finest wardens he'd ever known; in fact, Kent was the main reason he had decided to make wildlife his own life career. Kent had been with the Game Department all his working life.

No, he decided. It wasn't prejudice against the Game Department, it was Maimbo himself, and he recalled his first thoughts when he'd heard that Jombo had shot a buff in town: Did the animal really need to be shot? Was he aggressive, and had he become a danger to the townspeople or the rangers? Would he have left with the others to return into the park if he'd been given the chance? Or did Jombo just fancy buffalo steaks on his table?

Looking at the clock, he realized it was past four and everyone would be leaving the offices now. Picking up the rest of the Warden's Report, he proceeded to proof the remainder:

GAME NOTES:
General:
    The past 12 months have been the driest experienced in the history of this national park, and conditions have reached and passed the critical point in the area north and east of Main Headquarters in the vicinity of permanent water.

The heavy seasonal rains have failed completely in the drought area for the past year, and the only precipitation received there has been in the form of a few scattered and erratic showers. The budding growth which results from these brief showers is quickly consumed because of the large concentrations of hungry game in the northeast area. Gradually at first, and then rapidly, the vegetation has begun to thin and finally disappear in ever-widening circles around the few water holes and rivers in this area. The wildlife come for water at dawn or dusk and then, having satisfied their thirst, they move out in search of fodder from among those few sedges and evergreens which maintain their foliage during the dry season. At first, the distance was just a kilometer or so from the water, but soon the journey between water and the remaining vegetation became a distance of 10 kilometers, then 20, and the elephant and rhino, with their massive food requirements, have begun to die.

During the past 9 months, the tusks and lower jaws of more than 300 elephant have been recovered from the drought area by park personnel and were brought into the Research Center for study. The age and sex of each elephant fatality was determined by molar wear and eruption, and by the measurement of the lower jaw and tusks.

A detailed and scientific study of the situation is currently in progress at the Research Center, and I will leave the extensive reporting of these findings to Dr. Jeffrey Forbes, but I should like to include here a few of the major conclusions.

 · While the 306 elephant and 42 rhino fatalities have occurred over the past year, the majority of deaths have been concentrated in the dry seasons.
 · 95% of the deaths have occurred in the areas north and east of Headquarters in the immediate vicinity of permanent water.
 · The preliminary results of the studies made indicate that the animals most affected within the elephant population are:
   1. The very old males and females with their sixth and last molar wearing out.
   2. The young between 1 and 6 years.
   3. The sick or injured animals.
   4. And lastly, the lactating females.

Consequently, to date the die-off has occurred among the weak and infirm, and among females impeded by calves.

I must repeat my previous requests to conduct a total aerial count of every elephant and rhino in the Aruba ecosystem, because while I know that we can do little about the drought, I do feel that it is imperative that we know exactly how bad the situation really is. Therefore, I am again requesting authorization to schedule a total aerial count to be conducted as soon as possible, and I am requesting the sum of 50,000 shillings for operating expenses.

I also have to point out that it is absolutely impossible for me to effectively patrol this park without the full-time use of an airplane, and it has been over 8 months since the plane assigned to this park was taken to Nairobi for repairs, following the forced landing in the Northern Area after a power failure.

I am in the middle of a devastating drought, and the poaching situation is catastrophic. Without a plane I am virtually blind and unable to assess the extent of our losses. I cannot direct the Field Force from the air as in the past, and it is extremely difficult, if not impossible, to locate the carcasses resulting from poaching without a plane, because of the density of the bush in the problem areas. If my plane cannot be returned immediately, I suggest that Department Headquarters arrange the transfer of a plane from one of the smaller parks.

Let someone else do without. Because of its size, this park must have daily aerial patrol if it intends to survive.

Elephant:

Because of the drought, we have had a recurring problem with elephant invading the grounds near the gates and camping areas because of the presence of water and irrigated vegetation. Visitors at the self-help bandas have been startled to find elephant's trunks coming through their kitchen windows and into their sinks in search of water. The staff is complaining of elephant raiding the gardens planted near the junior-staff quarters, and the rangers are having trouble with the elephant eating the flowers, trees and lawns planted around the park gates. Elephant have taken to drinking out of the swimming pools and birdbaths at the two lodges, and regularly invade the grounds in search of something green to eat. We have used up all our thunder-flashes, and I have had to turn to peppering a few rear ends with a .410 shotgun and No. 5 pellets in order to frighten them out of those areas where visitors or staff might be injured.

During the first week of July we finally saw the last of the young bull elephant who had taken to chasing cars on the road between Aruba Dam and Nyache Gate. He never attempted to attack any of the vehicles; he only wanted to frighten the occupants by hiding in a thicket until the car was almost upon him, then charging out of his cover with ears flapping and tail extended as he screamed and trumpeted his victims into nervous collapse. All our attempts to drive him off failed, as he would always return at the first opportunity. Now, he's solved the problem for us. On 2nd July, he rushed out to confront one of our old Ferguson tractors, and as the driver and his passenger scattered, the tractor was left to clatter along by itself. Our young bull made another charge to clear the field, but the tractor was unmoved and continued to roll slowly along, belching bad smells and loud noises, until it bumped into a now-frightened young elephant and literally scared him silly. He rushed off squealing into the bush and has not been seen for three months.

Because of the increase in poaching, we have seen a marked increase in the numbers of animals found wandering about with horrible festering wounds from poisoned arrowheads which did not kill, but only left suppurating wounds. On 9th July, I shot a fine old bull who had been hit in the stomach area with poisoned arrows. It appears that in the case of these stomach wounds, the skin and flesh in the area of the arrow begin to rot away, and as soon as open sores appear the wound becomes infested with maggots, and the flesh is literally eaten away until the stomach and intestines fall through. This is the fifth elephant I have had to destroy because the poor beast was treading on his entrails.

During the past quarter I darted, tranquilized and successfully treated 4 elephant: a cow with an arrowhead in her shoulder; a young bull with 2 arrowheads in his left ear; an older bull with 3 arrowheads in his rump and right side; and a bull with an arrowhead in his left foreleg.

During the last quarter, 334 elephant have been recorded as poached.

Rhino:

This last quarter has proved to be a disastrous period for the black rhino. All of the rhino seen in the past few months have black patches on their backs, caused by coagulated blood, which indicates that they are suffering from acute anemia.

Dr. Silas Ndutu performed 3 additional postmortem examinations, and his report agrees with the previous findings: clinical analysis of the blood serum and examination of the stomach contents reveal that the rhino died of malnutrition. In many cases, the animals had a full or nearly full stomach, whose contents consisted of pure bits of chewed-up wood which were without nutritional value. During the past quarter, we've lost 12 more rhinos to the drought, which brings the total to 42.

On the night of 9th August, one of our Land-Rovers was involved in a head-on collision with a large male rhino near Mbilani. After the rhino regained his feet, he began to methodically bash in the front of the vehicle. The rhino suffered no injury, but the vehicle had to be sent by rail to Nairobi for repair.

During the period under review, 29 rhino have been recorded as poached.

Hippo:

Owing to the drought many hippo have been moving several kilometers from the Oreyiet and Ruui Rivers at night in search of grazing, and on 3rd August, Assistant Warden Mohamed Agaran had to shoot a female near Robi as the entire lower half of her left foreleg had rotted away owing to its having been caught in a wire snare.

Buffalo:

In the second week of August, a small group of 11 buffalo bulls discovered that by wading out into the Aruba Dam, they could work their way around the end of the elephant-proof ditch and gain access to the irrigated lawns that surround the guest bandas. During the day they would lie up in the reedbeds at the edge of the water and charge anyone who came near. The reeds were burned in order to prompt the buff to depart and find shelter somewhere else. One old bull proved a bit truculent and took to grazing in between the bandas and vigorously defending his new feeding area from all comers. A concentrated effort was made to drive him off before we lost one of our visitors; unfortunately, this operation only increased his belligerence, and in the end he had to be tranquilized and transported across the Lalaga Lana River to our "dumping ground" for problem animals in the Northern Area.

On 2nd September, one of the watchmen employed by the Kenya Sisal Estate was attacked and killed by a lone buffalo. The animal retreated back inside the park boundary, and the Field Force attempted to track him down, but he managed to join up with a herd of 300-plus buffalo and so was lost.

Giraffe:

On 3rd July, a bull giraffe was struck by a Nairobi-bound bus as it crossed the road 6 miles east of Moda village. The bus was extensively damaged, and 4 passengers reported minor injuries; the giraffe had to be destroyed by the Department of Wildlife station in the village.

Plains Game:

Last July, we received word that we would be receiving an additional 40 Grevy's zebra from Isiolo to increase our present population, who are the result of the original 22 animals first introduced here in 1964. We have constructed the required holding pens of blue gum and sisal poles on the edge of the Fafajaga Plain for their 6-to-8-week acclimation and reorientation confinement.

These zebra do well here since they rarely require water, and also because they are primarily grazers, so the most pressing threat to our Grevy's is not drought, but poachers. We know of 5 taken for their beautiful skins so far this year, but we don't know if these 5 represent all those poached, or only a fraction.

It is incredibly frustrating to know how many thousands of shillings are required, and how much work is involved, in the relocation of a small handful of threatened animals from a rapidly declining population, and then to see them poached. Dozens of our Wildlife personnel, including wardens, rangers, and veterinarians, spend months in building holding pens; in darting and capturing, feeding and treating, watching and hoping; in crating, transporting and unloading; to feed and watch and hope again until the operation is finally ended and it's time to set the animals free into their new range, only to see them go down, one by one, to a snare, an arrow or a bullet.

I doubt if the people in Europe or America realize that they inadvertently support poaching in Africa when they buy these skins. Perhaps one of the international wildlife organizations could do something about informing the public.

Predators:

In general, the predators and scavengers have done very well for themselves owing to the drought and its effect on the prey animals. Predators will invariably select prey who are physically below par as their potential meal. The lions, in particular, have taken to staying in the immediate vicinity of the water holes and rivers in order to intercept those seriously weakened animals within a group who are often unable to show much resistance in the way of fight or flight.

(a) *Lion:*

On the evening of 4th August, while returning to the staff quarters, the wife of a laborer was attacked and bitten on the knee by a lioness; the woman began to scream hysterically as she struck the animal repeatedly on the head until the lioness let go and ran off into the bush. Two armed Field Force Rangers with torches went out in search of the woman and finally found her in a tree where she'd sought refuge. She was treated for lacerations at the village dispensary and released.

On 11th September, a lioness captured at Ngong for killing 12 head of cattle was released on the Uiini Plain. She was obviously not a mild-mannered cat to begin with, and her normally cranky disposition was worsened by being captured, crated, and bumped about by train and lorry, so when released from her box trap at the back of the lorry, she rushed around to the front of the vehicle and promptly put fang marks through the metal fenders. The ranger, whose job it was to pull on the rope that had been tossed over a tree branch and attached to the top of the cage door, barely had time to let go the rope and get his arm in and his window up before she charged by. The driver attempted to start the lorry in order to drive slowly off and thereby force the lioness to let go her hold on the vehicle, but unfortunately the engine wouldn't start; it was to prove later to have a faulty battery connection. The lioness sensed her advantage and continued to express her irritation over the manner in which she'd been treated by leaping up onto the bonnet of the vehicle to glare balefully through the windscreen at the two un-nerved rangers and one driver, who was to be reduced to near hysteria before she was finished with the lot of them. After ripping off the windscreen wipers with the appropriate snarls and growls and clawing at the windscreen glass, she tried to chew her way through the top of the cab to get hold of the three inside; failing this, she tore off the outside rearview mirrors, bit into the bonnet again, slashed and punctured one of the front tires, tugged with her teeth on the door handles, and generally made a mess of the outside of the lorry. After leaving the vehicle on 2 occasions, only to return again to jump onto the bonnet to snarl and swat at the three men inside through the glass, she finally leaped off and disappeared into the bush.

(b) *Leopard:*

During the past six months we have set up another study project in cooperation with the Research Center; this field study of leopards by radiotelemetry will continue for a period of 2 years and is financed by the World Wildlife Foundation. During the last quarter, a promising site for the initial study area was located on the Gurujo Escarpment, and the old retired leopard poacher Mulu was recruited to assist the researcher, Mr. Richard Garroway.

Baited traps have resulted in the capture and collaring of 5 leopard: 4 male and 1 female. Immobilization of the leopard, after trapping, was effected with phencyclidine hydrochloride; after the radio collars were fitted, all of the animals recovered satisfactorily and took to the bush while continuing to transmit their 5 respective signals.

One leopard, who was collared within 6 kilometers of the Malathi

Lodge, was often monitored in the immediate vicinity of the lodge during the small hours of the morning after guests and staff had retired. He was followed and was seen to leap up onto the veranda which overlooks one of the water holes; he crossed the bar/lounge area and after passing the reception desk, he entered the deserted kitchen, where he proceeded to rummage in the garbage bins for the scraps of discarded cheese, bacon rind, meat and leftovers. Apparently this has been going on for some time, as the kitchen staff had remarked that food items were either misplaced or missing, but it was never suspected that the hotel had a visiting leopard. A locked kitchen door resulted in a few frustrating evenings for the leopard; his nocturnal scavenging forays ceased, and peace of mind was restored to the kitchen staff, who were threatening to terminate their employment.

(c) *Cheetah:*

Presumably as a result of the increase of the plains game and the opening up of the habitat, we have noticd an increase in the number of sightings of cheetah, and I can only hope that this represents an increase in the population by immigration and/or birthrate. Cheetah are quite reclusive, and while they are more frequently seen than are the more commonly distributed leopard, these more numerous sightings are the result of their diurnal habits, as opposed to the nocturnal hunting pattern of the leopard. Owing to the timid nature of this cat, and its reported inability to adapt itself to changing conditions and increased disturbance, I am aware of their precarious future, particularly in view of the very high cub mortality and the poaching of the spotted cats, and I can only increase our vigilance in areas they are known to frequent and hope for the best.

Primates:
Baboons:

It appears that a troop of baboons who live in the Moda River Valley has adopted a very young female impala. On several occasions, visitors and rangers have seen the impala with the troop. The young baboons are seen to climb onto and ride about on the doe, and she appears to enjoy the game, as she makes no effort to dislodge her riders.

Birds:
(a) *Ostriches:*

The last quarter was again mating season for the Somali and Masai species of ostrich, and groups of up to 20 birds were observed from the roads. The elaborate courtship display of the male birds was very impressive as they crouched with fluttering outspread wings while swinging their necks low from side to side before dashing toward a hen, as they puffed up their necks to deliver their deep booming mating call. While the visitors greatly appreciated the males' dancing efforts, it was unfortunate that the show usually left the aforementioned hens completely unimpressed.

It is disappointing that despite the dedicated efforts of the cock ostriches, there have been few nests this year.

Game Orphans:

We have a full house with the increase in new orphans because of the drought. In our semi-permanent herd of "big orphans" we have 3, soon to be 2, elephant: an adult female, Sarah, 19 years old; a male juvenile, Galogalo, 7 years; and the 13-year-old male, Dida, who has again gone off to join the wild elephants. I'm afraid that I will be forced to drive Dida away if he returns during the next quarter, since he has reached and passed that time when he would have been driven off by his mother and I understand fully why elephant females forcibly eject their male offspring from the family unit when they reach this age. His rapid physical growth, coupled with a developing aggressiveness, has resulted in destructive and unpredictable behavior, and I find I can't afford the liability of his presence any more than his mother would have done.

In addition to the elephants, the big orphans' herd consists of our young male rhino and female zebra, plus the pair of year-old buffalo.

(a) *Losses: Deportations/Deaths*

Two of the 4 warthogs raised in the Orphanage were killed and eaten by lion on 16th August. The remaining pair continue to spend most of their time on the lawn in front of the Main Head-quarters building. The female is hugely pregnant, so we should have a whole family in residence soon, all of them intently preoccupied with rooting up the grass, to the disgust of the head gardener.

This last quarter we transported our tame male rhino, Faru, to the area of the tented camp near the Lafaroge Plateau in order to rehabilitate him to the wild state. For several weeks it appeared that he was doing quite well, in spite of his affection for people which led him to spend much of his time in the camp area. The camp manager had no objection to his on-and-off residence, and the visitors so enjoyed his company that we felt no harm was done, particularly since Faru is so used to the affection of humans that he will walk confidently up to anyone, and this behavior leaves him terribly vulnerable to poachers. Consequently, his living near an

92

isolated tourist camp far in the bush offered him both a semi-wild existence and the protection of people should he require it. Now it seems he's discovered the pleasure of alcohol. He appeared at the camp bar once or twice in the evening, and after being given a drink or two by the tourists has taken to showing up every evening for a gin-and-tonic sundowner. Since neither I nor the camp manager want a tippling rhino on our hands, we've posted a sign over the bar to inform the guests that "No Alcoholic Beverages Are to Be Served to the Wildlife," and Faru is now allowed one cold Coca-Cola, straight, each evening.

(b) *Additions:*

The new additions to the orphanage began arriving on 12th July, with the appearance of the Kenya Sisal Estate Land-Rover, which brought in a very young female waterbuck who had been rescued from a pack of the town's dogs.

On 2nd July, Unit 3 Field Force rescued a young male duiker from a snare near Kithekani. He is now firmly integrated into the "pack" of little orphans.

On 10th July, two graders were trying unsuccessfully to level the Usi River road when the first machine passed by a cow elephant who had just given birth to a calf at the side of the road. The mother panicked and took off into the thick bush, while the now-deserted male calf looked about for something large like a mother to turn to, and at that moment the second grader came into view. The small calf promptly attached himself to the machine and proceeded to stumble along beside it. Since he could not be deterred from following the grader and the mother had completely disappeared, he was brought into Headquarters, where he quickly transferred his affection to Sarah. The calf measured only 2'9" at the shoulder at birth, and while we did everything possible to save him, he began to scour and decline after 3 months and died.

On 17th August, the Education Center bus found a young rhino wandering about by itself on the road. Since there was no sign of the mother and a lioness was nearby, the driver decided to catch the baby and bring him in. The calf was quite new, as his umbilical cord was still attached. He stood 20½ inches at the shoulder and weighed 85 pounds.

On 18th September, a very young orphaned buffalo calf was brought into Headquarters with one of its rear hoofs nearly severed, possibly the result of its being trampled on by its mother after birth. Careful doctoring has resulted in the successful healing of the wound.

On 27th September, 2 lion cubs from Northern Headquarters

arrived; the male was christened Neko and the female Neka, and both are doing well.

DAVID LEANED BACK in his chair and rubbed his eyes. It was very quiet. Standing up to stretch his legs, he crossed his office to the doorway and looked out. The corridor outside was empty, and the only sound was the faint sputtering from the Radio Room that told him that Duba was still on duty and standing by prior to the six-o'clock shutdown.

Returning to his desk, he riffled through the last few pages of the report and decided to finish proofing the rest before going home. He lit another cigarette, picked up the remaining pages, and began to read the most depressing part.

Poaching and Anti-Poaching Operations:

Several factors have contributed to a tremendous increase in the numbers of poachers operating in Aruba, and I cannot overemphasize the critical condition in which we find ourselves.

The situation can only get worse, since the price of ivory has gone up an additional 60% within the last year alone, and rhino horn has shown a still greater increase. Though poachers receive only about one-fourth of the value of the ivory, they now get 100 shillings per kilo for tusks weighing over 10 kilos. Even with the decrease in the average weight of the recovered ivory, a poacher with 2 tusks of approximately 20 kilos each will receive about 4,000 shillings, or $480, for the pair.

While interrogating a poacher last month, I learned that owing to the demand in India and the Far East, where it is erroneously believed that powdered rhino horn is a powerful aphrodisiac or cure for fever, the current price paid locally for rhino horn has spiraled recently from 500 shillings to 3,000 shillings per kilo, and is still going up. Taking an average weight of 3 kilos per pair of horns, this represents a profit of 9,000 shillings, or $1,080.

Consequently, we now find that some of our areas, which formerly had a high density ratio of 4 to 5 rhino per square mile, are reduced to only 1 or 2, and in too many cases, none at all. While it is true that drought has affected our rhino, the die-off from drought does not begin to approach the numbers lost to poaching. After the drought of the '60s, our population here was estimated at 6,000 rhinos. Eight years later, before the die-off began from the present drought, the population had fallen to 2,500 animals—3,500 rhino had disappeared and were obviously poached. In the year and a half since the last sample count, the poaching has continued on an escalating scale, and I have no idea how many rhino we have left.

The only thing that makes the situation more bearable regarding the elephant is that we're starting with a larger number of animals from which to subtract our losses.

As mentioned earlier, we've had a known mortality of 334 elephant poached in the past quarter. Known, because we've found the carcasses; but again, this park is huge, and I estimate the loss to be at least 500+ animals from poaching alone each quarter, for a total of more than 2,000 yearly. No park, and no wildlife population, can sustain losses like these, particularly during a drought such as we are facing now.

The problem is compounded by the fact that the present sentence handed down to a convicted poacher is only one year or 2,000 shillings' fine. In view of the tremendous profit to be made, this wrist-tapping is hardly a deterrent when 4,000 to 10,000 shillings is at stake. Too many are more than willing to take the risk. I feel it is absolutely imperative that we bring the punishment for this crime into line with the profits to be made from it.

In mid-September, 4 poachers tracked an elephant through thick bush, but before they could loose their arrows the bull caught their scent and charged; 3 men escaped, while the bull closed in on 1, whom he knocked down and tusked. It appeared from the spoor that the man was able to escape momentarily and succeeded in reaching a nearby warthog burrow, in which he attempted to hide, but the enraged bull grabbed the poacher's leg and after dragging him out proceeded to fling him some distance before trampling him to death.

The body of another poacher was found buried near Kwambusya. It seems this man had been paid some 12,000 shillings for illegal ivory and had then been robbed, murdered and buried in the park by persons unknown. The body was located and disinterred by the local police as the result of information received during the course of their investigations on poaching. No murder suspect has been arrested as yet.

I would like to express my gratitude to the Department of Wildlife Special Anti-Poaching Team who came down from Isiolo to assist us for a period of 3 weeks, and for the Government Special Unit who joined us for an 8-day operation.

For the detailed report covering poaching activity and anti-poaching operations for the period under review, please refer to Appendix A.

* * *

DAVID TURNED TO the first appendix and briefly scanned the heading and introduction before starting to read the day-by-day account that followed:

> 1st July 1977—3 elephant shot and killed by poachers on the Lafaroge Plateau. Tusks missing, tracks obliterated.
> —Armed confrontation between 4 Somali poachers and Unit 9 at Dakadiko. 1 ranger wounded; 1 wounded Somali captured, 2 killed, 1 escaped; 8 tusks and 2 rhino horns recovered.
> —Zebra found snared at Kijiji Tai. Destroyed.
> —2 rhino found poached near Kasiki Rail Station. Horns missing, arrowheads removed.

It went on, a grisly diary of every track followed, every carcass found; of horns missing, and tusks recovered; of animals shot and riddled with poisoned arrows; or snared, trapped, wounded, suffering, or dead. It followed the movements of Units 1 and 2 and Units 3 through 10; the poachers they reported, tracked, lost, or caught and arrested; the poachers who resisted arrest, the gun battles, the smoke grenades, and the reinforcements airlifted by helicopter; the poachers dead, the poachers who escaped, the rangers who'd been killed or seriously wounded, and the Flying Doctor who had made another trip from Aruba to Nairobi.

It reported on the hideouts found, the platforms discovered built over water holes, the pit traps and snares uncovered; it mentioned the pegged-out skins and the ugly naked carcasses thrown unwanted into the underbrush; the caves and hollow baobabs stocked with supplies and ammunition and sleeping mats. It described the hides and water holes ambushed; day or night, the men fleeing, and the rangers pursuing; the shouting and stumbling in the dark, a rifle butt connecting with a head, a scream of pain. Railroad *landhies* and village huts raided; the weapons, meat, skins, and trophies found, the men arrested, their women shrieking curses.

It told of a helicopter circling, directing the Land-Rovers and Field Force on the ground to the hides of the Wakamba secreted in the rocky outcrops, the hides of the Waliangulu in the thick bush, the thorn *bomas* built around the water holes to guide the prey into the pit, the snare, the trap.

It covered the wildlife fleeing the scent of man; impaled in the game pits, dragging their snares, caught in the gin traps; it followed their blood trails, found their putrefying corpses, and the rotting animals who still lived and suffered, and it mentioned another dying elephant calf, who'd stood alone with his head down in the sun beside the body of his mother.

DAVID RIFFLED THE pages through his fingers; three months, about ninety days, all neatly reduced to black type on twelve pages of clean white paper, and somehow it bore little resemblance to what had really happened. It didn't get across the physical and emotional exhaustion or the frustration lived with daily; it didn't even illustrate the problem. It was only a collection of words, words and numbers that failed to communicate the experience and the feeling of hopelessness.

David glanced at the last figures at the bottom of the last page under the heading *Arrests:*

July—108 poachers arrested; August—119; September—132; for a total of 359 men tracked, ambushed, and arrested in a 90-day period.

It sounded almost impressive. Unfortunately, he knew that it was probably less than 10 percent of the poachers who were there. He stared out over the bush that stretched for miles into the distance, and he wondered: How many are out there now?

He shook his head. Too many. Resolutely he picked up the report and signed the bottom of the last page. He stubbed out his half-smoked cigarette. He hadn't noticed he'd been chain-smoking while he read—he'd been too painfully engrossed in the summation of the park's problems, major and otherwise; and now his mouth felt like the inside of a seldom-washed ashtray.

Sighing heavily, he set the report aside and was thankful it was finished and not to be done again for another three months. He stood up, stretched, and decided that a cold beer sounded better than good. It was that time of day. He left his office to check with the Radio Room before walking the short distance home.

CHAPTER SIX

Night

VERA LEANED BACK in her chair, removed her glasses and slowly rubbed her eyes. Glancing at her watch, she saw that it was five thirty. With Adam to help, perhaps she'd get everyone cared for and gone by six. Calling to her assistant, she was reaching for the bell to summon the next patient when her attention was arrested by the sound of distant screams approaching rapidly.

She strode to the veranda door and stepped out to see a young woman running toward her with a very small child in her arms. Reaching the veranda, the young mother thrust the screaming child into Vera's arms, then quickly stood back, wringing her hands in agitation, her face distorted in panic.

Vera turned into the office and on to the examining room. Placing the shrieking child on the table, she began to remove the *khanga* wrapped about his hips and legs. As she rolled him onto his back to free him from the cloth, his body instantly stiffened. The child screamed again piercingly and thrashed about in a rigid, bowed position, his torso thrust up off the table. Vera swiftly turned him onto his stomach and held him down to examine the now-obvious reason for his screams. His thighs, buttocks, and lower back were a mass of burns, indicating he was another who had fallen onto his mother's cooking stones in his first uncoordinated attempts at walking.

After administering an injection of penicillin and a mild pain-killer, Vera began to apply a solution of glycerine, Epsom salts, sulfa powder, and silver nitrate. With luck, the child would heal quickly, with only a few small scars to show where the burns had been. But unless great care was taken, those badly burned areas would ulcerate and refuse to heal.

It was an oddity she'd seen among the local population here and in many developing countries: any sore, whether a cut, burn, puncture, or bad scrape, might refuse to heal properly and would instead form into a suppurating ulcer which could rapidly become worse than the original injury.

Reaching for the sterile prerolled bandages made from old bed sheets, she made thick pads which she placed over the burns. After securing the child's dressings with strips of heavy surgical tape, she gingerly picked him up. She felt the warm dampness of his small tear-streaked face press into her neck, and she smiled softly as he nuzzled closer, seeking comfort, his arms tightening about her neck. Moments like this were a rare reward.

She'd never married and never had children of her own. She'd spent her life helping those who could not yet help themselves; they were her family. As a familiar ache of loneliness swelled to fill an empty place inside her, she wondered: Was it enough? For a moment she doubted it. Then she looked down at the top of the small head capped with shiny black, tightly curled hair. The choice had been made years ago. It had to be enough. Just then the dark little face looked up at her. The round, brown eyes stared in wonder at the strangeness of her deeply lined white face, her hard and shiny spectacles. Then he smiled. A sob of gratitude welled in her throat and threatened to escape. She kissed him quickly and gave him to his mother, admonishing her to watch the child more carefully.

She returned to the office with Adam trailing behind her. Immediately the bell rang; the next in line entered, and all those waiting on the benches slid forward one place.

Slowly the veranda emptied, until finally the sharp ting of the small bell brought no response. Vera crossed to the door and looked out—no one. While Adam went about his evening routine of setting everything to rights for the following day, she began to count up the day's receipts. She'd just finished when she heard Adam call out good night and, rising, she locked up the office and stepped out onto the veranda for her evening walk.

It was just six thirty, and the sun would soon be setting behind the Dakagudiu Hills. The dusk here was a short affair, an almost unnoticed preamble to darkness. She walked slowly around the side of the dispensary, consciously enjoying the quiet.

In her memory's eye she saw the old stone building as she'd seen it the first day. It was situated a few yards off the dirt road, which took the back way through the village and on to the old railroad station, and had been surrounded by an empty and vast expanse of dusty nothing. The first thing done was to build two small staff quarters: one for the hoped-for assistant, one for the *shamba* man, whose hiring had been the second thing accomplished. Together she and Jamaa had planted a fast-growing hedge all around the two-acre property, and laid out narrow flower beds that ran along the front of the dispensary and down along the sides of the building. Now the hedge was seven feet tall, and it completely screened the dispensary compound; and the small flowering plants that had been set out sparsely had multiplied into a thick tangle of blooms.

The trees had gone in next: pathetically scrawny saplings then, but Vera had hungered for green shade and had the patience in those days to wait for the growth that would slowly transform them from leafless twigs into sturdy trees. Now the thick hedge surrounded a garden of not only flowers, but fruit trees and rows of thriving vegetables.

She stood silently in the small garden as the early-evening shadows darkened and the sounds of the surrounding village diminished. There was a last short flurry of birdsong as the occupants of the tall trees settled in for the night; a village dog barked sharply once; then everything was quiet.

Some days left her feeling shattered, as if the needs of others resulted in her own piece-by-piece dismemberment, with each supplicant carrying away a part of her until there wasn't enough left for her own survival. But whereas it took a day of constant and demanding work to undo her, it took only a few minutes of peace and quiet in her garden to put her together again.

A cup of hot tea had become a conscious thought and an almost tangible taste in her mouth. She turned from the garden and walked up the far side of the dispensary building toward her private quarters.

Putting on the water to boil, she turned to the evening ritual of lamplighting: paraffin lamps for the kitchen, where the dim light didn't matter, and the more-expensive-to-operate gas lamps for her parlor, where she read or sewed. After preparing her tray of tea things, she passed back into the parlor and settled into her old rocking chair.

The soft rhythmic squeak of the chair joined the muted twitterings from above to accentuate the silence. She thought of the small child she'd treated late that afternoon, and the memory of his arms about her brought back the sharp ache of emptiness inside. She wished for him now, just to sit and hold and rock quietly.

The large ornate clock she'd brought out with her from England began solemnly to intone the hour. Three hours left to fill before she could go to bed. The evening stretched out before her like a journey, and the feeling of loneliness grew until she couldn't deny it.

DAVID WALKED UP the driveway beside the Warden's Residence and passed through the gate in the fence that was supposed to keep the wildlife out of his back garden, but didn't.

Remembering the sharp whistle he'd heard at dawn, which had told him that something had startled the dik-diks feeding in his vegetable garden, he now looked about until he found their tiny hoofprints in the soft ground around the *pilpili* bushes; the lower branches were stripped of leaves from ground level up to a height of about three feet—just about the distance the pair of fifteen-inch-high antelope could stretch while using the lower branches to rest their forefeet on. He smiled and knew they must have found a hole somewhere in the sisal-pole fence; probably at the back behind the tomato plants. The shy little dik-diks were among his favorite animals, and he decided to leave the hole open. They didn't eat that much.

He passed through the back door into the cool of the kitchen, stopping at the refrigerator for a cold bottle of Tusker lager. As he popped the lid and replaced the bottle opener in the door, he glanced around the kitchen. *"Mzee,"* he called, *"wapi chakula?"*

Bubu's wrinkled brown face, split with a nearly toothless grin, appeared at the doorway. He was a small, wiry man of undetermined age and origin, whom David had inherited from Warden Nichols. When Nichols and his family left, they'd taken their house servants with them, but the old *shamba* man had been left behind. It was impossible to learn where he came from, or when, since he couldn't read or write, or speak. But the old man's familiarity with the bush, plus his affinity with all living things, led David to suppose that the *mzee* had been a scout for one of the park's earliest wardens. Of course, no one was left from the old days, but the *mzee* had been around as long as anyone could remember, so it was a reasonable assumption. A woman came up from the *campini* once a week to do the laundry and clean the house, and Bubu was adept at rough camp cooking, so they'd bumped along together somehow for over two years now, and the old man's proud and silent presence was welcomed as unobtrusive company.

David stepped out and down one step to his favorite place—the veranda. Running along the entire front of the house, the concrete-floored retreat was always cool, and commanded a panoramic view south to the Moda River Valley with the Karesa Mountain beyond, and the vast Fafajaga Plain as it stretched unbroken to the east and southeast of Headquarters Hill. The view was framed where white-blossomed bougainvillea had crept up the large acacia tree trunks that had been set into the concrete floor to support the thatched roof, and from there the vines had continued over the thatching to provide added insulation plus the welcome illusion of cool green.

Sitting in his bamboo armchair, thick with cushions, David put his feet up on the three-foot wall that encircled the outer edge of the veranda. The breeze from the south passed over him, drying his perspiration-dampened hair and face, and he watched in amusement as a pair of black-and-white pied wagtails marched single file, with long tail feathers bobbing, around the concrete edge of the large artificial water hole. Surrounded by green grass, the water hole was situated some thirty-five feet out from the veranda in the unfenced front yard, and the early morning and late afternoon usually found it congested with thirsty wildlife.

Watching the leaves fluttering in the breeze beside him, his eyes followed the progress of the creeper up onto the palm-leaf *makuti* roof. The thatching overhung the outside walls by three feet, leaving a space of several inches at the top of the wall, to allow the free circulation of air throughout the house. It was true that the *makuti* afforded a home to numbers of insects, mice, lizards, and bats, who regularly left droppings on every conceivable surface in the house, but the good far surpassed the negative points, and he was willing to suffer lizard leavings in his bathtub rather than be baked to death in one of the more modern parks' houses with their roofs of red tile.

The thought of lizards reminded him of one of his uninvited houseguests, and after taking a long pull of beer, he tipped back his head and looked up at the center ridgepole, which ran the length of the house and supported the thatching high above. The four-foot monitor lizard was still stretched out on top of it, legs and tail dangling, deep in the hibernation that had already lasted two months, as he waited for the rains to come and bring the hordes of insects he fed on.

"Perhaps," David murmured to himself, "it would be better to say '*if* the rains come.' "

The drought had gone on so long, and the rains had failed so completely, that it was almost hard to remember how the sky could darken during the day as thick, black clouds moved in on the strong monsoon winds from the southeast. The rumbles would sound occasionally, at first, then swell into the almost continuous booming of the thunder that announced the arrival of the rainy season.

When the clouds finally ruptured, the resulting rain was a deluge; there were no showers or drizzles, no tiny raindrops pattering on leaves. The rain came in huge visible globbets that pounded on the palm thatching with a thrashing hiss. Within minutes, the red earth began to run with water as the rain fell faster than the hardened soil could absorb it. Puddles formed instantly, their surfaces twitching and jerking under the onslaught of the falling rain. Soon the shallower depressions began to fill and overflow to run into any path of least resistance, and moments after the first drop fell, the ground was covered with shallow streamlets dashing this way and that.

Remembering the rains brought back the reality of the drought; the poaching; and the Warden's Report he'd just finished reading. What would the next quarter's report record? A continuation of the problems he faced now? His feelings of frustration returned and robbed him of his pleasure in the peacefulness of the veranda and his beer.

Bubu appeared silently with a tray which he deposited on a nearby table. David glanced without interest at the beef-and-cabbage stew, *chappatis,* and fruit, but he forced himself to nod and murmur, *"Asante, Mzee."*

The old man smiled and in his own peculiar sign language indicated that he was leaving. David nodded again, and Bubu padded off quietly to his quarters.

The silence was almost oppressive. He was depressed. He felt like sitting in a bar, with a glass of good Scotch and cold ice, and maybe someone to talk to. As he tentatively nibbled at a *chappati,* he made up his mind: dinner, a cool shower, fresh clothes, and the Safari Lodge, where, with luck, no one would mention the word "park."

STEPPING OUT OF the Main Gate ticket office, Gate Ranger Wambua Mulolo looked up the road approaching the gate; it was deserted. It was after 7 P.M., and the park entrances were officially closed until six the following morning. Taking the two padlocks out of the pockets of his shorts, he proceeded to lock the incoming and outgoing gates before returning to the ticket office to wait till his relief came on duty.

It was still hot in the little office. He removed his uniform hat and wiped his forehead and then the hat's damp leather sweatband. His fingers felt the bulge of folded bills, and he smiled—today had been a profitable day. Then he thought of the evening ahead, and scowled. He had to see Margaret—to learn if there had been changes in the Field Force patrols over the weekend.

He turned to look again through the open door and wonder where his relief was—probably taking a shower after playing in the regular late-afternoon soccer game. Like most people who intensely dislike physical exertion, he could not understand why grown men would want to get off duty at four o'clock, rush onto a dusty playing field, and run about yelling and pushing as they kicked a battered and often-patched leather ball into the thorns and one another. Screaming and sweating in the hot sun was not his idea of a good time, and he resented the fact that the park soccer game resulted in his having to wait to be relieved.

Not that his impatience was the result of any desire on his part to hurry to Margaret Githu; in fact, the idea of dinner at her quarters and the inevitable hour or so spent in her creaking bed was depressing. Margaret was little and skinny, with a thin flat chest and a scrawny rear end. Mulolo liked a woman with a large rounded *matako* that he could hold on to. He liked the laughing *towni* women, with their thick hair elaborately braided and their flashy jewelry and jiggling breasts. Margaret was plain and shy, a stupid *shamba* girl who had somehow learned to type. As far as he was concerned, her company was something to be endured, her bed to be avoided.

He reminded himself that there was more than one way to make a little extra, and Margaret was profitable, even if she wasn't what he would ordinarily pick for an enjoyable evening. As he saw the relief ranger approaching at last, the unpleasant expression on his face deepened into a scowl, and he grumbled in Swahili, "You're late."

The smile of greeting faded as the other man said in defense, "I had to take a shower."

"You could have quit playing a little earlier."

"I can't quit and leave before the game is over; I'm goalie."

Mulolo snapped, "Then end the game earlier."

The other Ranger spun around. He was a Luo; inky-black and very big. "We're not ending the game for you."

Mulolo forced a nervous laugh; he wasn't liked, and he knew it. And this time he'd gone too far.

"*Pole,*" he offered by way of reconciliation. "*Pole, Bwana.* I have a woman waiting." He spread his fingers and shrugged as if to say, "What can a man do?"

The Luo regarded him for a moment. *"Sawa tu."*

Mulolo wasn't pleased with himself. It was stupid to antagonize another ranger, particularly one who could twist his head off without effort. Apologizing again, he turned over the keys and was relieved to see that the other man appeared to have forgotten the incident.

Walking to the staff quarters in the early darkness, Mulolo thought back over the day. It had been good today, and Margaret wasn't really so bad, particularly since she didn't realize that the things she told him were worth money and so she never demanded a share. Yes, she was definitely an improvement over the other one.

ARRIVING AT THE Safari Lodge, David parked his car near the entrance in the place that was unofficially his parking spot, and passed into the bright yellow light that wasn't supposed to attract insects, but did anyway.

"Karanja!"

David turned and extended his hand to the owner of the voice— Salim Rajan. Salim's warm, dry hand shook his briskly. "Where have you been?" he asked. "We haven't seen you for a couple of weeks."

"I've been around; just too busy or too tired to get cleaned up and come over."

"Since when did you need to get cleaned up? Just come, dirt and all. You're always welcome," chided Salim, grinning. "Have a drink with me."

"Does that mean you're paying?" asked David with a smile. This was a long-standing joke between them. Salim refused to allow David to pay for a drink, and it was why David didn't visit too often and rarely had more than one or two beers.

"Of course."

"Mr. Rajan?"

Salim looked to the room clerk who had addressed him. "Yes, what is it?"

"May I see you a moment?" The man appeared to be getting the worst of a disagreement with a disgruntled German tourist over reservations.

Salim nodded and turned back to David. "I'll just be a minute, David."

David leaned back against the reception desk while he watched Salim deal with another of the hotel's daily problems. Salim had become one of his first friends when he was posted here, and he always enjoyed a drink and conversation with the manager of the

Moda Safari Lodge. He was Indian, a descendant of one of the hundreds of laborers imported from India who had come at the turn of the century to build the railway from Mombasa, across Kenya, to Kisumu, on Lake Victoria, thereby linking Uganda to the coast. Salim's grandfather had been one of those who had stayed in Kenya when the railway was completed, and he'd sent home for a wife and established a family line in this country.

The Indians had filled a gap in Kenya between the indigenous black population and the scores of British settlers who were beginning to arrive. The white settlers came for land, for farms and plantations, and the Africans wanted either to be let alone or, in the case of a few, to work for the *Wazungu* shillings on those farms and plantations. No one was really interested in supplying the needs of the growing white population, or the local people who were becoming familiar with, and developing a taste for, the things of the white man.

Many of the Indians saw a place for themselves in this void, and soon hundreds of small *dukas,* or general stores, sprang up all over the country to sell everything from paraffin to salt, cloth, sugar, and tools. The *Wahindi* soon became the small businessmen of East Africa, and as the years passed, many of them could no longer be classified as "small." Salim was the product of such a heritage.

He stood at eye level with David's six feet and was equally slim, but where David's lanky frame was usually encased in the khaki or dark green bush clothes his job required, Salim was invariably clothed in expensive, well-cut suits of European design, with the requisite silk shirt and tie, and gold jewelry that winked from ring finger and cuff.

Usually David didn't notice such things, particularly in men, but even he was aware that Salim was inordinately good-looking. The calculating stares of women tourists had once caused him to try to appraise Salim's appearance objectively from a European woman's point of view, and he had decided that Salim's medium brown skin, black curly hair, uncommonly large eyes, and strong, heavy brows combined to make Salim unusually handsome.

"Let's go and get that drink," said Salim. "I think I've earned it."

"Problems?" asked David.

"Just the usual. There are times when I wonder why I got into hotel management."

"Not you too," David commented wryly. "Aside from this," he said—he waved his hand to indicate the hotel—"how's business?"

"Fine." Salim's smile flashed again.

Salim's interests ran from dealing in precious and semiprecious gems to, David suspected, coffee smuggling, and like the majority of Indian businessmen, he was very good at what he did. While David didn't know the full range of his friend's business dealings, he did know that they were extensive and successful, which made him wonder all the more why Salim stayed on managing a hotel.

"Tusker?" Salim inquired. It was David's usual order.

"No. I think I'll strain our friendship by having a Scotch."

As they passed a hurrying waiter, Salim murmured, *"Lete* Scotch *mbili."* The waiter nodded his understanding.

"Let's sit here." Salim indicated a small table set into a recess between immense rough-finished stone pillars, which commanded an excellent view of the three flood-lit water holes just outside.

David saw that one of the thickly cushioned bamboo chairs was occupied by a woman.

"I know you're acquainted, but I'll make the introductions anyway," Salim said. "Halima Abdi, David Karanja."

The two men sat down, and David realized with a start that the young woman was the new Director of the Park's Education Center. She'd been transferred here about three months ago, and he'd seen her only three or four times. As usual when he had seen her, it had been in connection with official business, and he consequently hadn't really noticed her.

Hearing Salim apologize for his having been away so long, David realized that he was most likely interrupting their evening; he immediately felt uncomfortable and tried to think of a polite excuse to get away, but he was soon drawn into the conversation.

In between his replies, he looked again at Halima and decided that his job had made him nearsighted. How he could have failed to notice the woman was beyond him. Perhaps it was the park's uniform.

The Department of Wildlife had only two women as highly placed as Halima, and while it was necessary that they wear a uniform of sorts during the execution of their duties, it was obvious that little thought had gone into the design of a costume that was to be utilized by so few. Consequently, the uniform was a khaki bag that looked as if it had once held potatoes. But seeing Halima now off duty, and in her own clothes, David realized that she was an extremely attractive woman with excellent taste.

He watched her as she talked with Salim. Her face was in profile, and he decided she was of one of the northern tribes. He couldn't tell which one, nor did her name give much of a clue, but her finely sculpted nose, well-defined chin, high cheekbones, and dark brown skin indicated an origin in the north of Kenya.

He noticed the heavy, old-fashioned ivory-and-brass necklace around her neck and thought what a shame it was that so many other African women put aside their traditional costume and ornaments for the white woman's dress and jewelry.

"Am I going to be scolded?" Halima asked softly in amusement. She'd noticed his interest in her necklace.

"No," he replied with a smile. "Of course not." He, like the majority of wildlife conservationists, didn't care to have skins hanging on his walls or covering his floors; he didn't have stuffed or mounted trophies, wastebaskets made from rhino feet, or table decorations carved of ivory. That sort of thing was left to the tourists.

"I don't like the curio trade," he added, "because it supports poaching. But old, ethnic African heirlooms are a different matter. Did that belong to your family?"

"Yes," Halima nodded. "For several generations."

"What is your tribe?"

"My father and his people are Orma, but my mother was Borana." She indicated the necklace. "This was my mother's, and her mother's before her, and so on. I don't really know how old it is."

As the waiter served their drinks, Salim signed the chit and then looked at David. "I'm glad you came by this evening. It saves me a trip to see you tomorrow."

"Is there a problem?"

"I'm afraid so; it's the baboons again."

"Are they back into your garbage bins?"

"As always, but that doesn't bother me. Everybody's in our garbage bins—we can't get the stuff burned fast enough—and if it isn't the baboons then it's the elephants, so the staff just keep picking up whatever's scattered and not eaten. No, they're into the lodge itself now." He nodded in agreement with David's look of surprise before continuing, "This afternoon they raided the dining room during lunch. The first warning we had was when the cook at the barbecue grill gave out a yell and dived under the dessert table. The next thing we knew, we had about eight or ten baboons lunging over the balcony and onto the tables. The confusion was unbelievable. Women screaming, tables overturning, dishes smashing, and baboons grabbing food from left and right." Noticing David's concerned expression, he hastened to add, "It wasn't as bad as it could have been, because no one was hurt. A couple of small children and one lady were badly frightened, but the rest were just excited about it. Most of them regretted not having their cameras."

"How terrible," Halima said before turning to David. "Can you do something?"

"I'll send over two rangers in the morning, and you can position them in the shrubs and rocks just outside the balcony. If the troop returns they'll have to kill one or two of the dominant males, so you'd better warn your guests that there might be some shooting outside."

"I'll do it if I have to," answered Salim, "but is shooting them the only way?" He could already foresee the reaction of most of the tourists—they'd be screaming in protest.

"I'm afraid so. Once they've become this bold, then they've become completely out of hand and the leaders, the dominant males, have to be destroyed. We've tried everything else, but this is the only positive solution. We can't run the risk of having tourists savaged, even if they did create the problem by feeding the baboons in the first place."

"They're really terrible sometimes, and I don't mind admitting that they've frightened me more than once," Halima said. "They tear my wash off the clothesline, knock over my trash cans, and destroy my flower beds."

"Be careful when you try to run them off," David warned. "They'll usually run from a man's voice, but they have no fear of women." Turning to Salim, he added, "You'll have to explain to your guests that the big male baboons can be vicious and could easily inflict a serious wound. Particularly if they're thwarted, and if some guest decided to fight for his lunch rather than relinquish it."

A waiter appeared and held a whispered consultation with Salim, who turned back to them apologetically. "I'm sorry, you'll both have to excuse me again. Will you have another drink?"

David shook his head, and Salim turned to follow the departing waiter.

A long pause ensued, broken only when Halima ventured, "I understand you were educated in America. Did you go on a scholarship?"

"Yes and no." He paused to sip his drink. "Actually, I was raised by a missionary couple, and when Reverend Wallace returned to the United States, I went with him and was educated there. A scholarship helped."

"How did it come about that you were raised by *Wazungu*?" she asked in surprise.

"My parents died when I was fairly young. It's rather a long story."

"I'd like to hear it, if you don't mind telling it."

"No, I don't mind," he said, and added with a self-conscious grin, "but I warn you, it might be boring. Life stories usually are."

"I doubt that somehow," Halima replied with a smile of encouragement.

"Well, when I was very young we lived in a small village near Mount Kenya. My father was a tracker/gunbearer for a firm of professional white hunters in Nairobi, and I don't remember much about him because he was usually away on safari. My life revolved around the Mission run by Reverend and Mrs. James Wallace." He smiled in remembrance. "My mother was their cook, and a Christian—which was rare in those days because she was a Masai, and not many converted."

"But 'Karanja' is a Gikuyu name, isn't it?" asked Halima.

David nodded. "My father was Gikuyu. He met my mother near Kajiado when he was on safari, and he married her. They returned to his village afterward, and that's where I was born and raised. Then in 1952 the Emergency was declared, and two years later, when I was nine, my mother was killed accidentally in a crossfire between the forest fighters and the white Home Guard. That's when the Wallaces moved me from my mother's little house into their own. It was only natural that I would stay on with Mamaw and Papaw."

"But what became of your father?"

"No one knew at the time. He was always on safari, so he was only home for a week or two every few months. When the Wallaces tried to notify him of my mother's death through the safari company, they found out that he'd left weeks before. It seems he'd joined the Mau Mau and was fighting in the Aberdare forest. He was believed to have been killed in late 1956, but we never had proof.

"With my mother gone and my father presumed dead, the Wallaces took over and raised me. They both taught in the Mission School, and they taught me, and it was understood that I was to go on to university here. But just when I was ready to start, Mamaw died, and Papaw realized that he was too old to carry on without her, and that's when he decided that I should return with him to America. He wasn't ready to be alone, I guess, and neither was I. We went to California, and I started university there: biology, zoology, and whatever else came close to wildlife conservation. He died just three months after I graduated, but after his death my reason for staying in the States was gone, so I returned to Kenya. I went to an old friend of the Wallaces' whom I'd known all my life; he had been a Game Warden in our area and had retired. Frazer Kent was his name. He got me my first posting as an assistant warden with the old National Parks. A couple of postings as assistant warden, and then warden, and here I am."

Halima studied him for a moment before asking hesitantly, "Did you think of not coming back? Were you tempted to stay there?"

"No," he said, puzzled by her question. "I don't think it ever occurred to me. Oh, I enjoyed it there. People were good to me, particularly at university, and I made some fine friends whom I still write to; but no, it was a place where I went to become educated and it was where Papaw was. When I got my degree, and he died, I wanted to come home. And"—he chose his words carefully —"this is home; it always had been."

"The Wallaces never changed that," said Halima. It was more a statement than a question, and it conveyed approval.

"No. Not only did they not try to change it, but they were the ones who taught me who I was—an African. Both Gikuyu and English were spoken in our home, because one was my people's tongue and the other was theirs, and they wanted me to know both. No, they taught me that I was me; different from them and yet the same; and even though I was 'their boy,' as they put it, my future would always be in Kenya, because Kenya would need all her bright young men to build the new country. They were wise and sensitive people, and they saw independence on its way long before the Emergency came about. That was why I was to go on to university." He chuckled. "Like most family, they thought I was special, and head and shoulders above everybody else's kid, and I suppose they'd have thought the same if I had been a drooling idiot."

"I thought you said they were wise and sensitive," said Halima with a smile.

"I must have been their blind spot," he acceded.

Halima sipped at her fruit juice, and after a minute or two said, "You make me feel a little guilty—not for myself, but for my brother." Her expression was pensive.

"How?"

"Because the Wallaces were right. Kenya does need her promising young people. All the African countries do. Quite a few African students have gone abroad to Europe or North America to study and take their degrees, and too many don't return. My brother didn't," she added after a moment's hesitation. "He went to the United States to study medicine and he was going to return and do something about taking modern medicine into some of the remote areas of Kenya where it's really needed. A kind of portable tented hospital that could reach people who are a hundred kilometers from a dispensary." She glanced away before adding, "But he never came back. He's still in New York. He has a good practice and a big car, and he married a lovely black American. He has everything, I suppose, that he stayed for." She was silent for a moment, remembering. Then she added a little sadly, "They came to visit last year," and shook her head slowly. "It wasn't a success. He seems to have changed into someone I'm not sure I like. Perhaps in the end he gave up more than he gained."

Looking to David, she said, "That's why I suppose I was curious about you. You left to study abroad and you returned. I think I wanted to know why."

"Now you know," grinned David. He was surprised at himself. Usually he found it hard to talk about himself, particularly to people he didn't know well, and particularly to women. Yet here he was, perfectly at ease and ready to continue the conversation on into the night. Then he remembered Salim.

He finished his drink and collected his cigarettes from the table as he said reluctantly, "I've enjoyed talking with you, but it's getting late and I'd better be going."

"Would you mind taking me home on your way?" asked Halima.

David was startled. "Of course, but what about Salim? Won't he . . . ?" he floundered.

"Salim?" inquired Halima, uncertain of his meaning.

"I'm sorry, I thought you were together." David felt awkward.

She laughed and stood as she picked up her purse. "I came to have dinner with friends from Nairobi who stopped to see me on their way to the coast. When they left, Salim offered me a drink. I'm afraid that's all."

"Let's go, then." He was suddenly pleased. She didn't belong to Salim—at least, not yet.

After leaving a message of "Thank you" at the desk for their host, they passed outside, to meet the chilly gusts from the south, and walked quickly to the shelter of the car. During the short drive to Headquarters Hill, David recalled the meeting scheduled for the following morning, and on impulse said, "I'd like you to be present at a meeting at Headquarters in the morning. I think you'd find the discussion interesting, and it would give you a better idea of some of the problems we face here; problems we hope will be alleviated in time by education."

"That sounds interesting," she replied. "I'd like to come."

Pulling up the drive of the house next to the Education Center, he stopped and reached across to open her door. Before getting out, she said, "I enjoyed our conversation—and in case you're wondering, I wasn't bored."

"I'm glad, but now you owe me your life story in exchange for mine," he replied. Any self-consciousness he'd felt was gone now.

"Next time." She smiled and turned to get out of the car.

"Will there be," he insisted gently, "a next time?"

She turned back. Her eyes met his, and he was aware of a moment's hesitation before her smile returned. "If you like," she replied softly. "Good night, and thank you for bringing me home."

He waited until she reached her door and the light inside went on before pulling away. He found that he was looking forward to seeing her again, and as soon as possible.

Then he remembered another woman he'd looked forward to seeing—a young woman he'd loved—the only woman he'd ever wanted to marry. He hadn't thought of her in months, but now that he'd done so he found that the hurt was still there. It had been at the university during his senior year, and even though Papaw had never said so, he hadn't approved—she was a beautiful 24-karat ultra-liberal WASP. It was months before he began to suspect that her love for him was mixed up with a misguided desire to make a personal statement about human rights. They'd tried to work their problems out, but couldn't really. He'd tried to tell himself that she loved him enough, that subconscious motives didn't matter, and he'd turned to Papaw then for confirmation; but although Papaw refused to condemn, he'd said, "To her it matters too much, and you deserve better, David."

He'd been right. The first time they had a bad quarrel, they'd both said the first things they could think of to hurt each other, and that was the only time anyone had ever called him a "nigger." He hadn't known, until then, how badly he could hurt, but she had been the one who'd broken down and wept.

As he approached Headquarters Hill, he slowed down and turned at the small, discreet sign that read WARDEN'S RESIDENCE—PRIVATE ROAD. Driving up the incline, he noticed the resident group of waterbuck just below his house. Some of the animals were standing, others lying down with heads erect as they watched the headlamp beams pass by.

He slowed and searched for a moment until he spotted the young albino waterbuck standing between two other immature males just below the water hole. It was interesting, he thought as he remembered the old hurt, how animals accepted the variants of their species, and an albino was not treated any differently than its peers of typical coloration. But then, he thought with the touch of humor that age had brought, they're not as "intelligent" as people.

Pulling into his carport, he climbed out of the car and entered

113

the backyard gate; immediately there was a crashing sound as some-thing fled through the bushes. His torch flashed its yellow arc through the rows of garden vegetables, but whatever had been there was gone.

As he was about to enter his back door, a soft, rhythmic banging caught his attention. He stopped and listened, trying to identify the sound. It was inside the yard somewhere, and he began to look for its source. He approached the small house beside the fruit trees where Bubu lived. The flashlight illuminated the front of the house and followed the wall to the door, which stood open a few inches and then banged shut as another gust of wind tore through the yard.

"Bubu," he called. There was no answer. It was silent. Stepping to the door, he called out again. The wind rattled the banana-tree leaves together in reply overhead.

Reaching out, he took the door handle and pulled the door shut firmly until its latch snapped.

Glancing at his watch, he saw the luminous green hands indi-cating eleven thirty. Bubu was usually in bed by nine o'clock: Where was he? Then he remembered: it was payday today. Bubu wouldn't be the only one celebrating with copious bottles of beer at the park canteen. There would be a number of hangovers among the staff tomorrow. Smiling to himself, he turned back to enter the house.

THIRTY-TWO KILOMETERS to the north, in an area Mulolo had re-ported as being without a patrol, a large herd of elephants was on the move south toward the Lalaga Lana River. Their passing was not unobserved, nor had it been since the animals had crossed a little-known service road and left their huge spoor on the graded track. The two bush vehicles that tonight prowled silently over this rarely used trail through the dense thornbush had paused moments later when the dimmed headlamps illuminated the churned-up roadbed. Motors were cut, and a dark figure jumped from the lead vehicle onto the hood and up to stand motionless on the cab and search the area to the south with binoculars.

The bright moon washed the landscape a warm gray, to reveal the jagged bush striped and stippled with shadows, and through it, the broad, smooth backs of the larger elephants as they pushed through the agitated bush a few hundred meters away. The binoculars lifted a fraction of an inch to pick out the lead animals, who were headed due south toward the water, and noted, far beyond, the two large *kopjes* that formed a roughly broken half-circle. The elephants would pass through them within a short time.

The engines sprang to life and the headlamps flashed on high as the vehicles sped west to pick up the main track to Silanga. Reaching it, they cut south and backtracked as they followed the road southeast till they neared the small hills ahead of the elephants. Cutting into the bush, they approached the base of the rocky *kopjes,* where they stopped in the shadows. Soon the dark silence was broken only by the sound of heavy breathing as the men hauled their equipment into position on top of the boulder-strewn *kopjes,* where the dull wink of the moonlight reflected off a glass lens. It was soon quiet, and a hushed whisper from the man who stood with his binoculars trained northward carried far in the still night.

The lead elephants moved unaware into the uneven area between the two rocky hills, while those who followed were slowly funneled into a compact mass behind them by the broken ground. The huge spotlights flashed on simultaneously, blinding the animals. The herd matriarch's trunk lifted; her scream of warning was abruptly cut off as the rifles opened fire. The panic-stricken animals lunged forward sightlessly, only to trip and fall over the bodies of those in front who were being cut down in the merciless crossfire from above. They tried to turn, to escape the dazzling arcs of light that followed; again, those in the lead were dropped and the ones behind stumbled and fell under the continuous fusillade. The herd milled and heaved in terror, trampling the calves underfoot; their high-pitched trumpeting screams of fear drowned the sound of the shots. The number of fallen mounted: ten, twenty, fifty, a hundred struggled and thrashed on the bloody ground, and still the staccato chatter of the rifles continued.

III · TUESDAY

III-TUESDAY

CHAPTER SEVEN

Dawn:
Before the Meeting

DAVID STIRRED. His eyes opened and sought the window. It was barely perceptible; a square in a lighter shade of black stood out in the dark room. He lay quietly, listening to the silence, which was broken suddenly by the roar of a lion.

Lifting his arms over his head, he stretched his long frame luxuriously and felt every muscle and bone in his body yawn and come tingling awake. Kicking off the sheet, he sat up and groped in the dark for the clock to push in the alarm button, after which he gave it a vicious shake and banged it once on the table. He intensely disliked mechanical things; they seemed diabolically determined to malfunction in order to irritate him, and the clock's alarm would often fail to ring when it was properly set to do so, and at other times it would shatter his nerves by ringing when it was *not* set.

Crawling out from under the mosquito netting, he stood up, and after rewrapping his *kikoi* around his waist he padded barefoot through the dark hall and into the kitchen.

After making a cup of instant coffee and fetching a loaf of bread from the refrigerator, he made his way to the veranda. Depositing his coffee on the table, he crossed the lawn to the water hole, where he crumbled the bread for the early-morning birds. Then he returned to the veranda, to enjoy the early dawn.

It was going to be another spectacular sunrise. The sky, in the long dry season, usually cleared at night only to cloud over again by midmorning. But sometimes the thick racks of cloud failed to dissipate during darkness, and as the sun began to rise, the rumpled underside of the cloud cover would blush a pale pink, then gradually deepen to a livid magenta stippled with indigo. As the sky lightened, the emerging sun warmed the magenta to crimson, which passed to an orange and gold slashed with a paler shade of blue.

The tentative chirp and twitter of the waking birds had swelled into a deafening chorus. As David sipped his coffee he saw the first of his small tenants arrive for breakfast: a small, olive-buff bush squirrel started headfirst down the acacia-trunk pillar that supported the *makuti* roof over the veranda. Three-fourths of the way down, he hung on to the rough bark with the prehensile toes of his hind feet and slowly extended his small body, and after reaching out with his tiny forepaws, he flexed and stretched himself fully awake. Jumping the last foot or so, he stopped and sat on the ledge, rubbing his head with his forepaws; flicking his fluffy tail forward, he clasped it in his paws and proceeded to scrub his face and head with his built-in washcloth. Releasing his tail to flip back and cock itself over his head, he turned to David and proceeded to scold him in a trill of excited chattering, before scampering over to select a choice bread crumb.

David drained his cup and looked out to the water hole, where a horde of feathered bodies began to swarm and boil over the red earth. The red-billed and von der Decken's hornbills ran from bread crumb to bread crumb, while the superb and golden-breasted starlings slowly meandered around to peck and shake their heads. The smaller birds hopped and fluttered about, selecting the smaller bits, and as these white-browed sparrow weavers, Somali sparrows, and assorted barbets, finches, and bulbuls encountered one another, their pugnacious personalities often resulted in confrontations that saw the combatants rolling over the ground in a blurred flurry of feathers.

As David watched, Bubu stepped down onto the veranda and deposited a tray with a pot of freshly made coffee, cream, and coarse beige sugar. *"Utafanya nini leo?"* David asked.

Bubu waved his hand toward the southwest, made a walking gesture with his fingers, and then held up two fingers. David nodded: two fingers indicated that at *saa mbili*—the second hour of the day, or 8 A.M. *Mzungu* time—he was going to town. Today was the *soko*, or big market, day, when Bubu did the majority of the week's shopping.

After telling him about the bats in Vera's ceiling, David asked him to help remove them, and Bubu grinned, nodded, and turned back into the house.

Sitting back with the freshly ground coffee sending a pungently rich vapor up his nose, David sipped and watched as two young bush squirrels chased each other around and about the veranda floor beside his feet.

Suddenly he heard a loud snort. Looking up, he saw a large, grizzled waterbuck as she stood halted in her advance to the water hole ahead of the following herd. Again she snorted through her nose, and the flock of birds took to the air with an audible flurry and flapping of wings, while the red ground squirrels tore through the grass, tails trailing behind them, as they headed for their burrow in the old termite mound just outside the yard.

Slowly, two other females edged forward cautiously to join the leading waterbuck, who now stepped closer to the water before halting again. Staring at the house, whose presence she distrusted, she carefully scrutinized the veranda before her dark, questioning gaze moved on to investigate the yard and the trees for the possible presence of a lurking predator or man—one and the same. Her coarse, shaggy hide jerked and rippled forward over her back as she unconsciously reacted to one of the numerous ticks that fed upon her. Each creature fed upon another: some you survived in spite of; some took all, and you perished. It was this she watched for.

Boldly she advanced two steps and stopped, and again snorted her challenge and stamped her forefoot. She was very near the water and could smell its invitation. She was thirsty, but still stood with every muscle and nerve alert.

She stepped closer, and the water's edge was at her forefeet; slowly her head lowered as she continued to sift through the sounds, smells, and visions she weighed for a hint of danger. She drank deeply for a moment, and then abruptly threw up her head and glanced around to see if a predator had begun to creep up on her while her head had been lowered, leaving her vulnerable. She stood vigilant, her white-tipped muzzle dripping.

She was reassured, and slowly her head lowered as she spaced her forefeet farther apart to enable her to better reach the cool water. The rest of the herd—females, juveniles, and young calves—crept closer to the water hole; impatient to reach the water, and yet nervous because of the close proximity of the man smells. Forefeet tentatively splashed into the water as muzzles began to lower in expectation—then the silence was suddenly blasted by a shrill, un-natural sound which jolted the leading female into an explosion of straining muscles.

Her head shot up instantly, and her legs gathered beneath her as she spun away from the water hole and hurtled forward in an instinctive dash for survival. Dirt flew and pebbles smacked into the water as hooves scrabbled at the ground to gain the purchase necessary to propel the leaping, twisting bodies forward in their race to escape. Within a second or two the water hole was evacuated, and only the dust remained to float lazily on the breeze.

David sat perfectly still on the veranda and watched the retreating white-ringed rumps as they disappeared into the thick bush, and he listened as the erratic alarm clock finally wound itself down into silence.

"Goddammit," he growled in exasperation. Dawn was his favorite time of day, and the panorama of wildlife that passed quietly before him each morning was the best part of it.

Unpleasantly reminded of the oncoming day, he saw that the sun was climbing; dawn was over, and his mind had already moved ahead to face the day's agenda—the crucial meeting whose outcome might decide the future of Aruba National Park.

Getting up, he stretched his legs before passing through the house to his bedroom, where he unwrapped and flung his *kikoi* onto the newly made bed. As he started for the shower, he noticed the offending clock sitting smugly on the bedside table. Picking it up, he held it chest high over a metal wastebasket and let go. The wastebasket intensified the sound of metal striking metal and of breaking glass; the loud ticking was stilled.

ASSISTANT WARDEN Mohamed Agaran supervised as each man in Unit 1 checked out his rifle and ammunition for the day's patrol duty from Corporal Lugumba. Occasionally he would reach out and take one of the men's weapons to see it was cleaned and oiled. He made a habit of accompanying the various units on patrol on a rotation basis, and even though he had to return to Headquarters later for a meeting, he had a special reason for going out with Unit 1 today: the Waliangulu, Heekuta Neko, was somewhere near. He could feel the man's presence, and the feeling had given him an idea.

He only wished the eight Field Force Rangers would hurry up so he could get out of the foul-smelling armory situated below the Warden's office. The Headquarters main building was built on two levels and constructed of concrete blocks faced with natural stone, but while the offices and Radio Room above enjoyed the fresh air provided by huge windows, the armory was windowless by necessity, and the only available air gained access through four small slits in the steel door. This precaution against breaking and entering was important: the park's weapons were kept here, and the armory also acted as the storeroom for all the recovered trophies. However, the accumulated ivory, the rhino and dik-dik horns, plus the teeth of hippos, lions, and assorted other animals, besides the skins of the spotted cats, kudus, zebras, and lions, gave off a musty, slightly rotten smell of death that was hard to get out of your nostrils even after you left the room.

Periodically the trophies would be collected by the Department and transferred to the Ivory Room in Mombasa, where they were stored until auction. These auctions occurred twice a year and could involve a million dollars' worth of ivory, horns, teeth, and skins that had been recovered from poachers or collected from animals either shot on control or dead of natural causes.

Agaran glanced around. There hadn't been a pickup for several months, and it was almost impossible to move. Ivory was stacked everywhere: hundreds of tusks—everything from the last of the large-bull ivory down through the immature-bull and cow tusks and finally to the tusks of the small calves. Of course, some were the result of the drought, but the majority were from poached animals.

Noticing that the men were filing out of the room, he stood and followed. The sergeant approached and handed Corporal Lugumba a folded and sealed paper with his name and the day's date on it: Tuesday, 1st November. Agaran watched as the man opened it and slowly spelled out the patrol orders for Unit 1. He knew it wasn't easy for Lugumba because he couldn't read very well, but after a moment of study Agaran knew he had it: patrol the Moda River Circuit, from Shokoke to the Aruba Dam.

Picking up the two walkie-talkies and his rifle, Agaran walked toward the Land Cruiser. Shokoke, he thought, the old, heavily wooded site of the main Waliangulu settlement, just south of the Waliangulu poacher's last kill. The perfect hiding place.

As the vehicle pulled out, he leaned forward and reached for the VHF radio microphone to call up the Radio Room at the Headquarters they were just leaving behind in a cloud of boiling red dust.

"Six-oh-three, Lima-eight-five . . ." He verified that they were leaving for their patrol and signed off. A unit never went into the bush without first checking that they had radio contact with Headquarters; they might need help later.

Sitting back for the short ride, he looked ahead to the Moda River Valley. He could remember a time when the river had flowed through a thick, sprawling stand of trees which had earned the name of the Moda River Forest, but one by one the trees had gone down as the elephants pushed them over, or they'd stood dying after being ringbarked as solitary reminders of what used to be. Now many areas were completely stripped of trees, and the water that flowed during the rains ran between grassy banks dotted with the shrubs that would be tomorrow's trees. But in a half-dozen places there still remained dense stands of tall trees whose combined canopy offered shade and concealment for many elephants, rhinos, waterbuck, lesser kudus—and poachers. It was this last group which made frequent patrols a necessity.

He looked over his shoulder through the small window that afforded a view of the back of the vehicle. The men had rolled back and tied down the tarp that acted as roof, and now two of them stood braced against the brush bars as they each scanned one side of the road for the telltale footprints indicating the presence of poachers.

No one, except the Field Force, was allowed out of a vehicle once it was inside the park gates, except at one of the few designated lookout points, or on the grounds of one of the lodges or camping areas. Footprints anywhere else signaled poachers, and it was amazing how unthinking some poachers were. Many times they would use the park roads as the lions did, as an easy and direct trail on which to get from one place to another, rather than go through the bush, which tore at the traveler and made walking in a straight line impossible. Day or night, it wasn't unusual to overtake a pride of lions ambling along a road on their way somewhere; but the poachers used the roads only during darkness, without having the sense to know that the footprints they were unable to see at night showed up like signposts after dawn.

Agaran noted that the road now began to indicate the presence of a large concentration of wildlife in the area. The spoor of buffalo crossed the graded track, with the occasional dark, splatted droppings which resembled those of cattle; elephants had passed here and left their own huge wrinkled spoor, and these prints were accompanied by the cannonball droppings, laced with partially digested vegetation and seeds. As the vehicle approached, small flocks of birds flew up and away from the elephants' leavings; the seed eaters came for the seeds contained in the dung, and the insectivorous birds congregated to feed on the small beetles that had begun to arrive earlier while the dung was still warm. After the vehicle passed, the birds returned and resumed their feeding.

When the huge elephants passed over their range, they were responsible not only for the pushing over and ringbarking of many of the trees they fed on, but also for the dispersal of the seeds from yesterday's foraging, which would in time propagate elsewhere to grow into the forests of tomorrow. Thus not only did the elephant reap the benefit of the natural vegetation, but he cooperated in that he carried the seeds to a new place and he sowed them in a bed of fertilizing dung. The elephants did not necessarily destroy as man destroyed, but they did bring change.

The Toyota slowed as it approached Shokoke, and stopped. This area was closed to the public, and so a ranger jumped out to unhook the chain which spanned the service road that led into the largest of the remaining stands of forest. The Toyota then swung to the right onto the badly rutted service track that led into the dim grove of tall trees hung with vines and creepers.

The vehicle moved ahead slowly as the men scanned the area, seeking the presence of an interloper. A bush moved, and the rangers' dark eyes mutely inspected each twig, each leaf, until a yellow baboon stalked out to inspect the intruders before barking a warning to his troop. The grunting of another baboon acknowledging the warning was ignored by the patrol, as were the chatter of the birds overhead and the hum of the insects, but a snapping twig jerked heads around to seek the source, and when an ugly, piglike warthog sow burst from the undergrowth ahead of her four equally unattractive offspring, the dark eyes passed on to question elsewhere.

The Toyota continued to the edge of the now-dry riverbed and stopped. The men piled out, their rifle straps over their shoulders. Agaran passed one of the walkie-talkies to Corporal Lugumba and indicated the four rangers who would accompany the Orma corporal on his section's foot patrol along the north side of the riverbed.

Motioning the four remaining rangers to follow him, Agaran walked toward the sand river. The Toyota's driver would now return the way he had come, and after regaining the circuit road, he would continue east on the main road to where he would park near the approximated rendezvous.

Crossing the deep gray-white sand of the river, Agaran noted the spoor of three giraffes and one rhino without conscious thought or reaction. He was interested in the spoor of only one animal; he saw the others without seeing.

He walked at the head of his four men as they headed southeast toward the old settlement, and his eyes never ceased moving, scanning the ground for any indication that the Waliangulu had passed this way. Periodically, he looked up at the sky to watch for the vultures who could tell him of the man's next kill, and once he saw a growing circle of the birds to the south as they rotated slowly with outspread wings. He stopped to study their movements: they were only circling on a current, searching as he was searching. They had seen nothing—yet.

AUDREY FORBES LAY QUIETLY and tried to hear the singing of the birds outside in between Jeff's rasping snores. She gave up with a sleepy smile. No one could compete with her husband when it came to snoring. She thought of the nights spent sleepless and deafened besides him in the first months after they married and how she'd grimly hung on through each night until morning. Combinations of earplugs, earmuffs, and insulating pillows that nearly smothered her had all been tried and discarded: but she was determined to sleep beside her husband, and finally complete exhaustion accomplished what the other remedies failed to do. Now the rare occasions that saw Jeff away from home for a few days left her restless and wakeful because his braying burr, sizz, and whistle was missing.

It was probably after six, and she decided, regretfully, that she had to get up. Sitting, she pulled the pins from her hair and shook her head as her long, thick russet hair fell and covered her shoulders. Jeff loved her long hair; in fact, it was her hair that had first attracted him. He told her that he'd had an Irish setter when he was a boy, and her hair was the very same shade of deep rich red; not carrot or copper or any of the other words used to describe red hair. It was Irish setter red, and that was what he called it.

Really, though, she decided, she was too old to be still wearing her hair down; it should be cut short in something stylish, or put up somehow, not cascading everywhere and flying in her eyes and mouth. But Jeff wouldn't hear of it, so that was that.

Slipping under the edge of the white netting over the bed, she pushed her feet into waiting sandals and got up to wrap herself into a long fuzzy robe in order to keep the bed warmth in and the early-morning coolness out; days were hot, but a chill came with the wind at dawn and dusk. She shut the door softly behind her as she left the room, although she was well aware that her early-morning creep-around was unnecessary; nothing short of being gored by a rhino was likely to wake Jeff before his time.

Going into the kitchen, she was relieved to see Hassan busy with the preparation of the morning feedings.

"*Jambo, Hassan,*" she said, using Swahili's common form of greeting.

"Jambo sana, Mama," he replied, grinning over his shoulder.

"Unatengeneza maziwa?" she asked, hoping he was well ahead with the mixing of the formulas.

"Ndiyo. Nilitengeneza yote," he said as he wiped the last bottle.

They had a full house in the orphanage now, and it was all she could do to see the lot of them fed and doctored, even with the help of her cook and the two herdsmen. She was going to ask for another pair of hands if she got even one more; the additional elephant calf who'd arrived yesterday strained her resources almost to the breaking point.

Mentally she calculated. She knew the herdsmen would split up today. Lochoro would take the "big orphan" herd down to the valley to graze, while Joseph stayed here with Sarah, the adult elephant cow, and her newly adopted infant, plus the female calf, because the newcomer was too weak yet to trek the distance. They knew better than even to try to separate Sarah from the young male calf. The bond had been sealed instantly and irrevocably; this calf was Sarah's now and would remain so until it reached puberty.

She picked up the file cards from the counter and began checking the required feedings against the bottles prepared by Hassan.

As she ticked off each of them with its formula mixture, she moved them from the counter into a large *kikapu* at her feet; reaching the last card, she was reminded that as yet the newest orphan had no name. She'd have to think up one for him today, but she was running out of good names. She'd used them up over the years, and each one had a furry face attached to it in her memory, so she couldn't drag it out and give it to someone else like an outgrown garment.

She picked up the two bottles labeled NEKO and NEKA, crossed the kitchen to the large wicker laundry basket beside the oven, and lifted the lid. Two pairs of small bright eyes peered from their soft nest of clean, old ratty towels, and a series of shrill meows indicated that the lion cubs were indeed awake—and ravenous.

She reached into the basket and lifted first one and then the other by the scruff of the neck and deposited them in her lap. Taking the cuff of her thick long-sleeved robe, she pulled it down past her fingers and then repeated the operation with the other sleeve. Picking up the bottles in her now-protected hands, she offered the calcium-enriched formula to the squirming cubs, who lunged forward to latch on to the thick rubber nipples. Growling, they sucked violently at their respective bottles and periodically clawed at the warm pile of the fuzzy robe which covered her hands.

She studied the two hungry cubs as they concentrated on their milk; their coats were thick and woolly, and as for color they were a brindled tawny-buff, spotted and striped by nature to help camouflage them. After calculating their age at five weeks and some days, she decided that it was time to offer them meat; she would have to mention it at Headquarters so that if a fresh carcass was found they could lay in a supply of it. In the meantime she'd have to start them off on what she could buy in the village today, although it would be out of the question to consider buying meat on a regular basis for a couple of rapidly growing predators; it was almost impossible to get enough for herself and Jeff.

The little female finished and now slumped over on her back against Audrey's leg in the sprawled and clumsy attitude of the very young animal. Looking up at Audrey, she mewed a question: When was she going to be picked up? The male finished at last, and for once hadn't torn the rubber nipple off his bottle. After making a rude digestive noise or two, the male cub tried a tentative growl and liked the result so well that he continued to sit hunched over his bloated belly and rumble infant snarls to himself.

After giving the emptied bottles to Hassan, Audrey picked up the eager female cub and held her to her shoulder as she would hold a human infant after its feeding. The cub immediately began to purr, and pushed her small milky face along Audrey's cheek and into her hair while Audrey stroked the cub's head and back.

After a few minutes she got up and went to find the little male, who had scuttled off on an exploration of the laundry-room floor. After depositing the cubs into their sandbox, she went out the back door into the securely enclosed section of the backyard where the little pack of orphans waited impatiently for their breakfast. Hassan followed with the basket filled with formula bottles.

Immediately the young calves were pressing around her, pushing and straining as they lowed, bleated, whistled and snorted. Suddenly, without warning, she was butted in the back of the knees by the rhino calf, and as her legs buckled and went out from under her, she sat down hard on the ground. Hands on hips, she was just opening her mouth to scream in outrage when she heard a familiar roar, and she turned to see Jeff leaning out the bedroom window convulsed in laughter. After a moment spent in impotent fury, she began to giggle while the young rhino, Shetani, stepped all over her robe.

"You're appropriately named," she informed Shetani. "You are indeed a little devil."

Turning to Jeff, she called out, "If you think it's so bleeding funny, then you can come help me." He disappeared from the window still chuckling.

"You take Maji and Sawa-Tu," she told Hassan, indicating the young waterbuck and duiker, "and I'll take the other two."

Reaching into the basket, she selected the bottles labeled SHETANI and MBOGO-DOGO and stuck them into the impatient faces of the young calf rhino and buffalo. Soon the only sound to be heard was that of sucking and slurping as the four young animals pulled at the rubber nipples.

"I'm a filthy mess," she said out loud as she surveyed her mud-splattered robe and watched a huge speckled tick as it crept up her ankle.

"May I be of some assistance, madam?" Jeff inquired.

She turned to see her husband approaching in his pajamas and slippers. "Oh, you're absolutely—"

"Yes, dear?" he inquired pleasantly.

"Go . . ."

Her words were cut off as he leaned over the calves to plant a good-morning kiss tasting of last night's pipe on her mouth.

"Jeffrey Patrick Forbes," she exclaimed, glancing at Hassan, who was now displaying a pointed and slightly desperate interest in the sky overhead.

"Oh, dear"—Jeff faked consternation; "my whole name. I must be in trouble again."

Shaking her head at her husband and trying not to smile, Audrey collected the last two and largest bottles and started up the path that led to the elephants' *boma,* where the female calf squealed in impatience for her bottle. Reaching the top, Audrey noted with satisfaction that Dida's pen was still empty and that he wasn't hanging around the *boma* either. Good—she didn't trust the adolescent elephant since he'd lashed out with his trunk and sent her flying through the air, to land on her hip and so badly bruise the entire left side of her body that she'd hardly been able to get out of bed for a week. And all because she'd given the younger Galogalo a piece of sugar cane that Dida wanted, after he'd already eaten his share. The realization that he could have killed her was a little frightening.

There were people who were a little barmy when it came to animals, and who would insist that a potentially dangerous animal was as gentle as a kitten if it had been properly loved and cared for. She supposed that some individual cases were proof of that attitude; but still, kittens had claws, and while a kitten couldn't do much damage, an adult leopard could kill.

She thought of her cubs. They were adorable; soft, fluffy, funny, awkward, and vulnerable. She loved to feel them tumbling over her, pushing and mewling their demands. She understood their affection for her, and their dependence upon her, and she responded by loving them and caring for them, but she knew that the sweet little male would someday be an adult lion of four to five hundred pounds, if he had a full stomach, and he'd stand some three and a half feet at the shoulder and measure up to eight feet in length. Then the days of chewing on her fingertips would be over, and if she wanted to see him after he'd been rehabilitated to the wild, she'd be forced by reality to do her visiting from the safety of a Land-Rover.

No, she'd known Dida for more than seven years; ever since he was some six years old. She'd fed him treats, played with him, and doctored his hurts; but he was now entering adulthood, and he had needs that she couldn't fulfill. So it was either go and live the life nature intended, or spend a lifetime caged. Audrey well knew which of the two available choices she would choose for her charges.

"Yes, I know," she said to another series of hungry yells. "You're hungry."

Putting one of the huge thirty-six-ounce milk bottles under her arm, she deftly unlatched the hook that closed the only door through the tall, chain-link fence surrounding the elephant pens. Digging into the pocket of her robe, she produced an orange, and stepped over to the pen that held Galogalo to offer him the fruit through the six-inch iron bars.

"Poor Galogalo," she murmured. "You used to be her baby, and now she's got two new ones and you're out in the cold."

Lifting and extending his trunk, Galogalo reached out and took the orange and swiftly curled his trunk under and tucked the fruit into his mouth; immediately the trunk returned to question her hands for another. Rubbing over his trunk's corrugated surface, bristling with coarse, spiky hairs, she consoled the slightly jealous six-foot seven-year-old by paying attention to him first.

Ignoring the now-livid female calf, whose squealing shrieks were taking all of Audrey's willpower to endure, she offered the last orange to Sarah and patted her trunk as well; unwrapping the heavy chain that bound the pen shut, she swung open the gate and, after depositing the second bottle behind her, tilted Zimwi's bottle. Abruptly the trumpeting squeals ceased.

Looking past the suckling youngster, Audrey watched Sarah and the new calf, who stood underneath between the female's huge, pillarlike legs. Sarah was comforting the little male by caressing him all over with her trunk and reassuring him with a deep rumbling sound that emanated from somewhere inside her.

The new calf stopped regarding Audrey and began to grope at

Sarah; finding the nipple he sought, he sucked hard and then snorted in frustration and backed away. Sarah moved over him again and guided him back under her belly in the direction of the unproductive teat; again the calf groped and sucked to no avail.

Sarah was an oddity of sorts, thought Audrey. Of all the elephants raised here at Aruba, she was the only one who had never left to join the wild herds. She would move through them when a wild herd crossed the path of the big orphans, and on a few occasions she'd failed to return with the others at night, but within a day or so she always returned to her *boma*. These small calves who arrived periodically were her reason. Some of the very young died, and for these Sarah grieved, but the ones who lived and stayed on were the reason she never left for good. The maternal instinct is strong in a female elephant, and Sarah had matured quickly because of the presence of the little ones.

She was nineteen years old now, and for eighteen of those years she'd lived with people. She'd been the leader of the herd of big orphans for over seven years, and for all of those years she'd acted as a surrogate mother for every elephant orphan turned in. It was the reason she remained, and it was also the reason that she stayed as gentle and dependable as she was; the small orphans satisfied her maternal instincts, and to her they were her own offspring. The fact that she had never been bred, had never birthed and never been able to produce the milk she urged the calves to suckle was irrelevant. She cared for them, and that made her their mother. Nothing else was important.

"Almost finished?" asked Jeff as he stepped into the stockade.

Zimwi had finished most of the formula and began to lose interest in the bottle. "One more to do," said Audrey, putting down the nearly empty bottle and retrieving the full one before kissing Jeff lightly on his stubbly cheek in passing.

She approached the male calf, who was backing away beneath Sarah, and spoke to him in a soothing undertone. The calf was hungry, but the idea of a bottle was still strange to him, and it would take several days to accustom him to it. Sarah continued to rumble her mysterious communication to the youngster as she fondled him with her trunk. Backing the calf up against Sarah's hind legs, Audrey stooped and moved under the large female to offer the tipped bottle, and after much fumbling, she succeeded in getting it into his mouth. As yesterday, it was immediately rejected, and the first contest of today was begun; jerking his head away and pushing the nipple out of his mouth with his tongue, the calf continued to reject the bottle while Audrey kept shoving it into his mouth.

Finally, enough of the warm formula ran down his throat and he began to remember the idea behind this apparent torture. Haltingly at first, he ceased to struggle in resistance, and began to cooperate by swallowing the milk that had been running out of the sides of his mouth. Finally he began to suck.

Audrey stroked his small head and felt the coarse little hairs gliding under her hand; this year-old calf had lost much of his baby hair, but he was still much more thickly haired than an adult. He brought to mind the small calf whose birthing had been disturbed by the road graders, and who had lived for three long months, only to eventually die.

She'd first seen him in the late afternoon when he'd been lifted down off the back of a Land Cruiser, and the declining sun had backlit the calf so that his coat of reddish hairs had outlined him in a soft halo. He had been tiny—quite the smallest elephant she'd ever tried to raise—which was why she had tried so hard, half-hoping that he might be the first to live when hand-reared from birth. She had almost made it. The fact that success had been so close made the failure that much harder to bear.

She was so sure that she had finally found the right formula. Baby elephants were unable to tolerate the fat in cow's milk, and fat-free diets failed to provide the necessary nutrients, so infant elephants under the age of a year or so, who were not yet able to take solid food, either scoured or wasted away to nothing, and death was the inevitable outcome either way. But with this baby she had had success the first week after discovering an American baby formula whose coconut oil proved to be acceptable to the elephant infant's delicate digestion.

With three-pint feedings every three hours, starting at 6 A.M. and ending at nine thirty every evening, the calf had grown at least an inch, and had put on weight as he developed an intelligent and captivating personality that was almost elfin in character. He'd been called No-Name, because at first Audrey had feared that his case was hopeless and it seemed that his having a name would make his eventual death more personal. It was Jeff who first called him No-Name, after tiring of referring to "the new calf," and the name had stuck to the little elephant, who shuffled around the garden or rocked backward and forward, or from side to side, while exploring everything and everyone with his tiny and usually muddy trunk. Then after an unheard-of success for three long months, he had developed a scour that failed to respond to drugs. After twelve days the terrible symptoms of dehydration set in, and within hours he slipped into a coma that ended in death.

In retrospect, she felt that she knew the answer to his sudden decline and subsequent death, and hoped the lesson learned so painfully would provide the next infant elephant with a better chance.

The sound of sucking air announced that the latest arrival had finished with his feed.

"You were hungry," said Audrey, stroking his forehead.

The stubby trunk reached out tentatively to feel her face, and Audrey knew that within a few feedings the calf's apprehension would disappear.

Recovering the bottles, Audrey closed the *boma* gate securely. Soon the herdsmen would come and open all the pens to assemble the big orphans for their march to their feeding grounds along the Moda River.

"What were you thinking of when you were feeding the new calf?" asked Jeffrey as he put his arm across her shoulders.

"No-Name."

"I thought so."

Turning her head to look at him, she asked, "How could you tell?"

"Because you looked so sad." Smiling in understanding, he added, "Don't feel bad—you'll pull the next one through." Extending his forefinger, he wiped the side of her cheek and murmured, "You're dirty."

"I know," she said in contentment. "I always am."

LOCHORO, HEAD HERDSMAN for the big orphans, stood outside the door of his small one-room stone house beside the elephant *boma* and watched for the arrival of his assistant. Inside, his pregnant wife sat quietly on an overturned Kimbo can, long emptied of its cooking fat, and slowly stirred the pot of maize-meal porridge bubbling over the charcoal brazier beside her.

When it was done, she poured the thin gruel into a bowl for his breakfast and took it out to him. Silently taking the hot *uji* from her, he sat down on a three-legged stool in the sunlit doorway and began to eat while he waited for Joseph to arrive.

The woman filled another bowl and returned to the Kimbo can; after drawing the back hem of her *khanga* up between her legs, she reached out for her two-year-old son and pulled him toward her, nestling him between her knees as she cradled her arm about his small shoulders.

Picking up the cooling *uji*, she held the bowl in one hand and took up a spoonful, which she tested against her lips before offering it to the child. He hungrily slurped the porridge from the tip of the large spoon, and as his mother took the next spoonful, he stood quietly and observed the underside of her dark jaw. She continued to spoon up the *uji*, one for the child, one for herself.

As she offered the last spoonful to the small waiting mouth, she felt the warm stream of urine as it trickled over her foot in front of her son. Unconcerned, he finished the *uji*, and after placing his forefinger inside his mouth to explore the interesting texture of his bright pink tongue, he began to rub the sole of one wet foot over the top of the other.

Seeing Joseph striding up the hill's gentle incline, Lochoro stood, and after taking up the long metal rod that served as a walking stick and herding staff, he grunted his departure to his wife.

"*Aiyah*," she acknowledged placidly, and watched as his shadow disappeared through the bright doorway.

"*Habari za asubuhi?*" Joseph inquired of his well-being.

"*Nzuri tu*—Just fine," Lochoro replied.

Joseph stepped inside the lion-proof fence and unwrapped the chain that secured the gate to Sarah's pen. Swinging it open, he stepped in and around the cow and coaxed her out with a soft "Ugh, ugh."

The female calf needed no urging; she was out and heading for the water hole. Sarah nudged the male calf forward, and they followed as Joseph released Galogalo.

Zimwi snorted and snuffled the water in her trunk and managed to lose half of it before she got trunk tip to mouth; she was past that infant stage where she would kneel and drink water through her mouth while trying to keep her stubby trunk out of the way, but not yet as adept as Sarah, who now approached and expertly drew three gallons of water up into her trunk before curling it under and back to pour the contents into her open mouth.

When Lochoro saw that the four elephants had begun to drift away from the water hole, he began to open the small houses to release the rest of the big orphans while Joseph attached the hose to water down the mud wallow.

Hare, the female zebra, was the first out her door and the first to reach the water hole vacated by the elephants, closely followed by Worsesa, the young male rhino.

After releasing Gardissa and Nyati, the pair of year-old buffalo, Lochoro hurried back to the watering area to supervise the exuberant spirits of the just-released orphans, and was just in time to see Hare take a nip at Galogalo's bristly tail and dodge a dirt clod thrown by the irate young elephant's trunk. Swinging the metal staff which rarely came in contact with the orphans, Lochoro moved among them to deter any more scuffles.

Joseph was plastering the thick red mud onto the two elephant calves while Sarah supervised closely. Zimwi cooperated handsomely by lying down and thrashing her legs about; she was used to this game and enjoyed it enormously; but the newest orphan was clearly frightened, and a shriek of terror attested to the fact.

Sarah gracefully sank rear first into the goo, and after laboriously positioning her front legs and lowering herself, she slipped over onto her side and wallowed, while Galogalo nursed his nipped tail and sulkily contented himself with grasping a blob of mud in the curled tip of his trunk and then throwing it over his body: left side, right side, under his belly and over his head, and repeat.

Discontinuing her mud bath, Sarah spied the unattended water hose lying nearby and still gushing water, and she was up and after it. Picking up the hose several inches behind the flowing water, she curled it into her trunk and lifted it to her mouth, where her enormous molars, each the size of a loaf of bread, held it secure: not tightly enough to cut off the flow of water, but tightly enough so that removing it would prove to be impossible. Galogalo immediately noticed Sarah's treasure and sidled up alongside; running the tip of his trunk along the hose toward Sarah's mouth, he carefully curled the end around the plastic and without warning gave a tremendous yank. Sarah was not perturbed, nor had she been unaware of his intentions; her prize was secure, and the battle was on as the younger Galogalo squealed in outrage and began a furious tug-of-war.

Lochoro sighed and calmly turned the water off. After a moment, Sarah removed the end of the hose from her mouth and dropped it unwanted in the mud for Galogalo to eagerly grasp—only to twitch it back and forth in dismay before his disappointed face: the water was gone.

The mud-daubed young rhino, Worsesa, was rubbing his face affectionately against that of his favorite friend, Gardissa, one of the yearling buffalo, while the other young buffalo began to feed on the short grass behind Lochoro's house. Hare and Galogalo were at it again, but this time the young male elephant was the aggressor as, with outflung ears and tail tensely held out behind him, he swung his trunk at the zebra, who dashed nimbly away, only to prance back again.

Sarah stood maternally above it all and rumbled reassuringly to the two small calves, whom she'd herded back under her belly and out of the way. Lochoro glanced over the small herd; assembled and watered, they were hungry now and ready to go. He began to walk forward as he uttered the "Ugh, ugh" sound the herded animals knew so well.

Heads swung around; the feet began to move as they started to file along the road behind the Warden's Residence and down along the side of the Forbes home.

Sarah led the way, with her two charges closely orbiting her; periodically she would stop and graze or browse on a tasty bit of grass or shrub, while the calves would pick at the vegetation with inexpert trunks, only to lose it by bits and pieces as they stuffed it into their mouths.

Approaching the fence around the Warden's garden, Sarah stopped at a patch of tall grass that occasionally received a splash of water from the sprinkler inside the yard. Reaching out, she curled the end of her trunk around a clump of the still-green shoots and grasped it. Immediately her right forefoot came up, to kick repeatedly at the soil around the roots while her trunk exerted its pull until the grass came up, roots, dirt clods, and all. Flinging her trunk up and out with a swishing sound, and then back under her chest and up again, she expertly shook the bits of soil and dead grass from her meal before placing it in her mouth, where her tongue shifted the grass into position so that the dirt-encrusted roots extended from the side of the mouth; her huge molars came together, and immediately the roots were sheared off neatly, to fall to the ground. Meanwhile, her trunk and forefoot were at work dislodging the next mouthful: swish, swish, swish—stuff—shear.

Zimwi carefully watched Sarah's feeding; the calf's short, stubby trunk extended in imitation, roamed uncertainly over the grass, grabbed at a few stems, and pulled, while one forefoot stubbed the ground a foot or more from the tuft of selected grass. The calf yanked, and the tightly curled trunk tip slid along the grass stems with an audible squeak; legs braced and ears extended in agitation, the female calf gave another mighty heave, and the grass stems broke off. Zimwi stood uncertainly with her prize of mutilated grass stems clenched in her trunk; she slyly observed Sarah's swish, swish, and stuff. Confident now, Zimwi flung her stubby infantile trunk out in front of her face, and watched with amazement as the hard-won grass stems sailed up in the air and away on the early-morning breeze. Silently she watched them go.

Down the trail they filed behind Sarah and her two adopted offspring, Galogalo eyeing the frisky Hare, Worsesa plodding beside his constant companion, Gardissa, while Nyati wandered off to the side by himself and Lochoro and Joseph followed watching.

As the group approached the Forbeses' house, the herdsmen moved up and began the unpleasant task of separating the group; as Joseph headed Sarah off to the left, Lochoro cut in between her and Galogalo to swing his staff and urge the young male elephant and the rest of the herd to continue toward the valley.

Pandemonium broke out, and Audrey Forbes giggled at the kitchen window as she watched the insistent Galogalo race about Sarah, with a sweating herdsman sprinting behind. Meanwhile the plodding Worsesa continued on his way to the valley below; he knew where he was going, with or without the others. Now there were three groups: placid Sarah and the calves, a trumpeting Galogalo impeded by a rollicking zebra, and a single-minded rhino leading two buffalo.

Audrey stepped out the kitchen door and shouted a compromise. Joseph then herded all the elephants together, while Lochoro swung his staff at the zebra, who agreed to part with the object of her harassment and galloped off to pester Nyati. Peace was finally restored.

Joseph settled under a tree to observe the elephant family from time to time while Lochoro followed the others to the valley below.

Audrey Forbes turned to console her cranky husband, whose ankle had just been gnawed by the sharp milk teeth of a curious male lion cub.

And the pregnant woman on the hill sat quietly on a three-legged stool in the sunlit doorway with her son in her lap.

DUNCAN SHELBY had enjoyed his poached eggs on toast. His cook, Walter, had been with him for fourteen years, and knew exactly how his employer liked his food prepared, particularly his breakfast.

Finishing his guavas and cream, Shelby poured his coffee and sat back in his wicker chair as a slight breeze came up to muss his carefully brushed white hair. He was almost an old man; almost, because while the years testified to the truth of the statement, the willpower of a gently indomitable spirit proved it to be a lie.

Sixty-nine years old, he reflected. Not really ancient, but old enough; particularly for this country. He calculated; casting back in his memory, he sought the dates that gave him the figure he groped for: forty-eight years. He'd first come here forty-eight years ago.

He glanced around the wide veranda on the east side of the old house. Unconsciously, he shook his head. "No," he murmured, "it couldn't be that long." But he thought again, and realized that it was so.

He'd been so sure of himself then, so confident and so eager to live the "great experience" that he and Charles, his brother, had embarked on. Charles had been the one who had first mentioned the idea, but it was Duncan who had become excited, who had made the idea a reality.

Charles had had an old school chum whose father was one of the many British businessmen involved in corporations in East Africa in those days. One of his investments was a sisal estate, which had started out in 1904 as a sansevieria concession to harvest the wild sisal growing on ten thousand acres of East African bushland. The estate had been a financial success, but the corporation had decided to unload the holding because of constant problems with managers. They came and they went, or they stayed and they drank; and months would go by without the supervision necessary to keep the harvesting and factory operations functioning. Finally, the nephew of one of the major stockholders had gone out from London to East Africa to take over the management of the estate, and by Jove, there would be an end to this nonsense. Things were going to happen. He would see to it.

Things did happen. The young man had become involved with a Bombay-born Eurasian girl, and had married her in a moment of lonely tenderness. Intermarriage with exotic half-breeds was a thing not done by members of the British upper-middle classes, and the family's reaction had been swift and ruthless. Ugly, vindictive letters flew back and forth between London and East Africa, and one warm, windy night the young manager slipped out of bed while his delicately beautiful young wife still slept and proceeded to get quietly drunk on the veranda outside. And when the sun began to come up out of the Fafajaga Plain, and as the lavender-blue shades of dawn changed to gold, he blew his brains out.

So the estate was put up for sale, and Charles's friend Robbie was enthusiastic about becoming one of the future owners. He'd visited there with his father and had become enamored of the whole romantic wildness of it, clichés and all: the vast miles of bush teeming with wildlife, the smiling natives in quaint thatched huts, and a gin-and-tonic sundowner in the evening on the veranda.

Robbie hadn't been there long enough to learn that the wildlife not only destroyed the sansevieria, but could prove dangerous as well; the natives didn't exactly take to work with enthusiasm; and a drink on the veranda during most of the year entailed hand-to-hand combat with swarms of insects.

Robbie had money left him by a benevolent grandmother, and Charles and Duncan were similarly independent with the recent acquisition of a trust fund. Robbie's enthusiasm soon spread—

particularly to Duncan. News of the successful importation and transplanting of Mexican sisal by German plantations in Tanganyika, and of improvements in crops and profits, was all Duncan needed to prevail over his brother's hesitation. The purchase was arranged.

The three young men had decided that the only way to manage the estate successfully was for the owners themselves to direct and supervise it, and they would start out by each serving a two-year stint in East Africa. After six years and after all three had taken their turn at management, they would decide which of the three would stay on and make the sisal plantation his life's work, sending home to England the profits due the other two.

Shelby smiled to himself.

He had been the first to come; Robbie was to follow, then Charles. But Robbie never came; he married a young woman—of good family, of course—and her parents objected to their daughter's being removed to the wilds of Africa. The young lady had agreed.

"Later," said Robbie, "when she's had time to adjust to the idea. Later, when the honeymoon is over." Later was never to come.

So Charles had come instead, ahead of his turn. But Africa wasn't kind to a handful of the British who came, those who were perhaps more delicate in mind or physical constitution than the others; and these, who found the soil of Africa too exotic or too vigorous, withered and soon died.

Duncan Shelby leaned forward and poured himself another cup of coffee; he hadn't thought of this for years. Sitting back, he remembered how it had been when he himself had come.

It had been 1929. He saw himself as he had landed at Mombasa, fresh-faced, twenty-one years old, and done up in a stiffly new white suit and requisite pith helmet. He remembered his impressions: the heat—the hot, wet heat—and the people: coal-black to light brown, with the occasional beet-red countenance of the sun-scalded European. He had stepped off the boat at Mombasa into the thronging Indians, Africans, Arabs, and *Wazungu,* and their conversations had reeled around him in a babble of unknown tongues. He remembered the smell: the God-awful stench of a harbor that received the city's garbage, its sewage, and the occasional body; and he recalled the swarms of insects and the exotic street music. And he had loved it.

He tasted curry and wanted more; he heard Swahili and began to learn; he drank the homemade maize beer, *pombe,* and the local palm wine, and filled his drinking gourd again; and he made love to a dark Swahili girl and was incomparably sad when she took his money and ran away.

He'd arrived at the derelict plantation and found that the native workers had melted away into the bush; the factory machinery was either broken down, burned out, or rusted together; and the beautiful plantation house had become the residence of numerous bats, squirrels, and mice and the cook's chickens.

He had thrown himself into setting things to rights with an enthusiasm that could only have come from genuinely loving every moment worked, and his incredible ignorance had made him successful. There was no one to tell him how to work the tribesmen or how to get things done. Consequently, he did everything wrong, and it all came out right.

He had rounded up his house staff and illustrated how to wash clothes and scrub floors by cheerfully boiling up water, soap, and his underwear, and by getting on his knees with a brush. His extremely limited knowledge of their languages had led him to use one of the few words he did know over and over: *mzuri*—good. This perennial expression communicated his positive attitude, and while the local people thought he was a little crazy, they felt that his oddness was a nice kind of peculiarity, and they worked for him accordingly.

In return for his lessons in housekeeping, he demanded instruction in Swahili and the local Taita, Kamba, and Waliangulu tongues, and he spent hours each night painstakingly repeating new words and spelling them out phonetically in a little leather-bound book.

He wrote letters demanding machine replacement parts and bribed a mechanical engineer away from a rival plantation on the coast, and soon the factory was operational. He went on safari to the villages in the surrounding hills and begged, bribed, and cursed until he had another labor force, and within six weeks of his arrival he had the plantation operating.

The gracious rectangular two-story plantation house on the hill was scoured, and a barrel of white paint arrived to begin the restoration of the home built in 1907 and since ignored. Both floors were completely surrounded by wide verandas which faced all directions and were partially fenced with an iron grillwork that was now sanded free of its rust and painted. The beautiful wooden floors were restored and polished, the high-ceilinged rooms that caught and circulated the slightest breeze were painted and furnished, while new drapery was cut and sewn for the immense windows.

After admiring an imported tree he'd seen in Mombasa for its plumes of lacy light green leaves and clusters of purple-and-lavender blossoms, he acquired a hundred of the fragile saplings and laid out a sweeping circular drive before the house, and he carefully planted, staked, watered, and fertilized the avenue of young trees. The house was perfect in its construction, but it stuck up out of the African bush incongruously without the definition and setting of grounds. Duncan intended to remedy this at once.

The sprawling acacia bushes had been cleared away, as was the termite mound by the front steps, and when the avenue of jacaranda trees went in, he had the outline for the garden that people would one day come miles to see.

Leaving the mature acacias, and the other fully grown indigenous trees, he began to search the area for each and every exotic, attractive, or strange tree, bush, vine, cactus, and flower that the country had to offer. On horseback, he prowled along the river and into the hills, and he brought home his finds in bags with the roots carefully wrapped and watered.

It was a time of trial and error, not only for the young Duncan Shelby, but for the plantation and factory as well. And by the time his brother, Charles, was on his way, the trials had been endured, the errors had been learned from, and Duncan Shelby had become a man who knew that his was the life that was to be spent here. Not Charles's, and not Robbie's.

He remembered the trip on the train to Mombasa to receive Charles, and he remembered his trepidation when he wondered how he would broach the subject of his feelings. With Charles's arrival, Duncan was to return to England; but he knew that he couldn't, not now.

He needn't have worried. He remembered Charles's face; he had been a bit late, arriving at the ship's dock just moments after Charles had disembarked, and Duncan had seen Charles before being seen. His older brother was standing backed up against some stacked bales of goods in an effort to remove himself from the crush of alien bodies; his pale nostrils were pinched in revulsion, and his expression was one closely related to shock. Duncan had not understood, and had hurried forward in greeting.

"What is that ghastly odor?" Charles demanded almost immediately.

"What odor?" Duncan was nonplussed before thinking, Oh, yes. "Not to worry; it's caused by—"

But Charles didn't want to hear. "My God," he exclaimed in outrage. "Something should be done. It wouldn't be tolerated in England."

But this isn't England, thought Duncan, and still he didn't really understand.

It was just the beginning, and it became progressively worse.

Duncan wanted to introduce Charles to his favorite places and acquaintances, share the special spots and people it had taken him two years to know. They went to dinner, and it was not a success. Charles disliked the food and expressed the hope that Duncan's cook could prepare good solid English fare.

"As a matter of fact," replied Duncan, "he can't."

So Charles went without dinner, and Duncan wondered how it was that his brother had changed so drastically. He didn't see that Charles hadn't changed at all.

They went on to the plantation, and Duncan nearly strutted with pride as he showed off the wild sansevieria beneath the acacia and commiphora trees, the new young fields cultivated with the imported and improved sisal, the humming factory, and the sheds stacked with the huge bales of marketable sisal fiber.

He took his brother to the house and walked him through the gardens, then left him in his room to wash off the dirt accumulated on the train while he poured himself a stiff drink and sat in his favorite veranda chair to try to understand his brother's negative attitude. He went over their afternoon's activities.

"So that's sansevieria, is it?" Charles had said, when Duncan had taken him to the fields, factory, and estate. "I fail to see any difference between that and the sisal. I greatly doubt if there *is* a difference."

"Hmmm . . . the leaves go into that machine to be crushed and the pulp is washed out and then the fiber is dried on those lines . . . is that all there is to it?"

"What language are you speaking to those people? Don't they understand English? Well, they had better learn damn quickly, because I have absolutely no intention of talking like a native."

"My God, it's isolated! How far is it to the nearest white neighbor?"

"You don't really pretend to call this a garden, do you? I've never seen such plants. What is that odd spiky thing? Good Lord. And what is that print there in the mud? . . . A lion? . . . in your garden?"

"The house is too big, and it's drafty."

"Why would anyone want to sit outside on a veranda? Civilized people sit *inside* their houses."

"Why are there so many house servants? What do you mean, 'They work more slowly than English servants because their duties are still strange to them'? Well, we'll soon put a stop to that!"

It had gone on and on, and he hadn't been wise enough then to see that Charles would never stay in a place so utterly foreign to him. Duncan did decide, though, to evade the question of the exact date for his own departure. He offered to stay awhile until his brother was settled and familiar with his responsibilities, and he had been surprised at how quickly and gratefully his offer had been accepted.

He had stayed, along with Charles, and had watched with dismay the deterioration in the older brother who had seemed so admirable at home in England.

At first it was noticeable only in his surliness of temperament, which progressed to the point where a minor irritation resulted in a thunderous explosion of rage. Then, as time went on, comments regarding the heat, the wind, the insects, the wildlife, the natives, the food, and generally everything were expressed less often, but a petulant expression of long-suffering forbearance took their place. Soon the cook's unsuccessful attempts at English cooking were left uneaten, and a sundowner of gin took the place of the evening meal. The sundowners began to be poured as early as before lunch, and somehow Charles could never bring himself to accede to regular meals and weekly doses of quinine to suppress the malaria that came with the rains twice a year.

The weeks stretched into months, and by the time the second rains came since Charles's arrival, Duncan found himself coping with field and factory workers who failed to return to work on Monday morning after their Sunday visits to their family *shambas*, and he had house servants who simply disappeared because of his brother's total inability to work with the people. Half drunk on gin, he would bellow an instruction or reprimand in English to a man or woman who had no idea what he was saying. Sensing the African's incomprehension, he would yell even louder, as if the lack of understanding were the result of deafness instead of a language barrier. If yelling and swearing did no good, he resorted to a blow without thought of the consequences. In short, he did everything that Duncan had not done.

Duncan had spent long hours in talking with his brother. He'd tried to send Charles home; he'd told him then how he wanted to stay and live there, and that it wasn't necessary for Charles to stay when he hated it so; that he, Duncan, would remain. But no, Charles had agreed to manage the plantation for two years and that was what he was going to do. Duncan didn't have it in him to tell his brother the truth: Charles had been there five months and he hadn't actually managed the estate for one day.

For behind the scenes, it was Duncan who gave the orders and rescinded the wrong directions and instructions; he who covered up the mistakes and kept the plantation working, and the entire work force listened patiently to Charles and the orders they didn't understand and nodded their heads in agreement, only to slip off to Duncan to get their instructions delivered in Swahili or Taita or Kamba.

So somehow he'd kept it working, and somehow he kept the how of it from Charles; and whenever Duncan carefully brought up the subject of Charles's returning to England, the elder brother would pour himself another drink before reaffirming that as a gentleman, he had entered into an agreement, and by God, he would see it out. And then he'd add wryly, "Even if it kills me."

And it did.

One month later, the rains came again, and the mosquitoes bred, and soon the dusk brought the familiar whine that filled the dark hours of the day. At first Charles had a headache, not much different from the morning-after hangovers with which he was familiar. But this hangover didn't go away; the fever came instead. Even so, Charles refused to stay in bed. "I have responsibilities," he said; "I have things to do. These people don't work unless you stand over them."

They carried him home after he'd fallen from his horse and struck his head, and while the bleeding of the head wound soon stopped, the fever went on and mounted in intensity. Then the chills came. Delirious now, he roared at the servants who weren't there and he spoke of a girl in England. He called for the mother who had died years before, and then he whimpered a prayer to the God he wasn't sure of, before screaming a curse on the heat, the wind, and the insects.

Duncan had sent to Mombasa for a doctor, but before the man arrived Charles was dead. He was young, it was true, but his under-nourished and gin-permeated body had been unable to withstand that first violent attack of malaria. Duncan had sat awhile and held the still-hot, dry hand, and he realized that there hadn't been any-thing in his brother that he had liked. His love for Charles had been feeding on memories of a different brother in a different place.

Charles had been buried the day he died, as soon as the rigor mortis had confirmed beyond doubt that he was indeed dead and not sunk into a deep coma, but before the hot, humid climate could begin to decompose the body. Duncan buried him at the foot of the garden which Charles had disliked. The servants and the field workers stood by silently without grief. They hadn't liked him, and there was no pantomime of sorrow because they knew that Duncan knew them and would understand.

He was placed beneath a huge flat-topped acacia tree, and the grass had just finished spreading itself over the mound when the stone arrived from the coast, along with a few bedraggled primroses, rhododendrons, and azaleas. Soon there was a garden within a garden whose center was the acacia tree and a grave; a tall wrought-iron fence enclosed the area and kept the wildlife from feeding on the delicate, but thriving English blooms which were somehow a rebuke to the man whose transplantation had been so much less successful.

Duncan's grief was short-lived; not because he didn't care, but because he instinctively knew better than to regret the inevitable; and there was still the plantation. He turned back into the estate, and more fields were painstakingly cleared for the new sisal plants; better housing was needed for the growing number of workers, and a village sprang up of small rondavel huts with conical thatched roofs. He consoled himself with work, and was thankful that so much remained to be done.

Three more years passed and Robbie never came. Eight thousand more acres were added, and the transition was made from the original harvesting concession to outright ownership of the land, and before Duncan realized how quickly the years were passing, he had celebrated his twenty-eighth birthday alone in the big house.

He hadn't known it was his birthday until two days after, when he checked the date for some of his correspondence, and he saw that the day had come and gone without his being aware of it, and this had bothered him all day. That evening before dinner, he sat on the veranda and sipped his one drink of the day and he felt alone for the first time.

Looking around, he appraised the results of nearly seven years of work: a successful plantation and a beautiful home, and yet it needed something. He'd decided then to return to England for a visit. He told himself that it was necessary to see Robbie on business, although Robbie's less-than-one-third interest in the plantation began and abruptly ended with the draft received promptly each quarter, and Duncan chose not to admit that the reason for his going home was to find a wife.

He found her, of course; it happens that way; and within a fortnight of meeting her he knew that he loved her and had to have her. He had always been fascinated by the exotic, but the strangeness of Africa had long ago been accepted as familiar and was no longer alien to him. Instead, he found Britain foreign now, and the overcrowded cities and villages, the verdant green countryside, and the pale women were unfamiliar and somehow exciting.

She was small; small and delicately boned. Her large blue eyes set off the flawless pink-and-white porcelain complexion that occurred rarely among English girls, but yet often enough to create a platitude. The top of her head clutched a tumble of curls that habitually escaped their pins to stray in wispy strawberry-gold tendrils at the nape of her neck, and he was captivated. Her soft, carefully cultured speech with its barely perceptible lisp delighted him, and he spent hours trying to amuse her so that he might again enjoy her bubbling laugh. She made him feel ten feet tall and as strong as a bull elephant when he stood beside her, and he was impatient to get her home.

He endured the lavish wedding and the traditional honeymoon on the Continent, but all he thought of was installing her at the plantation with the now-well-trained servants to wait on her hand and foot. He looked ahead to see her walking in the garden, reclining on the wide, shaded veranda during the hot afternoons, and greeting him when he returned home. That most of all; those evenings when he had returned to an empty house had stretched into years of evenings so spent, and they were over now. She would be there.

She lived exactly seven months to the day after she first stepped ashore at Mombasa, and when she died, she took with her the stillborn son whose conception had eventually drained away her life in her last bloody effort to birth him.

This time grief won, and he had slipped into a chasm of anguish that threatened to overcome him. It was only the necessity of immediate burial that snatched him back from instant madness and forced him to function. The coffins had to be made, and they had to be lined to receive the bodies he had to wash, lay out, and prepare for burial himself. Two more graves had to be scratched in the hard red soil, while the grass was carefully set aside to cover the rawness of the new mounds that would mark the burial places. And when the ugly reason for the haste registered itself on Duncan's consciousness, his mind recoiled, and slipped even closer to insanity.

Once again he followed a coffin to the garden within a garden. The people came, and expressed their grief in the way of their people, because it was real now and they grieved for her passing. But most of all they grieved for him, and again he understood.

He lived through the day, although he'd been sure that he couldn't, and he lived the next and the one that followed, and the insanity never came, although he had a nodding acquaintance with it for several months. But in time that too was over, and the days passed one by one.

The days became years, and for a while there had been a comfortable Indian mistress, but no children, and now he guessed that she was old and fat; he didn't know for sure. He had sent her away years ago, with a tidy sum of money to express his gratitude for the time she'd spent with him, after he had noticed that his urge for a woman had begun to fade. He supposed it was gone now.

The breeze was stronger now, and a gust of wind lashed his face to water the pale blue eyes, and the need to blink recalled him to the present.

He saw that the breakfast dishes had been quietly removed and that he still held a half-cup of cold coffee in his hand.

He chuckled to himself; he always enjoyed a joke on Duncan Shelby. Not old, hmmm? You're a damn sight older than you'd like to think you are. When your mind begins to wander in the past, you're not only no longer a young man, you've become a silly old ass.

Glancing at his watch, he saw that it was after seven thirty. He'd be late getting to the factory. Briskly rising to his feet, he stretched stiff legs and walked to the edge of the veranda and looked down over the garden to the spreading acacia tree that protected the little patch of transplanted England.

With time, he had learned that some were strong and others were weak, some were survivors while others perished; and at this moment he regretted his strength and his ability to survive. It wasn't that he envied their fragile failure; just that they had left him and he was alone.

Glancing up from the garden, his eyes were caught by the panoramic view that spread itself before him as if in consolation.

"Yes," he murmured. "I suppose you were worth it." What else could a man say when his life was nearly done?

As he was about to turn away and leave, his eyes unconsciously picked out that which was wrong and out of place in the far-off fields below and held it up to the conscious mind to see and evaluate. Immediately, he swung back and his eyes narrowed to study the strange dots that littered the distant southwestern fields.

Picking up the high-powered binoculars that lay on a nearby table, he swept the area in question, and saw the dots magnified until they were recognizable as elephants.

"Damn," he muttered; "they're back."

MARGARET GITHU rubbed her thin black arms with her hands; it was *baridi sana* this morning, and she'd been in such a hurry to catch the seven-thirty lorry, which brought the Headquarters staff up from the *campini,* that she had failed to snatch up the worn cardigan which hung over the back of one of her two chairs.

The lorry hit a hole in the dirt road, and she stumbled and fell against the man standing beside her. Hot now with embarrassment, she whispered an apology and stared hard at her feet. She was painfully aware of herself when she was around other people, particularly the men; and her awareness only made her trip or drop things or do something equally clumsy. But she wasn't awkward with Mulolo. She smiled secretly to herself. He had come to dinner last night, and she had carefully hoarded the few shillings she had left, after sending the monthly postal order home, in order to have a special meal for him. *Steaki.* Not the cheaper *nyami ya ngombe,* full of fat, gristle and smashed bones. No, it was *steaki* with *ugali,* and potatoes cooked with cabbages, tomatoes, and onions and flavored with curry. They had talked a long time after eating, and he had been in a happy mood; he seemed pleased with her.

Sometimes it wasn't like that and he would be moody; he would come and sit with her awhile and talk about the Field Force and then he would go. Perhaps his moodiness was because he wanted to be in the field units and he was still a Gate Ranger. She could understand that, and she would fit her moods to his, as her mother did with her father. As all wise women did with their men. If he wanted to talk, she would talk; if he wanted silence, she would not speak; if he was angry about something and yelled at her, if he struck her because he could not reach the thing that angered him, then she would keep her head low and put her hand to her mouth, and no one would hear. She looked up from her feet, and her eyes stared ahead at the road in front of the lorry, and instead of the rutted, dusty road she saw his face.

I am his woman, she thought again, and she whispered the warm words to herself.

When the lorry pulled up behind the Headquarters offices, she filed down toward the back with the laborers, mechanics, and artisans, and jumped down to the ground in her turn. Yes, he had been in a good mood last night, and while they ate she had told him about the big meeting this morning.

"The drought is bad, and the poaching is very bad too," she had told him, "and the Warden is going to do something about it." That was why Dr. Forbes, the Research Director, was going to be there besides Warden Karanja and Assistant Warden Agaran.

"And," she had added with the excitement of a child sharing someone else's secret, "the Senior Warden of the entire Coast Province is coming too."

He had been very quiet then. He had just smiled and told her how good her cooking was, and she had been so happy. Last night had been very good, particularly since he stayed with her all night. He'd never done that before.

Stepping into the large office she shared with another typist, the assistant accountant, and a clerk, she saw that she was the first one to arrive, and so she proceeded to roll back the wooden shutters before going to her small, cramped desk. Yes, last night had been good, but not this morning. Absently she began to fiddle with a pencil.

She had fixed him breakfast for the first time, and she even had sugar for his portion. Everything had been perfect until he was dressed and ready to leave and he'd told her that he would come back that evening; he wanted to know all about the meeting. Without forethought, she had said she didn't think that she would have anything to tell him. She wasn't present during the Warden's meetings; there was no reason for her to be there.

Immediately he was angry. "You be there this time. I want to know what happens in this meeting. I want to know what is said. You be there!"

He'd stamped out then, and she had remained sitting at the table where he'd left her. She had been frightened by his sudden change of mood. It had all been so good, and then she had somehow made him very angry with her and she didn't know what she had done.

"Margaret."

She had heard her name spoken, but it hadn't been said nicely; it had been growled at her.

She had turned and faced the open door; he had come back and he'd stood there.

"*Nitarudi jioni hii.*" His voice had been low, and she'd sensed a threat in the tone. He would return this evening.

"Yes," she'd whispered.

Now her pencil continued to tap on the desk as she thought about what had happened.

"*Habari.*"

The greeting startled Margaret and she jumped. It was Rose, the other typist.

"*Salama tu,*" she responded with a forced smile before turning away to rummage in her desk for something to do, a paper to look at, or hide behind. She bit her lip, tears close. What was she going to do? How would she be able to get into the meeting?

* * *

AS DAVID WALKED out his front door and down the flagstone walk along the side of his house, he felt a soft flutter as a small gray Somali sparrow landed on his shoulder. Turning his head and glancing out of the corner of his eye, David remarked, "And where have you been since yesterday morning?"

Mdomo ignored him and continued to ride along on his favorite perch with tail feathers bobbing as he accompanied David to Headquarters as usual.

One evening, several months before, David had found the sparrow in the grass outside Headquarters after he'd apparently fallen from one of the nests in the acacia high over head, and he'd put the nearly featherless chick in his beret and taken it over to Research. At the time, Audrey was in Nairobi shopping, but Jeff had told him what it was and what it ate, so there was nothing he could do but return home with the hungry chick and the small pair of forceps donated by a chuckling Forbes.

Following instructions, he had mixed up tiny bits of bread crumbs with a liberal dash of egg yolk. Then, adding milk, he'd stirred the thick, lumpy mess in the cap of a bottle of imported Scotch which served as a tiny feeding dish. With the chick in the bowl of his cupped hand, he'd picked up a piece of the sodden bread crumb in the tips of the forceps and gently pressed the offering against the side of the chick's beak. He'd waited expectantly for some response, but there was none. Dragging the wilted bread crumb around the chick's beak, he'd begun to swear silently in frustration while the little bird continued to stare at him with wide, unblinking eyes.

He had decided to try another, fresher, bread crumb at that point, and while trying to figure out another approach, he'd inadvertently let the bread crumb hover above the chick's bill. Immediately, a tiny cheep erupted as the beak flew open, revealing a huge mouth which shot upward and gobbled the tidbit. After that, the chick couldn't get the food into his mouth fast enough, until after several minutes of voracious feeding, the little beak snapped shut and that was it. Taking a teacup, David had carefully wadded up a few sheets of blue *choo* paper and put it inside; dumping the chick into the cup, he'd been relieved to see him settle down under a fold in his new nest and go to sleep.

By the time Audrey returned five days later, he was used to the little bird's presence and had turned down her kind offer to take over the care of the orphan. *Mdomo,* or "Mouth," as he quickly came to be called, had grown into a small but handsome bird, and it was acknowledged without hesitation that he had the run of the Warden's house and Headquarters.

David passed into his office and sat at his desk, where he began to scribble notes to himself and others. Calling out for the sergeant, he sent for his typist.

What this office needs is an intercommunication system, he thought absentmindedly, and a telephone hookup with town. And a lot of other things, like at least two hundred and fifty additional Field Force Rangers, and the return of my plane.

Mdomo left his shoulder and flew to the desk top, where he began to push the papers about with his beak. Margaret entered quietly, and after a moment he noticed the splash of her print dress on the far side of his desk.

"Oh, yes," he murmured. He'd almost forgotten that he'd sent for her. "The meeting is scheduled for ten o'clock." He glanced at his watch; it was ten minutes to eight. "I want tea served about midmorning—say, eleven or so. Do you have everything you need?"

"Yes, Warden."

"Good." He extended a folded-over paper to her. "When you leave, give these Field Force patrol reassignments and instructions to the radio operator, and tell him I want them relayed immediately. I expect the units to be at their new patrols by eight thirty and operational."

Margaret took the radio message form. Without thinking she opened it and read:

Units 1 and 4—withdraw from present positions and proceed to area of village. Patrol inside the park boundary on foot in the vicinity of the village and outlying shambas. Shoot on sight all domesticated dogs and cats found inside the park and any of the wildlife that appear sick or diseased. Deliver carcasses to the Research Center.

Margaret was dismayed: a change in the patrols, and she hadn't known last night, as was usual. She was beginning to feel panic: the meeting and now a change; he would be angry with her. The thought flickered—What did it matter? Why was it important?— then died. The meeting. She had to be present at the meeting or he would be angry.

She glanced up and saw the Warden watching her closely.

David spoke slowly and concisely: "It is not necessary for you to read orders that do not concern you."

Her heart began to pound. She said nothing, knowing her voice wouldn't come. Dumbly she nodded.

He studied her closely. "Give that to Duba"—he indicated the message—"and that's all."

Her feet began to move toward the door while her mind re-

151

peated, The meeting—ask about the meeting. Her feet carried her on to escape the room and his watchful eyes, and the words came more urgently: You've got to go to the meeting—the meeting. The door closed behind her and the words stopped. Her head felt light; she was dizzy. She knew she'd failed, but she didn't know how to make it otherwise.

David sat in his chair and watched the door close. That was odd. Why did she read that radio message? Perhaps she thought I meant her to. But no, why should she think that? The movements of the Field Force are none of her concern. She's only a typist. He frowned. She doesn't look well either. Perhaps she's sick . . . or pregnant. He seemed to recall that she wasn't married—not that that was likely to make a difference these days.

CHAPTER EIGHT

Midmorning: The Meeting

THE SENIOR WARDEN for the Coast Province read the Poaching and Anti-Poaching Operations section of David's Quarterly Report. Senior Warden John Shepherd had been with the National Parks since their beginning, and it wasn't possible to find a man more dedicated to wildlife conservation anywhere in Africa. He was in his mid-fifties now, and his thirty years of experience had made him one of Kenya's foremost authorities on wildlife. Besides which, his quiet, understanding manner made it possible to go to him with a problem, knowing that you had his complete attention and that he would respond wholeheartedly.

Finishing the last page, Shepherd looked over to David and acknowledged the seriousness of the situation: "I knew you were up against it here, but this is worse than I thought."

"It's bad," David agreed, "and getting worse each day."

"Is that why you asked me to come?"

"Yes. Ordinarily this is a regular operations meeting between me and my assistant warden in charge of the Northern Area, but today I've asked for the attendance of both of the directors of the Research and Education Centers, besides yourself."

He paused a moment before adding grimly, "The situation has reached such critical proportions that I may soon be Warden of an eighty-five-hundred-square-mile faunal desert. I need help—and quickly."

The conference-room door opened as Mohamed Agaran entered, closely followed by Jeff Forbes. After a few moments of genial conversation, David saw Halima step through the door, and he turned to his superior.

"I don't believe you've met our new Director of Education. Halima Abdi, this is our Senior Warden, John Shepherd."

As she stepped forward to shake the Senior Warden's hand, the older man said, "It's certainly time Nairobi sent us someone young and pretty."

Halima's confusion was appealing as she struggled to respond to the gallant greeting.

John Shepherd was as well known for his appreciation of an attractive woman as he was for his knowledge and love of wildlife. He seated Halima on his left next to the window before taking his chair at the head of the large leather-topped conference table, while Forbes and Agaran found seats on his right. As David watched them he realized how much he hoped for as a result of this meeting. The park was endangered; relief was imperative. Now he studied the people who were the only ones who could provide it: Forbes, the scientist, who interpreted Nature and all her nuances for him; Agaran, his second-in-command, and the best Field Force commander in the Department; Shepherd, veteran conservationist and Senior Warden, the only man in the province with a voice loud enough to be heard in Nairobi; and Halima, the educator, whose teaching today might spare the parks of the future.

After seeing everyone settled comfortably, he took his seat and proceeded to establish the purpose and objectives of the meeting as he stated the critical condition of the park and its wildlife:

"I've asked you here in order that we might discuss both our problems and the reasons behind them, and I hope that each of you will have something to offer the rest of us—in the way of information, and also in suggestions as to how we can best cope with the situation."

He continued: "First of all: our vegetation is decimated, and our stocks of animals, primarily the elephant and rhino, are declining drastically each day. There are two reasons why this situation exists: one, an extended drought, and two, poaching."

Looking around the conference table, David saw with relief that he had their concentrated attention. "I know the first question any of you will think of is: Yes, the critical condition of the park is caused by drought and poaching, but then, we've had drought before, and we've had to deal with poaching since the park was first gazetted thirty years ago. Why have these two factors now resulted in the critical position in which we find ourselves?"

Standing up, he stepped behind his chair before answering his question. "There are several reasons why, and all of these reasons represent changes that have come about in the vegetation, the wildlife, and the human settlement in the area, and their cumulative effect upon one another has resulted in the circumstances in which we find ourselves now."

He proceeded to check off the important points. "I want to reestablish in your minds the main reason why this area was set aside as a game refuge, as opposed to other possible locations. It wasn't a desert, because it could support wildlife, but the area's rainfall was so marginal that it wasn't sufficient for successful agriculture, and ranching was prohibited because of the lack of good forage for domestic stock plus the presence of the tsetse fly. So the wildlife got it because it didn't seem at the time that man would want it. To a certain extent, that has changed.

"When the park was originally gazetted in 1948, Kenya's population was five and one-half million, and the park area and all the thousands of square miles adjacent were virtually uninhabited, so the wildlife was free to roam throughout the entire Aruba ecosystem. In the past thirty years our population has trebled; we've now got three people for every one we had, and all these additional human beings need a place to live and a plot of ground in which to plant their maize. The good, well-watered farming areas near rivers and along the coast filled up with people years ago, so areas that were undesirable in the past have become populated out of necessity, and this increasing population explosion has resulted in the human settlement of the areas outside the park; as people came in they cleared the bush for cultivation, planted their crops, burned down trees for charcoal, and hunted and poached the wildlife population. The existing wildlife found their range shrinking as settlements encroached upon them, and they were forced to fall back into a habitat that was steadily decreasing in size.

"In 1948, the major portion of the park was covered in dense bush, which consisted mainly of trees of the *Commiphora, Delonix,* and *Acacia* genera; there was little, if any, grass cover. As the wildlife were condensed into a smaller area, the elephant began to make a noticeable impact on the vegetation. Where before they roamed over vast areas and allowed the vegetation to recover, they were now trapped in the immediate area of the park as humans closed in on them and cut off their migration routes. As the destruction of the bushland continued, the resulting accumulation of combustible material allowed the ingress of fire, which proved to be even more destructive to the bush than were the elephants.

"Prior to 1948, this area supported a considerable population of elephant, rhino, and lesser kudu, but the other animals existed only in very small numbers. As the vegetation pattern changed, so

155

did the wildlife populations; the falling back of the bush opened many areas to grass, and this conversion from bushland into open grassland resulted in a tremendous increase in the numbers of buffalo, zebra, oryx, impala, hartebeest, and gazelle. At the same time, the elephant populations were under heavy poaching pressure, but a successful anti-poaching operation in the late fifties literally eliminated this as an ecological factor. When poaching was suppressed suddenly, the removal of the predation by man resulted in a rapid increase in the numbers of elephant. An important side effect of poaching was that prior to the late fifties, the elephant spent very little time in the immediate area of permanent water because such places were frequented by poachers, and this irregular watering probably resulted in increased mortality among the young elephant during the dry seasons. When poaching was suppressed, the elephant returned to the permanent water; the mortality dropped among the young, and the overuse of the riverine strip ensued.

"Now," he said, "What's changed here in the past thirty years? In 1948 the park was part of a seventeen-thousand-square-mile ecosystem virtually free of human habitation which consisted primarily of a dense bushland that supported elephant, rhino, and lesser kudu. Now that area has shrunk to only eighty-five hundred square miles of grassland interspersed with tracts of bush, and this smaller area is required to support the original condensed populations of elephant, rhino, and lesser kudu, as well as the additional plains game and all the other species of the entire ecosystem.

"Consequently, while we've always suffered the effects of dry seasons and periodically recurring drought, the situation is worse now because we have a much larger wildlife population, particularly elephant, who are condensed into a smaller area where the vegetation has changed to a grassland that seems to react more unfavorably to the effects of a sustained failure of the rains."

Here David paused for comments. "Does anyone have anything to add to this?"

After a moment Jeff Forbes said, "I have a few things I'd like to mention about the drought and the vegetation."

"Good," said David. He wanted their participation, and most of all, he wanted their suggestions.

Leaning forward over his folded hands, Jeff said, "We've all heard about 'The Destruction of the Habitat at Aruba by the Elephant'—all in capital letters—and I'm glad to hear David say that while the elephant began the initial destruction, the result-

ing fire has been the determining factor in this vegetation change.
I'd also like to add that as far as the change to grassland in the
east is concerned, it is my opinion that the change is for the better. Fifteen years ago you couldn't have found a worse game-
viewing area in East Africa. The elephant and rhino may have
been there, but for all you saw of them through the dense bush, they
might not have bothered to come around at all. In fact, in 1961, the
previous warden's estimate of the number of elephant in the park
was between two and four thousand, depending on the season.
That doesn't mean that a population explosion resulted in twenty-
three thousand elephant in the park by 1973, with an additional
twelve thousand on the outskirts of the park area. It means that
before the bush was opened up, you just couldn't see the damn
things."

Shepherd nodded. "It's true, and in those days both pilots and
planes were beyond our means, so aerial reconnaissance was out of
the question, and without planes it's next to impossible to know
what's out there."

"Of course," Jeff Forbes continued. "It was startling for people
to come here later and see acres of dead and dying trees standing
about, and all they saw was destruction. I've found," he commented
wryly, "that that's what many people call change; and it's not the
same at all. Yes, the woodland or bushland, whatever you prefer to
call those short, scrubby trees which proliferate around here, has
gone in the northeast area of the park, and grass has taken its
place; and no, I don't believe the vegetation change is responsible
for the mortalities we're seeing in the elephant and rhino now."

Here he paused for several moments before he continued: "At
the moment we're compiling data that have taken one of our scientists nearly four years to gather. It's been an exhaustive study that
if put into as few words as possible would be called simply a 'Soil
and Vegetation Survey' of this area."

"Is that the study done by the soil scientist Philip Otieno?"
Halima asked. "He's given some fascinating lectures to our groups
visiting the Education Center, and he's made soil and geology
interesting to the schoolchildren."

Forbes grinned. "That's the man. Only Philip could be enthralled
with a handful of dirt." Serious again, he added, "I know that a
'Soil and Vegetation Survey' sounds rather unprepossessing to the
layman, but I don't want anyone to underestimate the amount of
work that went into it or the value of the eventual conclusions. It
was a huge undertaking that was designed to investigate the fact
that the vegetation pattern had been changed, and to answer the

resulting questions of: What exactly is happening here? Why is it happening? How is it happening? And what are the long-term effects going to be?

"From these studies we see two important facts: the mineral content and consequent nutritional quality of the vegetation depends on the chemical properties of the soil, and the primary production, or standing crop, of the vegetation is the result of the rainfall. In other words, how good the vegetation is depends on the soil quality; how much of it there is is determined by the amount of rain it gets.

"I can't encapsulate four years of research and the results in one meeting, particularly since it will take another six months to correlate and study the data before we can present conclusive findings. When it's done we'll have a volume of maps and information that will identify every foot of the park in terms of soil properties, the species of vegetation to be found growing on that soil, and the quality and quantity of the vegetation."

Turning to David, he added, "In a few months you'll have a map on your wall and a report that will tell you everything you want to know about the vegetation in a remote corner of the park. You won't even have to go there. Just point to a place and ask us for the recent rainfall records; turn to page one-twelve, or whatever, and you'll see that the soil is a deep reddish-brown luvisol that is moderately well drained and a neutral sandy clay that was developed on the sedimentary plain. It has moderately good physical properties and good chemical properties, and its dominant vegetal species are *Dobra glabra, Aniosotis parvifolius,* and *Maerua denhartiorin,* plus a dozen others. Your rainfall will tell you exactly what the primary production is in terms of kilograms of standing crop per square kilometer, and therefore how many kilos of the four-legged biomass it will support."

Shepherd exclaimed, "That's marvelous! It's what we need for each and every park we've got."

"It's a good management tool," Forbes agreed, "but it won't make it rain."

After a moment he added, "I didn't mean to bring down the spirits of the meeting, nor do I intend to denigrate the importance of the study. Its value is incalculable. It means we're no longer stumbling around in the dark about how many animals this area can support in the dry season, the rainy season, or during a drought. And that brings me back to your question: bushland versus grassland, and the future of this park.

"I say grassland definitely, because contrary to earlier opinions, we've found strong indications that grassland will support twice the biomass that can be supported here if it's bushland. I can't give you specific numbers to the last ounce of the biomass right now, but the rough figures are that bushland will support twenty thousand elephant, and grassland will support thirty-five thousand elephant, and that means in time of drought as well. I'd also like to mention here that the figures I just gave you are conservative." He sat back and began to fill his pipe from a battered leather pouch while the others sat in various attitudes of confused silence.

Finally David exclaimed, "But if the vegetation isn't declining in value as we thought, if it's actually an improvement . . ."—he paused, perplexed—"then why are some of the elephant and rhino dying in the drought?"

"No water," Forbes murmured as he drew on his pipe.

Shepherd interjected, "But there're the Ruui, the Oreyiet, and the Lalaga Lana, plus the permanent water holes."

"They're too far apart, and in some areas there is no water at all now for a hundred square kilometers," replied Forbes. "You can't expect an elephant to trek fifty kilometers a day between water and forage without finally giving up. Open up these grassland areas with catchment water holes, and boreholes where it's possible, and get these huge herbivores dispersed throughout the park. Then you will eliminate the drought die-off.

"But is that what you want?" He glanced at David and answered his own question. "I don't think you do, because it's only a temporary measure that buys a little time. Our recent studies indicate that with an average rainfall, the park will produce eighty percent of its potential in terms of vegetation, and that is sufficient to carry thirty-five thousand elephant, plus the rest of the wildlife. If you supply additional water, then you can carry more, but only for a short time, because the elephant population is increasing by three and a half percent a year, and that yearly increase will escalate as more animals reach puberty. In ten years you'll have fifty thousand or more, and what do you think will happen to your park?"

No one answered.

"We *must* stop pushing our use of our resources to the absolute limit," Forbes warned. "We need to maintain a small safety margin for the years in which the conditions are less than favorable. Increase your demands and you will eventually get less, because our use of the land will then become misuse, or overuse, and we have the deserts to prove it." Sitting back, he added, "We have a name for this concept."

"What is it?" asked Mohamed, who had missed the twinkle in Jeff Forbes's eyes.

"It's called conservation," Jeff replied wryly. "The important thing to realize," he continued, "is that the Ruui, the Oreyiet, and the Lalaga Lana Rivers have been here for hundreds of years, and the soils and the vegetation along these permanent water sources have adapted to the stresses of constant overuse during the dry seasons and droughts. This will not be the case with artificial watering areas when the vegetation is subjected suddenly to thousands of elephants as permanent residents.

"Look," he explained, "it's like this." Taking a box of small wooden matches from his pocket, he slid off the lid and dumped the matches onto the table. "Think of these matches as elephant. Now, when the rains come, this whole area becomes dotted with hundreds of small, impermanent water holes, and"—he pointed to the scattered matches—"the elephant disperse all over the park to feed and water. The vegetation is lush and green, there's plenty of water, and everybody's happy. Then the dry season comes, and as the vegetation dries out, so do these small water holes, so the game falls back on the rivers or the few natural and permanent water-catchment areas." With this he swept the space in front of him free of matches and looked up. "The majority of the vegetation is left to go into its dormant state and recover, to regenerate when the next rains come.

"Now suppose"—he moved his ashtray into the center of the table—"that we put a big unnatural water hole right here."

Abruptly he returned the matches and scattered them about the ashtray. "The wildlife don't leave the area; they stay near the water, and the vegetation is stripped to the ground. It doesn't get a chance to recover, and after even the dried-out grasses are consumed, the rains will come in their proper time, and you've got the beginnings of erosion and a lot of other problems. In the areas of permanent water, you have a balance in nature that's taken a millennium to evolve. If you put water into virgin areas that don't have and never have had permanent water, you'll cause deterioration of the habitat by reducing the grass cover and the carrying capacity of the vegetation, and possibly cause permanent damage through erosion and compaction of the surface sealing of the soil.

"Remember, I mentioned that one of the important questions to be answered by the soil research was: 'Is the soil becoming degenerated through changes in the vegetation as the result of the elephant's feeding?' The answer is a conditional 'no.' I say conditional because of all the trouble spots studied, the only one that is a *maybe* is on the Moda sand river. The other places are definitely not suffering soil deterioration because of the elephant-induced vegetation change; but at the Aruba Dam on the Moda River we are seeing the soil begin to blow away, and we are not yet sure what the ultimate results will be, although we do know that they won't be pleasant. This river flows only during and after the rains; when the runoff from the Dakagudiu Hills is over, the river dries up. So what made it change? We put in an artificial dam in order to trap the runoff some thirty kilometers back so we could provide water for the wildlife throughout the year.

"Now they don't leave, and in the area of the dam we have reduced ground cover, and erosion, and the topsoil has become airborne. If you blindly construct more water holes to open up more areas to year-round grazing, you'll multiply your problem." His voice rose slightly; the concern of the scientist began to show itself. "And for what?" Looking around the table, he waited for an answer that didn't come.

"Enough is enough," he said emphatically. "In the good years that are coming immediately following the drought, the vegetation will be producing close to its maximum capacity for the rainfall we have available to us, and that vegetation will comfortably support thirty-five thousand elephant, plus the rest of the wildlife, and that's it." The sound of his open hand's hitting the table was loud in the quiet room. "Put in more water holes and the vegetation will begin to go as the wildlife increases, and in a few years you'll see the whole damn park blow away, and what's left won't support a dieting ground squirrel."

He looked around the table with an angry accusing stare, which softened to reflective dejection and apology.

After a moment he said softly, "I suppose I'm what you would smilingly refer to as a 'dedicated scientist.' " He looked away and smiled wryly at his description of himself. "If you give me the time and money necessary for research, I can tell you the maximum potential for a given use in a particular area; but I can't make it more productive than it can be."

He looked appealingly at David. "What is happening here is happening all over the world; and it's happening to people, not elephant." Shaking his head despondently, he added, "Five million people have grown into fifteen million people here in Kenya in just thirty years, and they all want: they want land; they want water; they want food; and they turn to the Government, which turns to the scientific community to provide the answers on how to get it. All we can do is evaluate the maximum potential and devise improved methods. But we can't make it rain. Then they say, 'More, we want more,' and we somehow provide a little extra in the way of technology, and that appears to help for a little while, but someday soon, when they ask again, we're going to have to tell them the truth." Forbes glanced over to the Senior Warden and said somberly, "There is no more."

The room was quiet. David's voice, when it came, was heavy with pragmatic resignation. "Then we have the resources for only thirty-five thousand elephant, plus the rest of the wildlife, and more than thirty-five thousand because of annual population growth. Is that right?"

"Right," said Forbes as he sucked furiously at his extinguished pipe.

"So the die-off is of surplus animals that we can't now or ever in the future support here at Aruba?"

"That's right," Forbes agreed again as he selected one of his matches from the table before him.

"If I put in more water holes it will give us only a few years, while the elephant reproduce until they overgraze the area into a desert. So, in your opinion, the drought is a built-in climatic population control: every ten years it will starve out the elephant in excess of thirty-five thousand or so."

"You'd better hope so."

"Hope so? Why?"

"Because if the drought doesn't come around, you'll see the beginning of real habitat destruction. When the bushland went out in areas, the grass came in; but," Forbes warned, "if the grass cover goes, nothing will replace it but the sound of the wind. So if the drought doesn't crop them, then," he said as he struck a match to get his pipe going, "you'll have to shoot them."

Shaking his head, he continued, "The drought isn't really your problem. In fact"—he pointed at David with the stem of his pipe—"it's functioning in your favor. We had a few too many elephant when the drought began, and now the drought is cropping the population, and it will ultimately result in the survival of the fittest.

"I think I'm beginning to see something odd, and it's what I've wanted to discuss since this meeting started, but it's taken forever to get past the drought, which I feel has acted rather like a blindfold on all of us.

"The drought is continuing," he explained, "and the die-off should be at its maximum, but we're seeing fewer mandibles and tusks coming in from drought victims. There's been a very slow decline in the weekly total of recorded deaths from drought, and it wasn't until the day before yesterday that the implications of the situation came to my attention.

"Audrey and I flew to Nairobi last weekend with some friends from the coast, and as we returned Sunday afternoon, we flew over the extreme western side of the park and I observed the number of elephant carcasses below. There must have been one or two every kilometer, and it bothered me as somehow not being right. It wasn't until later that evening that it dawned on me why it seemed peculiar."

He looked around the table before explaining, "The drought is centered on the eastern side of the park. The western side is almost untouched in most places, and the rainfall is just a bit less than average. So where," he questioned, "did all those carcasses come from?"

David's eyes narrowed slightly in speculation, and he felt a presentiment regarding the answer.

"By the time I thought of that," went on Forbes, "sleep was out of the question, so I put on my bathrobe and slippers and went to the center to check the rainfall records. I was right about the rainfall, and the consequent available vegetation, so I got the records for the weekly recorded deaths from drought, and after studying them I realized that the die-off was slowly decreasing. It's true that many of the elephant in the eastern area are wandering around in an emaciated condition, but they've ceased to die. It didn't make sense. The deaths should be increasing at an alarming rate now, yet they've been slowly, almost imperceptibly, decreasing over a period of months. It was only because I got away for a couple of days that I was able to see, really see, the abnormality of elephants dead in the wrong place.

"The next morning I sent four of the research assistants in two vehicles to the area where I saw the carcasses on the western boundary, and they returned late last night. Their preliminary report was thirty-five carcasses in the immediate area; only three possible deaths from drought—two calves, and one old bull. The remaining thirty-two carcasses appeared to have been poached.

"No, the drought isn't really your problem, and how many elephant we have a year from now won't be determined by the drought die-off, but by the amount of our losses to poachers." With that, he sat back with folded arms and continued to puff on his pipe.

Forbes's unexpected prediction was met with consternation, followed immediately by the hum of questions.

Just then the door opened and Margaret Githu entered, precariously balancing a huge tea tray, which she deposited at the end of the conference table. The conversation continued, and as she prepared to set out the cups to pour the tea, David looked up and saw her. Absently dismissing her with a "Thank you, Margaret," he turned to Halima and asked if she would please serve the tea.

Margaret stood for a moment in confusion as she tried desperately to think of another reason to stay in the conference room. They were discussing poaching, and she wanted to know what they were saying. She had to know. He would ask.

As David accepted his cup of tea from Halima, he noticed that Margaret was still standing by the door. Thinking there was something of importance which required his attention, he inquired, "Yes? Is there anything else?"

Margaret started visibly, and with a stricken expression she turned and fled.

With his teacup arrested halfway to his lips, David stared at the closing door and wondered, *Now* what's the matter with her?

His attention was recalled to the meeting in progress when the Senior Warden addressed him.

"What is the problem with your plane, David? I noticed a heated reference to it in your report."

David was only too glad to explain his difficulties to someone who he felt would be inclined to listen, and he quickly described the crash landing in the north over eight months before, and the subsequent difficulty in getting it repaired and returned.

"Do you mean to say that you've been eight months without a plane?" Shepherd inquired incredulously.

David nodded. "I still have the 'copter, but it's not as effective as a plane in a park this size, particularly for anti-poaching work, and I'm having a lot of difficulty with funds for maintenance and fuel because there's always a holdup regarding the payment of my suppliers. Consequently they refuse to honor my purchase orders, so I'm left without fuel."

After a moment he continued: "Some weeks ago I bought eight drums of fuel with my own money, but I use the 'copter now only for emergencies, because I can't afford the expensive operational costs for daily patrol." He added wryly, "The cost of the petrol would be several times my monthly salary."

Shepherd exploded. "Things have come to a pretty end when the Department can't get a plane repaired in eight months and our wardens are required to buy their own fuel!" He sat quiet and angry before adding, "I've been out of the country quite a bit during the last few months, so I didn't know about this. It seems as if everything's gone to hell; but I'll take care of it. Don't worry, I'll get you your plane and the fuel to operate it. Now, I'd appreciate it if you could review the poaching situation for me, David. Exactly what's happening, and when did it start?"

David put down his cup and moved to the wall at the head of the table, where a huge map of the park and the area adjacent was prominently hung. "One of the major hot spots is the highway," he said. Tracing his finger over the Mombasa/Nairobi highway where it bisected the park, he continued, "Roughly one-half of the park area lies east of the road, with the remaining half to the west, and its presence makes it possible for a poacher, or poachers, to quickly and easily gain access into the interior of the park anywhere along this ninety-mile stretch of road between the southeastern and northwestern boundaries.

"It's been going on since the park was gazetted, and it's getting progressively worse. The incredible price of ivory is in all the Nairobi papers, and it's giving too many people ideas. We're picking up poachers and would-be poachers armed with everything from bows and arrows to homemade rifles and shotguns. They hitch a ride into the park from a lorry that's just passing through, and they're usually well dressed to avoid arousing the suspicion of the lorry driver, so they carry their poaching clothes in a small bag and have their weapons concealed as parcels."

"Are the lorry drivers involved?" inquired Jeff Forbes.

"I'm sure some are, but the majority aren't," replied David. "We also believe that there are groups who have their own transport and are thus able to enter and leave the park along the main road at prearranged places and times."

"A more organized operation?" queried the Senior Warden.

"We think so, but we have absolutely no proof."

"How do they operate once they're inside?" asked Shepherd.

"There are dozens of slightly varying methods of operation, but they usually have the two following points in common." He ticked them off on his fingers: "To get in and out in as short a time as possible, and to get as many trophies as they can by shooting every elephant and rhino they see in hopes of getting at least one set of trophies before taking off to avoid the patrols.

"What we usually see is this: two to four men come in on lorries as hitchhikers. They head for a rocky outcrop where they can hide, and where they have elevation to look over the immediate area; after changing into their rough clothes, they prepare their weapons and wait for the early evening, when they'll be harder to spot by the rangers, and when the large animals have moved out to forage and water. Usually one or more of the group have been here before, so they're familiar with the area, and they head for any nearby watering places, where they proceed to shoot their poisoned arrows, or whatever, into any rhino or elephant they see. After dawn, they'll proceed to follow up one or more of the wounded and dying animals, and after they recover the trophies they hide them under brush and rocks near the highway. Then one of the men will change clothes and flag down a ride out of the park, and they go to find a buyer, of whom there are many who hang out in every *pombe* club in every village near here. After dark, the poacher and his buyer return by car to collect the ivory or horn, and the poachers are paid off. They may leave then and return in a few days or weeks when they're broke, or they may stay to hunt again immediately. Usually two to three men work together in this; sometimes one man will work alone, but the important thing is that usually these lorry-traveling poachers aren't really professionals—not like some of the others we have to contend with."

"We've had to put down dozens of elephant who had been shot in the ear, trunk, foot, or anywhere the arrow landed." Gesturing to a folder on the table, David continued: "I've information here about three amateur poachers from Nairobi who not only killed one rhino, but added five more animals to the walking-wounded list in one night. At least we managed to catch them. Good hunters, like the majority of our local tribal people, have made and used bows, arrows, and poisons for generations, and those few who continue to hunt generally know what they're doing. They get the animal they're after, and there's no waste.

"These others"—he gestured again to the folder—"come from anywhere, and they don't know a damn thing about hunting. They generally buy their bows and arrows and poison, because they don't know how to make them and because they find it impossible to get rifles. Then they come here and are responsible for the killing or maiming of six trophy animals in one night because they let fly at anything in hopes of getting something. The five elephant and rhino who escaped will wander around now with those badly placed arrowheads starting infection and causing the animal to rot on its feet, until it either dies in a thicket somewhere or is shot by one of my rangers. The number of elephant and rhino we're losing to this type of poaching is astronomical."

"What are you doing about it?" inquired the Senior Warden.

"The only thing I can do," replied David. "We regularly ambush the rocky areas along the road that we know are favored by the poachers. We check the watering areas near the highway for tracks and signs of blood or wounded animals, and watching the sky for circling vultures has given every man here a permanent crick in his neck. We patrol the road itself and check the road shoulders for footprints heading into or out of the bush, and any vehicle stopped on the road is approached and questioned. My problem is that I don't have the men and vehicles necessary to maintain a constant twenty-four-hour-a-day watch on nearly two hundred kilometers of road. It's impossible to do. Our only chance is to catch them in the bush before they reach the highway, because once the poacher gains the road he can flag down a ride and be gone in ten minutes. The traffic is fairly heavy, and any car or lorry could be carrying poachers and trophies, so we are literally powerless once the poacher gets into a vehicle."

"What exactly do you need?" asked the Senior Warden.

"I need the cooperation of the police and the C.I.D., plus the authority to set up two round-the-clock roadblocks for an indefinite length of time. One roadblock would be at the southeastern side of the park and one on the northwest, to check all vehicles and passengers leaving the park area. I'd like to maintain these two positions for a few weeks and then start moving them about without warning to cover the few side tracks that might be used as alternative routes. That way, I could completely disrupt the poachers' usual methods of entry and exit, and after apprehending a good number of them for possession of weapons and trophies, we would be able to discourage the rest."

The Senior Warden had been making notes as David spoke, and now he looked up and said, "I'll see what I can do. I can't promise anything, but I'll back up your request." He smiled.

"Thank you. I'm hoping that they might listen to you in Nairobi, because they aren't hearing me."

"Where else are you having problems?" asked Shepherd.

"Let's start with the Northern Area," said David. Turning to his assistant warden, he added, "That's your area, Agaran. Would you explain the situation there?"

John Shepherd looked to the wall map and studied the huge three-thousand-square-mile Northern Area, which lay north of the Lalaga Lana River and constituted one-third of Aruba National Park. It was closed to ordinary tourist traffic; the purpose was to maintain the area as a sanctuary for plant and animal life, as free as possible of human influence. Small groups were allowed to travel north of the river only when accompanied by experienced professional guides. The professionals were a necessity, because the area was huge, featureless, and almost totally lacking in water for most of the year. A tourist on his own, without a radio or knowledge of the area, or how to survive in case of a car breakdown or other emergency, would probably never get out alive.

Agaran moved to the map and ran his finger along the north and northwestern boundaries of the area. "Here we border on the Wakamba Land Unit, and many of the tribesmen are doing the same thing they've done for generations. They plant their crops, tend their goats, raise a family, and hunt a little on the side. Before gazetting, they hunted all through the western side of what is now the park; afterward they fell back and hunted close to their *shambas*, near the boundary and for a few miles inside. The last two years have seen them moving farther in, and now they've come as far as the extreme southern portion of the Park. I have no idea how many there are. I just know how many we've caught, and the number indicates a big increase in poaching. The Kamba almost always use the bow and poisoned arrows, and they're more efficient than the average road poacher, but not quite as good as the Waliangulu. I'm also seeing a lot of snares and traps in the western portion of the Park. As usual, the Kamba poaching is heaviest along the Ruui and the Oreyiet Rivers, and on the Lafaroge Plateau. They prefer to build well-hidden hides on the rocky outcrops and hills and often near water, and when they come in to poach they usually number anywhere from three to a dozen men, who stay and hunt for several days or a couple of weeks before leaving. They're mainly interested in the trophies, because of their increased value, but they also take hides and meat. They aren't easy to find, and all we can do is patrol regularly and look for tracks to follow up, and we systematically ambush the few watering places, because they have to come for water, as well as the wildlife."

Gesturing to the northeastern and eastern boundary lines, Mohamed said, "Here we have the worst problem in the park. The Somali. Most are from Somalia, but some are our own Kenyan Somali people, and they've only taken up poaching here recently. Originally they entered across our eastern boundary in search of leopard, and worked along the watercourses and around rocky outcrops, setting their snares and gin traps wherever they saw signs of leopard. But it appears that what money they received from the leopard skins was quickly invested in high-powered rifles, which they smuggled into the country, and we first became aware of their hunting elephant and rhino about a year and a half ago. Their knowledge of bushcraft is far superior to that of the more agrarian Wakamba and Wataita, and the Somali are as vicious as a wounded cat when they're cornered. When a Kamba or Taita poacher is flushed by the Field Force, the question of whether or not he escapes often depends on who can run faster, the poacher or the pursuing ranger. When our Field Units encounter the Somali poachers, the result is often a gun battle that can last for the remainder of the day. In addition, the Somali have shot at patrolling rangers when the rangers were totally unaware of the near presence of the concealed poachers, so the motive was clearly murder, and not an attempt to escape imminent arrest."

"Was that what happened to Dan Boyd?" asked Shepherd quietly, referring to a well-known rancher whose land adjoined the park.

David answered, "Yes, sir, it was."

"That was a good man and a good friend," murmured Shepherd. After a moment he said, "I was on my long leave in England when that happened, after the public relations nonsense in which I was asked to participate in Europe and North America. I was told when I returned that he'd been shot while riding in a vehicle on his ranch and the people responsible were never caught. Can you tell me anything more about it?"

David answered, "Well, we were called on VHF radio immediately, and I flew over in the helicopter, hoping that there would be a chance of getting him to Nairobi in time, but he died just a few minutes after I arrived. It seems he'd been out patrolling with his men, looking for some poachers who'd killed one of his Boran cows during the previous night. He was standing up in the back of the Toyota with the canvas roof rolled back, and was scanning the area for movement, when the driver said he heard a shot and felt Boyd slam against the back of the cab. He fell across the brush bar and must have hung there a moment till the driver heard a second shot almost immediately, and then Boyd fell back into the rear against the men seated on the bench seats. They got him to the ranch house as quickly as possible, and since they'd radioed our Headquarters from their vehicle, I was able to arrive shortly after them. He'd been shot twice in the back with a large-caliber rifle."

"In the back?" exclaimed Shepherd.

"Yes, sir—they shot him twice, in the back."

"The bastards," muttered the Senior Warden. After a moment he looked at David. "But why, for God's sake? The man was a rancher. All he wanted to do was protect his cattle. Why kill him? And most of all, why shoot him in the back? If the patrol had already passed the poachers, why shoot him at all?"

After a moment David said, "That's what we're trying to explain about these Somali. Kill an elephant or a leopard, or kill a man— it's all one and the same."

The Senior Warden was silent, apparently studying the tabletop before him, and David waited a few moments before continuing: "These Somali poachers obviously feel that it's their inalienable right to hunt where, when, and for what they please. In the park or out doesn't seem to matter to them. The fact that Dan Boyd employed a private antipoaching squad to protect the wildlife on his ranch, plus his cattle, put him high on their list of people who were getting in their way. It might have been a trap."

Shepherd exclaimed, "Is that possible?"

"I believe it's a distinct possibility," David answered gravely. "When our Field Force Units showed up a bit later, we went out to the area where the Boran carcass had been found, and we followed the same tracks that Boyd and his patrol had followed. After about four kilometers the tracks just seemed to melt away, and it was about a half-kilometer farther on that Boyd was shot, when they were driving about trying to pick up the trail again. We figured out approximately where the shots had come from, and we combed the area on foot until we found where five or six men had gone to ground among the rocks on a nearby outcrop. They had obviously been there for several hours. They might just have been waiting for night to come so they could move out of the area undetected, or they could have been waiting for the patrol. Their tracks were as clear as a posted sign until they disappeared near the outcrop. Perhaps they deliberately lured Boyd into the area where they were waiting, perhaps not. We'll probably never know. The fact remains that he's dead and Somali poachers are responsible."

"How is it," asked Shepherd, "that these people are proving to be so much more of a problem than the local tribesmen who've poached in this area for years?"

"First of all," answered Mohamed, "they're not an agricultural people like most of the local tribes. When a group of people become tied down to a particular place because of their crops, their whole way of life changes, because they have to coexist with others on a permanent basis. They become more restrained as they lose much of their independence and aggressiveness. The nomadic peoples are different. That's one of the reasons the Field Force is made up of our northern tribes, like my people, the Turkana. For fieldwork we prove to be more effective, not only in attitude, but because we have a superior knowledge of bushcraft. We know and understand the bush—it's our home; whereas the Wataita think of home as a cultivated *shamba* field. They've lost their affinity with the virgin bushland and the wildlife. So when our Field Forces go out against the Wakamba, the Field Force has the advantage if you think in terms of hunter versus farmer. But when you pit the Field Force against the Somali you've got hunter versus hunter, and not only have we lost our advantage, but the advantage has passed to the Somali poachers."

"How so?" asked Shepherd.

"Because we have rules that we have to play by," replied the grim-faced assistant warden; "they don't. We can't shoot down our adversary from ambush. They can."

He continued: "There are other reasons why they're more of a problem than our usual poacher. One, the local people use bows and arrows, because it's their traditional weapon and guns are impossible for them to obtain; the Somali use smuggled rifles, and where we still have World War Two Enfield three-oh-threes, they have superior and modern high-powered repeating rifles. Two, the local people surrender if apprehended, because they have a respect for, or fear of, authority; the Somali resist until they're dead or hopelessly outnumbered, because they have no such respect or fear, and they refuse to recognize anyone as having authority over them. And the third and most important reason is that we're seriously outnumbered. Gangs numbering over twenty-five men are not uncommon, and while they split up into smaller groups once they're inside the park, it remains that there may be as many as twenty-five within a small area, and into this we're sending patrols of Field Force who at maximum strength number twelve men. That's why I say the Somali are the most serious threat to our stocks of rhino and elephant."

"Good Lord!" said Shepherd. "It doesn't sound like an anti-poaching campaign; it sounds like a war."

"That's the point we're trying to make," replied David as he studied the Senior Warden's expression.

"We've had poaching ever since we had our first game-control laws in 1935, so that's nothing new," mused the Senior Warden; "but this," he continued, "this is on a scale I've never seen before."

"Not even during the fifties?" asked Forbes.

"No, not even then," answered Shepherd.

"I've got a staff of over five hundred here," said David, "but only about one hundred and twenty are Field Force personnel—the rest are everything from carpenters to clerks. Out of these one hundred and twenty men, I've usually got twenty who are either on leave or recovering from sickness or injury, so that leaves only one hundred on duty at all times. Spread those hundred men over eighty-five hundred square miles and you'll see that I have each man covering eighty-five square miles. It's too much. This park is too big to protect with my limited personnel and equipment, particularly without air support."

Moving to the map, he pointed to the northwest boundary. "If a patrol reports signs of heavy poaching in this area, I pull in some of the other Field Units and deploy them there; and then"—he pointed to the eastern side of the park—"I'm hit hard here. Move the Field Units east and I'm hit in the south."

He paused; he'd thought of something odd. It had flickered across his mind and was now gone. He lost his train of thought and stood for a moment in confusion before collecting the thread of the previous conversation.

He turned back to the Senior Warden. "I've got my men jumping all over this park, and I'd swear that we spend more time traveling than tracking. Yes," he volunteered, "we're making a decent number of arrests; but no, it doesn't begin to slow down the poaching activity, because for every one we pick up, ten more are ready to come in to take their chances at getting a rhino whose horns will bring them ten thousand shillings."

The Senior Warden nodded in understanding. "What's the situation in the Southern Area?" he asked.

"Pretty much the same," answered David. "Somali coming in from the east and filtering down from the Northern Area. Wakamba in the western area, Waliangulu and Wataita in the east and Southern Area of the park, plus the road poaching and the nuisance groups."

"Who exactly are the nuisance groups?" asked Halima.

"Fishermen on Lake Konogudiu. Squatters in the Dakagudiu Hills; illegal trespassers who come in to scavenge the ivory and horn from the drought victims; and those blasted Masai with their bony cattle."

"Aren't you Masai?" queried Forbes in confusion.

"Yes, my mother was Masai," replied David, "but it doesn't make it any easier for me to understand or to sympathize with the tribe, when they insist on running large numbers of cattle on limited and marginal pasturage. These people I refer to as a nuisance are not as serious a threat as poachers, because they're always few in number and they don't really poach on a large scale. Their presence in the national park is more like trespassing. But their presence demands that I find and arrest them, and that spreads out my Field Force even more, because if they are ignored and allowed to bring in their cattle to graze, or to squat in some secluded valley in the hills, then we won't have just one or two herds of cattle on the plains and two or three families hidden in the forest; we'll have dozens of them, because the word will go out that the law isn't being enforced, so everyone and his brother will be moving in. That's what's happened to poaching. Too few are being caught and prosecuted out of the vast number of poachers operating. Every time a man comes into the park for ivory and gets away with it, he becomes a walking advertisement for poaching, and he influences others to do the same."

"Do you have any idea of your monthly losses to poaching?" asked Shepherd.

David thought a moment. "That's impossible for me or anyone else to answer, but in my Warden's Report I estimated a loss of five hundred elephant per quarter, two thousand a year; but it could be more."

The room was quiet as they all realized the implications of what a sustained loss of two thousand elephants each year could mean. Halima's troubled expression caught David's eye, and he felt the warmth of her empathy. He found that he was glad she was there, to a degree that surprised him.

Jeff Forbes broke the silence by saying softly, "In my opinion, that is a conservative estimate considering what I just saw on the western border of the park."

"I agree," said David.

"We've got to have a count," said Shepherd.

"Yes, but can you convince Nairobi?" asked David. "I've been on my hands and knees for months and I've got absolutely nowhere."

"Yes, you have," Shepherd corrected. "I saw the Acting Director of the Department the end of last week, and as a result of your previous reports, he authorized the funds for a total aerial count if I felt that it was necessary. I planned to base my decision on the information you'd present at this meeting, and it's obvious; we're seeing too many dead elephant and rhino, and I agree with Jeffrey that it's more than possible that the drought has acted like a blindfold. We expect to see the carcasses of drought victims, and so every time we see a dead elephant we automatically say 'the drought,' but it may be that there's a six-inch poisoned arrowhead or a bullet inside that rotting hulk."

"We can't visit and study every carcass in the park," said Jeff Forbes. "And besides, a severely deteriorated carcass or a pile of bones can't tell us anything."

"But," said Shepherd, "animals dead where there is no drought tell a lot."

"True," agreed Jeff Forbes.

"So you've got your count," said Shepherd emphatically. "Later we'll work out the timetable for the count, and we'll try to be in the air next week. With the cooperation of everyone in the Department, we should know exactly what's going on out here within a few days. We'll not only see exactly what's happening in the drought-stricken areas, but we'll be able to assess the situation in the thickly wooded areas in the more remote sections of the park. And most importantly, what this total count will tell us is how many elephant and rhino are surviving, and that's really our main concern."

He turned to Forbes and asked, "If we take the last count of thirty-five thousand elephant and subtract the known drought die-off, what do we have?"

Jeff Forbes considered the question. "Well, we've recovered over three hundred lower mandibles and pairs of tusks as of last week. My estimate would be four to five hundred fatalities as of now. You have to understand, though, that I'm giving you an educated guess."

"Fine, but we have to have some kind of figure to work with now," said Shepherd. "All right, using the absolute maximum of five hundred drought victims, subtracted from the last known count of thirty-five thousand, means that there should be at least thirty-four thousand five hundred elephant left here. How about rhino?"

David said, "Last sample census indicated roughly twenty-five hundred rhinos."

"What's the drought die-off?" asked Shepherd.

"We've got forty-two recorded as of now," replied Forbes. "But it could be twice that."

"All right, then," said the Senior Warden; "as soon as possible we'll do a total count of every rhino and elephant in the entire ecosystem from the air. And what we're looking for is approximately thirty-four thousand five hundred elephant and nearly twenty-five hundred rhino. Every one that's missing from that roll call is poached."

David leaned back in his chair, conscious of a feeling of relief, as if a tremendous weight had been lifted from him. The enthusiastic conversation which continued around him began to fade from his hearing as the realization grew in him that he wasn't alone anymore. But as it did, he became aware that something of importance had passed him by. His forehead creased and his brows drew together in concentration. It happens often that a confused jumble of ideas reveal the obvious when the ideas are spoken aloud. It had happened today, and he'd been aware that he had said something vital, something he'd not thought of before. For a fleeting moment, something had seemed almost clear.

He turned in his chair to face the map behind him as he tried to recall his previous comments regarding the poaching. He felt the answer wavering on the edge of his memory. It was just there, nearly in his grasp. Haltingly he cast back in his mind: What had he said? Something about increased evidence of poaching in the east, and when he pulled in his units and sent them east he was hit in the south, and after he concentrated his men south they were hit somewhere else. The feeling that something was becoming ominously clear mounted, only to disappear completely as his concentration was broken.

"David . . . David . . ."

Hearing his name spoken, he turned immediately and saw that the Senior Warden was looking at him in a peculiar manner.

"I'm sorry," David apologized; "I guess I was wandering."

"Is it something important?" inquired Shepherd.

"No, I suppose not," answered David. It was gone.

"Well, then," said Shepherd, "let's discuss what has to be done."

"It would seem," said Jeff Forbes, "that what is needed is a stronger deterrent in the form of stiff penalties for convicted poachers. David is right when he says the possibility of a year in jail isn't enough in view of the profits to be made."

"True," agreed Shepherd, "particularly when the maximum penalty of five years is already provided for by law. But really stiff sentences aren't going to happen anytime soon. I'm positive we can get magistrates to hand down two-year sentences for each offense as soon as we convince them of the enormity of the problem, but anything much heavier will take months, if not years, to accomplish. Don't forget that the Swahili word for 'poaching' and 'hunting' is the same, and that's how many Africans still look at it."

"What about reinforcements?" David asked.

"We'll get them," said Shepherd. "I'll be flying to Nairobi this afternoon so I can get to work on importing some tough magistrates and to get authorization for the roadblocks. I'll be at Department Headquarters tomorrow to ask for the Department's Special Anti-Poaching Team from Isiolo. I'll also arrange to get the Government Special Unit back here, and I'm going to radio each and every warden in Kenya from Headquarters to beg, borrow, or steal every man who can be spared from every national park and reserve in the country."

"Let's work out the sequence of events," suggested David. "Our first priority is the aerial count, and I want a total count not only of every living rhino and elephant in the ecosystem, but also of every carcass as well. Every elephant and rhino, alive or dead, will be pinpointed on a map that will tell us not only how many we still have, and their exact whereabouts on the day they were counted, but also where the fatalities are taking place and how many."

"From that," volunteered Forbes, "we can tell you how those pinpointed carcasses compare with the recorded deaths from the drought. We've kept very good records of the drought victims' whereabouts, so as the locations of carcasses start coming in, we can either confirm them as possible drought victims or send out a team to check the remains and give us an opinion: victim of drought, poacher, or whatever."

"So the count comes first," said David. "And a major anti-poaching campaign can then be planned, based on the intelligence we get as a result of the count. Where the poaching is heavy will determine where we send our reinforcements."

"How soon can we get started?" asked Jeff Forbes.

"When I can get enough pilots and their planes," answered David. "I'll begin organizing the count this afternoon, and I should know by tomorrow when we can start."

"Good," exclaimed Senior Warden Shepherd. Glancing at his watch, he added, "Now perhaps we'll get an early lunch, so I can be on my way to Nairobi. Besides, I think we've earned it."

The meeting broke up as everyone enthusiastically endorsed the suggestion. The predominant attitude was one of hopeful determination now. There was something to do, affirmative action to be planned which would define the problem and ultimately bring results. As chairs scraped back and papers were gathered, a hum of conversation erupted with additional suggestions and comments.

David heard Halima address him: "I'm afraid that I had little to offer the meeting. I'm sorry."

He looked up in surprise. "I didn't expect you to," he said. "I know the situation here is different from that in Nairobi, and I wanted you to understand our problems." He sat on the edge of the table and grinned. "You might say that today was an exercise in educating the Education Director."

She smiled in relief, then her expression sobered. "It was certainly that." She looked up and added simply, "I had no idea of the range and complexity of the problems here. I don't know what I could do to help, but if I can, please let me know."

"I'm afraid," he said ruefully, "that today's problems are mine to deal with. But perhaps you'll be able to help reduce our problems in the future through education. Although in the meantime"— he grinned—"a little moral support now and then would be very welcome."

"You have that," she said with a laugh.

"Good," he said, alert to the opportunity. "Then perhaps you'll have dinner with me tonight. Having that to look forward to would brighten up what will probably prove to be another difficult day."

Once more he was aware of a moment's hesitation before she said, "Yes, I'd like that." Then she added tentatively, "But perhaps it would be that much nicer if I fixed dinner for us at my house."

"It would definitely be nicer," he replied with a smile.

CHAPTER NINE

Noon

Vera batey bumped slowly along the deeply rutted road toward the dispensary, carefully steering the car wheels in between the deep gullies on either side of the roadway.

"When," she muttered to the striped tabby cat beside her, "are they going to grade this ghastly road?"

Immediately the right rear wheel landed in the gully on that side, and the sound of dirt smacking the underbody of the car was heard before the worn tire caught hold and the car lurched forward with a jerk that sent Vera's glasses skidding down her nose. After peering at a fuzzy, lopsided world for a moment, she reached up and shoved the spectacles up to where they belonged, and grimly held on to the bucking and jerking wheel until she pulled up out of the gully and into the driveway beside the dispensary.

She sighed. The veranda out front looked busy, and Adam had been working by himself all morning. After parking the car, she reached across the seat and retrieved the large shopping basket.

"Come along, you nasty little brute," she said to The Cat, who promptly jumped out of the car and followed the basket, which held his fish; he had no intention of letting it out of his sight.

Vera opened the screen door and held it with her foot while she unlocked the main door before passing inside, with The Cat following closely behind. The banging screen door narrowly missed the bent tail whose crook indicated that he'd lagged behind one time before.

Setting the heavy basket on the plastic-covered kitchen table,

Vera began briskly to store away the results of her morning's shopping, while her companion sat on the table waiting for his catfish to appear.

At last the stained, newsprint-wrapped bundle appeared, and a loud meow of recognition returned Vera's attention to her pet.

"I suppose you're hungry," she said, and another shrill yowl agreed with her. Chopping up a small saucerful of raw fish, she continued to talk to him as he stepped on and around her sandaled feet, rubbing himself on her legs and purring his anticipation.

After setting the saucer down on the floor with a small bowl of milk, she finished putting away her few groceries and deliberated as to whether she had time for a cup of tea before going to Adam's assistance. Deciding that she did, she set the water to boil and took down a biscuit tin, from which she took out two of the thin imported wafers that were her only luxury. Her tea ready, she passed into her small parlor and sat down in her rocking chair. Immediately her narrow lap was full of the fat presence of The Cat, who began to carefully lick his forepaw before rubbing it over his head.

She absentmindedly stroked his back, and the rattling purr resumed. "You're a dreadful animal. I don't know why I keep you," she said softly.

The Cat turned around a time or two on her cotton dress, preparatory to curling himself into a tight ball on her thin thighs. She wasn't very comfortable, but he didn't mind; he was used to her, and her rocking.

Vera had always had a pet—a dog or cat, and once even a small mongoose—but something always happened to it. A sickness, an injury, or the hungry presence of a jackal, and another pet would never reappear. And each time Vera would say, "No more." But it wouldn't be long until a stray would hang around the house to peer at her with frightened, hungry eyes, or someone would come to the back door with a wretchedly dirty kitten or puppy, all bones and supplication, and once more the chipped china saucer would be filled.

She sat and quietly stroked the sleeping cat. Through the open doorway to the ward room she saw the passing figure of Adam, and called out to him.

"Yes, Mama?" His round black face appeared at the door.

"Are there many waiting?"

"No, Mama, only five or six. It has been very quiet, but then, many came together. I am almost finished with them." He looked closely at her; she looked tired. "You rest," he added. "I will finish and close the doors for lunch."

"Thank you, Adam. I'll open at two."

He smiled and nodded before disappearing, and the doorway was empty again.

"Thank heavens," she murmured. She'd been up before dawn and hadn't stopped once. David's man, Bubu, had arrived early and he and Jamaa had crept about on the rafters above, capturing bats and shooing them out of the large hole they'd discovered under the eave. Then that hole, plus two smaller openings, had been carefully screened. At last the area between the roof and the ceiling was unoccupied. With luck it would stay that way.

As soon as that had been finished, she'd hurried off to talk with the local chief about the rabies problem. Then there had been the shopping to do. Now, it seemed, she was going to get an unexpected rest. Bless Adam.

The Cat had vacated the warm lap and stood at the door howling to be let out.

"No, you're not going out," she said.

The Cat was the village Don Juan and spent a good number of nights on the town, causing Vera to notice several small versions of his distinctive gray-and-black-striped person in various litters scattered about. One more howl brought no response, and when he saw she meant it he returned to her lap and his nap.

She had talked with the chief and some of the elder *wazee,* and now the village dogs and cats were being shut in, as advertised by the various howls of the dogs that protested the unaccustomed confinement.

She glanced at the large clock: its face reminded her that it was time she started her lunch. In a minute, she thought. A cool breeze sifted through the screened window and the curtains billowed softly. The creak of the rocker continued and then began to slow. Another breeze lifted the edge of the curtain, and The Cat stretched in his sleep and flexed one paw as the creaking stopped. Vera's head nodded, and again her glasses slid slowly down her narrow nose, to rest unnoticed on the flare of the nostrils as she dozed.

ASSISTANT WARDEN MOHAMED AGARAN glanced down at the dog he'd just shot. It was small and scrawny, its coat ragged and matted with burrs, while colonies of bloated ticks were scattered over its head and back and clustered around its rectum.

There was a regulation in existence which stated that no dogs were allowed in the national parks, and that any found inside would be shot on sight. However, this regulation was sometimes overlooked, particularly when there was a village or town nearby. But with the possibility of a rabies epidemic there was no choice now. He shook his head in resignation. It was just one more problem with which to contend.

Squatting down on his heels, he ran his hand over the dog's side and felt the protruding ribs and hollowed stomach of a perpetually hungry animal. He picked up a stick and drew the dog's lip up, to expose abnormally red gums. It looked sick, all right. He'd thought so when he'd noticed the animal's unnatural gait through his gunsight, just before he'd squeezed the trigger, killing it instantly. But sick with what?

Standing up, he called to the driver, *"Lete mfuko."*

As the dog's carcass was bundled into a jute bag, Agaran glanced at the sun: past noon. He'd finish this patrol with Unit 1 before leaving for Northern Area Headquarters. Situated in the far northwestern end of the park, Northern Headquarters was where he lived and worked the majority of the time. It was his job to look after the vast area north of the Lalaga Lana River and to direct the Anti-Poaching Forces operating there, but he tried to spend at least one week a month in the larger Southern Area to back David up.

He had another, special reason for staying in the Southern Area now: the Waliangulu was operating in the south. He'd been disappointed when the morning patrol at Shokoke had failed to reveal a trace of the man. He'd been so sure. Shokoke was the perfect hiding place. Thickly wooded, well watered, and situated south of Headquarters and west of Aruba Dam, it was an ideal area where a man could go to ground in the daytime and come out at dusk and dawn to hunt. The man had to know the area better than he or his men did; he had to have been one of those displaced when the park was gazetted. He was the right age. It was possible that he'd been born and raised there, and it would explain so much. But there had been nothing to indicate his presence, or even that he'd passed that way. Still, he wouldn't leave signposts; they might have just missed him.

He swore softly under his breath as he picked up his rifle. He'd give anything to be able to return to Shokoke with two units and scour the area, but the Waliangulu wasn't their only problem. He had Unit 4 patrolling north of the village while he and Unit 1 covered the eastern side, and when those areas were free of potential rabies carriers he had to head north with supplies and new patrol orders for the northern units. Thursday he'd be back. Thursday he'd go through Shokoke and personally look under every rock.

He called his men together, and they fanned out and moved slowly through the bush.

The afternoon wore on. The heat had intensified when Agaran noticed the tracks, and he abruptly halted the line of rangers before squatting down to inspect the footprints. The direction from which the prints came was the interior of the park; glancing up, he followed the tracks' obvious destination: the village.

Someone had come from inside the park and had gone toward the village. That was not an uncommon occurrence, since many times goats or children wandered away from the outlying *shambas,* and that was why the regulation regarding village dogs wasn't rigidly enforced; but these tracks did not accompany the small prints of a retrieved child or goat. Perhaps the man who left the tracks had gone into the protected area for a little firewood; it wasn't supposed to be done, but it happened now and then anyway. He would see.

He stood up and moved on beside the tracks. The path diverged from the previous direction taken by the rangers. Early yesterday, or perhaps the night before . . . They weren't fresh, but they were clear. His men fell in behind him as he moved along beside the footprints. The tracks came and went as the ground passed from hard sunbaked soil to soft sand, and he unconsciously came to several conclusions based on his previous knowledge and experience: it was a man—women placed their feet differently; and this one was possibly old or sick, because the stride was uneven and occasionally faltered, and too, this person had stopped to rest occasionally; the length of the sandals, which had been made from an old tire, indicated one of medium height, since the foot was neither very large nor very small; but perhaps this person was of heavy build, since the tracks were fairly deep, or perhaps the one who had walked here had carried a heavy load.

Agaran saw that he was approaching the boundary, and looked beyond to the village. Stopping at the edge of the fifty-foot-wide graded boundary line that marked the edge of the park area, he glanced up to the north, then south; the boundary stretched away in both directions like a road, and the exposed red soil cut a red slash through the gray scrub. He continued to follow the tracks across the boundary and into the dry thornbush on the other side, outside the park.

The tracks began to veer away from the village, and after another kilometer had passed, the trail cut sharply into a thicket of what appeared to be impenetrable scrub, and the tracks' progress was obscured in a tangle of footprints that trailed into and out of the wall of thornbush. Agaran stepped back and surveyed the area. He was at the edge of what appeared to be a large and thick stand of gray, scrubby bush that looked dead and lifeless. It wasn't, of course: when the rains came, these apparently dried-out branches and twigs would erupt with tiny green leaves; but now it all looked dead.

He reached out to the branches just before him and took a twig between his fingers. As he applied pressure he heard the snap of dead wood. He reached out again, but two feet away, to the right of the trail, and took another twig. This time it did not break under pressure, but slowly returned to its former position when released. Extending the end of his rifle barrel into the thick tangle of thornbush in front of him just above the ground, he lifted up and back over his shoulder. The bush came away with a minimum of resistance. He pressed forward, opening up the narrow trail so cleverly concealed by branches of cut thornbush.

He pushed through for several feet, and the bush opened to reveal a small clearing. Agaran stopped to examine the apparently deserted house ahead as his rangers came up behind him silently.

It was an old mud-walled house, whose thick coat of hard red soil had begun to fall away to reveal the latticework of the poles inside the walls. The roof was constructed of large flattened cans that were thick with the rust accumulated over a period of years. There was no sign of smoke from a cooking fire or of life, and the clearing was piercingly quiet. He saw that it had been years since the bush-enclosed field had been cultivated, since the once-cleared area was now a thick tangle of regenerating scrub.

Studying the ground before him, he saw that the same tracks he'd followed were here inside the clearing, and as he moved about and noted the direction and approximate age of the prints, he knew that the same man had come here perhaps yesterday and then left, only to return and leave again apparently as recently as last night. Approaching the house, he observed the door and examined the rusty lock that hung there. The door hinges, he noticed, were inside. He considered slipping his knife between the door and the doorframe and cutting through the hinges, which were probably made of leather, but decided against it. Circling the house, he examined the wall closely until he saw what he was looking for—a small crack that had worked itself through the old wall. Cupping his hands on either side of his face, he cut out the glare from the bright sunlight outside as he peered inside, to see only dim emptiness stabbed with faint beams of light from small holes in the rusted roof.

He resumed his walk around the house and returned to the door. Again he contemplated forcing his way in, and again decided against it. The Field Force had unlimited authorization for pursuit and arrest inside the national park area, and they could follow tracks out of the park and make an arrest if they were in hot pursuit of a fleeing poacher; but that implied that the rangers were only minutes behind the suspect, and such was not the case here. He knew he had no right to break into and enter a house outside the park; and for what? He had a feeling; that was all. He'd seen tracks that came out of the park and which led to this *shamba,* but there was no carcass and no evidence of illegal trophies on which to base his suspicions. He only had a feeling about an apparently deserted *shamba* that was visited occasionally; that, plus the fact that whoever came here didn't want it to be known; otherwise why would he have gone to such trouble to conceal the entrance?

"Una kiberiti?" asked Corporal Lugumba, as he put a cigarette in his mouth.

The question interrupted his thoughts. Absentmindedly shaking his head, he returned to his speculation as Lugumba cadged a match from one of the other rangers.

Deciding that there was nothing he could do here, he turned to Lugumba and explained what he wanted done before they left.

He stood to the side and watched as all the rangers departed the way they'd come in, except for the three men who carefully removed all traces of their patrol's visit by sweeping and patting the soil with tufts of dried grass to obliterate the tracks they'd left in the dirt around the house—just enough to brush away the prints, but not hard enough to sweep away the normal surface litter.

After replacing the dead brush as they'd found it and withdrawing a distance of some two hundred meters, Agaran stopped and turned to survey the thick stand of bush they'd left. It was as if they had never been there, except that now there were no footprints at all: not theirs, and not the tracks of the one who had come before. Perhaps he was being overly suspicious, but something nagged at Agaran's mind, and again he wondered why someone would go to such trouble to conceal the hut and his visits to it. It wasn't right, and it bothered him. That was why he intended to have Unit 1 return to the house tomorrow and he didn't want their presence here today discovered.

He turned to the corporal, and after a moment's conversation the unit split up, as it had done earlier at the riverbed. Agaran and four men cut back through the bush into the park and returned to their patrol of the boundary as they watched for stray dogs and sick wildlife, while Corporal Lugumba backtracked along the trail they had followed before, to discover where the tracks had come from inside the park.

AUDREY STOOD for a moment beside her car in front of the old *duka* with its high cement steps leading into the cool and crowded interior and went over her shopping list. She drew a line through *Shell Petrol Station,* and ticked off the list below: *2 pkg. butter, 4 torchlight batteries, 1 large cooking-gas cylinder* and *1 kilo bacon.* She shook her head in exasperation. Shopping day was a dreadful succession of errands, picking up this or that in a series of odd, out-of-the-way places that carried unlikely goods, like bacon at the petrol station.

She dashed another line through *duka;* she'd been to several of the shops which carried packaged goods, canned goods, nails, sacks of beans, bicycle tires, and brassieres. She smiled to herself as she thought of the bright red-purple-and-orange-patterned bra she'd seen dangling from a rope stretched high above the counter in this last *duka* she'd gone to in search of fresh garlic; there it had hung, flamboyant and flyspecked, between an umbrella and a dangling pair of yellow rubber sandals. She should have bought it—but really, it was too hideous even for a joke.

Flour, sugar, rice, powdered milk: she ticked them off one by one. *Canned goods.* She shook her head in irritation. Half of what she wanted hadn't been anywhere; but then, she really hadn't expected it to be. When she got home, the unavailable items would be transferred to the big shopping list headed *Nairobi* which had several entries added to it weekly.

She came to the next-to-last item on her list—*meat*—and checked her watch. It was about time for the carcasses to arrive from the slaughtering area outside the village where the marabou storks congregated. Deciding to leave the car and walk, she retrieved the large plastic bag from the front seat and crossed the rocky, pitted side street that led to the square in the middle of town where the Mombasa- and Nairobi-bound buses stopped.

As she stepped over an oval reed basket that held a half-dozen bedraggled and protesting chickens, and through the maze of the wheelbarrows of fruit, warm sodas, and hard-boiled eggs being offered the hungry bus passengers, she glanced over the square. It was a bustle of confusion: buses pulling in and pulling out; people calling their wares—*ndizi, mayai, machungwa; matatu* drivers yelling their local destinations—Wundanyi, Mwatate; and people coming and going as they laughed and talked. Market day was a noisy procession of people and things, and she loved it.

She looked at the Muslim women swathed in their shiny black *buibuis* beside the Somali women wrapped in filmy *khangas* and the Taita women with their faces etched in swirling patterns of blue-green dye; and all carried baskets in their hands or balanced them on their heads, while they wore their infants and toddlers strapped securely to their backs. The men sauntered by: some in the uniform of the national park, one or two in the khaki-and-gray of the police, while most others were in the pants and shirts of the European. Here and there a man was seen wrapped about the hip with the *kikoi* worn along the coast. There were the lighter brown complexions of the Indian or Arab, and the dark brown to black of the tribal people who came from all parts of East Africa, and here and there the pale white faces of the few Kenyan citizens of European descent.

Audrey noticed a small group of tourists standing by a minibus from one of the better-known tour companies. They were busy taking photographs and gesticulating. An old *mzee*, with his pierced and distended earlobes nearly brushing the lapels of his tattered khaki bush jacket, walked by leading a plodding goat behind him on a long strip of black inner tube. The tourists immediately pointed their cameras in the direction of the approaching *mzee*, who passed them by with head erect and his solemn eyes facing forward.

Audrey frowned in sympathy. Tourists often got out of hand. Didn't they know that most Africans were reluctant to have their pictures taken—sometimes violently so? Did they care? She doubted it.

As she approached the corrugated-tin butcher's shack across the street from the square, she saw a large wooden barrow piled with carcasses approaching up the dirt road. A small crowd of villagers followed closely. Quickly stepping inside, she took a place at the rough wooden counter as the crowd surged through the door, while two men with blood-spattered white coats carried in the skinned carcasses to hang on huge hooks at the back before piling the severed heads and legs at the door. As the butchers gutted the animals, and handed the livers and hearts to the health inspector standing by to examine them for disease, Audrey counted two goats and a whole cow. She was incredibly lucky. There would be enough meat not only for her and Jeff, but also for the cubs. She could start them on minced liver today.

As she brushed away the flies that had begun to swarm about, the

185

inspector finished and the pushing, shoving shoppers broke into an excited babble of requests: *"Kilo mbili nyama," "Kilo ya tumbo."* Audrey's voice joined the others, and she was rewarded when a butcher wielded a huge *panga* to hack her order from the largest of the dangling carcasses. After throwing the two-kilo slab of steak onto the scales, the butcher retrieved it; brushed off the flies, dirt, and miscellaneous hairs; and wrapped it in newsprint before weighing the liver he retrieved from a pile of intestines.

Relieved of thirty-six shillings and clutching her plastic bag of hard-won meat, Audrey escaped into the street. "Really," she muttered to herself as she headed for her car, "it's enough to turn you into a vegetarian for life."

After settling herself in the car, she pulled the hem of her skirt up over her knees; it was hot, and she was beginning to perspire. She'd best hurry and finish her shopping or she'd have two liters of spoiled milk when she got home, and she and Jeff didn't like *maziwa lala,* or sleeping milk, as the Africans referred to the soured milk they loved served with their *ugali.* Thank heavens, all she had left to do was the *soko.*

Threading the car slowly between the vehicles and people, she pulled away from the square and crossed the road to a dirt track which meandered through a field of dried cornstalks and led to the back entrance of the open-air vegetable-and-fruit market. After parking the car, she retrieved a huge empty *kikapu* from the back seat and approached the people congregated beneath the tall trees, where the fresh produce from miles around was displayed in piles on sacks laid on the ground.

"Momi, Momi, karibu."

Audrey glanced up to see the hugely fat Kamba woman from whom she bought many of her fruits and vegetables grinning and gesturing at her. Again, Audrey wondered where the woman had heard the term "mommy"; she obviously thought it a preferable form of address for Audrey to the Swahili *mama.*

Squeezing her way between the crowded people, who stood or squatted while they carried on a furious dialogue with the farmers and traders who sat in the midst of their fruits and vegetables, Audrey finally arrived at the pile of cabbages that marked the edge of the Kamba woman's produce.

"Karibu, karibu," the woman repeated happily as she sat behind the stacked cabbages on a small collapsible stool that threatened to do so immediately. Her hair was twisted into tight little black braids that stuck up all over a small head which looked out of place perched on top of her large body. Breasts the size of her monstrous

cabbages swayed between hugely fat arms and swelled over immense hips which completely obscured the seat and most of the legs of the stool on which she sat. Her bare feet were widely spaced and flat to the ground as if rooted in the soil under the shade provided by a battered umbrella clutched in her hand.

"*Unataka nini?*" inquired the woman as she abstractedly wiped away the streamlets of sweat that trickled over her cheeks.

"*Nataka vitunguu,*" said Audrey as she sat down on her heels and began to pick through the large pile of purple onions. "*Bei gani kwa kilo moja?*" she asked.

"*Shilingi kumi,*" answered the huge woman. She laid aside her umbrella and bent over to exchange the brass weights on her scale before weighing the onions, which were then dumped into Audrey's large woven basket.

Ten shillings for a kilo of onions, thought Audrey glumly; it was dreadful the way prices kept going up. Her order went on: two heads of lettuce, potatoes, sweet peppers, and carrots. Again she wished she could have a nice garden like David's, but she knew it was impossible; her orphans would devour it faster than it could grow. She had crossed many items off her list, and there were just a few things left on it that weren't available here. After paying the large, good-natured woman, Audrey said, "*Asante, Mama,*" and turned to go.

The woman called out, "*Asante sana, Momi,*" before turning to another potential customer: "*Karibu, karibu.*"

Picking her way through the narrow aisles left between the heaps of sun-warmed fruits and vegetables and the milling, gesturing people, Audrey again checked her list as her eyes flickered over the produce searching for the things she needed. Sweat trickled down her sides and into her eyes as a brisk gust of wind suddenly plastered her damp cotton dress to her body and threw grit in her face. Momentarily blinded, she stumbled into someone, and as she wiped her eyes she had an impression of a khaki back topped with grizzled-white hair just before he disappeared into the crowd. She murmured, "*Samahani, Mzee,*" and after dabbing at her sweating face with her handkerchief, she turned back to her shopping.

Let me see, now, she thought: avocados—I want three; and limes, if there are any. Her eyes continued to roam over the piles of fruits and vegetables. Oh, yes, and oranges—lots of oranges.

THE OLD *mzee* left the *soko* and hurried along the narrow path that led from the village in the direction of the old *shamba*. Heekuta Neko was irritated; he had meant to be there by *saa nne,* the fourth hour, but he had been delayed in getting away this morning, and now again in the village. The afternoon was passing, and he needed several hours in which to boil the poison until it reached the desired consistency and concentration. He realized that he'd have to stay and finish it this evening, because he was planning to hunt again tomorrow night. He had seen a herd of fifty or sixty elephants who had moved into the area and were just south of the Park Headquarters, and he wanted the one large bull tusker that had stood off to the side of the herd. With luck they would stay in the area through tomorrow night.

The faint track he followed began to die out as he passed the last of the outlying *shambas,* and he glanced around to see if anyone had observed him. No one had; the people were all at the market. That was good; he didn't want his passing by noted. He continued for another two kilometers as he watched for any herds of goats or cattle which would signal the presence of a herdsman, who might wonder what an *mzee* was doing going nowhere into the bush, and who might remember.

He began to slow only as he approached the thicket in which the house was hidden. Satisfied at last that he was alone and unobserved, he pulled back the thick bush and squeezed his way through into the clearing. Setting his things down, he returned and rearranged the thornbush so that it again concealed the small opening.

As he approached the house, he noted with satisfaction that all was as he had left it the night before.

He unlocked the dangling padlock, then kicked at the bottom of the door, which tended to stick, until it flew open. Once inside, he went to work immediately. After gathering some dried grass and twigs from outside, he got a small fire going between his cooking stones, and slowly the larger pieces of dried wood and the small bits of charcoal were added. He left the glowing fire to grow and then fall back on itself until it was reduced to a small hot fire that would provide an intense and even heat over which to boil down the poison.

He turned to the clay cooking pot that stood in the corner. Picking it up, he carried it to the doorway to inspect the color of the contents in the sunlight; it was a very dark brown and ready for boiling. After inspecting his hands carefully to see that there were no open sores or scratches through which the poison could enter his own body, he took up a stick and stirred the mixture before carefully removing the waterlogged slivers of wood and the few bits of bone from the elephant shrew.

By the time he was done, his fire was ready. He carried over the pot and set it on the cooking stones. Then, taking up a sharp stick, he gathered the bones and small pieces of wood he'd removed from the pot, and dug a small, deep hole at the edge of the clearing. Next, he buried the remains and stamped down on the disturbed place until it was invisible.

Returning to the house, he checked on the poison and fished out a small stray sliver or two of wood that rose to the surface; these he dropped into the red coals, which briefly sizzled a protest. After adding a few more pieces of charcoal, he sat back on his heels in satisfaction. This would be good poison. The tree he had selected from which to take the wood had been a good specimen of its species, as evidenced by the number of dead insects and the occasional bird carcass around it. The water it had soaked in was dark and very potent as a result, and the end product was going to be one of the most *kali* of the poisons he had made.

He got up and crossed the house to a dark corner. Reaching up into a recess in the top of the mud wall, he extracted a smaller round-bottomed clay cooking pot with a stopper made of giraffe hide and a bundle of old cloths, from which he shook numerous mouse droppings. Sitting on a stone just outside the door, he inspected the pot, which would hold the fresh poison; once securely sealed with the hide stopper and then wrapped in the cloth, the thick, gummy mixture would be kept airtight, dry, and at a fairly even temperature, to last for years if necessary.

He estimated the length of time necessary to boil down the mixture until it was the consistency of *uji*. Perhaps ten hours. He would be very late tonight, and the fact bothered him. His many years of success were based on the fact that he did not appear to be what he was; that, and the fact that he never drew attention to himself. No, he wasn't pleased, but it couldn't be helped. He decided to put it out of his mind and enjoy a short nap in the sun before it was necessary to add more charcoal to the fire. He closed his eyes and leaned back against the warm mud wall.

Almost immediately he was conscious of an irritation: there was a piece of meat wedged between his back teeth from the meal he'd taken in town earlier. He prodded at it with his tongue; then without opening his eyes stuck his thumb into his mouth and dug between the molars with his fingernail to try to dislodge a small remnant of goat meat. The thick nail failed to reach it. Opening his eyes, he glanced about for a twig or stick, and immediately spotted the very thing. Sitting up, he reached for it, and again using his thumbnail began to pare it down to a sharp thin toothpick.

Then it struck him. With a stab of awareness he knew something was wrong. He was in danger.

Like an animal he froze, while his heart pounded and every muscle tensed. His eyes darted up, to probe every inch of the clearing as his mind raced over and around the object he held in his fingers. A matchstick. But he didn't smoke, and when he started a fire in the house he threw the match into the flames. Someone else had been here.

Slowly he stood up and surveyed the clearing. No one else was here now, but someone had been before. His mind ran ahead. The entrance through the thicket was as he had left it. How did this one get in? Push through the thornbush? He doubted it, but he began to move slowly around the edge of the clearing to look for an opening forced through the bush, a piece of cloth on a sharp thorn, a trail or track which would indicate the point of entry into the clearing; but there was nothing: no hole, no shred of cloth, no tracks. No tracks.

He stopped at the place where he himself had come in just recently and studied the ground. There were his footprints entering; but where were his tracks from last night? And the day before? He bent nearly double and followed the small, almost imperceptible pathway to the house.

Nothing. Not even the tracks of a bird or mouse. He reached the house and circled it, his eyes sweeping the ground between the edge of the encircling thicket and the house. Then he saw it. Half of a heelprint. He knelt and studied it, and a half-formed conclusion was reached before he moved on and continued the search until he found another. This time the print was nearly perfect, overlooked because it was not near the house where the soil was bare. Someone had walked away from the house, and the clumps of knee-high dried grass had concealed the prints.

He knew those footprints had been made by ankle-high black boots issued to the rangers, because of the distinctive pattern on the heels. Somehow the Field Force had discovered the thicket and the house, and they had wished to keep their presence here unknown. Otherwise, why had they gone to such trouble to brush away their footprints? That was another reason why he knew it had to be them; only they would be so aware of tracks. The average inquisitive person would have left without thinking of the spoor he left behind.

He briefly considered the possibility that they had prepared an ambush, but discarded the idea. If there was one it would have been sprung by now. But they obviously meant to return; he had to get out.

190

He went back to the house and put out the fire. For a moment he wondered what to do with the contents of the cooking pot, and then he decided. Going to the far corner of the house, he reached up and withdrew his bow and a quiverful of arrow shafts and heads, then wrapped them in the cloth that he'd used to cover the pot of poison. Taking the wrapped bow and arrows and the still-hot cooking pot outside, he returned for his large woven basket and the remains of the sack of charcoal, and these he took outside as well. The house was now empty, the fire out. He locked the door as before.

Consolidating his belongings, he placed all the oddments together in the basket of food he'd purchased earlier in town, and laid the wrapped bow and arrows across the top. Now all he had to carry was the bulging basket and the clay cooking pot, which was quickly cooling.

He took them both to the entrance through the thornbush thicket, removed the dry bushes that concealed the opening, and set them outside. He went back to the house and carefully brushed away his own footprints from around it, then the path as he backed out, brushing the soil lightly till he was outside. Carefully he replaced the concealing branches, and moved the pot and basket some distance away, then ran back to erase his approaching and departing tracks. Five minutes hadn't elapsed since he had discovered that the Field Force had been there.

Wrapping the warm cooking pot in his jacket and taking up the basket, he began to walk toward the village as he tried to guess how they had found the house. He must have been tracked, but where had they come on his trail?

CHAPTER TEN

Afternoon

DUNCAN SHELBY REPLACED the telephone receiver and reached for the carafe of water standing on the corner of his desk. He'd yelled himself nearly hoarse during his call to Nairobi, since the connection had been a particularly bad one, and now his throat felt raw.

Through the open window he watched his workers going about their business in and out of the factory sheds. If things didn't improve soon, he'd have to start laying off men. He didn't want to do it, but the effect of the drought was to be seen in the crop, and the stunted sisal leaves were hardly worth harvesting.

With the ten to fifteen inches of rain his plantation usually received, he could figure on harvesting 250 leaves from each plant per year, with each leaf weighing about one pound, and it required approximately twenty-five tons of leaf to produce one bale of fiber. A lot of plants and a lot of leaves were required to make up just one quarter-ton bale, and now it was worse. The growth of the leaves was so retarded by the drought that they were producing fiber close to the absolute minimum of two feet in length; anything less was not acceptable on the market. It was requiring more work and more leaves to produce each bale, and the quality was falling.

As if that weren't enough, he'd had to abandon over four thousand acres of cultivated sisal because of the depredation of the elephants, who ate the heart of the plants, chewed the leaves for moisture, and trampled the rest. Four thousand acres. Over a million-shilling investment. He sighed. If it wasn't the elephants, then it was the buffalo and baboons. But it was the elephants who did the most damage because of their sheer size and appetite. It required the full-time employment of twenty-two men who did nothing but sit under little *makuti* shelters out of the sun and wait for the troops of marauding baboons to appear before dashing out to scream and beat on a pan. The Baboon Guards. It would be funny if it weren't such an expense. Twenty-two baboon chasers and twelve elephant guards scattered over the plantation, and still the wildlife came back.

For a moment he thought about the professional hunters he'd employed briefly several months ago. He'd felt he'd been driven to it, but one morning nineteen elephants had been shot in a milling stampede in one of the fields closest to the park, and the sight and smell of nearly two hundred thousand pounds of rotting flesh had caused him to send the hunters away and to abandon the fields.

Still, something had to be done. Things couldn't be allowed to get worse, because he was barely making ends meet now. There was no question of profit these days: it was all he could do to keep his people working. He realized that for him, at his age, the plantation was no more than a fifty-year-old habit, something to do for his remaining years. But for his men, it was more. The grandsons of the men he'd rousted out of villages five decades ago worked for him in the factory and fields, as had their fathers, and their fathers before them. They lived and raised their families in the village he'd built, and he felt he owed them the right to continue to do so. Three generations had built their lives around this plantation, as he himself had done, and they looked to him to keep it going. They were, in a way, the closest thing to family he had.

He was the *Bwana,* the *Mzee.* He'd earned their trust and their respect—the numbers of small black "Duncans" his men had named after him proved it. He had to keep that trust, to see to it that the operation made enough to cover their salaries. And it would, if he could keep the elephants out. They made the difference between staying afloat and going under.

DAVID RETURNED TO Headquarters after dropping off John Shepherd and his pilot at the airfield. As he pulled his Land-Rover behind the Headquarters building and parked, he reflected that he was in a marvelous mood; and he thought, Why not? After months of frustration and worry, he finally had the authorization for a count, and the Senior Warden was even now on his way to Nairobi to arrange for the reinforcements to help contain the poaching and protect the game.

Briefly the question of how many elephants and rhinos were left to protect crossed his mind and brought an immediate sobering of his high spirits. "I'll know soon enough," he muttered to himself. Then he recalled the prospect of dining with Halima, and his spirits rose again.

Passing through the hallway and into his office, he saw with amused irritation that Mdomo had managed to shove most of his papers and all of his pens and pencils onto the floor before leaving to spend his afternoon elsewhere. He retrieved his things and sat down, flicked a few small bird droppings from his desk to the floor and glanced at his notes.

He'd spoken to Shepherd about the need for a vet, and yes, the man would arrive the following morning. He scribbled a fast note of explanation to Warden Jombo Maimbo and asked him to meet the vet and get him settled in the village. Calling for Sergeant Lemboko, he explained that he wanted the message sent over right away.

Lemboko left, and David crossed that item from his notes, plus the point about the assistance he needed from Research. Jeff Forbes had agreed to send out a team to capture a few of the predators to send to Nairobi for a rabies study, along with the brain tissue from the stray dogs that were being eliminated from the park areas near the village. Good.

"Afendi?"

David glanced up and noticed the Field Force lance corporal who had stepped inside the door to address him.

"Njoo," David replied as he motioned for him to enter. As the man stepped into the office, something in his manner made David decide to speak in Swahili. The ranger appeared to be agitated about something, and what little English the man knew had probably escaped him.

"Ndiyo, sema basi," he said.

The man stood rigidly before the desk and proceeded to tell him that his father, who was a very old *mzee,* had come to visit his son and family, and that this morning a ground hornbill had stood before the staff compound and called. The ranger went on to stress how the large black bird, with its red unfeathered face and neck, had walked about before the staff quarters repeating its grunting cries, and now his father had taken to his bed and had turned his face to the wall. He was going to die.

The man wanted emergency compassionate leave to take his father home. He wanted to go now, immediately. If he didn't leave now, his father would die before the next morning.

David asked several questions, which were promptly answered by the ranger, who stood before him staring at a fixed point somewhere above David's head. The man's breath was rapid and uneven, and his rigidness testified to the tremendous effort he was making to refrain from trembling.

David considered quickly. This was one of his best men, and he needed him in the park during the count—and soon for the anti-poaching campaign—but he couldn't ignore the very valid plea for compassionate leave. The man was a Luo, and the Luo were not the only tribe who attributed supernatural powers to the ground horn-bill. They believed that when such a bird cried out its strange lionlike grunts before a village, it meant that an old person in the village was about to die. This ranger's father obviously believed the bird had come for him, since he was probably the eldest person in the staff quarters. David glanced up at the ranger. He knew he could assemble a lorryload of doctors to assure the old man that it was all superstition and that he wasn't going to die, and it wouldn't do a damn bit of good; if the old man was kept here he would be dead by tomorrow.

He would be dead because he believed that death was inevitable, and so he would turn away his face and die resigned to his fate, and that was why these old superstitions were still believed. Terror and the willpower of resignation made them come true.

"*Babako ni Mkristo?*" David asked.

The man replied that yes, his father was a Christian.

David didn't want to have to let him go, so he tried once, in spite of his foreknowledge. Would it help if they brought a minister from town for his father? To try to convince him that this would not happen, that he would not die?

The ranger shook his head dumbly.

David silently agreed; he didn't think it would work either. He jotted down the man's name and the permission for his leave of absence and handed it to the ranger. After telling him to take it to the office clerk, he added that an advance on his wages could be arranged if it was necessary and to speak to the Assistant Warden—Accountant about it. And to try to return as soon as possible.

The man murmured his "*Asante sana, Afendi. Asante mengi,*" and saluted before quickly leaving.

David sat back and thought about the matter. It was funny how the old superstitions hung around, even after a conversion to Christianity. But then, many Europeans would walk out of their way to avoid a black cat, or a ladder in their path, and it was done without thought or reason.

He figured that the *mzee* would be instantly reassured once his son got him away and traveling home. Once in his own village, the son would be able to take care of the father's fear through either the family minister or, more likely, the local witch doctor. He hadn't inquired about that—mainly since that sort of thing was illegal and usually dealt with harshly by the authorities, who wished to put an end to witchcraft and the trouble it could cause; and also because it was none of his business.

"Whatever works," he murmured philosophically as he turned back to the preliminary plans for the game count.

Glancing up at the map that illustrated the park and the adjacent areas which made up the Aruba ecosystem, he began to consider the area to be covered and the planes it would require. He and Jeff Forbes would be working together to coordinate the count, but he wanted to have an outline of the operation in his mind before they got together the following morning. He went over to the large metal file cabinet and found the old Warden's Reports. Flipping back through the years, he located the folder labeled "1973," withdrew it, and returned to his desk to read the particulars of the last total count, which had been done two years before he was posted here.

A light tap at the door interrupted his concentration, and he looked up to see Duncan Shelby standing at the door.

"I hope I'm not interrupting something important."

"Of course not. Come in." David rose and extended his hand. "It's good to see you. Sit down." He indicated the chair beside the desk. Resuming his seat, he added, "I hope it hasn't taken a problem to get you to drop by."

"I'm afraid so."

"Elephants?"

Shelby nodded. "Approximately a hundred and fifty are back into the fields west of the village near Tari Hill."

David swore under his breath. "I wish I could do something to keep them out, but I can't," he said regretfully. "Unfortunately, all we can do is continue to come out and drive them back into the park and out of your fields." Damn these elephants, he thought in exasperation; why won't they stay put inside the park? Shelby's plantation was here for twenty years before the park was gazetted; he must hate our very existence.

Shelby's blue eyes took in Karanja's morose expression, and as if he could divine his thoughts, he said, "Don't feel responsible. I've been contending with these unwelcome visits for too many years to get excited about it now.

"Besides," he continued, "I think that perhaps the answer lies in prevention, and you may be wrong when you say that there's nothing we can do."

David leaned forward; this must be the idea of Shelby's that

Warden Maimbo had referred to. "How do you mean, prevention?" he asked.

"Take a look at these," said Shelby as he passed over some diagrams.

David took the sheaf of papers and spread them on the desk. The first diagram was of the fence that enclosed ten square miles of the Addo National Park in South Africa, and the method of construction was carefully explained: fourteen-foot sections of railway track had been driven six feet into the ground at intervals of twenty-six feet; the eight-foot track sections that projected up out of the ground were linked together by steel mini-cables under great tension. Thick hardwood stakes were driven into the ground every eight feet between the projecting sections of railway track, and logs studded with sharp nails linked the mini-cables together and kept the elephants from trying to grip the fence with their trunks.

"Impressive, isn't it?" asked Shelby.

David nodded his assent without looking up.

"Unfortunately," Shelby went on, "it isn't practical here. It can stop a charging elephant, but it was six years in construction, and it cost a fortune."

"It looks like it," agreed David. He turned to the rest of the half-dozen diagrams, all illustrating methods by which elephants were kept either in or out of areas in and around national parks in Africa, and he guessed at the cost and the length of construction time of the fences, ditches, and various barricades illustrated. When he was done, he sat back in his chair and looked to Shelby, who was quietly puffing on a pipe.

David ventured a guess. "You're thinking of a ditch?"

Shelby nodded and pointed to the huge wall map. "As you can see, the estate's fields lie outside the park to the south and west of the village, and since we abandoned those fields to the east . . ." At this David winced, while Shelby continued without noticing: ". . . the elephants have been circling around Tari Hill and entering the plantation between the west side of Tari Hill and the east end of the Koche Hills. That narrow corridor is their only access to the plantation. If they try to go around the other way, east of the village, they run into the Karesa Mountain, and that will take them ten miles east before they round it and start back on the other side toward the plantation. It's roughly the same if they try to go around the Koche Hills to the west.

"So"—he glanced back at David—"I'm proposing that we dig a ditch some six feet wide and six feet deep between the Tari and Koche Hills just inside the park."

"Do you think that will stop them?" asked David speculatively.

"I think it will."

David got up and crossed to the wall map and studied it for a moment before asking, "What's the distance between Tari and the Koches?"

"Just over two kilometers."

"It seems plausible," David decided out loud. "But on the other hand, you know those hills seem considerable to us when viewed at a distance from the flatlands, but neither can be referred to as a steep precipice, and elephant are good at mountain climbing. They've been recorded at twelve thousand feet on Mount Kenya and sixteen thousand feet on Mount Kilimanjaro. I've seen elephant trails in the mountains that looked better adapted to mountain goats, not elephant, and yet they were elephant trails. And"—he paused and grinned—"while I haven't seen it myself, I've heard that a determined elephant can cover fifty miles in one night. So how can a ditch two kilometers long help if they just go over the hills on either side, or take the longer, easier way around the ditch, hills and all?"

"I don't really think they'll bother," replied Shelby. "It's not as if sisal were their favorite food; it isn't. Besides, it's not so much what they eat as it is how much they trample."

"I know," agreed David. "Elephant destroy twice as much as they consume foraging."

"I believe they come into the sisal fields just because they're there," reasoned Shelby, "just outside the boundary, and not because they are particularly hungry for sisal. It would be different if I had groves of oranges. And," he continued, "during a drought they come in herds, but only because there isn't much else around and sisal is a little better than nothing."

"But you don't believe that 'a little better than nothing' is enough to motivate them to climb a mountain or trek twenty miles to get to it?"

"No, I don't. We may get an occasional one or two, but not herds; not like now."

"It's possible you're right," said David thoughtfully.

"Do you agree," asked Shelby, "that the best of those ideas"—he gestured toward the sheaf of diagrams—"would be the ditch for this particular problem?"

David nodded.

"Even a narrow ditch will stop an elephant, because they're totally incapable of jumping," Shelby went on. "I think that many of these fences were started before the idea of a ditch occurred to anyone. Besides, it just costs too much to construct a really elephant-proof barricade."

"So what are your plans?" asked David.

"That's what I have to discuss with you. You have earth-moving equipment and I don't. The cost of renting such equipment would be prohibitive for me. What I'm hoping is that we could come to an arrangement."

"Go on."

"Your equipment isn't in use now, so if you could supply the equipment, then I could provide the fuel and the labor, and together we could put an end to this problem."

David considered the proposition. On the face of it, it sounded good. His equipment was lying idle at the moment, so if Shelby provided petrol and laborers with picks and shovels, then the ditch could become a reality that would cost the park little or nothing; and he had no money budgeted for this kind of extra, particularly with the count and anti-poaching campaign imminent. But would it stop them? He turned to the map and studied the area. It might. He'd check with Research. He turned to Shelby.

"Let me think about this for a day or two," he said. "And I'll have to check with the Senior Warden of the province to make sure that I can release the equipment for this kind of project."

Shelby smiled. "If you'll seriously consider my idea, then I can't ask for more. Thank you."

"In the meantime," added David, "I'll send Unit Four of the Field Force to your factory this afternoon. You can take them out to those northwest fields and they'll run the elephant back into the park again."

Shelby nodded his appreciation. "Say, in about an hour?"

"Fine."

After a few minutes of conversation, Shelby picked up the wide-brimmed straw hat he was never seen without and stood up. "Thank you for your time, Warden."

AS HALIMA CROSSED THE lawn of the Education Center at the head of the group of twenty-two children she'd just taken on a nature walk, she was thankful her day was nearly done, and her evening about to begin. She turned the children over to Patrick, her assistant, and the two teachers who'd accompanied them up from their school in Mombasa, and passed by her office for her things. Then she left by the back way to take the path between the Center and her own small house nearby.

After lunch she'd dashed home to get something out of the freezer in order for it to defrost in time for dinner, and now she laughed at herself when she remembered her momentary consternation as she'd wondered what to fix; it had been that long since she'd cooked for a man. The novelty of the occasion had been a pleasant intrusion into her thoughts all afternoon. It seemed a long time since she'd looked forward to a man's company.

She unlocked the back door, put down her things and crossed to the refrigerator, where she poured herself a cold orange squash before passing into the sitting room to sit down and rest a moment before taking her shower.

As she sipped her drink her thoughts returned to David. She remembered how it had been at the university and after, how she and her friends had been acutely aware of and interested in the men around them, as potential friends, lovers, possible husbands. It was only natural. But then the young biologist had come along, and for three years she'd seen only him. Even afterward, when it was all over, she'd failed to respond to the men she met through acquaintances or work. It was as if the intensity of her loving and then the depth of her hurt had numbed her. She saw now that it was as if, battered by emotions, she'd crept off somewhere where nothing could touch her until she recovered.

She'd lived quietly, engrossed in her work and the occasional company of a few old friends. Then had come the transfer and the getting settled in a new place, with different people, new friends. She thought of Audrey and smiled. Audrey and Jeff. You couldn't think of one without the other, and she'd been drawn to them from the first time they'd met.

She'd known a number of *Wazungu* at school, and later through her work, but never intimately. Not as close friends; not until Audrey and Jeff; and when she knew them well she knew what it was she'd wanted, what had been missing from the one relationship she'd thought would last her forever. Jeff and Audrey were together, a couple, two halves of a whole. Neither one dominant, neither submissive, but equal in their strengths and weaknesses. She'd seen Audrey scold her husband as if he'd been a naughty child; and seen Jeff comfort his wife like a father when she burst into tears as an orphan died in her lap. She'd seen them each turn to the other for help or advice, or to share a joke or a triumph, and she'd envied Audrey.

Envied her because Audrey wasn't caught between the traditional past and the modern present; envied her because Audrey's culture had accepted her both as a woman and wife and as a being of intelligence and capability. With her education, her femaleness did not preclude her from any profession she chose to pursue. European and North American women were generations ahead of other nations in that way.

In contrast, Halima's mother could not read or write, because when she was a child such things were not thought of for girls. She'd been taught how to carry heavy loads of firewood or water, and how to tend a *shamba,* her father's herds of cows and sheep, and her younger brothers and sisters, for that was the sum of a woman's usefulness and subsequent life. It was Halima's father who had seen that things were changing, that his daughters would have a different life which would need different lessons.

Had he known, she wondered now, how difficult it would be to be in between? To be one of the generation who took a step forward out of the past, only to find in mid-stride that they didn't know where they were going?

What, exactly, did the future hold for her? Was there a man of her race she hadn't yet met who wanted her to be everything she felt she could be, and wanted to be? Not only as a woman to reach for at night, and as a wife and mother, but also as a companion, a human being who could help, who could be respected and relied on as a full partner? Or would it be like before, when the only man she'd loved had sought companionship from his male friends in bars, his challenges in the work he would never discuss with her; a man who, if he had problems or disappointments, never spoke of them and who'd come to her only like a bull to a cow?

Is there such a man, she wondered, or am I asking too much, too soon? So many questions. Perhaps such men won't be until my daughter's day, when the young men of her generation have grown up with mothers who were no longer thought of as procreating beasts of burden. If so, then what about us—what about me and the others like me? Shall we do with so much less, when we have so much more to offer?

She thought about the evening ahead and David. What sort of man was he? What sort of woman was he expecting? A traditional woman, whatever that was, or her, whatever she was? She didn't know anymore.

Finishing her drink, she went into her bedroom and opened the closet door. Without thinking she reached for a pair of *khangas* to put on after her shower, and then she laughed softly. At her office she wore her uniform, and for business, dresses or suits, but at home she wore the traditional *khangas,* draped in the way of the northern tribes. One tied over one shoulder, leaving the other bare, and one wrapped around her hips, covering her to the ankles. It was comfortable, and it suited her.

Perhaps I'm a mixture of the past and the present, she mused as she unbuttoned her uniform and dropped it into the clothes hamper. Perhaps I'm neither, or both. As she stepped under the shower she asked herself, And what shall I be tonight? Shall I wear the *khangas* and deny the rest? Shall I sit quietly and offer no opinion, no idea, just listen and applaud before following him to bed, where again I'll pretend to be what I'm not? Or shall I be me?

Whatever that was.

CORPORAL LUGUMBA LIT his last cigarette and inhaled deeply as he reviewed the results of his unit's patrol with the assistant warden, before Agaran had left to return north, while he waited for the radio operator to finish his regular call-up of the various gates and stations in the park. When he was done, then Lugumba would give him the information that Duba needed for the Field Force Patrol Report.

Each day, the corporals of the ten Field Force Units stationed at either Main Headquarters or Northern Headquarters would report to Duba in person or by radio, and inform him where they had gone, what they had done, what they had found, and whom, if anyone, they had arrested. The resulting daily report illustrated the area covered by each patrol, plus the carcasses, tracks, hides, and suspects discovered.

Today, after an unprofitable morning at Shokoke looking for the Waliangulu, they'd covered the eastern edge of the village, where they'd shot two dogs and found one set of tracks. Not much in that— but that secluded house had bothered Agaran, as it had him. That was why he was to return tomorrow to check it out, even though they really had nothing on which to base their suspicions. After leaving the house, he and Agaran had split their force, and he had followed the tracks into the park and found where they led—to the road. Perhaps, he thought, someone had hitched a ride and got out where the tracks began, to walk the remaining distance. He shrugged his shoulders; but a deserted house so close to the park and the road bothered him. It ought to mean something.

He turned his attention to Duba, who was now involved with some problem of a visitor's car disabled near Nyache Gate. Lugumba sighed. He wanted to get done and go home for a beer and a shower. Noticing the clipboard with the previous day's Patrol Reports on it lying beside him, he began to spell out the words to himself out of boredom.

The last entry was from yesterday's report by Unit 3 here in the Southern Area. They must have been late coming in after following the trail that led away from the carcass discovered near Headquarters the previous morning.

He picked up the clipboard, his finger tracing a line beneath the written record as he painstakingly picked out the letters and formed the words in his mind. As the meaning became clear, he reconstructed the progress of Unit 3 on the wall map before him, and his attention was caught.

After pinpointing the location of the cow's carcass and then referring to the Patrol Report, he saw that the poacher had cut southwest and the trail had been lost at the highway; he noted the position on the road with a pin, and then he found the area his unit had patrolled today. Placing a pin on the map at the house's location, he then backtracked the trail he had followed, which had swung in a southeasterly direction until it too ended at the highway's tarmac, and here he placed a third pin. It was possible; even probable. The tracks of the Waliangulu who had taken the cow night before last had disappeared at the road just about two kilometers east of the trail that reappeared the same night and which led to the deserted house. He saw the poacher's strategy in his mind.

Komora Duba finished with Nyache Gate, and after scribbling down the information he'd received in the logbook, he turned to Corporal Lugumba and said, "Now, *Bwana*." He stopped and looked around the small room. Lugumba was gone.

DAVID STOOD AT THE kitchen window and took another long pull at the chilled bottle. He was thirsty, and he drained the short beer quickly.

He'd been able to get a lot of work done that afternoon, and now he felt ready and eager for the operations meeting with Jeff in the morning.

He continued to look out the window into the garden area, and after a moment a small grayish-fawn head, with the crest of long hairs on its forehead and between its tiny horns alertly erect, appeared through the dark green leaves of the *pilipili* bush; the large dark eyes ringed with white surveyed the garden, while the elongated nose twitched in reconnaissance, before one dainty, pale fawn leg advanced, followed by the rest of the body. The little male dik-dik began to select suitable twigs, against which he rubbed his face to deposit a globule of the dark substance secreted from the small glands below his eyes with which he marked his territory. Meanwhile, the tiny female behind him began to feed rapidly on the narrow green leaves; periodically her small head would abruptly lift from its browsing and glance around while the mouth continued to chew the leaves before swallowing them in a blob.

David smiled and was glad he hadn't told Bubu to close up the hole by which the dik-diks gained entry into the garden. He liked watching them. He turned and left the kitchen and headed through the house to the veranda, where he saw Corporal Lugumba coming up the walkway carrying a map that fluttered in the late-afternoon breeze. The corporal saluted.

"Karibu," David said as he acknowledged the salute and indicated the veranda chairs. Sitting down, he said, "What is it?"

Lugumba also sat, and spread the map on his knees. Then he told him about the previous day's tracking by Unit 3 and the results.

"Yes," replied David, "I read the report."

Lugumba related Unit 1's patrol with Agaran and the finding of the house, and he pointed out its position on the map and the place where the tracks had originated on the road. David instantly saw the relationship, and he moved forward in his chair to study the map. Yes, it was possible that they had finally got something tangible on the Waliangulu poacher.

"You think he'll return?" he asked Lugumba.

"Yes, sir."

"But won't he be scared off, now that you've been there?"

"No, I don't think so. We didn't see anyone, and we removed our tracks and replaced the brush as it was before."

David smiled again; his men knew what they were doing. "Very good," he said.

"I'd like to go back now and set up an ambush in the surrounding thicket. Assistant Warden Agaran wanted us to return to the house tomorrow, but I think the Waliangulu may return tonight. He was there last night."

"Will one unit be enough?"

"Yes, sir."

Another bottle of beer and a glass were set down quietly on the table beside David, and the two men continued to talk without noticing Bubu's presence as he began silently to rearrange the pillows on the other chairs.

"What was in the house?"

"Agaran said he couldn't see anything, but he didn't want to break down the door."

"No, he couldn't do that," David considered; "but the police could do something if we had more information to link the house and the tracks that left the carcass together." He thought for a moment. "You have more than enough time before dark. Go back to the carcass and take another look at the tracks there, and then compare them with the ones that leave the road and lead to the house. I believe you said they were the tracks of sandals made from tire treads."

Lugumba nodded his understanding. "The treads may match."

"If the pattern is at all distinctive they may match perfectly, and if the man doesn't return in the next day or two, then at least we'll have enough evidence to enable the police to enter the house."

"I'll go now, sir," Lugumba said as he got to his feet.

David smiled; he could see that the corporal had one thing on his mind, and that was the poacher. "Good enough," he said as he stood and offered his hand. "Very good work, Lugumba."

David stood a moment watching him go. I have some fine men, he thought as he turned and headed for his bedroom and a cool shower. I only wish I could have more of them.

Bubu plumped up the last pillow and rearranged it in the chair before picking up the half-finished beer and glass to return to the kitchen. After putting the dirty glass into the sink to wash later, he stood with his back to the kitchen door and finished the contents of the bottle. A smile slowly spread across his face.

ASSISTANT WARDEN Mohamed Agaran's Land-Rover crossed the Lalaga Lana River just above Maika Faya Falls and left that part of the park which was open to tourists behind. Now it had the long distance through the Northern Area to cover before reaching his Headquarters. As the vehicle rattled and banged over the corrugated road, Agaran gave up trying to take a nap beside the driver. It was too hot, and the noise of the vehicle made sleep impossible; or perhaps it was his thoughts.

He was looking forward to returning within a day or so, and then he'd go back to Shokoke. With two units he might possibly discover the Waliangulu's trail. But what if he didn't? The thought was sobering.

He studied the problem. Perhaps an informer. Someone, somewhere, must still be around who knew of the man. The problem was that the Waliangulu had never been a populous tribe to begin with, and then their villages and settlements had been broken up twenty-five years ago and the people scattered. Many had drifted back into the area to resume their former way of life, but the anti-poaching campaign of the late fifties had come along, and it had ended with the majority of the men of the tribe going to jail. During all this upheaval, a new generation had grown up and away from the old way of life, without the training and influence of the tribe and the elders with which they could identify and emulate.

The result could be seen in small settlements on the Lalaga Lana River outside the park, and along the main Mombasa/Nairobi road. There were only a few *wazee* Waliangulu left, with the filed teeth and tribal scars of their people and still speaking their distinctive tongue; they lived with their grown children and grandchildren, who were unmarked Swahili-speaking Africans. The hunters were gone, and the tribe, as a tribe, existed only in the minds of the old ones, as a memory.

It was very possible, Agaran concluded, that there was no one left who could lead him to the man. He knew the man hunted alone—that was in his favor. He didn't appear to live in or near any of the Waliangulu settlements—that too was in his favor, because no one had a clue as to where to start looking for him. We know where he's been when he's poached an elephant, he thought, but where the hell is he before and after?

He'd have to wait and see what developed. If Shokoke was a dead end, he'd have to wait till the man made his next kill. Then he'd be right behind him. It was all he could do.

As he bumped along engrossed in his thoughts, his seemingly sightless eyes absorbed every detail of the passing bush and suddenly transmitted a message of alarm.

"*Simama*"—his raised voice superimposed itself over the noise of the engine and the rattle of the vehicle. The driver immediately skidded to a stop.

Agaran scanned the thick bush to the right of the road; nothing moved and there was no sound. He looked up and watched the huge brown birds as they continued to plummet to earth at a point some fifty meters off the road. He pointed toward the descending birds and murmured, "*Pole-pole*" as he reached for the loaded .303.

The driver turned the Land-Rover into the bush and slowly weaved an erratic course between thick clumps of thornbush while Mohamed's eyes searched every thicket and studied every rock. Gradually the bush thinned and Mohamed could see a reddish-gray hump, decked with jostling birds. As they came closer, the brush continued to thin to reveal the huge corpse, and then another beyond, and one off to the side—and more.

"*Simama hapa,*" he repeated softly—not because he was afraid of being overheard, since he could see that only they two, plus the vultures, were there, but because he was awed by the evidence of the massacre which had occurred here.

He sat perfectly still, with the rifle butt on the floor between his feet and the hot metal barrel pressed against his inner knee. Finally he opened the door and stood on the running board, and his eyes swept the area before him. He ignored the great flocks of vultures who slowly lifted off the nearer corpses and flapped and fluttered away, and he ignored the others farther on who tore and gobbled at the hacked and bloody faces of the victims, who lay on their sides, bloating under the hot sun.

The carnage was unbelievable. In all his years with the Field Force he had never seen poaching on this scale before.

The area was flattened; bushes and thickets were smashed to the ground, and where the red soil showed through, the earth was lacerated from the milling stampede that had taken place, and the scarred depressions in the red dirt had filled with the now-blackened blood of those who had fallen. Cows, juveniles, calves—even the tiny ones—and the occasional bull littered the ground before him on a bed of bloody and broken vegetation, and scattered everywhere were the severed trunks and the splintered pieces of shattered faces in pools of coagulated blood. The cloying smell of death filled his nose and overwhelmed his senses, while his breath caught in his chest and hurt.

He began to count: one, two, three, four—and on. His eyes were drawn from those carcasses near him and moved on and out to the ones farther away as he mentally recorded them one by one.

He stepped down from the vehicle and quickly strode to one of the nearby rocky outcroppings he'd noticed before. It would give him a little elevation from which to survey the area. As he began to clamber up over the rocks, he saw the prints scattered about on the dirt, and he stopped. Slowly he began to examine the tracks and follow them about, and he saw that several men had been here. Perhaps four or five, maybe more. The rocky soil was crisscrossed with the tracks of a number of poachers; and when he reached the top and looked down onto the other side of the kopje, he saw in the sand at the base of the rocks the clear imprint of tire tracks. A vehicle. They were inside the Northern Area in a vehicle.

He turned around and surveyed the trampled area below that he'd seen from the Land-Rover. He held his breath against the mounting stench of putrefaction as he automatically reconstructed what had happened here.

A herd had wandered into the area at the foot of the *kopjes,* and either the poachers had been waiting for them or they'd arrived soon after and gained the height of the outcroppings unnoticed by the elephants; then the poachers had opened up and caught them in a crossfire. He saw that the stampeding animals had tried to break toward the south and that the leaders had been shot and dropped, which had caused those who followed to veer east, and

207

again those in front had been dropped to panic the others, and again the terrified animals had veered away to double back, and each time they attempted to break from the milling center they had been turned back and picked off one by one.

He knew how it was done. Yes, he'd seen it done on control in a heavily overpopulated park when two wardens with rifles had brought down twenty-nine elephants in less than five minutes. Two men, five minutes, twenty-nine dead. These were not indigent Somali tribesmen with their first rifles. Whoever had done this knew how it was done.

He stood stunned as he realized how many dead elephants there were, how large an area they covered, and in the near distance he saw more of the vultures arriving to flutter earthward onto the carcasses of still more, who had finally fallen some two or three hundred meters away in the bush out of sight.

He turned away and climbed down the rocks again and moved slowly toward the vehicle. Who? How? The vehicle. Where had it come from? The expended shells among the rocks. The number of tracks. How can it be? Who are they? His mind raced among the evidence presented and stopped to pick up each fragment of information, to turn over, examine, and drop before stumbling on to snatch at something else to consider a moment and discard before whirling on in confusion.

Returning to the vehicle, he reached for the microphone. Depressing the button, he mumbled, "Six-oh-three. This is Field Two." He repeated himself and heard his own words as if spoken by someone else, and then he heard the rustling, disembodied voice of the radio operator at Main Headquarters.

"Field Two. Six-oh-three reading you."

"This is Agaran. I am requesting reinforcements. All available units in the Northern and Southern Areas. My position is approximately five kilometers north of signpost two-one-six, between Maika Faya Falls and Silanga. Request aerial support and reconnaissance. Is the Warden there? I repeat, is Warden Karanja there?"

"Negative, Field Two. The Warden is at home," replied Duba, who wondered what the hell was going on. The assistant warden wanted *all* units?

"Six-oh-three, tell him . . ." Mohamed's breath caught again, and the smell of blood was strong. "Tell him there are more than one hundred poached elephant here. Tell him the poachers have a vehicle. Tell him"—again he paused—"to come."

CHAPTER ELEVEN

Evening

MARGARET SAT AT HER DESK. It had been nearly an hour since everyone had left, and still she remained in the deserted office with the shutters drawn and the door closed.

She didn't want to go home and she had nowhere else to go, so she continued to sit and dread seeing Mulolo. Glancing up at the clock, she saw that there were still two hours before he was off duty; then he would come to her quarters to ask about the meeting, and she didn't want to be there. He might even be there now if he had been able to get someone to take his place at the gate.

She remembered this morning and the unspoken threat in his voice, and again she wondered what she was going to tell him. How would she explain her inability to find out what he wanted to know? What was he going to say? What would he do? She didn't know, but she was instinctively afraid he would leave her and that he wouldn't come back. She thought of future evenings spent alone, without his occasional company or even the hopeful expectation that he might come by to look forward to, and the prospect left her numb and cold.

She had always felt shut out. She'd been the first and last child of her parents, because her difficult birthing had made future children impossible for her small, frail mother, and the two of them had borne in silence the anger and the sometimes brutal retribution of her father's frustrated disappointment at his lack of sons.

She had always been lonely; just herself and her shrinking mother, and when her father came home she'd been put into a corner and hushed. Her placating attitude had been learned early. It had been her only method of survival, and her painfully withdrawn and self-effacing shyness had become the adult result.

Margaret knew that she was often considered to be stupid. It had been so in school, until her teachers had noticed that her written work was really far superior to that of anyone else; but they had only to ask her a question before the class and she was instantly struck dumb, and her wits seemed to fly out her ears. But she wasn't stupid and she knew it, and so she continued to sit quietly and think desperately by herself. There had to be something she could do to make up for her earlier failure.

She knew the meeting this morning had been concerned with the poaching and the drought, and she knew who had been there, but what had been discussed? It was obviously something that needed the approval of the Senior Warden; otherwise Warden Karanja would not have asked him to come. What could they have decided on? Why had the Warden been in such good spirits this afternoon? What was he going to do?

She was still studying the problem when she vaguely heard the Radio Room door fly open and bang against the wall, then the running footsteps of the radio operator as he rushed past the closed office door and out of the Headquarters building. Unconsciously she realized that Duba had left, but still she continued to worry: On what had Warden Karanja and the Senior Warden decided?

Then the answer slowly presented itself as obvious: the Warden's list. He had so many things to remember and so much to do that he relied on the notes he made to himself to supplement his memory. She smiled. Of course he would have written down everything he wanted to remember; listed all the things he had to do immediately plus those that wanted seeing to during the next few days; and the notes would be on his desk. She jumped up and went to the door to listen. There was no sound outside, since it was the quiet time between the closing of the offices and the arrival of the night duty guards.

Shutting the door behind her, she stepped quickly to the corner and peered around to look into the main corridor: no one must see her and wonder why she was going into the Warden's private office after hours. But no one was there to observe, and the only sound she heard was that of the muffled static from the radios.

She turned the corner and slipped past the Radio Room and glanced in; she was right: Duba was gone. She hurried past the door of the now-deserted conference room and approached the closed door of the Warden's office. Softly she tapped; she had seen him leave, but then he might have returned. There was no answering call.

Breathlessly she tried the door handle, and it opened with a loud snap. She slipped in and pushed the door to, but not till it clicked. Duba would be returning soon, and she wanted to leave the office without making a sound; it would look shut from the outside unless it was inspected closely.

Quickly she crossed the room to the desk and looked around. There it was, under the large ashtray. She slid the papers out from under the improvised paperweight and found that she had two lists: one titled *Rhino & Elephant Aerial Count,* the other labeled *Anti-Poaching Campaign.*

Hardly daring to breathe, she scanned both, and her attention was drawn to the second paper: *Field Forces on hand: 10 units (recall those on leave). Expected reinforcements: Anti-Poaching Special Forces, Field Forces (other parks). Roadblocks: positions/rotation. Co-op personnel: police, C.I.D.* She didn't need to read further. This was what she needed.

Quickly she snatched up a pencil and a blank piece of paper and began to copy down the information.

DAVID STEPPED DRIPPING from the shower and began briskly to dry himself off as he hummed a Masai song he'd learned from his mother; the same one she used to hum to herself contentedly as she moved about the hut doing her work while he had played by himself on the floor.

Opening the medicine cabinet, he reached for the *mswaki* with which he brushed his teeth. He'd never liked the bristly plastic things he'd had to use in America, so even though they were also sold in the Nairobi chemist's shops, he preferred to use a twig, the end of which he had chewed until the fibers formed a brush. It left his mouth feeling clean, but not scoured.

Looking into the mirror, he considered whether or not he would shave. Like most Africans, he didn't need to scrape off his slowly sprouting whiskers daily; usually once every three or four days was enough, and he'd last shaved the day before yesterday. He grinned self-consciously at himself as he decided to shave again before going to Halima's for dinner.

He carried on with his song as he lathered, scraped, and washed off the last of the soap, and as he put his razor away he noticed the small bottle of after-shave lotion he'd received as a gift a long time ago, and rarely used since. Unscrewing the top, he sniffed and wrinkled his nose in distaste.

Well, he reasoned as he thought of the glossy magazine ads for men's after-shave lotions, she'll probably like it. He splashed it liberally into his hand and rubbed it over his face and neck.

Wrapping his *kikoi* around his waist, he left the bathroom, to hear an insistent banging at the front door. "Now what's wrong?" he muttered in irritation.

By the time he reached the living room the door had been answered by Bubu, and Komora Duba was inside and asking for him.

"Yes, what is it?"

"Radio message from Assistant Warden Agaran," Duba replied as he offered the radio-message form. He didn't like being the bearer of bad news, and he'd rather the Warden read the message than have to hear it aloud from him.

David snatched the paper from his hand. He knew it had to be a problem by Duba's expression, plus the fact that the message had caused him to run over from Headquarters. He was still out of breath.

Quickly he read the note, and the explosion was loud and instantaneous.

"Dammit! The bastards," he muttered. "One hundred elephant poached at once." He was in a fury, and his orders were barked in rapid succession to a dazed Duba.

"Call out all units except Unit One. Immediately. Send them to Agaran's position. Call the airfield. Tell the attendant to move out the helicopter. Have two armed rangers standing by at the airfield to accompany me. Radio Agaran and tell him I'm on my way. Have you got that?" he demanded. Duba nodded, stricken.

"Then move!" David took off past Bubu and headed for the bedroom, where he hastily flung on the dirty, discarded clothes he'd taken off only a half-hour before. As he rammed his bare feet into his boots, his mind asked a score of questions, but foremost among them was: How did the sons-of-whores get a vehicle into the Northern Area?

Snatching up his rifle and ammunition and running out of the house toward the Land-Rover he'd left parked outside Headquarters, he saw that he had only an hour of daylight remaining, but there were no more oaths left in him. His growing rage had passed beyond his ability to express himself by swearing.

Unlocking the Land-Rover's door, he threw the rifle and ammunition into the seat and got in to start the engine. Glancing about, he saw that his sunglasses weren't there. He must have left them in his office, and he'd be flying into the setting sun. Grinding his teeth in irritation at the delay, he jumped out and ran into Headquarters.

Passing the Radio Room, he heard Duba's voice, loud in its urgency, as he called out the now-off-duty Field Force Rangers. It would be a while before the units were on their way, and the men would be in everything from half-uniform to sandals and hastily grabbed *kikois,* but they'd be armed and moving as soon as possible.

Soundlessly flinging open his office door, he stopped and stared in surprise before growling, "What are you doing here?"

BUBU FINISHED THE LAST of the stew left over from the night before and thought about the conversation he'd overheard less than an hour ago between Corporal Lugumba and Warden Karanja, and his earlier self-satisfied smile returned.

After putting the dirty dishes in the sink, he went out the back door into the garden to the toolshed and got the yard broom made of twigs lashed to a pole with strips of black inner tube. Slipping off his sandals and walking barefoot over the grass, he passed around the house to the front and down the driveway to the road that led to the Headquarters building nearby. Glancing toward Head-quarters, he saw that the Warden's Land-Rover was missing from its parking place. The Warden was gone and must be at the airfield by now, he guessed, and ready to leave for the place where the assistant warden had found all those poached carcasses that he'd heard mentioned in the radio message. He shook his head in bewilderment: one hundred elephants. The enormous number was nearly beyond his comprehension.

He began to sweep the dirt driveway carefully, and a cloud of dust soon rose, through which flew the occasional small rock or leaf. As he worked his way up toward the house, he left the dirt behind clean and free of all marks except for the small scratches left by the broom and the prints of his bare feet. Working around the front yard and the sides of the house, he soon reached the back garden, and the dirt continued to fly in dusty puffs, accompanied by the scratching sound of the dry twigs brushing over the soil. He slowly worked his way up and down the garden between the rows of green growing things and around the trees, and he paid particular atten-tion to the area around his small house by the back fence.

When he had finished, he paused and glanced around to survey his handiwork. The Warden's house now stood in a carefully mani-cured setting of lawn and garden, and only his bare footprints remained on the ground where before there had been telltale tracks that could say too much if noticed.

Returning to the toolshed, he put away the yard broom and hunted about until he located a cardboard box containing small tools and the strips of old inner tube that were good for a hundred household uses, plus a large piece of rubber tire tread. Taking the tire tread and a hammer and a pair of pliers, he left the shed and picked up his old pair of sandals from where he'd kicked them off on the grass before proceeding to his little house.

Sitting down, he took up the pliers and began to remove the nails that held the straps to his old pair of sandals, and when he was done he used the old sandal sole as a pattern, to which he cut new soles from the piece of tire tread. This done, he compared the old soles with the new ones and smiled in satisfaction. They were nothing alike, since the tire from which the new ones were fashioned was different from that of the old. He quickly hammered the old straps onto the new soles and tried on the result. They were perfect.

After returning the hammer and pliers to the toolshed, he got a shovel and returned to the garden, where he began to dig a deep hole near the back fence by the banana trees, and into this he dropped the incriminating sandal soles, the soles which could link him to the carcass and to the house in town. After filling up the hole and replacing the shovel in the shed, he dragged out the hosepipe and hooked it to the garden faucet and began to carefully water the banana trees. He was very proud of the way he cared for the Warden's garden.

DR. JEFF FORBES sat on a tall stool beside the wide counter that ran along the length of the Research Center's laboratory and studied the map spread out before him. Periodically he would refer to the clipboard he held in his left hand, as he rapidly made notations and figured on a piece of scrap paper while muttering to himself in meaningless grunts and murmurs.

The other scientists and research assistants had left more than two hours before, but Jeff had been mentally nibbling at the same problem for two days, and he'd decided that he couldn't go home and relax until he answered some of the questions that nagged at him.

Hearing the door open, he growled out without looking, "Go away."

"I will not" came the spirited reply.

His features relaxed from irritated concentration into a half-smile as he felt Audrey's hand on his shoulder.

"Hello, there," she said.

He grunted pleasantly and chewed on the end of his pencil as he continued to study the figures before him. After a few more scribbled notations, he flung down the pencil and rubbed his eyes. He had his answer. And he didn't like it.

Audrey began to massage his tense shoulders and neck muscles through the white lab coat he had on: his badge of identity, as he called it; so that the visiting dignitaries would immediately know who the ringmaster of the Research circus was.

"What are you doing?" she asked.

"Trying to answer a question that doesn't really have a definite answer yet."

"What's the question?"

He hesitated for a moment before answering, "Why aren't the elephant continuing to die off from the drought?"

She stopped the massage and moved to his side to study his face before asking, "Are you serious?"

"Perfectly," he sighed.

"I don't understand."

"Neither did I, my dear, and that's the point." He sat and frowned at the map before him and at the paper covered with scrawled figures before continuing: "I've just been over the mortality figures for the past several months, and I'm seeing the reason for an inconsistency we noticed before when we were trying to analyze the fatalities and come up with a projected figure for the total estimated die-off.

"It's like this"—he reached for a clean scrap of paper and began to write across the top: *1976—short rains,* and then *1977—long rains.* Up the left side of the paper he jotted, *10 . . . 20 . . . 30 . . .* and on.

"Now," he said. "In the eastern area of the park, the short rains failed at the end of 1976, and the drought fatalities began with the first recorded deaths of some very old rhino and elephant, plus the odd calf or two." He began to draw a line, illustrating the number of deaths that occurred during the last two months of 1976, and the pencil began to climb higher as the deaths escalated during the beginning of 1977.

"During the short, hot dry season, the deaths rose, and then fell back during April and May in the long rainy season of '77, because a few showers fell there and temporarily alleviated the situation." The pencil line began to dip again before resuming its climb. "However, it was a short-lived respite, because the showers were too few, and very soon what little vegetation there was was consumed. So the death rate began to increase during the succeeding dry season, and now some calves and a few lactating females began to die as well as the old."

Audrey watched as Jeff's pencil climbed higher: 30, 40, 50 fatalities per month, and still the line rose through the long dry-season months of June and July.

"Now, on the basis of my calculations, this is what should be happening"—and he consulted his notes and figures before filling in the graph for the months of August, September, and October.

When he finished, he asked, "What do you see?"

Audrey studied the graph a moment before replying, "Well, it looks as if the number of deaths is much higher." She compared the long dry season of 1977 with the long dry season of 1976. "See. The fatalities are twice as many or more each month, as compared with last year during the same period of time."

"Why?" he asked.

"I suppose because of the length of the drought. The very old and very young animals are getting weaker and less able to find enough to keep alive. Besides, the vegetation is getting worse in the east every month."

He nodded quietly. "That's right, and that's what we've been basing our projected figures on. But," he added as he tapped the graph, "I said that this is what *should* be happening—not what *is* happening."

Snatching up a red-leaded pencil, he began to draw another line from August through October, and when he was done he said, "Those are the actual recorded deaths for the past three months."

She was amazed. Finally she blurted out, "But they're much lower! In fact"—she paused to compare the graph lines—"in August they're only a fraction of what they should be, and in October they've stopped."

She turned to him in perplexity. "Why?"

"That's the same damn question we've been asking ourselves," he replied in irritation with himself. "And the answer is obvious, but we couldn't see it for the drought. In fact, that's all we did see—the drought. We checked rainfall records and we wrung our hands. We raced around in the bush collecting mandibles and tusks from animals dead of starvation in the drought-stricken areas of the park, and as scientists we never looked beyond our noses at the rest of the park. We barely," he added in frustrated contempt, "had time to record instances of elephant obviously poached in the drought areas, because after all," he snorted, "*that's* not *our* concern."

He was nearly breathless with anger. "But we did manage to record those animals riddled with arrowheads and bullets, although we never bothered to analyze them.

"At least," he continued, "until now."

Audrey reached out and placed her hand on his arm. He didn't notice. She was alarmed; she'd never seen him so upset. It was true that he was volatile and outspoken at times, but never like this, not distraught. Not filled with anger at himself; she sensed that there had never been a need before.

She heard him murmur softly, "The worst part of it is that he has relied on us."

"Who, dear?" she asked.

"David," he replied, looking at her abjectly. "He relies on the Research Center for the scientific *why* of things, in order to make many of his decisions, and we let him down. Or rather," he corrected himself, "*I* let him down; and I've let him down very badly."

"Please," she urged him, "explain. I don't understand."

He passed his hand over his face, and after a moment he asked, "What would be the result of my bringing home five or six people unexpectedly for dinner when you've planned a meal for just the two of us?"

"I'd kill you," she promptly replied in an effort to lift him out of his mood, and she was rewarded with a half-smile of understanding.

"Seriously," he reminded her.

"Well, there wouldn't be enough food."

"So we'd all get a little, but not enough," he added, "and so we'd all be a bit hungry."

She nodded.

"What, then, if they changed their minds and decided not to stay for dinner after all, and they left?"

"Why, then we'd be back to dinner for two and there would be enough."

"That's right," he said, and his eyes bored holes into her.

"I'm sorry," she said, "I still don't see."

"All right, look at it this way," he said. "During the past year and a half we've had an almost complete failure of two rainy seasons in the east, and consequently the vegetation there has failed to regenerate normally. Brief isolated showers in places brought a flush of green periodically, which was quickly consumed. It's like your dinner I mentioned: only enough for a few thousand, and more than thirty-five thousand came to dinner."

"I see," she said slowly. "So the rest are going hungry."

"That's right: they're going hungry to the point of starving to death. Now, the longer the drought continues, the longer they go hungry, the more animals eventually succumb to the cumulative effects of continued starvation. That's why the monthly mortalities now should be so much higher than this time last year, and it's why the fatalities for each succeeding dry month should climb higher than the month before. But it isn't happening."

Audrey studied the red line on the graph before venturing, "It appears that perhaps there are fewer coming to dinner so there is more for the others, and now the death toll is dropping."

She looked up at her husband, who was studying her closely. He removed the white lab coat and handed it to her; she took it and folded it neatly over her arm, her perplexity registering itself on her face.

"You obviously deserve this more than I do," he said, "and I believe you're wasted at home and hearth, my dear, because you saw the only possible reason *why*.

"It's obvious." His voice rose. "The reason they aren't dying is because there are damn few left to compete for the little remaining vegetation."

Audrey watched him quietly as he lapsed into silence, and she saw that this was not one of the periodic frustrations of the scientific career; this was a confrontation with a failure. She hesitated, afraid of offering a word or gesture that would appear to him to be a face-saving placebo, and yet her first impulse was to reach out, to comfort. She wanted to remind him of all that he had done in the past, affirm his cleverness and deny that anyone would have done better. But she didn't because she knew he'd turn away, and so she bit her lip to hold the words back and felt her long nails press into the palms of her hands. When he finally turned back to face her, she said the only thing she could think of to say: "I'm sorry."

"What?" he asked softly as his eyes explored her face.

"I'm sorry that you didn't see it before."

His miserable expression softened a little, and then he said, "Thank you." He paused and smiled. "I'm sorry too."

His arm stole around her, and he stood quietly beside her while his mind began to collect the pieces of facts, known and guessed at, to arrange neatly like interlocking puzzle pieces, and she saw that he'd accepted his previous failure and was beginning the rebound to continue his search for solutions, without wasting valuable time on pointless self-recrimination. That would come later. She stretched up and kissed his cheek.

"What was that, a consolation prize?" he asked in mock severity.

"No, love. Consolation prizes are only for the losers."

They stayed together, each with an arm around the other.

"I have a question." Her voice came muffled from where he'd buried her head against his chest.

Relaxing his arm, he asked, "What?"

"How many have died from the drought?"

"Roughly four to five hundred."

"Is that enough to enable the survivors to find sufficient food to stay alive?"

"Absolutely not," he said emphatically. "A decrease of five hundred elephant is nowhere near the necessary drop in population that would account for this kind of recovery. No"—he shook his head—"the gradual decline in fatalities that we've noticed has reached such proportions that it can be accounted for in only one of two ways: either by heavy rainfall in scattered areas which would result in a marked regeneration of the vegetation, or—"

"But that hasn't happened, has it?" she interrupted.

"No, it hasn't," he answered. "So by a process of elimination I arrived at the only possible answer. Yours."

"Mine?"

"It looks as if fewer are coming to dinner."

"How many fewer?"

"Thousands." He thought carefully before venturing a suspicion only hesitantly confronted in his mind. "Many thousands."

"Good Lord, Jeff!" she exclaimed. "You're not serious!" She watched his face and waited, and the silence confirmed that he was. "But where are they?" she finally asked. "If they aren't in the park, where have they gone?"

"That's the question I mentioned earlier, the question that doesn't yet have an answer. There are two possibilities"—he sighed —"and I'm hoping the answer is that they've migrated."

"Where?"

"South into Tanzania, north to the Tana River, or perhaps just to the western section of the park."

"You don't seem very positive about that possibility."

"I'm not—because I'm afraid they're too weak and malnourished to travel far, and mainly because they've appeared to be disinclined to move far from the dry-season areas they're accustomed to. Still, it's possible they may have been forced to migrate because of the extreme drought here now. I don't know, but I'm left wondering why we've had no reported sightings of large numbers of elephant on the move; someone, somewhere, would have noticed it. No," he said, shaking his head, "I'm desperately afraid that they haven't migrated."

"Then where are they?"

"If they didn't migrate out of the area, then they must still be here, and if they *are* here, they are no longer competing for the little remaining vegetation; which means that they must be dead."

"Dead?" she asked. "But how?" And then the realization dawned on her: "You don't mean to say they've been poached? Not that many?" Her voice was incredulous.

"I'm afraid that it's a distinct possibility," he replied, "and that's why I've let David down. I should have realized that a declining rate of fatalities indicated that there were many fewer animals competing for the existing remnants of the vegetation, and perhaps something could have been done sooner. As it is, we never saw, we never suspected—because we couldn't get past the drought. We blamed everything on the drought and we never realized that the poaching had become so much worse."

"How many do you think are gone due to poaching?"

He shook his head. "I'm almost afraid to estimate. Not having an airplane here has crippled our power to observe what's going on. I can only guess."

"Then guess, please. I would like to know how bad it might be."

After a moment's hesitation he said, "I'm afraid that there might be somewhere between five and ten thousand elephant poached."

She was shocked, and for a moment she stared at him in disbelief.

"Not fewer than five thousand, or more than ten," he continued, "because fewer than five thousand would not really affect the drought die-off, and not more than ten because I cannot conceive of such a thing." He looked up at her, and she saw the desperate anguish on his face.

"My God," she whispered, and she felt her heart sink inside. Her expression was a mirror of his own, and she said finally, as if it were a prayer, "For the first time ever, Jeff, I desperately hope you're wrong."

DAVID LISTENED TO the 'copter blades as they ceased their furious whirling and began to slowly wind down. He couldn't see the blades, but he was conscious of their subsiding revolutions. Landing after dark was not his favorite exercise, but sometimes it was necessary, like tonight. At least the helicopter was easier to put down in late dusk without instruments than was the plane.

Releasing his seat belt and removing his earphones, he addressed the two rangers—"*Sawa-sawa*"—and indicated that they could un-buckle their belts.

He noticed that the ranger beside him was fumbling ineffec-tually, so he leaned over and released the buckle, and the man shot out of the 'copter to wobble off on shaky legs.

Only a handful of rangers had ever been in a plane or helicopter before, and the first time they were singled out to accompany the

Warden they wavered between high excitement and sheer terror. A year ago, he'd had the misfortune to draw an individual who had finally roused himself from his paralytic terror, after lifting off, to decide that he'd had enough and that he wanted out and he wanted out right then; the fact that the 'copter was one hundred feet off the ground and traveling at seventy knots didn't seem to matter. David had at once become aware of the furious struggle going on behind him as the second ranger attempted to subdue his wall-eyed companion, and he had had barely enough time to clear a tree and plop down in the nearest small clearing before the terrified ranger wrenched himself free to fall the last twelve feet into a thornbush, where he promptly passed out cold.

From that time on, David had drawn two rangers from a pool of ten who took turns accompanying the Warden in either plane or helicopter, and who had all become used to flying.

Unfortunately, this evening Duba had sent the first two Field Force Rangers he'd got hold of, and David had seen that familiar look of panic in the man's eyes as soon as he approached the 'copter, so he'd put that ranger beside him, where he could keep an eye on him. Thankfully, this one hadn't tried to jump.

He continued to sit in the helicopter after the departure of the two rangers, his mind returning to the scene he'd left north of the Lalaga Lana River. The extent of the massacre had shaken him. As he'd approached the area in the 'copter and circled slowly, the incredible number of carcasses below had had the effect of numbing his senses. He had counted 107 carcasses, and the magnitude of the slaughter went beyond his ability to feel anything but despair.

As he flew over the area, disturbing the squawking and hissing vultures whose white droppings had begun to stripe the carcasses they collected on, he had noticed that an effort had been made to pile cut brush onto the fallen elephants. Several had been nearly obscured with brush and dirt, others only partially covered; it was apparent that the poachers had started to conceal the bodies and either had been frightened off by approaching aircraft headed for the coast, or had simply given up their efforts because of the sheer number of carcasses and the obvious devastation in the vicinity of the slaughter which no amount of brush could cover. It made him wonder how many other concealed graveyards there might be scattered throughout the park, yet to be discovered.

He opened the door, and after retrieving his rifle from where he'd strapped it down under his seat, he began to walk toward his parked Land-Rover. Agaran had shown him the tracks of both men and vehicles, and together they had estimated that the gang of poachers numbered approximately eight to ten men in two four-wheel-drive vehicles. All together, some forty-six Field Force Rangers had been rounded up from the various off-duty units, and Agaran had deployed them along the road to follow the deep tracks of the poachers' overloaded vehicles, while David did what he could in scouting the area from the air. Unfortunately, darkness had forced him back to the airfield all too soon, but the ground units would continue on as long as possible, and then sleep on the track tonight in order to be off again as soon as possible at dawn.

Once more he considered the implications of the incident. The snatching of over a hundred elephants by poachers armed with sophisticated rifles and possessing vehicles indicated that these people considered themselves a match for his forces, if not superior to them. And that kind of boldness could come only from knowing David's limitations. They had to know that he was without the means to carry out daily aerial reconnaissance; they would never have dared to bring vehicles into the park otherwise. They also had to be pretty damn sure that no Field Force Units were in the area at the time, because somewhere between two and three hundred rounds of ammunition had been expended back on those kopjes, and it must have sounded like a full-scale war. They hadn't been in any hurry, either. Not one carcass had been overlooked; all the ivory was gone. They hadn't wasted time, but they hadn't been in a rush to get away, and that could be accounted for only by the fact that they felt safe because they knew that there was no plane to spot them and no rangers bivouacked nearby to hear and respond to the shots.

Getting into the Land-Rover, he put the rifle on the seat and lit a cigarette before starting the engine. He recalled the meeting this morning, and he remembered the first feeling of suspicion when he'd been discussing patrol movements and how they seemed to have been anticipated, and again he saw Margaret's frightened face as he'd last seen it when he'd returned to his office for his sunglasses.

"The little bitch," he muttered between clenched teeth. Again he marveled at his own stupidity as he recalled the scene earlier that morning with the radio message redirecting Units 1 and 4, and how she'd avidly opened and read it right before him, and still he hadn't seen, hadn't suspected her.

Starting the car, he pulled away from the airfield and turned toward Headquarters while his barely contained anger seared inside him.

Pulling up behind Headquarters, he parked and went directly into the Radio Room, where Duba stood by his radios waiting. He knew that Duba had been on duty since 6 A.M. and should have left at 6 P.M., after his shift, and yet he'd waited because he'd known that the Field Forces were out and that David was in the air, and the night guards would not have been as effective in his place.

"*Asante sana*," he said.

Duba jumped up to salute and grin deprecatingly.

"I want you to arrange for food and extra ammunition to be sent out to the Field Forces first thing in the morning."

"Yes, sir."

"Where is Margaret?"

"In the armory under guard, sir, as you ordered."

"Who knows about her presence here tonight?"

"Only myself and the sergeant, sir." He paused. "One of the Gate Rangers came by about seven and asked about her. I didn't know what to say, so I told him I didn't know where she was. I said that I hadn't seen her since this afternoon."

"Good," replied David. "I don't want anyone to know anything about her being detained, so don't mention it in the staff quarters. Not to anyone. Do you understand?"

"Yes, sir."

"Now tell the sergeant I want Margaret brought to my office, and then see about the ammunition and food; I want it to leave here by four o'clock tomorrow morning, so arrange for a vehicle and driver tonight. After that's done you can turn over to the guards, but check in with me before you leave."

He turned as if to leave, hesitated, and then turned back to Duba to ask, "Who was the ranger who asked about Margaret?"

"Wambua Mulolo," responded Duba.

"He's on the Main Gate, isn't he?"

"Yes, sir."

David remembered the man; a Kamba. He'd not particularly liked him the few times he'd seen him around. There was something about his attitude that irritated.

"That's all, Duba."

"Very good, sir."

David passed into his office and flipped on the light, to see Mdomo hunched over his perch on the back of David's chair. Slipping his forefinger under the sleepy bird's chest, he felt the small talons grip, and he transferred the blinking bird to the edge of the IN box, where Mdomo obligingly stepped off, and where, after another blink or two, he went back to sleep. Sitting down, David drew the notes he'd made that afternoon toward him, along with the nearly finished copy Margaret had been scribbling, and as he studied them he heard the door open, to admit Sergeant Lemboko and his typist.

Glancing up, he watched coldly as Margaret approached to stand beside his desk. Her legs shook so that she visibly quaked on her feet. Her hand reached out to the table for support. Wordlessly, he indicated the chair nearest her, and she sank into it, covering her face with her hands.

David turned to Lemboko. "What has she said?"

"Nothing, sir; she hasn't spoken since you left."

David nodded. "Stand guard outside, and don't mention this to anyone."

"Yes, sir."

The door shut with its familiar click behind the departing sergeant while David inspected the top of Margaret's bowed head. He had an almost overwhelming desire to break her thin neck.

All these months, he thought, she's been . . . and then he stopped. She'd been here for only three months or so. After considering that fact for a moment, he weighed what he knew of the girl and calculated how best to find out the reason and purpose behind her spying on the activities of the Field Force.

After a moment he barked out, "Look at me!"

Her trembling hands withdrew from her face and dropped into her lap. Slowly her head came up from its bowed position until she faced him, with averted eyes that clung to the floor. Her skin was a ghastly shade of wet ash, and her features were set in a deadened, vacant expression. Nervously her tongue licked over dry lips that quivered before being caught and held by her teeth.

"I said, look at me," he repeated.

With an obvious effort she slid her eyes up from the floor to David's face, and a shuddering moan broke from her; tears began to course down her face, and her hands clutched and wrung at each other.

"Why?" he demanded.

Her features were convulsed with fear, and her body twisted in agony. She was very close to hysteria.

He slammed his hand on the desk before her and bellowed, "Answer me!"

Her closed eyes flew open and her squirming ceased abruptly at the sound of flesh slapping the wood before her. Her huge eyes stared unblinkingly into his face. "He . . ." she murmured, and broke down.

This time his fist hit the table, and the sound rattled the windows as he roared in Swahili, *"Sema!"*

"He told me . . . he . . . Oh, he will," she stuttered, "be angry." Her hand went to her mouth in fear. Whether fear of him or fear of talking, David didn't know, but he'd had an idea.

Leaning forward, he put his face close to hers and growled out, "Mulolo will—what?" Her widening eyes locked with his, and he knew he was right.

"What did Mulolo tell you?" he probed. "Why will he be angry?"

Then she broke. Gibbering a stream of disjointed words and phrases, she babbled out a story that made no sense at all to him, but certain words were clear, and they struck home to convey something of a woman's loneliness and fear. He let her go on and on, and slowly it began to make some sort of sense.

In spite of himself he pitied her. She was an ugly little thing and obviously believed some incredible nonsense about Mulolo wanting to join the Field Force when all the time he'd been pumping her for information. He sat and watched her as he pieced together the bits and pieces she'd told him. Many things were becoming clear in his mind. After a moment he started to rummage about in his desk until he found what he was looking for. Handing her the battered box of paper tissues, he poured a glass of water and set it before her.

She wiped her face and drank the water, and he saw that she was beginning to calm down. There was a tap at the door and David called out, "*Karibu.*"

The door opened and David saw Duba's alarmed face peering in timidly. He realized that from outside it must sound as if he'd been beating her to death.

"Come in and shut the door," he commanded.

Duba did as he was told, and hesitantly approached the front of the desk, studiously avoiding looking at Margaret.

"Yes, sir?"

"You live in the staff quarters near Margaret, don't you?"

"Yes, sir."

"How long has Mulolo been coming around to see her?"

Duba thought for a moment before replying, "I think, ever since she came."

"I see," he said, and glanced over at the girl, who had now resumed staring at the floor.

"Tell me, has Mulolo paid much attention to any other woman in the staff quarters that you know of?"

"Only Emma, sir."

"Emma Ndumo?"

"Yes, sir."

David reached for his keys and handed them to Duba. "Go into the accountant's office and get me Mulolo's personal file."

After he left, David turned to the girl and said, "Margaret, do you know who Emma was?"

She looked up at him and shook her head. "No," she whispered.

Duba returned with the file and keys. "*Asante*. You can go now, Duba. And remember, I don't want you to mention Margaret's being here tonight."

"Yes, sir." He saluted and left.

David quickly read the information pertaining to the Gate Ranger before saying to Margaret, "Emma Ndumo was my typist before you came here."

She looked up at him with large wounded eyes that seemed not to understand the significance of what he said.

He continued, "Did you know that he was married?"

Mutely she shook her head as her eyes welled tears that refused to fall.

"Of course," David went on, "there's no reason why he can't take two, even three, wives if he can afford to; but still, he might have mentioned to you that he already had one." She continued to stare at him in dumb misery.

"However," he went on, "I don't believe that he's interested in my typists as potential wives. I think he's interested only in the information they might have." He waited. "What do you think, Margaret?"

He saw the understanding flicker and grow in her dark eyes and he knew that it hurt, and again he was aware of the fact that his anger was going and pity had come to take its place. He'd seen animals in snares that looked as she did now. He felt uncomfortable, and it was he who finally looked away to stare at the floor while he wondered what he was going to do with her.

There was no doubt in his mind about her complicity. She had admitted to telling Mulolo the daily patrols assigned to each Field Unit, plus any other related information concerning the Field Force, besides both his own and Assistant Warden Agaran's movements. It was obvious that Mulolo knew as much about the Anti-Poaching Forces as he himself did; but what was more important to him was the question of who knew besides Mulolo. Obviously he was selling the information, and it was the buyer whom David wanted most of all. He'd have to leave the smug little bastard at the gate until later. But how to get to the buyer?

He glanced back at Margaret, who continued to sit and mutely watch him, and again he wondered what to do with her. He could call in the sergeant to have her removed to the jail in town, where she'd be held and booked, and she'd eventually be found guilty and sentenced—and for what? He knew she'd been Mulolo's eyes and ears, and yet he was equally positive that she hadn't known what he did with the information.

No, he wouldn't send her off tonight to the police station; but yet he couldn't send her home either. Mulolo would come looking for her, and as yet he wanted the Gate Ranger to be unaware that he was under suspicion. He couldn't take her home with him, so what? . . . and then he thought of Halima. Perhaps she could . . . He stopped and quickly glanced at his watch. It was almost nine, and he'd completely forgotten about dinner. Inwardly he groaned. That did it; the end of a perfect day.

He abruptly made up his mind. He'd take her to Halima and see if she could be kept there for a day or so while he considered what to do with her. It was possible that she'd be of some use, but first he wanted to see what was going on behind those wounded eyes.

"Margaret."

Her gaze was still glued to his face.

"Do you understand what you've done?"

She nodded, and the tip of her tongue flicked out to lick her lower lip.

"Do you see that Mulolo was using you to find out where the Field Force Units were deployed?" She nodded, mute.

"Do you know that this information would be valuable to some people? Do you understand now why he came to you?"

Her staring eyes finally fell, and she seemed to slowly shrink into herself as she took a deep shuddering breath. Her attitude too plainly said, "Yes, I know. I'm not pretty and I suppose I knew he wasn't really interested in me, didn't really care about me, but I hoped. Yes, I hoped." Her mouth trembled like a child's, and a tear slipped down her frozen face. She nodded; her "Yes" was whispered.

After a long moment she straightened up and wiped away the last of her tears; he watched as a muscle jumped wildly in the small jaw. She turned to face him and said, "I am sorry." She hesitated a moment to collect herself and to will the trembling mouth still, then plunged on: "I wanted . . . I wanted to please him."

She sat straight, and he had to admire her just a little. It wasn't much of an explanation, but he understood.

"Do you still want to please him, Margaret?" he asked softly.

She seemed to consider this question for a time, and her eyes turned inward upon her thoughts. Whatever she saw there served to calm her. Her head shook slowly from side to side in a measured and deliberate motion as her opaque eyes and her voice returned to normal.

"No," she said. "No, I don't." Her eyes met his, and her gaze was direct. He knew that she was telling the truth.

He nodded. "Good. I've been thinking about what to do with

you," he said. "Do you realize that I could turn you over to the police?"

"Yes," she replied. She didn't flinch; she didn't implore him. Her answer was candid and without emotion.

"I don't want to have to do that, though."

She said nothing; she only watched him.

"And yet I can't send you home either, because he'll come looking for you, and I don't want him to know that we've had this talk together."

Her eyes probed his face for the meaning behind his words; a small wrinkle appeared between her brows to indicate her concentration.

"It's possible," he added, "that you can undo some of what you've done. You may be of some use to me. I haven't decided how yet, but we have an advantage over Mulolo because we both know now what he's doing, only he doesn't know that we know. I'd like to use that advantage if I can."

Understanding began to flicker over her face. She nodded, and a small smile pulled at the corners of her mouth. She obviously didn't know exactly how she could be of help, but the will to try was there.

"We'll think about it tonight and discuss it together tomorrow." He knew he was taking a chance, but it wasn't a big one. She might run, but he didn't think so; she might warn Mulolo, but that was even less likely. There was something about little Margaret in the last few moments: he didn't know what it was—perhaps an indication of strength not noticed before; and because of it he liked her better.

"I'm going to take you over to Miss Abdi's house. I think you can stay there tonight." He watched her closely, then asked, "Will you promise not to try to run away? And not to speak of this to Mulolo?"

"I promise." Her voice was stronger now, and more definite than he'd ever heard it. There was a strength of purpose behind it. He wondered what it was.

She hesitated and then added, "I would like to help."

He nodded and smiled. "Let's go."

After dismissing the sergeant with a reminder to keep quiet about Margaret's presence and her short incarceration in the armory, he proceeded to the Land-Rover with her trailing behind him. During the short drive to Halima's neither of them spoke, and David wondered about his reception. Halima might slam the door in his face, but he hoped not. Arriving at the house, he said to Margaret, "Stay here. I'll be back."

He walked up the path and was relieved to see the lights on inside; at least she hadn't gone to bed yet. He tapped at the door, and after a few moments it opened as the porch light went on.

Obviously not expecting callers so late at night, she was wearing a dressing gown, and for a moment she stood there in the doorway taking in his filthy, sweat-stained uniform and sheepish expression. Then she smiled, and her hand came up to hide her sudden amusement. "You're just a little late for dinner, Warden."

"I'm sorry," he said, relieved. It was going to be all right. "But I've had a few problems."

She opened the door wider. "Come in and tell me."

She sat on the sofa and listened sympathetically. When he'd finished explaining about the poachers in the Northern Area and Margaret's indiscreet babbling, she asked, "Where is she now?"

"Waiting outside."

"Do you think you can trust her, David?"

He considered for a moment before saying, "Yes, I believe I can."

"All right, you bring her in and I'll get the sheets for the guest room." She smiled and left the room.

After Margaret was settled into the spare bedroom, a beer appeared on the low table before the armchair where he sat.

"You sit there and drink your beer while I heat up the dinner," she said as she tied on an apron over her robe.

He started to protest: "It's too late, too much of a bother."

She smiled at him and shook her head. "It won't take long, and you must be hungry." Forestalling any further argument, she added as she went into the kitchen, "Besides, if you don't eat it I'll be stuck with leftovers all week and then I will be angry with you."

He chuckled to himself, and then for the first time in hours he allowed himself to lean back and relax. He was tired; tired but comfortable, and the beer revived him somewhat. He listened to the domestic sounds in the kitchen in contentment, and then a remembered conversation teased his memory. What was it? Oh, yes, something Vera Batey had said, something like "What you need is a woman . . . to see that you get a warm meal at whatever hour you get in."

He smiled. She was right.

BUBU DOZED. Half awake at times, he listened, and hearing nothing, he nodded off again.

The sound of an approaching vehicle registered on his consciousness, and he became alert to listen in the darkness behind closed eyes. It came closer, and he heard the hum of the engine increase, and soon the crunch of tires rolling over the rough, rocky driveway became audible. As the Land-Rover pulled into the confinement of the carport, the sound of the engine increased, then ceased abruptly. The car door slammed, and soon the garden gate squeaked open, then shut with a click. He heard the muffled footsteps on the flag-stones, and after a moment the sound of the back door opening and closing.

He sat up immediately and with his flashlight he checked his old battered clock. It was ten thirty; still early. He was satisfied that he had plenty of time. Moving to his small front window, he looked out across the yard to David's bedroom window just as the light there went on, closely followed by the adjoining bathroom light.

Bubu went back across the room and picked up the charcoal brazier he rarely used—he usually took his meals in the main-house kitchen—and carried it to the far side of his quarters beneath the large window at the back of his little one-room house. He soon had an intensely hot charcoal fire blazing, and he returned to the small window in front which afforded an excellent view of the back of David's house. The bathroom light in the big house was out now, and he stood and watched until the adjoining bedroom light blinked out as well, to leave the Warden's house in darkness.

Drawing the thick curtain across his window, Bubu turned to the bed, from under which he drew the clay cooking pot. Settling it onto the brazier beneath the open window, he checked to see that the fire was hot and steady before noiselessly opening his door and stepping out into the garden. Shutting the door, he squatted down on his heels and pulled the stopper from the small gourd of snuff that hung around his neck. Taking a liberal pinch of the dark, pungent powder, he placed it under his lower lip and began his nightlong vigil.

There was little smoke from the charcoal fire, but the boiling poison would soon produce a *kali* smell, which was why he'd decided to wait until everyone had gone to sleep before proceeding. Not that anyone would be likely to notice it: the Warden's house was west of Headquarters and behind; no one lived near; besides, the breeze tonight was blowing briskly, to effectively disperse any lingering fumes escaping through the back window.

For a moment he was tempted to be pleased with his audacity, but he rejected the idea as foolish. He hadn't survived as long as he had by taking unnecessary chances. Tonight was a necessity, and an unfortunate one, but the possibility of discovery was very slim indeed, and he knew it; otherwise he would not have dared boil down the poison here.

He considered the reason that demanded he hunt again. He'd stopped two years ago when the new Warden came. He hadn't really needed the money for years, not since his wife had died and the children had scattered like dust on the wind. He'd kept it up only because of the old anger; the anger at the *Wazungu* who had taken the land and the animals for their park, for themselves.

It had not been theirs to take, he'd reasoned. It was not no one's land; it was the land of the Waliangulu. True, they had not planted crops as the Kamba had; and no, his people did not keep vast herds of cattle like the Masai; but it was their land all the same, and he had often said to himself: Just the fact that we did not put our mark on the land does not mean it was not ours.

But since those who apportioned the land had seen differently, his anger had demanded that he continue to hunt and take the ivory he didn't need, for the land was still his to roam over and the elephants still his to take, and he would not let the *Wazungu* forget.

He'd been immediately interested when he heard that the Warden, Nichols, wanted another man to work at the big house for him and the *Memsaab*. He'd gone to see about this job, and his hiring had made it possible for him to hear much of what was going on inside the park whose boundaries tried to shut him out, and he was pleased that he not only hunted there, but now he lived there as well, and the shortsighted *Bwana* never knew because he never really looked at any of the people; he never really saw them.

Time passed, and the changes came so slowly that Bubu had not foreseen the inevitable result. The young assistant wardens were more and more often Africans, not Europeans; but still the Warden himself was not, and so he continued to hunt because he had always done so. And then the day came when the ailing Nichols received his long-hoped-for retirement, and the new Warden came to take his position, his park, and his house.

When Bubu saw David Karanja, he knew that his hunting days were over; his anger had cooled with time, and now the reasons for his anger were gone as well. The Warden of Aruba, the *Bwana Mkubwa,* the big boss who oversaw the park and everyone in it, was African, and so it could no longer be said to belong to the *Wazungu*. It seemed that the *Wazungu* wardens had merely kept it for a while, until it reverted to the people to whom it belonged. True, it did not come back to the Waliangulu; but then, how could it? They were gone now. After thirty years they were no more a people, and how can the land be given back to those who no longer exist?

So the reasons for his anger were no longer there to motivate him to do what the passing of years had made more difficult. He was growing old and was only waiting for the natural end of a life that had already outlived its people and its time. He ceased to hunt and stayed on in the only home he had left to him, and after a time he began to take an interest in the new Warden. He was young; young enough to be his son; and he was the kind of son Bubu would have liked to have.

He'd been content these last two years as he waited; he was satisfied with what little he had, and was resigned to the impossibility of demanding what could not be. He had a nice little house and all the food he needed and enough work to pass away the hours of the day, so it was not a bad way to spend the last few years of an already overlong life. Yes, he'd been content, until the woman came.

She'd come to the back door of the Warden's house six days ago and had asked for him by name: his own name—Heekuta Neko; and he'd been very thankful that he, and only he, was in the house that day. He'd quickly got her away from the main house and into his own smaller one in the back garden, and as he sat her down he'd studied her carefully and wondered how she knew of him, how she knew where he was.

She was small, slightly built, and painfully thin. Her face was drawn and tired as if now beyond the repair of rest. Her feet were bare, as was her head, and her *khanga* was ragged but clean. He could see by her tribal markings that she was Waliangulu, and she seemed familiar, yet greatly altered beyond his immediate recognition.

He wasn't really surprised to learn that she was the wife of his son Boru. It was sad to realize that of the four children born to him and Diramu, none remained. One by one they'd left, or died, and now the last and worst of all—his younger son, Boru—was gone.

He'd run off when he was a young man and after an absence of five years had returned. He'd offered no explanation of why he'd gone or where; only that he was back and needed a place to hide. Bubu had taken his son with him into the bush to hunt, and after a time he thought the boy had settled down, so Bubu had bought him a fine wife to help keep him settled.

He looked closely at the woman now before him. Yes, he decided, ten years of life with Boru could do this to a woman. Several years ago, his son had gone after a big bull while drunk, and had been brought home crushed and crippled to the woman who waited in the hut hidden on the Lalaga Lana River. Bubu had gone to him then and had helped for a while with money, but his son's constant drunkenness, and the resulting arguments, had succeeded long ago in driving him away.

Now the woman told him listlessly that Boru was dead. He'd

recovered some use of his legs and, again while drunk, had managed to climb up a doum palm to collect a gourd of the tree's tapped sap, with which he intended to make more palm wine, and had fallen headfirst onto the rocks below and killed himself.

Bubu wasn't surprised and he wasn't grieved. Looking at the wife, he saw that there was no sorrow within her either, and he briefly regretted purchasing the beautiful young girl she had been, for his son to reduce to the resigned and spiritless woman who sat before him now.

She'd come to ask him for help; she knew where what was left of her own family lived, near the Tana River, but she had no money, no way to get there.

He nodded. He understood—a woman must go to her family. He would help.

He'd drawn a map in the dirt at his feet and shown her where to meet him that night in the village, and when he'd arrived with the few hundred shillings he'd saved he saw the boy; it was Boru's young son, and obviously the only good thing he'd ever done, and Bubu knew that the few hundred shillings wouldn't be enough.

The child was only seven, but he had the look of Bubu's elder son, the one dead of fever. He had the look of Bubu himself, and he knew that this grandson was the last of his line. He knew that when the mother went he'd never see the child again; this was his last and only chance to do something for him, to be of value to him. Gone were the days when the grandfathers helped to educate the young; and besides, what had he of value to teach the bright-eyed child? To hunt? No, all he could give him was money, and he knew only one way to get it. He had to hunt again.

They waited now, in a small shelter he'd made for them outside the town. The mother had carefully buried the money he had first brought, plus the almost 3,000 shillings he'd received for the cow's ivory. He thought of the big bull with the herd across the river: soon there would be a few thousand more shillings to add to the little hoard that was to help raise the boy in the new way of things.

It wasn't much, he realized. Just a few thousand shillings. And it could not compare with the value of a father and grandfather. But of what value had Boru been? A drunken and crippled fool who was a pathetic example of what could happen to a once-proud people.

And himself? Of what value was he, except as a living memory of days past; a living relic of a way of life that was over before he himself was even born?

For a moment he regretted again the loss of the old ways; his contentment faltered, and he wished for more than was possible.

Not for himself, but for the child. It had been a good life, he knew, and because he did not understand the future, he distrusted and feared it. He would not be here to guide the boy, to lead him into manhood. He couldn't.

No, all there was was money now. It was all that had value anymore. It was all he could do for him. The money would help smooth his path; remove some of the obstacles and help him find the way to whatever the future held for one of the last of his tribe.

He thought of the bull across the sand river and nodded in resignation. Yes, he thought. It would be enough; it would be the final hunt. Getting up stiffly, he turned to reenter the small house to prepare his poison for the last time.

IV · WEDNESDAY

CHAPTER TWELVE

Morning

As David walked into his office, he quickly scanned the radio message he'd been handed as he passed by the Radio Room. It was good news for a change, and the slightly depressed feeling he'd awakened with lightened.

So far there was no word from Agaran in the Northern Area; but still, it was early. He checked his watch: seven thirty. The Field Forces would have been on the move since before six: an hour and a half. Not long enough to have come up with the poachers, if they were going to be able to catch up with them at all. He opened the folder containing yesterday's notes regarding the count operation and got back to work.

A light tap on the door announced the arrival of Jeff Forbes, who walked in with a monstrous pile of paper, which he dropped with a thump on the only cleared corner of David's desk.

"Good morning," he said cheerfully. "You look as terrible as I feel."

David smiled in spite of himself. "I've got problems," he admitted.

"Really? I can't believe it."

"It's true. Nothing much, mind you—just one or two minor irritations."

"Like what?"

"Like the discovery yesterday of a hundred and seven elephants slaughtered in one go, and a lovesick typist who's admitted blabbing the Field Force movements to someone who I believe has been selling the information to the highest bidder."

Jeff's bantering mood changed immediately. "You're not joking?"

David shook his head. "No, I couldn't joke about something like this." He smiled wryly. "Actually, my imagination is just not that fertile."

"I'm sorry," Jeff muttered as he sat down. "Tell me about it."

David briefly filled him in on the occurrences of the previous afternoon and evening. After his few questions were answered, Jeff fumbled for his pipe and said, "As a matter of fact, I've been fighting a depressed state myself since I got up. The attempt at light-hearted humor when I came in was to jolly myself out of the doldrums."

"Did it work?"

"No." Forbes lit a match and began to puff at his pipe before asking hesitantly, "Can you take some more bad news?"

"No," sighed David in resignation, "but tell me anyway."

"All right—I spent at lot of time yesterday struggling to find possible reasons why the drought die-off is slowing down. Now, before giving you my best guess, I have a question I'd like you to answer."

David nodded.

"Tell me," continued Forbes: "in your opinion, could a massive migration of the elephant have taken place recently?"

"No," said David without hesitation.

"Why not?"

"Because we would have heard something about it from somewhere. People complaining about elephant damage to their crops—that sort of thing. That, plus the fact that I personally don't believe elephant migrate over long distances. I think they're more territorial than we thought at first. The early accounts of vast migrations were taken at face value, but what little we've done with radio-collared elephant tends to disprove that theory. They definitely move about a lot within their particular home range areas, but massive migrations over hundreds of miles? No—I don't believe it. Why do you ask?"

Jeff Forbes sat quietly and stared at him for a moment; then he sighed. "I agree with you, but I suppose it was a last straw to grasp at rather than face the only alternative." He glanced toward the large window looking out over the Fafajaga Plain.

"It's strange," he said, "in fact, it's almost unbelievable, how little we know about what's out there." He indicated the bush that stretched off into the horizon. "Do you know," he asked, turning back to David—"do you have any idea just how many of anything is out there?"

"All I know is what your center has been able to tell me, based on your sample census of the various wildlife populations. No one can expect you to deliver the exact population of each species, and I realize that; besides, I don't need to know the exact figure right down to the last animal. Thirty-five thousand elephant with a plus-or-minus variation of seven point two percent, and a ninety-five-percent confidence limit, is a good enough indication of the population."

"Yes," said Forbes, "but all our figures are based on our periodic sample counts, and the last one done on elephant was four years ago. In the meantime the elephant have been badly hammered by poachers; we can estimate a population growth based on their reproduction, but we can't estimate losses due to poaching."

"Neither can I," said David. "But another count can tell me the answer."

"That's what I want to prepare you for," replied Forbes. "The figure is going to be lower than we might anticipate."

"What makes you think so?"

Forbes briefly explained what he thought was the reason, and ended with the summation: "The elephant are responding as if the drought were over."

"But it's not," replied David.

"That's right, but the effect is the same if there are that many less to feed."

"How many do you think have been poached out of the original thirty-five thousand?"

Forbes pushed his fingers roughly through his hair in frustration. Leaning forward, he put his elbows on David's desk and studied the tabletop before replying. "Five to ten thousand, I'm afraid."

David's expression didn't alter, but his mind reeled. It was more than his own worst guess, but it wasn't an impossible figure. All he could hope was that Forbes was wrong.

"Well," he said resignedly, "we'll know soon enough."

"When will you be able to actually start the count?"

"Today's Wednesday—I'm hoping to be able to begin flying early Friday. A two-day total aerial count will give us the answer late Saturday or early Sunday."

Jeff sat open-mouthed. "You're not serious?"

"Yes, I am."

"But that's impossible. There's seventeen thousand square miles in this ecosystem and we've got to fly over every inch of it, to say nothing of the coordination and planning. The aircraft and personnel, equipment, supplies; the—"

David held up a restraining hand. "I know. And I know we can do it. Let's just say that yesterday's events made it a little more urgent. I need the information. I need it now. I want a full scale anti-poaching operation to go into effect next week, and I must have the information from the count."

He leaned forward and handed Jeff the radio-message form he'd received when he arrived that morning.

Jeff read: *Arriving Thursday evening with 2 observers. You don't give a fella much notice, do you? Bob Njonjo.*

A series of knocks at the door announced the arrival of two assistant wardens: Bruce McKinney of Works and Daniel Balaga of Accounting.

"Find a chair," David said, and when the men were seated he added, "On Friday we begin a two-day total aerial count of all rhinos and elephants in the area, and I need your assistance."

Balaga's expression was one of disbelief. McKinney chuckled.

"Whatever you're doing, drop it. I need your full cooperation because we have a lot to do."

"*That,*" murmured Forbes, "is a gem of understatement."

David's glance returned to Jeff, and he nodded. "Now," he said, "this is what we're planning on. We've got a lot of park to cover and two days to do it in. That means ten pilots and planes, thirty observers or counters, and ten standby observers, for a total of fifty people." He indicated the radio-message form. "The first reply to my radio-message appeals for pilots and planes has already come in this morning. Warden Njonjo of Samburu National Park will be here tomorrow. I make the second pilot; you"—he turned to Jeff Forbes—"make three, and Senior Warden Shepherd makes four. We'll have six more by tomorrow. Between ourselves and Department Headquarters in Nairobi we can come up with the observers and their standbys. All right?"

Jeff nodded affirmatively.

"Balaga"—David turned to the accountant—"you're leaving for Mombasa immediately with a pile of requisition forms. I need fifty drums of aviation fuel. Arrange for that first and then go to the Senior Warden's Office and get back to me on the radio for additional instructions. When you check in, give our radio operator the whereabouts of the fuel so that McKinney's lorry drivers can pick it up this afternoon."

Turning to Bruce McKinney, he continued: "Here's a map illustrating the airfields in the park and on neighboring ranches and estates where I want drums available for refueling. The majority of the fuel will be here at the Main Headquarters airfield, because this will be our departure point each morning, but I don't want the pilots to have to return from their blocks each time they need to refuel. Double-check my figures later, when I give you the plane assignments, to make sure I've allocated sufficient fuel at each refueling airstrip for the number of planes that will be requiring it. If you get the drums here from Mombasa this afternoon, they can be transported to the outlying airfields tomorrow. Any problems?"

"No," muttered McKinney, shaking his head as he studied the map.

"Balaga?"

"No, sir."

"One other thing—after you purchase the fuel, get me a hundred and twenty rolls of black-and-white film, and I want the fast kind. You'd both better get going now. Check in with me later."

He turned to Jeff as the assistant wardens left.

"Now," he said, "let's see if we can get this thing together."

MOHAMED AGARAN stood beside the idling Toyota and studied the maze of vehicle tracks in front of him. He and his men had been on the move since first light had made tracking possible; they hadn't even stopped to eat, just thrown the provisions sent out before dawn into the back of their vehicles and taken off.

He felt someone nudge his arm. Turning, he saw the can of water extended by the driver. Murmuring, *"Asante,"* he drank it down before returning to his study of the ground before him.

The rising sun had enabled him to study the two sets of vehicle tracks seen only briefly the evening before. He's found where the two sets merged, and had followed their trail east on one of the main service tracks to the eastern boundary of the park, north of the Lalaga Lana River and Nyache Gate on its southern bank. About a kilometer short of the gate, the two sets of the poachers' vehicle tracks had cut north off the road and continued through the bush to escape detection by the Gate Rangers on the other side of the river. Two kilometers beyond the gate they had cut south, crossed the shallow river, and proceeded to double back through the bush to the graded boundary.

That was where he was now, and as he examined the shallow excavation and the scattered remnants of slashed brush before him, he reconstructed the poachers' movements of the day before.

The poachers had been unexpectedly successful in their attack on the elephant herd. So much so that the job of hacking out the

241

ivory and moving it out of the park had presented a problem. Agaran was well aware of the time and labor involved in axing a pair of tusks out of a freshly killed elephant, and also of the total weight and bulk of more than two hundred tusks. The poachers had consequently been required to make two trips hauling the ivory out.

Sometime during the previous day they had taken this track east, crossed the river, and cut back to the boundary, where they had dug a shallow ditch, buried the load of ivory, and covered it with brush. Then they'd returned the way they'd come and picked up the second load plus the men and had returned along the same route, but instead of stopping here, they had continued on down the boundary cut which stretched like an arrow to the south and the main Mombasa/Nairobi road. Agaran knew what they were going to find when they followed their trail: nothing but lovely clear tire tracks all the way down the boundary line—all the way to the tarmac road, and disappeared.

They must have returned for the buried ivory during the previous night, he thought; when there was no one to see them here, or later when they pulled onto the main road. He glanced south and swore silently; still, he had to go, had to follow the trail until it disappeared.

"*Twende,*" he rapped out as he climbed back into the vehicle and reached for the microphone to check in with Headquarters.

MUTTERING AND SHAKING his head, Komora Duba swiftly jotted down the message from Agaran after signing off. Everything seemed to be going wrong at once. All those elephants shot yesterday, and now Assistant Warden Agaran was trying to catch up with the poachers' vehicles on the boundary. He shook his head in disbelief: poachers' vehicles inside the Northern Area. And if that weren't enough, it seemed that the Warden's typist was in trouble, and he didn't know why or anything about it, except that today she had disappeared altogether and he'd been told to say nothing. Balaga had run off to Mombasa, and McKinney was bellowing something about lorries to his mechanics outside. He got up and closed the louvered windows in an attempt to shut out the workshop clatter.

Gathering up the radio messages for Warden Karanja, he continued to worry himself. Everyone was running about, into meetings and out of meetings, and now it seemed that all the other park wardens were coming here. Duba didn't like it. It wasn't the normal thing at all.

Most of all, though, he found himself concerned about Margaret.

What was the matter? What had she done? He was surprised to find how she returned to his mind.

"BUT IS TWO DAYS enough?" inquired Jeff Forbes.

"Absolutely. Besides," replied David, "it's important that the count take the shortest time possible. The longer it takes, the greater chance we have of the elephant's wandering from one block to another and being counted twice. With ten planes, we'll have time to finish before dusk on Saturday. By the way," he added, "did you find the block illustrations?"

Forbes pointed to the huge pile of papers he'd stacked on the far corner of David's desk. "There they are. I finally found them in a cupboard labeled 'Herpetology Specimens.' "

David chuckled, "Where else?" as he reached out to take a handful off the top. After reading the heading—ARUBA NATIONAL PARK—GAME COUNTS—BLOCK I—he studied the line-drawing map illustrating the boundaries and features of this one of the twenty-seven blocks which together constituted the park and the adjoining areas within the ecosystem.

"This goes with the block maps," said Forbes, handing him a mimeographed paper.

David read it quickly. It was the data sheet to be used by each observer and pilot to note the number of animals seen in each given spot, the species of animal, the frame numbers of photos taken of them, and the information needed regarding carcasses spotted.

The door opened after a tap and Komora Duba's head popped in. "Radio message, sir."

David quickly scanned the messages. "Good," he grunted. "The warden of Amboseli is coming, and so is one of the assistant wardens—Marsabit. That makes six, and they've got two observers."

"And only four to go," added Forbes as he watched David's pleased expression change as he read the next message.

"What is it?"

"Agaran is on the eastern boundary cut, following the tracks south."

Forbes's eyes turned to the huge map on the wall, and after a brief study he said softly, "They're gone."

"The bastards," muttered David, in spite of the fact that he hadn't let himself hope for too much.

"Will there be any answers, sir?" asked Duba, indicating the messages.

"No, *asante*." He forced his mind away from the men responsible for the massacre in the north. He'd deal with them in their time. The count came first now.

After Duba left, David stood and began gathering up maps and papers. "Let's move to the conference room, where we can spread this lot out." He led the way.

"Now," he said as they settled around the long conference table next door, "the first thing I need done is the pilot assignments." Opening and spreading out four different Survey of Kenya maps, he aligned them together and taped the edges to create a huge map covering the Aruba ecosystem.

"Starting here—Block One"—he pointed to the far western area of the park—"and the adjoining blocks Four, Five, and Nine, should be about the maximum area that can be flown in two days by one plane."

Forbes scribbled it down as David continued, "The plane assigned here will fly Blocks One and Four on Friday and the adjoining Five and Nine on Saturday." After studying the map, he added, "On Friday he'll refuel at the western substation airstrip and on Saturday at the Malathi Lodge airfield.

"Remind me," he added, "to give McKinney a copy of these assignments so he'll have sufficient fuel at each refueling depot. I don't want to be losing planes out there."

Forbes nodded.

"All right," David continued as he settled down with the map of Block I. "Imagine that you're flying this monster. First of all, pick out any visible landmarks which the pilot can sight his position on. Now, based on that . . . you decide whether he is to fly north to south and back across his block, or east to west, or whatever, in order to keep the sun out of his eyes and the wind with him, instead of pushing him too far off course. One other thing," he added: "As we go on with these, we have to make sure that no two adjoining blocks are being flown at the same time by different planes."

Jeff nodded. "We don't want two of them overlapping on the boundaries and flying into each other while everybody, including the pilot, is preoccupied with searching the ground for rhino."

Reaching for a ruler, he asked, "What altitude?"

"Let's stick to the standard three-hundred-foot altitude, and speed at a hundred and twenty miles an hour."

Starting at the extreme southeast tip of Block IV, Forbes aligned the ruler north to south and lightly drew in the first flight path, or transect. "One-kilometer intervals between flight paths?" he double-checked.

"Right."

They continued working; estimating flight paths and turns, fuel consumption and refueling stops, landmarks, sun and wind.

"Finished," murmured Forbes.

"We're making good time," said David as he completed the first block, and then he quipped, "and only twenty-five blocks to go."

Jeff glanced up smiling from beneath his shaggy brows. "You can be replaced, you know," he observed sardonically before starting to work on Block IX. After a moment he glanced up questioningly. "You said a three-hundred-foot altitude."

"Yes."

"Isn't that a bit low?"

"No," replied David, puzzled. "It's the standard for flying game counts. The higher you fly, the greater the possibility of overlooking something—particularly the rhino. Elephant are generally more sensitive to low-flying aircraft and will take off when they hear a plane approaching, so they're fairly easy to spot when they're moving and out in the open. But the rhino usually just lie low and skulk about in a thicket and they're hard to spot even at three hundred feet, unless you catch them out of the deep bush."

"Actually, I wasn't thinking in terms of rhino. Last year a poacher fired on a low-flying plane taking aerial photographs, probably because he thought the plane was looking for him."

"It crossed my mind yesterday, but I think the chances of its happening here are one in a thousand, if that."

"Good enough," replied Forbes. "I agree with you, but I thought I'd ask." He went back to work with his ruler.

JAMES MUGALU shifted his slight frame a foot to the left to stay under the meager shade of the euphorbia whch offered some protection from the burning sun. It was hot and still at the edge of the thicket near the dried-out riverbed in the Moda River Valley; only the droning hum of the insects was heard, besides the occasional rumble from Sarah as she grazed on one of the small patches of *Cynodon dactylon* remaining from the lush meadows that had spread across the valley floor before the drought.

One day a week, for several weeks now, he'd accompanied the big orphans and the herdsmen into the bush and he'd recorded everything eaten by either Sarah or Galogalo. It was his first independent study—Feeding Habits of Elephant During the Dry Season. Today not only was he meticulously recording every species of plant Sarah selected, but he also noted what part of the plant was eaten and how often. He was very proud, not only of the responsibility and trust conferred on him by Dr. Forbes, but also of the way the project was progressing. It would prove to be a valuable study, and he was already anticipating a like study done in the wet season.

His boyish grin illuminated his face. He loved his work, and the park's Research Center was a long way from the sterile and eroded *shamba* he'd grown up in near Mwatate—the *shamba* which had been divided into tiny parcels for his four older brothers. He'd been the lastborn, and because there was no land left he'd been kept in school and gained the secondary education which had led in time to Aruba. He was very fortunate, and he knew it; the inch-long fingernails he'd cultivated on his little fingers proved it—he did no manual labor. Dr. Forbes gently teased him about those nails, but he didn't mind. He knew Forbes couldn't understand, really, what they meant to young men whose fathers couldn't write their names.

He noticed that Sarah and her orbiting calves had moved away from the patch of grass, and he was up and after them. Sarah paused under a tree and began to grasp loose dirt in her trunk tip to fling over her back to ward off the hot sun. James leaned against the tree, and his mind wandered among his blessings: he had a fine, clean job; a small, but weathertight and comfortable house in the staff quarters; and a handsome wife who just this week had presented him with his third child—another girl, and at this he frowned a little. That made three girls; but then he brightened. The boys would come later, and girls brought bride prices to their fathers when they were older.

And, he grinned to himself, this week I will fly in a plane for the first time. He could hardly contain his excitement. Just this morning Dr. Forbes had told him that he was to be one of Forbes's observers, along with Dr. Sorensen, the primatologist, and he'd wanted to whoop for joy. It was a great honor to be chosen to assist in the game count with the senior Research staff, and it seemed as if everything happening this week was an augury of the future that stretched brightly before him.

MARGARET TURNED off the gas burner, and the high-pitched whistle stopped its scream and quickly fizzled out. After pouring the boiling water from the teakettle into the pot, she leaned against the stove to wait for the tea to infuse.

She was alone in the house. Halima had left early, telling her to fix herself breakfast when she got hungry and to make herself comfortable. She was nice, thought Margaret. She knew that Halima was aware of what had happened at Headquarters, of what she'd done, but she hadn't said anything about it, hadn't treated her as if she were a . . . a what? Her eyes swam, and she swallowed something that persistently caught in her throat.

She hadn't slept well; in fact, she hadn't slept at all. Her mind had refused to slow down enough to allow sleep to come. Instead it had swirled with images of Mulolo, her home, the face of her mother, her father's hand raised in drunken anger, Mulolo again, and her room in the staff quarters, where she'd sat alone and listened to the laughter and the voices of the rest of the people who were not alone. She resolutely shook her head and pushed the bad thoughts away.

Adding milk and sugar to the cup, she poured the tea and wandered with it through the house. A whole house, she thought, with two bedrooms like an *Mzungu* house, only it was Halima's. An African's house. An African woman's house. She sat in a large overstuffed chair carefully as if afraid of rumpling it, or being seen there. It was Halima's, and not because she was the wife of a clever man, but because of herself. Margaret was awed at the idea.

Briefly she wondered if Warden Karanja was Halima's man. She doubted it. She had heard him leave last night. Perhaps he had left because she was here? No, it wouldn't matter, they wouldn't pay any attention to her. No, he had gone home because he didn't sleep here.

She thought about him—Warden Karanja. He was nice, very nice, and he was nice to work for. He had never shouted at her, even when she'd been slow or made a mistake. He'd just ask her to do it over. She'd always been afraid of him, though—afraid of doing something wrong, of making him angry. He was the Warden; he was a man, so she had feared him.

Involuntarily her mind crept back to the night before. He had been angry then, very angry. She tried to turn away from the memory, but David's face returned, contorted with rage as he hit the desk and yelled at her.

She couldn't remember everything she had told him, but his anger had gone. At lunch today he was coming to talk with her again, but she didn't fear him anymore. He had been angry last night, but he hadn't struck her, hadn't knocked her down as her father would have done. He hadn't even sent her to jail. He'd told her that perhaps she could help him—help undo what she had done.

247

She wanted to help. She wasn't afraid of him now. No, it was something different—was it shame, perhaps? Yes, she was ashamed, and she remembered how she had felt when the office door opened and she'd turned from the notes she was copying to see him standing there. "What are you doing here?" he'd asked, and she'd felt as if she had been discovered doing something dirty.

The shame she'd felt earlier washed over her and made her feel almost physically sick. She had never done a bad thing before, and she was humiliated, but most of all she was consumed with self-loathing for having been used, been tricked, been lied to and, she knew, laughed at. Yes, Mulolo would laugh at her. She could hear his laughter now, and her small, thin face hardened.

Having spent most of her life trying to avoid making others angry, she was slow to realize the name of what began slowly to stir and grow inside her. It was born of humiliation and fanned by a desire to hurt back, if only a portion of the hurt he'd caused her; it brought a calm of sorts: the calm that comes with a resolution made, a course of action decided upon. The cringing self-disgust inside lessened and turned its ugly face elsewhere. Mulolo, she thought; yes, he was the one.

DAVID DROVE DOWN the hill from Headquarters and brooded on the last message received from Agaran before the assistant warden had left once again for Northern Headquarters. He and the men had followed the tracks down the boundary cut to the main highway, where the tracks had turned right and disappeared into the tarmac. The poachers could then have headed for the village of Moda or anywhere on the main road clear to Nairobi, 350 kilometers away. It was an effective dead end; but then he hadn't really expected the Field Force to catch up with the poachers, because of their head start and his lack of aerial support.

They had to be the recipients of the information Mulolo had been getting out of Margaret, and they knew the park as well as he himself did, right down to the obscure and little-used service tracks. Their cutting through the bush to avoid the gate, and then cutting back after crossing the river farther on, told him that whoever was directing the poachers had spent some time inside the park and was familiar with every outpost.

Turning at the Education Center signpost, he passed the main buildings and continued on to a modest cement-block staff house beyond. Pulling into the driveway, he jumped out of the Land-Rover and knocked lightly.

The door opened a crack, and the top of Margaret's head peeped out. Recognizing him, she opened the door enough to allow him in while she continued to hide behind it.

"Are you feeling better today?" he asked as she closed the door.

She nodded and stared at the floor, and he knew that as usual, talking to Margaret was going to be difficult. Noticing the teacup on the small table, he decided to give her something to do, something to occupy herself with while he told her what he wanted of her.

"Are you having tea?" She nodded again.

"Would you fix me a cup?"

As she went into the kitchen, he wondered again why she always appeared to be frightened. Again her likeness to a snared animal returned: she must be the most timid human being he'd ever seen.

He followed her into the kitchen, and after she put the water on to boil he said, "Come sit down here," and pointed to one of the two chairs at the small kitchen table.

"Look at me, Margaret."

Her dark eyes darted up to his face and then away.

"I'm not going to hurt you, and I'm no longer angry now—I want you to help me, and I can't talk to you if you won't look at me."

There was a long pause. Finally she looked up and said softly, "I'm sorry." Her eyes tried to slip away again. "I am ashamed." Her voice was a whisper.

"I know you are, but that's past, and you're going to help me now, and then what you did will be forgotten. Do you understand?" He reflected that it was all a bit incredible—here he was consoling her for the nearly irreparable damage she'd done. But punishing her would serve absolutely no purpose. She was as much a victim as was the park.

"Last night you told me that Mulolo asked you about the Field Force patrols, and about what Assistant Warden Agaran and I were doing about the poaching. Did he ask about anything else?"

She shook her head, then said, "Only that, and about your plane."

"What did he say about the plane?"

"Nothing; he just kept asking if it had been sent back."

Right, thought David grimly: he would want to know about that. "Did he ever mention anyone's name to you? Any friends or acquaintances?"

"No."

"Did he write or receive letters?"

"No."

"What did he do when he wasn't on duty?"

She thought for a moment before saying helplessly, "I don't know—sometimes he came to see me, and sometimes he went to town. But I don't know what he did or where he went—he never talked about it."

"Did he ever take you to town with him?"

She shook her head.

He sighed. He didn't doubt she was telling the truth. The whereabouts and activities of men were not a woman's business; but still, he'd hoped for some thread to follow. He studied her for a moment.

"What I'm really interested in, Margaret, is what Mulolo does with this information. I want to know whom he's selling it to. Mulolo isn't very important except for the fact that he can lead me to someone who is important—the one who's responsible for the large-scale poaching operation that is functioning successfully because of the information Mulolo sells."

She nodded, but looked a little disappointed.

"Mulolo isn't important?" she asked. "You don't want Mulolo? He isn't in trouble?"

"I want him very much; and yes, he's in a hell of a lot of trouble. It's just that I want these other people first. When I've got them, then I can get Mulolo, but right now I need him to lead me to the leaders of the poaching operation."

"Will he go to prison?"

"For a very long time," he assured her.

She smiled softly, and he saw that she was satisfied—now he realized what Margaret wanted. What was that bit about a woman scorned? He didn't blame her one bit. Still, he was a little surprised —he hadn't expected meek Margaret to have claws. But then, that was good, because neither would Mulolo.

She brought his tea, and as he sipped it he said, "I want you to continue telling Mulolo what he wants to know. He's used to asking you questions and getting the answers. I don't want that to change. I don't want him becoming suspicious."

Margaret's eyes opened wide. "But—"

"It's all right." He smiled. "The difference is that now you'll be telling him what I want him to hear. Understand?"

She nodded.

"Now," he added, "it's going to be impossible to keep the game count a secret. Already the Radio Room and accounting and workshop departments are working on it, and tomorrow planes will be arriving from all over Kenya, so they'll hear about it, and if you haven't told Mulolo then, your credibility will be damaged and he'll suspect something. So tonight you tell him. Tell him whatever he wants to know, because it isn't important—it isn't connected with poaching. But your telling him will relieve any suspicions he has about your disappearance."

"What should I say about last night and this morning—about where I've been?"

"I've been thinking about that, and I want you to say that the Research and Education Centers are assisting with the count and you've been working yesterday and today with Miss Abdi. Typing and mimeographing forms, that sort of thing. And by the time you quit working last night, it was dark and you were afraid to walk home alone because of lion, so you stayed here. He'll believe that."

She nodded, smiling, and looked a little pleased.

"Now tell me what you're to say."

She repeated her story quite believably, and he saw that by the time she delivered it to Mulolo it would be practice-perfect.

"Good. At the moment I don't want you to mention the big antipoaching campaign. That may be the trap we'll set later. Just say that the daily patrols are deployed as I directed last week, and that a large number of poached elephant were discovered yesterday in the north, but the poachers' tracks were lost at the tarmac. Got it?"

She repeated it parrot fashion and waited expectantly for his appreciation.

"Good, very good," he said.

She smiled.

He leaned forward and took her small, nervously plucking fingers in his hand. "Can you do it, Margaret?" he asked.

"I can do it," she said distinctly and definitely.

CHAPTER THIRTEEN

Afternoon

WAMBUA MULOLO peered through the window and called out again softly, *"Hodi."* There was no answer, and no one could be seen inside.

Turning away, he wondered again where she was. He'd come yesterday evening and she'd been gone. Where could she go? She had nowhere, no one, to visit. She was always either at Headquarters or here in her own room in the staff quarters. She went to town only once a week to buy a little food.

He began to walk back to the Main Gate, where he'd left another ranger in his place for a few minutes. He'd come twice last night and once this morning and again just now, and still she wasn't there. Perhaps she was sick? He brightened a little before deciding that it wasn't likely. If she really was, he'd have heard. Mentally he began to run through her acquaintances: Whom might she be with? He automatically discarded the idea of another man—but perhaps a woman friend? But she was so quiet, so shy; she didn't seem to have any friends. At least, none that he knew of.

He reached the gate. He thanked the off-duty ranger who'd helped him out. As the man left, Mulolo continued to worry. Where was she? He was getting very nervous. And when he got nervous he became angry.

"KARANJA! Come in. *Karibu.*"

David stepped into the sitting room and shook the extended hand of Joseph Kiboko, head of the local Central Intelligence Department. He was a slender, clean-cut man of less-than-average height who had an air of intense vitality. The two of them had worked together often in the past when they'd pooled their resources in a collective effort against the illegal ivory trade, and David respected Kiboko's sharp professionalism.

"I hope you don't mind my coming to your house during your lunch, instead of to the office during working hours, but frankly, I didn't want it common knowledge that I've seen you."

"Anywhere is fine," Kiboko replied. "Sit down and tell me the problem. Is it a fiddle? Or are those half-tamed spearmen from the north tearing into one another again?"

"Neither," smiled David, "and don't malign my Field Force." This had been a favorite topic of Joe's ever since he'd seen the result of a fight between two Turkana Field Force Rangers who'd gone at each other with wrist knives.

"Who's maligning them? I envy you your Field Forces. They have a kind of courage that I wish I had more of in my Department. Too often we'll get a recruit from some *shamba* whose only idea of resistance is to run away."

David laughed. "No, my problem is unique this time; at least, it hasn't happened to me before." He proceeded to explain about Margaret and the presence of what appeared to be a large, well-run poaching organization.

"How long have these people been operating?" asked Kiboko.

"I can't say, but I'd guess that it's been quite a while. This ranger, Mulolo, was more than very friendly with my last typist." He considered a moment before venturing, "A year, maybe more."

Kiboko's response was immediate. "Shall I have this Mulolo picked up for investigation? He might have a lot to say."

"I don't think so. I'm not sure he'd talk."

The C.I.D. man studied David briefly. "He'll talk, don't worry about that. I'll see to it."

David wasn't surprised, nor was he shocked. As Forbes had remarked during the meeting Tuesday, "It's not an anti-poaching campaign, it's a war." And it was; it hadn't been very long since David's orders had gone out to the Field Forces: "At the least sign of resistance to arrest—shoot; and shoot to kill, because if you don't, they'll kill you."

"It's possible, though, that his fear of talking may deter him just short of breaking his neck," replied David, "and once he's picked up then he's no good to us as a link. They won't go near him; they may even kill him to shut him up."

Kiboko nodded. "You might be right. You want me to have him followed, then."

"For the moment, yes."

"I have a new man from Nairobi," mused Kiboko. "He's not known here. How do you propose to get him close to this Mulolo?"

"Does this man of yours know anything about gardening?"

"Gardening?" inquired Kiboko, at a loss for once.

David grinned. "I noticed that the landscaping at the front gate looked a bit unkempt. It's been a while since the gardeners were there. We'll put your man in the blue coveralls of the subordinate staff and he can putter around the Main Gate for days. Mulolo won't pay any attention to him."

"Good. That's it, then. During the day he'll keep watch on him at the gate and then follow him wherever he goes after he's off duty. Meanwhile, what do you want done about this typist of yours?"

"Margaret Githu?" said David. "Nothing, I suppose. Mulolo has been seeing her off duty, and he asked questions about the Field Force, which she answered. She gave him the daily patrols and information about anti-poaching operations, but I don't think she was conscious of any wrongdoing until she was caught."

Joe shook his head in disgust. "Is she stupid or what?"

"Actually, she's not. It's surprising how much people say just in normal conversation, and they fail to realize how much should be left unsaid. Besides, he's her man, so she'd normally answer any question he put to her without wondering why he asked."

"But now she knows."

David nodded.

"Will she tell him?"

David considered the question before answering, "No, I'm sure she won't. She doesn't have much left in the way of affection for him—I think she's more interested in a little feminine revenge. She's agreed to tell him what I tell her to tell him."

"What are you thinking of?"

"I've got an aerial game count coming up during the next few days. Following that I'll be mounting a major campaign against poachers with the help of large numbers of reinforcements, and I'll be needing your cooperation. I've asked for the G.S.U. and several units of the Special Anti-Poaching Forces from around the country. We'll be deploying a large force on the ground, with extensive air support plus roadblocks. I want to seal off the area and beat every bush and thicket in the whole park. I want to clean up the road and clear out the bush. Any poacher caught inside the park will get out only in handcuffs. I'm hoping to use Margaret to pass information to Mulolo that will effectively draw this organization into the trap before we spring it."

Joe Kiboko's eyes were bright with anticipation. "You can rely on whatever help I can give."

"Where I really need help from the police and C.I.D. is with the middlemen, the buyers. The park is my concern, and with reinforcements I can go a long way in apprehending the hunters inside, but I know that within a few weeks the poachers will start filtering back in. The price of ivory guarantees it, and there'll always be a handful who are willing to take a chance. But if we can put enough middlemen away, we can constrict the traffic, because it's the receivers who are responsible for getting the trophies out of the bush and on their way to the coast. There's where I need your help. I'll take care of what's going on inside the park. I need you and your Department to concentrate on what happens when the ivory and horn reach the highway and start moving to Mombasa or the borders."

"Let me see what I can start putting together. When do you plan to begin this campaign?"

"A week to ten days from now—I'll be more definite when the Senior Warden returns from Nairobi."

"That's not much time," said Kiboko reflectively.

"I know; I don't have much time to waste. I've a feeling that it's getting late now."

"If you're thinking of trapping this organization in your anti-poaching campaign, I see two difficulties. One—if this is going to work you'll have to keep it quiet. The minute reinforcements start arriving, your big fish will pull out and wait until the pressure's off. They'll know something's up."

"I've thought of that—that's why I don't want anyone to know about this except those of us who have to know. The reinforcements will be taken to Northern Headquarters and kept there until they're called into action."

"It might work if you don't have any more like this Margaret."

"I don't think I do. What's the other difficulty?"

"You'll pick up the hunters, but rarely does an operation like this get the big fish we were discussing. You don't find them *bundu*-bashing with the boys. They only come on the scene when it's time to collect the ivory and move it along. At the maximum profit, I might add."

"I know; that's where you and your lot come in. If we get the men in the bush, we'll have done about all we can do. It's up to you to get the information out of them in order to go after the ones on top. We've had some success with informers; let's increase their benefits and maybe we'll get lucky."

"I hope so," replied Kiboko. "I know what you're fighting out there, and I don't envy you. We'll do all we can to help. I'll see that your Gate Ranger is under surveillance as of this afternoon."

PULLING AWAY from Kiboko's house, David's vehicle rattled and bounced over the rutted dirt road he followed back the way he'd come earlier. The C.I.D. man's house was on a meandering side road above and behind the Police Department building, which also housed the C.I.D. offices, and as he approached the more densely populated village area he heard a shot.

Quickly braking, he stopped and glanced around. A shrill yelp followed by another shot brought silence, and David picked out the dark green of a Department of Wildlife vehicle off the road in a field of dry cornstalks some distance away.

Releasing the brake, he continued on until he was parallel with the other vehicle, and then he turned off the road and approached as two rangers appeared carrying the thin, dirty carcass of a stray dog, which they threw into the back of their Land Cruiser before acknowledging David with a brief salute.

David nodded and returned the salutation. These were Maimbo's men. Former Game Rangers with the old Game Department station in Moda, but now, like himself and his Park Rangers, reorganized under the Department of Wildlife. He remembered now. It was Wednesday. The cleanup of all strays in the area. The department veterinarian from Mombasa would be in the village for the next two days vaccinating all domestic animals, and Maimbo's men had started eliminating the strays in the village as his own men had been doing inside the park area. He'd forgotten about the whole thing as soon as he'd sent the note to Maimbo the previous morning after the meeting. He'd forgot about Maimbo as well. The count and the upcoming anti-poaching campaign, plus everything else on his mind, had shoved the Game Warden into the background. Now he wished he'd stayed there.

Backing out of the cornfield and onto the road, he turned and continued on his way back to the park. Theoretically, Maimbo was his counterpart. They were supposed to work together; but it had been his experience that he worked better without Maimbo's assistance. Not that the Game Warden didn't try; he did, to the point of being ingratiating. The plain fact, David knew, was that he didn't particularly like the man. And he really had no reason not to; nothing specific, at any rate. Still, Maimbo should be included in the count and in the anti-poaching campaign. That was what he was here for, it was what he was paid to do. But he didn't want him.

Pulling his handkerchief out of his pocket, he wiped the stream of perspiration from his face and opened the dash vents wider. It was hot, and the thick, heavy clouds from the coast brought an oppressive humidity. He considered what to do and decided to hell with it. Maimbo would be busy with the rabies problem for several days; there was no reason to include him. He wasn't a pilot, so his value was negligible; any of Forbes's research assistants would be just as competent as an observer; and besides, Maimbo's direction was needed in town to halt the rabies epidemic. As far as the anti-poaching campaign went, he'd worry about that later. He'd think of a small role for Maimbo to play, perhaps on the roadblocks, but that would be at the last minute. He definitely would not be in at the planning stage. There were enough senior officers already involved, counting the Senior Warden, himself, and his own assistant wardens. Between them there was no reason to include Maimbo, particularly since it was vitally important to keep the campaign quiet until after it was in operation.

He remembered Joe Kiboko's words of caution, and his own decision that only those would know who had to know. He knew he could trust Senior Warden Shepherd, and he thought of his own men: Agaran, McKinney, Balaga, Jeff Forbes in Research, and his radio operator, Duba. He knew them all and trusted them. There would be no indiscreet blabbing; but Maimbo? He didn't know him that well, and he knew nothing of his staff, but the fact that they lived in town, instead of being isolated out in the park, and the fact that Maimbo was known to spend hours talking and drinking in certain bars in town made the Game Warden and his men a security risk. A risk he wasn't prepared to take now.

AS DAVID PASSED the Radio Room, he heard his name called out. Komora Duba scrambled out of his chair and handed him a sheaf of radio messages.

"These came in at fourteen hundred hours, sir."

"*Asante.*"

David quickly flipped through them: Balaga had the fuel—good. Two more pilots and planes with six observers were responding from Department Headquarters in Nairobi. And the first communication received from John Shepherd since he left: *Arriving Thursday afternoon with two planes. Mine and yours.*

David grinned. "It's about time," he muttered to himself as he passed into his office. Eight months had been too long to wait, but at least it was on its way back again; it would make all the difference in the world. Now he could get back to regular daily patrols.

A huge park and only a hundred-odd Field Force Rangers; the plane was what tipped the scales slightly in his favor. The knowledge that it was to be here tomorrow caused his spirits to lift.

Sitting at his desk, he saw the folded note with his name on it. Opening and unfolding the cream-colored paper, he read:

Since you couldn't make it last night until late, why don't we try for a nice dinner tonight? It won't be leftovers this time.

Halima

Smiling, he scribbled a note of acceptance. At least, he was forgiven. With any luck he'd be able to make it on time this evening. His social life was nonexistent; not only were there few places to go, but it seemed as if fate decreed that if ever there was a get-together or party at someone's house, he ended up dealing with a lion in the staff quarters, or a visitor lost in the bush.

He tapped his finger against the messages from the two additional pilots and mentally calculated. These two made eight pilots and planes committed as of now, with the count scheduled to commence two days later, at dawn. And he had the fuel as well. The additional observers needed could be rounded up at Research, so they were going to make it. If the additional planes came through it would help tremendously, but eight was good enough; they'd just have to fly a third day, but it would be done. The count was definitely on.

He quickly jotted a note to the Safari Lodge manager, Salim Rajan:

Book ten doubles for me for Thursday, Friday, and Saturday nights. I also need 40 box lunches delivered to Headquarters airfield at dawn on Friday and Saturday—and please, don't send that slimy bologna you give the tourists. Sliced chicken, ham and beef will do nicely.

Thanks,
David

"Lemboko," he shouted.

The door opened and the sergeant popped in to salute, with Margaret trailing behind him.

"Yes, sir."

David saw Margaret and turned to Lemboko. Thinking quickly, he said, "That's all. I just wanted you to fetch Margaret."

"Very good, sir."

He departed, and as the door shut, David said, "I didn't expect to see you here this afternoon."

"I wanted to come to work. I thought it would look more natural," she explained. Her small face was earnest.

"You're right, of course," he agreed. "Since you're here, you can take care of this." He handed her the note, which she took, but didn't open. She stood waiting expectantly. Good, he thought, a lesson learned. No, he didn't think there was going to be anything to worry about as far as Margaret was concerned.

"Find my driver and have him take you up to the lodge. Ask for Mr. Rajan, and give him this note."

She nodded and turned to go.

"One other thing."

She stopped and looked at him questioningly.

"As of tomorrow morning, Mulolo will be watched and followed every minute of the day and night. Do you remember what you're to tell him?"

She didn't speak; her head nodded, and a small smile hardened the corner of her mouth.

After she left, David reached out for the maps of the five blocks he intended to fly himself; he'd left those to do last. Picturing the areas in his mind, he began to draft the flight patterns, when again a knock sounded at the door and Komora Duba came in.

"Yes?" he muttered in irritation. Was there never a whole five minutes when he wasn't interrupted?

"Units Three and Seven reporting, sir."

David looked up as the radio operator continued, "Corporal Bagaja in charge of Unit Three picked up the fresh tracks of six poachers in the Valani area. He radioed Unit Seven and requested that they assist, and the two units surrounded the poachers, who opened fire. Two Somali poachers were killed, three were captured, and one escaped. Corporal Leleliti of Unit Seven reports Lance Corporal Guraha wounded by a bullet in his leg, sir. He requests to know if he is to take him to dispensary or hospital."

"Have him taken to the dispensary in town for first aid; then proceed to hospital in Mombasa and return immediately. Where are the prisoners?"

"Unit Three is bringing them to Headquarters now, sir."

"Very good."

"Yes, sir."

David sat back and reflected. Only one of his men wounded; sometimes they weren't so lucky. Guraha—which one was he? Then he remembered a tall, slender, medium-brown Boran—always grinning and cheerful. A good man. They were usually all good men. He rarely had trouble with his Field Force. Only when there was a bad one in charge. They, like everyone else, were as good as the man who commanded them.

He got back to work on his block maps, and had just finished the last one when Lemboko opened the door a crack and said, "Corporal Bagaja, sir."

David gestured for the Unit 3 corporal to enter.

Corporal Akbalo Bagaja was a short, wiry Orma; very dark and sharp-featured. Small, unevenly spaced and stained teeth combined with deep-set eyes, whose whites were not white but yellow, made David think of any one of a number of the small carnivores in the park. The corporal stepped up to the desk and saluted, and as he made his report in Swahili, David listened to the familiar maneuver of track and surround while he watched the man. Bagaja was speaking slowly and quietly, and yet the impression given was not of softness; on the contrary, the man's still attitude hummed with contained violence. There was a savage core in him that David knew and recognized; something feral and primitive that was still a part, deep inside, of every man, but in some, like Bagaja, it simmered visibly just below the surface.

He could picture him smiling with his small children on his knee, and at the same time he could see him in the field as he would have been today, exploding viciously to run down and capture his prey. He was ruthlessly single-minded. His job was to catch and, if necessary, kill anyone armed and inside the park for the purpose of poaching. And that was what he did, and did well.

Every society has its killers, reflected David, and we have ours. Usually they're found in the military or in law enforcement, or as criminals on the street; this one is in the Field Force. He's like a wounded leopard on a leash. But then, no one in Bagaja's unit is ever shot or killed in a skirmish. It isn't Bagaja who's taking one of his men to hospital in Mombasa. And no one in Bagaja's unit even attempts to think about secreting a found rhino horn or tusk to sell on the side; nor would I ever worry that this unit might decide to shoot a trophy animal themselves and split the profit. No, Bagaja would smell out treachery as he would cowardice, and he'd crush it before it became more than a conscious thought in the mind of one of his men.

He realized that Bagaja had stopped speaking and now stood waiting quietly.

"Where are the prisoners?" David inquired.

"Hapa, Afendi."

"Bring them in."

David studied the three handcuffed Somali as they were led in

260

to stand against the far wall. They were all a little above average height and slimly built, with narrow shoulders and hips and long, slender bones. Thin, finely molded faces with high cheekbones and brown skin told of a homeland in the Horn of Africa. And before that—the Middle East. Africans yes. But not of the Bantu peoples, not of the Negro races. They were Caucasian in origin, with bloodlines lightly mingled with those of the black peoples through whom they'd passed in their hundreds of years of wandering. Their language was one of the Afro-Asiatic tongues of northeastern Africa and southwestern Asia, and they were Muslims, the followers of Islam's prophet, Muhammad.

They were a tough and resourceful people; fearing little, they were good fighters and dangerous enemies, and they were David's most serious problem. Eighteen months ago, when his rangers had apprehended the first of what was to become a flood of Somali poachers, David had gone to Nairobi to impress upon his superiors the seriousness of the situation, but somehow he'd failed to make them understand. The unrest and political upheaval in the Horn of Africa had had far-reaching effects among the wandering pastoral tribes, and roving bands of heavily armed *shiftas,* or guerrillas, had turned to cattle raiding and poaching across the borders into Kenya. In the countries to the north and northeast, the wild game had been decimated, and Kenya's protected wildlife plus her unarmed villagers with their stocks of cattle proved to be a powerful magnet for unsettled men uprooted by civil disturbance at home.

As a nomadic people, the Somali tribe was scattered throughout northeast Africa, and families had relatives on both sides of adjoining borders. So as the Masai followed their cattle from Tanzania to Kenya and back again when the border was closed to all others, the nomadic Somali trailed their herds from Somalia into Kenya and no one was asked for a passport or identification papers, for what were those? The nomadic way of life was one of the oldest, and like the herds of wild game, they came and went as the seasons and their needs dictated, and no one had the right to stop them any more than one could halt the migrating wildebeests of the Serengeti.

David looked at the three who stood before him now and studied their remarkably similar features. Even their expressions were the same—sullen truculence was reflected in varying degrees on all three faces. As a ranger brought in the poachers' confiscated possessions, David turned to Bagaja and asked, "What have you got out of them?"

Bagaja shook his head and murmured, *"Sikupata kitu."* Nothing. It was the answer David had expected. When these people fought, they didn't give up. If apprehended, they wouldn't speak; well aware of the Kenyan authorities' difficulties in sorting out and dealing with Somalia's Somali and Kenya's Somali, they all professed ignorance of the Swahili spoken in Kenya, which made interrogating them difficult. There were few Somali-speaking rangers, and no officers.

Glancing through the poachers' possessions, David noted that as usual they traveled light: two water calabashes, one small axe, three knives, two strings of salted *biltong,* or dried meat, and two rifles: a Lee-Enfield .303 and an Italian 6.5 Carcano.

He leaned forward to pick up the finely crafted Italian rifle, which he knew was not quite enough gun for the game it was intended for, as a ranger added two medium-sized ivory tusks and a pair of rhino horns to the pile.

Addressing the Somali who stood nearest him, next to Bagaja, he asked in Swahili, "Is this your rifle?"

The man stared at the floor, silent and expressionless.

"Are these your trophies?"

Silence.

"Do you have a permit for these things?"

No answer.

"What is your name?"

The quiet was broken by a loud thwack as Bagaja took off his black beret and rolled it in his hand before smacking the Somali on the side of the head with it.

"Sema," Bagaja said softly. Speak.

There was no reaction; the man didn't even flinch when struck, nor did he try to avoid the blow that followed.

"Enough," said David. He stood and crossed the room to stand before the man, who looked up. David was conscious of the stoically mocking awareness in the dark eyes.

"Ma agani [I don't understand]," the man murmured in Afsomali.

David knew the man lied, and he was aware that the Somali knew of his knowledge. If he'd been caught poaching elephants in Somalia, he wouldn't be answering—or rather, avoiding answering —questions: he'd be dead. He'd have been shot on sight, with no questions asked, and left for the birds to pick at. It was one of the reasons he was now David's problem.

There were, he decided, occasions when a democratic government had its drawbacks: when the rules laid down for the protection of society at large provided sanctuary for its criminals.

He wanted some questions answered; questions whose answers

would help to wipe out the poaching; questions like: Where did you get your rifles and ammunition? Who supplies them? Where do you take the ivory and horn? Who's the buyer?

He wasn't at all averse to making the man talk by whatever means necessary, and yet he knew he should be. He accepted the fragile thinness of civilization; he knew he had that in common with mankind in general, irrespective of race or religion. And he didn't have to speculate on what would happen to him if his and the poachers' positions were reversed.

He returned to his desk and sat down. There were about a half-dozen Kenyan Somali in his Field Forces—all of whom were out on patrol—and only when confronted with a Somali-speaking interrogator would these men consider answering questions. After being persuaded, of course.

"Take them into town and book them," he said to Bagaja.

Joe Kiboko in the C.I.D. had a Somali on his force, and by the time he had gently "worked them up" without leaving a mark, the answers might be forthcoming.

As the men filed out ahead of a prodding Bagaja, David tried to return to work on the aerial census, but a question nagged at the back of his mind. Was it right to force a man to speak, just short of breaking something, or leaving permanent damage? Was it right to hurt him just enough to make him fear not to speak? He decided it wasn't. Then the picture of 107 elephant carcasses rotting in the Northern Area returned to his mind, and he added, But I'll do it, because I can't accept the consequences if I don't.

AUDREY STOOD UNDER the tepid shower and let the water run down her back. Marvelous, she thought; lovely clean water to wash away the sticky heat and at least a kilo of dirt. She watched as the water swirled about her feet before disappearing down the drain with a gurgle that told her that for once a frog or toad was not keeping itself cool in the drainpipes. Usually, she came in hot and dirty and had to bang on the shower floor and scream down the hole to get the little beasts to vacate and allow her to take a shower without flooding the bathroom floor.

"Housekeeping in the bush!" she muttered with closed eyes under a thick layer of soapy bubbles before shoving her face under the spray to feel the tiny jets of water wash the soap away and leave her face feeling clean and tight. Frogs in the plumbing, cobras in the garden, and rats and mice in the pantry and kitchen eating *everything,* including the plastic canisters and hand soap, and leaving mouse droppings on every dish and in every spoon. Sometimes it was more than you could stand. This morning another pair of her lace panties had been found chewed to rags behind the sitting-room sofa, and she knew that somewhere a nest of squirrels or mice were bedding down in shredded black lace.

Stepping out of the shower, she reached for the fluffy towel and without thinking she shook it violently, and then glanced at both sides before wrapping it around herself. Certain actions were performed without conscious reminding; they were done because you had been advised to by the people who'd lived here for a long time, or always, and if once you forgot and received a painful reminder, then you never forgot again.

Never leave clothes or towels on the floor; hang them, and even then shake them well before putting them on or around you; never put shoes on without checking to see who's taken up residence in the toe; never put your hands or feet anywhere where you can't see well, and that goes for cupboards, closets, or your own handbag. Never go outside at night without a flashlight, even if it's just to the car parked by the side of the house. Never go barefoot; always sleep under netting; never assume you know what something is unless you can see it well enough to identify positively. The list went on, and the few times it had fallen to her to give the old look-where-you're-going litany to new research people who were fresh out from antiseptic places like Boston or London, she had been met with a raised eyebrow and an "Oh, really, it can't be that sinister" attitude.

It wasn't sinister, it was plain good sense, but it was hard to convince the occasional one whose idea of a housekeeping trauma was a trail of meek and well-bred English sugar ants. So she told them about one of the park's near neighbors, an older couple who'd spent their life here ranching and who should have known better. They had a houseful of cats, and the favorite napping place of one of them was under the bedspread at the foot of the bed. Every day for ten years, that cat crawled up under the spread and curled itself into a ball and went to sleep, and every afternoon the elderly lady would slip under the bedspread, nudge the cat aside, and lie down for a quiet hour's nap. One day she lay down, said, "Move over," and pressed her feet against—what was supposed to be, had to be after ten years—the cat. But it wasn't the cat, and as the first thought crossed her mind that it wasn't furry, the cobra struck and struck again before she could get out of the bed and away. Miraculously, she lived, although her foot and most of the leg were withered and useless.

Of course, it didn't mean that you'd get bit by a scorpion every time you put on a shoe without looking inside; it meant that sooner or later you would. Nor, as Audrey had found out the hard way, did every towel contain a six-inch centipede, with an orange-legged turquoise body and ugly little head, which delivered an extremely painful sting—as bad as that of those monstrous black scorpions with big claws like crabs'. She shivered when she remembered the wriggly thrashing against her hip, after she'd flung on a towel quickly when she heard the cook coming down the hall with a message for her. So much for modesty, she grinned; or at least, she'd remember to shut the door next time.

She sat down at the dressing table and pulled the ribbon out of her hair. As she brushed out the gritty dust, she considered makeup—just a bit; some eye shadow maybe—and decided against it. It was late afternoon, yet still unbearably hot, and she knew any attempts at face paint would merely turn to a streamlet of rainbow-hued perspiration that would run down her face and drip off her chin. So much for the feminine arts, she thought wryly. "It's all I can do to stay reasonably clean and not smell like an old sweat sock."

Poking through her lingerie drawer, she found a pair of blue lace undies overlooked by the squirrels, and then she slipped into a simple cotton dress. She'd never got over her love of expensive and filmy lingerie—silk, lace, satin, it didn't matter as long as it was luscious; but her dresses were strictly practical. Loose and easily laundered, they covered you up decently, but did nothing *for* you.

"Oh, dreadful," she murmured when she caught sight of herself in the mirror. She wriggled her feet into her old leather sandals.

"What are you up to in here?" demanded Jeff, coming through the bedroom doorway.

She smiled and hugged him. "Is it that time already? I didn't expect you yet."

"Obviously," he murmured as he kissed her shiny-clean forehead, "or you wouldn't be hiding in the bedroom muttering to yourself."

They walked down the hall and into the kitchen as she said, "Well, you see, I was looking at myself in the mirror and I decided that I look tacky."

"Ummm," he replied, "and 'tacky' means . . . ?"

"Worse than dreadful," she answered unhappily. Popping the lid off a cold beer, she poured it into a glass as he looked her up and down.

"Actually, you don't look as if you're done up for anyone's parade." He paused, and sipped the beer she handed him before continuing, while he ran his hand over the curve of her hip, "but then, I always think of you as an exciting something wrapped in plain paper."

She smiled and, as the cook, Hassan, came in, moved out of his encircling arm with a conspiratorial murmur. "Down, Rover."

"I still am, my dear," he chuckled. "But not for long."

"Oh!" She fled out of the kitchen into the back garden and sat on one of the wicker chairs. "You are terrible—and in front of the servants, too," she said. "Hassan is scandalized."

He sat down beside her and said, "Hassan is always scandalized. Besides, I'm going to be more terrible still when you hear what I've done to you now."

"What's that?" she asked suspiciously.

"We were looking a bit short in observers for the game count, so . . ." He eyed her slyly and anticipated her reaction. "I put you down as a standby."

"Oh, no, Jeff," she exclaimed. "I hate flying counts."

"I know, but so do I, and we may need you. You know how much we need this census, and we've got precious little time to arrange it. I think we'll have enough observers, but I had to have a half-dozen extra standing by who've done counts before."

She scowled at him and took his beer to sip on. "Please use me last. Absolutely last. I get so awfully sick—back and forth—back and forth, up and down, and it must be a hundred and ten degrees in the plane. From dawn till dusk, and by the time I get down, my head is just spinning. Oh, Lord," she groaned, "I'm sick already."

He continued to nurse the beer as he glanced out over the bush below the house. His expression was thoughtful; that and a little dispirited. His thick brows drew together in a brown study, and she reached out and took his freckled hand with its short and blunt, yet so sensitive fingers. Rubbing her thumb over the little tuft of hair on the back of his hand, she murmured, "Oh, Jeff—you know I'll help if I can; and we can always hope it will be better than you think." His pale blue eyes looked into her brown ones; his crooked smile came up to light his face.

MARGARET left the door open wide; it was musty-smelling and hot inside her little room. Opening the three small windows to let in the fresh air and the evening light, she saw that a film of dirt and bits of leaves had blown in under the door. She reached for the thin, short broom she'd made of coarse grass stalks, and began to brush the debris into a small pile. With her back to the door, she became aware of a shadow that came to block the sunlight. For a fraction of a moment her heart came up into her throat, but the feeling passed and a chilly calm settled over her and took its place. She continued sweeping the floor with long, unhurried strokes that never broke the steady rhythm of a task done many times.

"Where have you been?" he growled.

She straightened and turned inquiringly, as if only just aware of him. She stared at him silently, and the first thought that ran through her mind was: Is this all there is of him? It was as if she were seeing him for the first time, and the mingled love and fear she'd known before remained only as the dregs of a bitter tonic tasted a long time ago and barely remembered.

"I've been working," she replied shortly, as she bent to resume the sweeping of the floor.

His eyebrows shot up, and the castigating remark he'd prepared and had ready for delivery died in his imagination. The longer she'd been missing, the more alarmed he had become. Where was she? What was she doing? Whom was she talking to? Did anyone know that he'd been getting information from her? The more he worried the angrier he became. How dare she! The little fool—she was his to see or not to see as he chose. How dare she go off without his knowledge and consent! All day he'd planned what he'd say, what he'd do, how he'd reduce her to cringing supplication. But he wasn't prepared for this terse unconcern.

"Move," she said quietly.

He remained standing in the doorway before the pile of litter she wanted to brush out the door. He watched her languidly sweep the dirt over his feet. Patting the broom on the step to dislodge any bits of trash, she said, "Come in."

After lighting the paraffin burner, she filled her small kettle with water from the four-gallon plastic *debe* and put it on to boil.

"I went to Headquarters looking for you," he stormed in frustration. "Duba said he didn't know where you were."

She continued to prepare the tea as she thought how strange it all seemed. It was as if she didn't want to be bothered with him, and she examined this new feeling. She felt like turning about and telling him to go away, and then she remembered her previously consuming adoration, and the sick feeling of humiliation returned. Warden Karanja's words came back to turn her indifference to something else. "He used you . . . used you . . . used you . . ." It reverberated inside her head, and she knew mere indifference wasn't enough for her. Besides, she'd made a promise to Karanja, and she always kept her word. As she filled the teapot she began to smile to herself; it was going to be like a game, a game she would win because, loving him or hating him, she'd always known he wasn't very smart.

She reduced her smile to one of shy conciliation before turning to face him. "Duba didn't know where I was because the Warden sent me to the Education Center to type forms and mimeograph them for Miss Abdi."

She sat at the table to pour the tea and kept her eyes cast down; she was afraid they would reflect her thoughts, and he would know she was lying; know that she had changed toward him.

He accepted the cup she handed him and studied her silently. He was perplexed. She had never lied to him; she wouldn't dare. What she'd said was possible—but it didn't sound right somehow. And her attitude had been strange at first, although she was acting more natural now. He watched her closely and observed her bowed head, her downcast eyes with their fringe of short crimped lashes.

"Then why didn't you come home last night?" he demanded angrily.

She sipped her tea. "Because there was so much work to do that it was late before I got done, and the lion were out. I could hear them roaring nearby, and I was afraid to walk home by myself, so I stayed at Miss Abdi's house." She lifted her eyes to his face, and concentrated on the thought of being out alone when the lions were hunting.

He considered this and knew she was telling the truth. No one left his or her room when the lions were heard near the staff quarters. Besides, he knew the Director of the Education Center didn't have a car, so she wouldn't have been able to drive Margaret home.

"What work were you doing there?" he asked nonchalantly. "What kind of forms?"

"Just different forms for the game count the Warden wants done this week on the elephant and rhino."

His attention was alerted. A game count. Airplanes.

"Is that what the meeting was about?" he asked suddenly.

She nodded as if it didn't matter.

"Well, what about it?" he demanded in irritation. She was so stupid; just sat there like a cow with no idea what was important, what was worth knowing. He had to talk to her like a child, worm things out of her.

She flinched and forced tears up into her eyes; putting her hand to her mouth, she whimpered, "I'm tired. I worked so hard and I worried so last night because I couldn't come home and you wouldn't know where I was, and now you're angry. You're always angry." She dropped her head on her forearms on the table; she was tired, very tired, and her sleeplessness of the night before, coupled with her present tense excitement, added credibility to a performance that was not all acting.

He gritted his teeth and swallowed. This was no way to handle her and he knew it. He'd have to be nice to her, cajole her, and then she'd tell him anything he wanted to know; everything he had to know.

"*Pole-pole,*" he murmured and reached out to touch her arm. "I was worried, *Malaika,*" he said softly. "I didn't know where you were, or what had happened to my angel." She felt his arm around her shoulders, and she forced herself not to draw away. Her face was still buried in her crossed arms, and he couldn't see the sardonic smile there as she exultantly asked herself a silent question: Who's the fool now, my Mulolo?

CHAPTER FOURTEEN

Evening

DAVID ACCEPTED A DRINK and leaned back in what was becoming a comfortably familiar armchair. He watched as Halima passed back into the kitchen to check on one of several pots on the stove. He couldn't help noticing her slim, but still generously feminine figure as revealed by the *khanga* bound tightly about her hips. She was tall for a woman, with long and slender limbs; yet her buttocks were generously curved and of a shape denied other races. The thin cotton cloth was wrapped loosely across her chest and over one shoulder, and as she leaned forward, her breasts moved sensuously beneath the material.

Realizing that his imagination was making him uncomfortable, he forced his attention away from the doorway that framed her and studied a wall hanging until the soft tinkling of her ankle bracelets announced her return.

"I'm surprised you were able to get away on time," she said smiling as she sat down on the sofa across from him and crossed her legs.

"To tell the truth," he answered, "I've wanted to do this census for so long that I've had it half planned out in my mind for months. All I needed was the authorization and the funds, and Jeff Forbes and I were able to get right to work and finish the rest. The aviation fuel arrived this afternoon, plus the confirmation of eight pilots and planes and most of the observers . . ." He broke off, and then added, "I didn't think to ask: Would you like to fly the count? We could use another observer, and I think you'd find it interesting."

"I would very much like to, and I'd love to see the park from the air, but the Center is booked solid for the next several days. We have groups coming from the Nairobi area and the coast, plus some day visitors, so I can't get away. But perhaps," she ventured hesitantly, "you might be able to take me up another time."

"Of course," he replied with a smile, and then asked, "Now that you've been here awhile, how do you like Aruba?"

Her face lit with pleasure. "I like it very much. It's almost like coming home." She added thoughtfully, "I'm afraid I was more than ready to leave Nairobi."

"Nairobi isn't your home?"

"No, I'm from Isiolo," she said, smiling. "At first I thought Nairobi was exciting, but after so many years of school, and then working at the Education Center at Nairobi Park . . ." She shrugged her shoulders. "I suppose I was tired of living in a city."

"How was it that you went to Nairobi in the first place? I'm curious. Few Orma have left their villages for higher education, particularly women."

She laughed. "I know—I'm an oddity, along with the rest of my family. The reason is that my father is a District Officer in the Eastern Province, and educating his children was very important to him. There are four of us, and we all went to university."

"You've told me about your brother, the one who's a doctor. What about the others?"

"My younger sister is a home economics teacher, and my other brother is now in law school."

"Very impressive," he said, smiling. "And how did you come to be with the Department of Wildlife?"

"I majored in biology and thought I'd go into teaching later, but I became involved with the Wildlife Clubs of Kenya, and somehow they all came together when I accepted the post of Assistant Director at the Department's Education Center at Nairobi Park."

"And now you're Director of Aruba's Center."

She nodded, then paused, looking at him for a moment as if weighing something in her mind. Then she added with a hint of reservation, "The education program seems to have more meaning here. Not only for the park, but for the surrounding area." She added hesitantly, "I realize that you're primarily interested in the conservation of the wildlife, but there's so much more to our program than that."

"Tell me," he said. "I'd like to hear."

Her dark eyes studied him in what seemed to be surprise. Then, as if to seek reassurance, she said, "Would you really?"

271

"Of course," he said, before adding apologetically, "I'm afraid I have to admit to a great deal of ignorance about the Education Center. I've got the rest of the park to deal with and I work closely with Research, but I've been to your department only once or twice. So tell me. It's time I knew."

"Well," she ventured, as if not knowing where to start, "we try to educate the young people about the importance of preserving our wildlife and the natural habitat in the national parks, but we also explain the necessity of the preservation of the forests as well as the rivers and lakes. And while the main purpose of our program is to educate children, we also deal with other groups as well. This week we had a visit of Taita chiefs and subchiefs. We took them on game drives, of course, but mainly we stressed soil and vegetation conservation through films and lectures."

She glanced up at him before explaining, "They're developing quite a problem in the *shamba* areas in the hills, where the topsoil is eroding rapidly in places because in the past they burned back the grass and bush for fields and grazing without any thought of erosion from the wind, the rain, or the overgrazing of stock, or of the silting up of rivers and streams from the eroded fields, and they had no idea of the damage they were doing to the soil by the repetitive planting of the same crop in the same soil without the addition of nutrients. When the land was worn out, and all the firewood and game within walking distance used up, they moved on to a new area and started again."

"I know," David replied. "And what's happening here with our condensed elephant population is not much different from the problems we're facing with people. As long as the elephants had room to move around in, the vegetation and soil could recover, but when too many were confined to one place permanently, then we began to have problems because the land couldn't recover from overuse. That's what's now happening with our people. The tremendous human population explosion has resulted in too many people everywhere. There's no question of using the land till it's no good and then moving on; there's not enough as it is."

She nodded in agreement and said, "This is what we're trying to explain to the young people, because only one-fourth of all the land in the country is able to produce crops and good grazing—the other more than three-fourths is desert, or close to it."

David finished his drink and leaned forward to set it on the table between them. He looked up at the young woman across from him, and as had happened before at the lodge and the meeting, he sensed her sympathetic interest. He felt drawn to talk about the things that really mattered to him; the things that crowded into his mind at night, holding off the quiet restoration of sleep.

"I'm worried about the future of the national parks," he said hesitantly. "I'm afraid that if our people aren't taught how, and then forced, to take care of what they've already got, then we're going to see the end of the parks."

Halima's expression was uncertain. "The end? How do you mean?"

"Well, for one thing," he explained, "we're experiencing a constant trickle of squatters who are moving into the recently annexed Dakagudiu Hills, because the land there is still virgin and it has a tremendous rainfall, while the land they leave is worn out because of their misuse of it. The areas north and northeast of the park are marginal and below in terms of rainfall, so that's safe for the moment; but the Wataita want the southern part of the park for agriculture and pasturage. Meanwhile, the Masai are moving their herds into the southwestern area, and the Wakamba have their eyes on the Dakagudiu Hills on the western side."

"I didn't know it was so bad already," answered Halima thoughtfully. "I thought we had more time."

David shook his head; his expression was grim. "No, there's very little time left. The country is developing, and I know that it's necessary for a better life for the people; but still, we've got to make everyone realize that they have to find a way to meet today's needs without wrecking the interests of future generations."

He sat quietly for a moment and then added, "I'm reminded of a quote I read somewhere that was attributed to a visiting dignitary. He said, 'There is no way we can win the fight for conservation of natural habitats and wildlife in the long term, but none of us should give up in despair.' "

He looked up at her and said dispiritedly, "I've thought of that often during the last few months. It seems that if people aren't blasting the wildlife for their trophies, then they're petitioning the Government to release protected areas so they can be raped like the land already in use. It's made me wonder . . ." He paused, and then shook his head despondently.

"What?" Halima asked gently. She was beginning to understand the pressure of the responsibilities he was under. The park, the drought, the poaching: all had combined to set him apart, a man who stood alone, and she sensed what it was he felt—the hopelessness of caring, because no one else appeared to.

She reached out and took his hand, and he glanced up at her. "I can only imagine what you're feeling, and it isn't true," she said.

"We have over six percent of our country's land set aside to protect the wildlife and the natural habitat. That's a tremendous commitment for any developing nation. And I think we have more time than you feel we do. Not much more, but enough."

She stood up and crossed the room to a small bookcase, from whose top shelf she drew a small book. Flipping through the pages, she found what she was looking for and returned to hand him the book opened to the page she indicated. "Here," she said. "I'd like you to read this while I get you another drink."

As she left the room he glanced at the cover; it was written by Elspeth Huxley. Turning back to the open page, he began to read:

Africans in the tribal state never, so far as I know, plant the seeds of trees. For trees are something put there by God; they are His business, not ours; if they vanish, that is His affair; there is plenty of bush for shade and firewood, and of what other use is a tree? As to the notion that, in twenty years' time, trees can be sold for money, that is all too remote and problematical. In twenty years we shall be old, perhaps fire will have destroyed the trees, and why should we work to help a future generation? Rather it is their task to help us when we are old.

He glanced up as she returned to sit by his chair on a small footstool. As she set his drink on the table before him, she noted his puzzled expression and began to laugh softly.

"Don't you see?" she asked animatedly with her arms wrapped around her drawn-up knees. "That book was written less than twenty years ago and it was perfectly true then! And *then* was just the last generation. They are the heads of the families of today, and it's their children who come to the Education Center from their schools all over the country, and it is these children who are learning to plant trees."

David frowned doubtfully and said, "Perhaps you're right—about trees. But as far as protected land and the wildlife are concerned, I don't see much in the way of change, and there have been game laws for several generations. Not just one."

"Yes," she conceded, "you're right—there have been laws against hunting for fifty years; but they were laws handed down from a dictatorial colonial government to illiterate tribesmen who didn't understand what was going on, except that their way of life was being changed for them. They were no longer allowed to hunt unless they paid gun taxes and bought hunting licenses—and how many tribesmen could afford to do that? So really, the laws came across as '*I* can hunt, but *you* can't.' So the whole concept of conservation, in all its forms, seemed to the African people to be a way to exclude them from what was theirs by right. Traditionally, land and wild-life have been regarded by Africans as communally owned—a tribe controlled a certain area and that land belonged to everybody in the tribe. Then parks and reserves were established, and people were no longer allowed to hunt, farm, or graze stock, or to collect water, firewood, or honey there. So it all appeared to be an elaborate scheme by which the *Mzungu* stole the land and everything on it."

"Yes," interposed David, "but they were told why."

"True, but telling and understanding are two different things." She sighed and observed in amusement, "It's obvious that you're not a teacher."

"You're right," he said in agreement, and then admitted, "I haven't the patience."

"That's what I mean," she answered eagerly, the last of her un-certainty and rectitude swept away. "Teaching requires patience, and very few have it. And what's more important is that the lesson taught must be taught by ourselves to our own people, for it to be believed and absorbed."

She studied the book on the table before him reflectively. "We're not doing badly, you know," she said as she looked up into his face.

"You mean as far as time goes?" asked David.

"Of course," she answered. "Using Europe and North America as examples, you can see that it took them hundreds of years to learn the necessity of conservation. How much wild game is left in Europe or the United States?"

"Not very much," he admitted.

"Exactly," she said. "No one values what there is too much of; it seems to gain value only when it becomes scarce. No one cared about the passenger pigeon in America until after the turn of the century, when all those billions of birds were gone and only a few remained. Now, of course, they're extinct. And the American bison, what they call a buffalo—sixty or seventy million wiped out in just a few decades." She shook her head in irritation. "No one cared until a large number of species began to decline rapidly to the point of extinction.

"It's always the same, and it's been happening here since 1900 when one by one, areas were opened to settlement by the Europeans —the Athi Plains, the Uasin Gishu Plateau, the Rift Valley—all had tremendous populations of wildlife, but the *Mzungu* wanted his crops and stock, so he shot the predators to protect his sheep and cattle, and he shot the plains game to protect the grazing and his crops. All game was classified as vermin, and it was mowed down

275

and left to rot in the sun. And don't forget that the only species of animal in Africa that have become extinct during the past hundred years, like the Cape lion, the quagga, and the blue buck, were wiped out by the white man. Not Africans. Besides, it's still going on all over the world. No wild animals are allowed to exist side by side with man and his crops and stock, because their very presence is a threat to man's profit.

"Now, of course," she added, "the developed countries have learned that wild animals have a right to life because they have an aesthetic value no one realized before. I say aesthetic because a wild animal doesn't *do* anything; he just stands there and you're supposed to enjoy watching him do it."

David started laughing. "So you're saying," he commented in amusement, "that man has finally found a value for the wildlife, besides that of pests, so now they too are worthy of consideration and existence."

She nodded emphatically.

Still amused at her point of view he teased, "Surely there's more to wildlife conservation than that?"

"Of course," she said, before adding pointedly, "but you have to admit that you can enjoy the aesthetic quality of a herd of impala dashing across a savanna only if you're not suffering from a protein-poor diet, and it's not your crops they're trampling. The more-developed nations have passed the point where their people have to fight nature to survive, and only when a nation reaches that point can it turn to the aesthetic enjoyment of what used to be its adversary."

She broke off to glance at her watch and gave a small cry. "Here I've been talking forever and you must be suffering from starvation yourself. I'm sorry."

"Don't worry, I'm enjoying the conversation. Besides, you never did get around to why exactly we're not doing so badly as far as time goes."

"That's true—I got carried away and wandered off the subject. What I meant to say was that conservation of habitat and wildlife is a relatively new concept to mankind in general, and that this concept took centuries to develop. Our critics are fond of criticizing us for not moving fast enough in terms of changing our people's attitudes toward wildlife. Well, the British handed down laws regarding game, but they did little in terms of educating our people. But then, how could they? Only thirty years ago, during World War Two, the British Colonials slaughtered tens of thousands of animals in the area between the Aberdares and Mount Kenya to feed prisoners of war captured in Abyssinia and North Africa, and then after the war they completely wiped out the game on the Kinangop to make way for thousands of acres of cereals. All day horsemen rode down the herds and shot anything that moved, and at night spotlights allowed the massacre to go on. What did that teach?

"Just fifteen years later we were to be given our independence, and the colonials predicted that once the British left, we would slaughter the game. I'd like to ask, What was it called before?

"When we gained our independence we didn't kill off our wildlife, but we did do something the British didn't. We began to educate our people about 'Our African Heritage'—and the important word here is 'our.' We *are* learning; thirty-three parks and reserves say so, and so do twenty-seven thousand young people in the five hundred and fifty Wildlife Clubs of Kenya, who plant trees and march peaceably down the streets of Nairobi with placards saying 'Ban Hunting' and 'We Protest the Sale of Animal Trophies in Curio Shops.' They helped bring about the ban on hunting, and in time they'll effect the inevitable ban on the sale of wildlife products. So we're *not* doing badly," she said earnestly. "We're doing very well, thank you. The important thing is that we're not taking centuries to learn, it's taken only one generation to get where we are, and we are doing it in spite of being an underdeveloped and protein-poor society.

"Now"—she jumped up—"I'm going to feed you. I promise."

After she left the room, he continued to sit and think about what she'd said. Much of it was true; but yet it was still colored by her optimistic view. But then, he decided, why shouldn't it be? She dealt with the young people who planted trees and joined the Wildlife Clubs, while he had to deal with the fathers and grandfathers who poached the wildlife, cut down the trees, and tried to invade and destroy the protected habitat and animals.

Owing to our respective jobs, he reasoned, she has the new generation and I'm dealing with the old one. She sees the future promise and I confront past failures. So she's optimistic, and I—he chuckled to himself—I am in danger of becoming a pessimist.

He watched her moving about the kitchen beyond as she finished her preparations for dinner and observed to himself, Between us we'd be two realistic people, neither up in the air nor in a depression, but somewhere in the middle.

As they sat down at the table, she remarked, "I thought of something while I was in the kitchen and I'd like to mention it. Then I'd like to drop the subject and talk about the weather or whatever."

"What is it?"

She handed him the rice and asked, "Why do Africans hunt—I mean, for what purpose?"

He thought a moment and wondered what she was getting at. "Well, they hunt for meat or for trophies to sell."

"So it's food or money."

He nodded as he watched her dish up the hot spiced-meat dish.

"I just wondered if it's ever occurred to you," she added with an amused expression, "that we Africans are not 'civilized' enough to kill for sport?"

MARGARET LAY QUIETLY beside Mulolo and only half-heard his heavy breathing. As usual, he'd finished with her and rolled over only to fall asleep instantly. She shifted slightly away from him, and the movement brought about a corresponding restlessness in the sleeper. Mulolo mumbled and stretched in his sleep; the bed creaked, and Margaret thought wildly that if he awoke and reached out for her again, she'd scream. A laugh sounded somewhere down the line of rooms in the staff quarters, and the baby across the way cried out, while she waited tense and listening. His slow, rhythmic breathing took up where it had left off, and she slowly relaxed.

She was tired; bone-aching tired; and yet she continued to lie sleeplessly and to brood. The evening had gone quite well. After he got over his earlier sulky behavior, he'd listened carefully and with a growing cheerfulness while she'd told him about the count. She'd been surprised at how easy it had been. All afternoon she'd dreaded his coming; dreaded seeing him and having to talk to him. Most of all, she'd been afraid that he would sense something wrong. But when she actually spoke to him, she realized that he heard only the words, that he discerned nothing of her tone, saw nothing in her eyes. She gained confidence through his inability to observe what to her was obvious, and his lack of perception so reassured her that her conversation became more relaxed, more believable. What she'd told him tonight had been the truth, yet she knew that when Warden Karanja gave instructions to tell him complete fabrications, she'd be able to do it convincingly and that Mulolo would believe unquestioningly.

She'd prepared a small dinner, and by the time it was over she'd run out of information, so she had assumed that he would go. When his leering at her indicated otherwise, she'd been startled and then alarmed. In all her imaginings she'd thought of everything but this, and for a moment she almost panicked. He'd turned down the paraffin light, and when the flame winked out she had a mad desire to run out the door. But she hadn't, and by clenching her teeth she'd managed to get through it. It had occurred to her that this marvelous condescension on his part was her reward. She remembered the night she'd been so happy when he'd stayed with her for the first time, and she knew that that too had been payment for information rendered about the planned meeting and his desire to know more about it. It was all she could do to keep from pushing his flabby, sweaty body off, away, and onto the floor; but she'd resisted, because the irony of the situation occurred to her. There they were, joined together like a mortar and pestle, and it would be hard to decide which of them detested the other more. She had been right when she'd compared it earlier to a game; an ugly game. But she would play; yes, and she would win, and the ultimate reward for her would be to see him cutting brush at the side of the road in his white uniform, along with the rest of the men in a labor gang, while a prison guard stood watching with a rifle in the crook of his arm.

CHAPTER FIFTEEN

Night

BUBU SAT ON the edge of his bed and slipped the top off the stiff leather quiver of arrows. Tilting it, he drew out the three-foot arrow shafts and began to inspect them. Selecting the two most perfect, he set them aside and returned the others to their case. Taking up the half-dozen forged arrowheads, he again picked out two, and with his thumb tested the edges of their points. He smiled in satisfaction and put the remaining arrowheads back in the quiver which he hid beneath his bed behind a box.

For a moment he studied the metal arrowhead and the wooden foreshaft into which it was set. The slender shaft was carved neatly with the spiraling X that denoted his clan. As a young man he'd taken that symbol and centered it between two slash marks as his personal signature, and this was filed meticulously into the metal of the arrowhead itself. Satisfied with his handiwork, he picked up one of the long flight shafts with its four rows of vulture feathers and inspected the gutbound fletchings and the reinforced bow-string nock at the end. Again reassured that they were as perfect as when he had made them three years ago, he proceeded to fit the arrowhead foreshaft into the main flight-shaft socket, bound and heavily reinforced with wet strips of sinew which had contracted and dried long ago into a hard, protruding ridge. This thick ridge had two functions: it prevented the flight shaft from splitting on impact, and it kept the shaft from becoming embedded in the elephant's hide; instead, it fell to the ground after striking the animal and delivering the poisoned arrowhead.

After both arrows had been fitted securely with their heads, he pulled the hide stopper from the clay pot of fresh poison and, using his knife blade, began to apply a thick coat of poison. Working over the wide mouth of the pot, he dipped his blade into the poison and rolled the foreshaft over the knife, adding more and more of the thick, tarlike substance to the arrowhead's foreshaft. Finishing the application, he picked up a long strip of cured dik-dik skin, and starting at the flight-shaft socket, he carefully wrapped the now-lethal arrowhead in a protective covering. Setting the first aside, he repeated the process with the second, after which he stoppered the clay pot securely, wrapped it in several sections of cloth, and secreted this too beneath the bed. He lay the prepared arrows on the floor and began to hone his knife and the small axe to a razor-sharp edge. Soon these too joined the arrows. Now only one thing was left to prepare.

Standing on the bed, he reached up and drew his bow from its hiding place in the palm thatching overhead. It was huge—the big bow of the Waliangulu elephant hunters, and five feet six inches in length—the height of the hunter, Heekuta. He stood down from the bed and inspected the bow for damage. The small bush squirrels had been known to nibble the bows and arrows made of some woods to bits. This bow was made from the wood of the *madera* tree and so was a light honey color. It was long, slender, and almost straight, since it was unstrung, and the wood was hard and only slightly flexible. He inspected the bowstring, made of the leg sinews of a giraffe; unwinding it from around the bow, he checked the end where it was fastened before reversing it, to brace that end of the bow against the instep of his foot. Grasping the other end and forcing the shaft to buckle slightly, he quickly secured and wrapped the twined sinew string around the other, only slightly tapered end of the bow, then wrapped the eight or so extra inches of bowstring above the knot. The bow was now strung, and so lightly curved that the distance between string and bow at the center grip was perhaps six inches, requiring twice the power to draw as did the famous English longbow.

Heekuta felt his pulse quicken as he held the massive bow in his hands. If any single object could be identified as a symbol of a people, this bow would characterize his tribe and their way of life.

What he knew of his people's past was the result of the tales told by his great-grandfather, who'd still been living when Heekuta was a very small boy, and later the stories heard from his grandfather's lips before he too died an old *mzee*. If a thing had happened before the time of the oldest living person within the tribe, then the particulars of that happening were lost to the succeeding generations. Time held little meaning unless it could be related to an outstanding occurrence within memory, such as "She died when the rains failed for the third time during the great drought and we moved our village south to follow the game," or "He was born at the time of the sickness that killed all the buffalo." All would nod their heads in acknowledgment of their understanding—yes, that was the time; but none could say if it had been ten or twenty years ago, or even more, because such things had little meaning.

It was said that the Waliangulu, or the *Wata,* as they referred to themselves, had come from the Orma, who had in turn come from the Galla of Ethiopia many, many generations ago. But the ancestors of the *Wata* had turned away from the Galla way of life and become hunters. They had turned away from the cattle and the spear of the pastoralist, and they had gone into the bush to follow the elephants with the big bow, derived from their spears, and at one time they had ranged from the Tana River south to the land now called Tanzania.

His great-grandfather's stories still remained vividly in his memory, and again he recalled sitting beside the frail white-haired man before the warm fire that flickered and danced over his wrinkled and shrunken features.

"It was during my youth," the wizened great-grandfather had said, "that the Wata stopped wearing the cured skins of animals and first began to wear the *hidhu,* the long cloth wrapped about the waist covering a man to his ankles. The Arabs from the coast had passed through *Lafawata* and had brought the cloth to trade; and this," said the old man, "was the beginning of the end."

Up to that time the people had drifted over their land in extended family groups, or clans, following the movements of the elephant. When a kill was made, the entire clan would settle beside the huge carcass and feast on the tender slabs of meat cut from the elephant's face and the stomach fat before drying the rest into long strips for future use. Everything of the elephant was used, for he was their way of life, and when the hunters went out again and brought down another, the clan packed up their shelters of elephant hide and moved again, leaving only the whitening bones behind. That was when the people of his tribe were at their strongest and most numerous; when the customs and traditions were followed and adhered to, the customs that brought order and security of the spirit and made the *Wata* proud and self-sufficient.

There had been perhaps fifty clans in his great-grandfather's time; each clan wandered on its own, following the game and perhaps meeting up with and staying with another if the water nearby was good and the game plentiful. Each clan had a council of elders who advised the people and gave judgments in disputes, plus one or more of the *abamuruati*—the men or women who were gifted in healing and foretelling the future.

The leader of all the *Wata*—or chief, if he could be called that— was the *Duressa,* and this man was the elder adviser of the entire tribe; he was their prophet. He could see into the future in his dreams and interpret the meanings for his people, and they listened and followed his words because the *Duressa* was close to Waka, the Universal God whose face the old ones could still see as a shadow in the clouds above.

"It was in my own father's time," said the old great-grandfather, "that the *Duressa* dreamed a great dream, and sent messengers to all the clans of the *Wata* to tell them, 'There will come from the coast a snake with feet, but without life, and his coming will bring destruction to the *Illm Wata.*'

"They did not understand then," said the old man, but he had understood a lifetime later, when as an *mzee* he'd watched from the bush while the *Wazungu* came and brought the *Wahindi,* and he saw them work with tools to lay the iron metal across the face of their land, and he understood when later he watched "the monstrous shining snake creep over its trail on short spinning round feet. It carried the *Wazungu* inside, and it screamed and belched smoke at its head, but it was not alive; it was a dead thing truly, and it brought death to a people."

The great-grandfather had heard the prophecy as a child from his own father, and he had watched the people begin to turn away from the ways of Waka, as He had known they would when He had sent them warning. They left off the skins of their ancestors and turned to the cloth the Arabs brought to trade for the tusks of ivory. And as the Arabs brought more to trade, the people began to accumulate more possessions, and slowly the elephant-hide shelters were re- placed with more permanent beehive-shaped huts made of grass thatching, and the hunters went to hunt in a group and left the clan behind to await their return, when they would come laden with dried meat. The people no longer moved as often; they might stay in a village for years before the game was all gone within trekking distance of the hunters, forcing them to pack up their belongings and move after the dwindling wildlife.

The coming of the Arab traders had brought many changes, and not least among these had had to do with the hunting of the elephant.

In the past, the hunters would bring down a young animal, because the elephant was to provide them with meat and an old elephant was tough, but the Arabs wanted the ivory, so the people hunted the *wazee* with the big ivory, and much of the meat was left. That was the beginning of waste, and the face of Waka retreated even further from His wayward people, and the old ones could no longer see Him in the shadows of the clouds.

Then the Arabs had brought much of the potent palm wine, and a new evil was let loose among the people, as men took to the hard drink. When the wine was gone they were forced to hunt again, and still more meat was left to waste, and slowly the customs and the traditions that held them together began to disappear.

It was not many years after the appearance of the snake spoken of in the *Duressa*'s prophecy that he himself had been born at Okote, the water hole named for the clay pots used to fetch water beside which his people had built a small village of grass-thatched huts. It was there that he had first heard the stories of his people from his great-grandfather, and it was he who had made him his first small bow and arrow and taught him how to use them. He'd learned much from the old man, and as a child will do, he had expected that the old one would always be there to run to, but before the clan moved again the *mzee* had been returned to the earth beneath a large *dalacha* tree at Okote.

His grandfather had taken over then, and between him and Heekuta's father, his training and education had continued until it was time for his circumcision and, soon after, his first big bow. By then they had taught him everything there was to know of *aruba*, the elephant; how to track him, where to find him, how to interpret his every movement and sound. He'd learned how to move up upon him and how to place his arrow in one of those few places that would bring death quickly; he'd learned how to escape the charge of the maddened animal and how to follow and find him.

How proud he had been to be counted among the men and to begin living the life of the hunters of his people; the life that he'd heard spoken of proudly by the old men as they sat warming their old bones and memories by the fires at night. How would he have felt if he'd known that the old ways were to be ended for them within a few short years?

He stood and looked at the bow he held in his hands, and his memory recalled the changes that had occurred in his lifetime. Changes that had quickly brought his people to the edge of extinction.

He remembered the *Mzungu* who had tracked them down in the

bush and had taken their bows and arrows, even their knives, and who had told them they could no longer hunt. He'd given them hoes and the seeds of maize and then he'd gone away, taking their weapons with him and leaving them to stand there with the strange things of the farmer that they did not know how, or want, to use. He remembered the breaking up of their villages and their banishment to the strange lands of other tribes who did not want them, and he remembered the way back; the hiding, and the hunger; the sickness and the fear; and most of all, he remembered and mourned the loss of his clan. No longer were they together; no longer did a man feel secure living among his own kind, to whom he could turn for advice or help. There were no seers of the future; there was no council of elders; no brothers, sisters, aunts and uncles. The *wazee* were gone, and who was to teach their young? Where was their *Duressa,* their prophet, their leader? They were all gone. And now a man, an old man like himself, had no one. No wife, no children, no fire around which to gather with the friends of his youth. Nothing.

His eyes traveled the length of the big bow, and he remembered the first day he'd been able to draw it; and he knew that tonight would be the last time.

Suddenly his right hand moved forward and gripped the taut bowstring with three fingers as his left hand tightened on the bow handle, and he quickly raised both arms as if to aim at the sky, only to bring his arms down suddenly with a simultaneous and powerful thrusting out with the left hand and pulling back with the right; for a moment his now-thin chest was framed between the drawn bow and its string, before he slowly returned the string in silence.

Quietly he gathered his things. He took the well-known and cherished things of his young manhood into his old and gnarled hands, and as he touched them, he appreciated them as one can do only when it is the last time he will know their feel. His knife, so often honed that its blade was thin, and his axe—the one that had outlived many new handles. He took up the arrows and ran his scarred fingers over the smooth wood and the stiff feathers, and he enjoyed his own exquisite workmanship a moment before picking up the big bow and moving to the window.

The lights in the main house were out; the Warden asleep. When he thought of David, he briefly regretted the necessity to hunt again, but he knew it was the last time, and so the regret faded away. Turning to the small table, he extinguished the paraffin lamp before opening the door to slip outside. The moon was rising; he had to hurry to be away from the Headquarters buildings before it would be light enough for anyone to see an old *mzee* carrying the big bow of the Waliangulu.

He left the yard and melted into the bush nearby; passing the Forbes house, which was also in darkness, he saw the bright lights of the Headquarters Radio Room, where the night duty guards sat talking and chewing the sleep-destroying *miraa*. He dropped below Headquarters and down on past the airfield, and as the moon continued its climb, he reached the sand riverbed in the valley below. Crossing the pale sand that lay gleaming in the moonlight, he plunged into the thick stand of trees on the other side and walked swiftly on. As he emerged into the thin bush, he stopped to get his bearings, and his eyes roamed over the short scrub thornbush before him; he picked out where he'd last seen the elephant herd at dusk, traveling northwest, and he calculated their position now.

He heard the distant roar of a lion, followed by the chattering howl of a hyena, and was aware of something near that pushed itself through the dry bush. He stepped back into the shadows of a tree and stood close beside the trunk as he patiently watched the bush some twenty feet away where the animal was. He had no fear, only curiosity, and just as he decided that it was a buffalo, the expected head became visible with its massive, heavily bossed horns widely spread. The buffalo bull stepped out of the thicket and paused as the bush continued to crackle until his two companions appeared. Then the three old bulls continued plodding heavily on their way toward the green forage near the dry riverbed, unaware of the man in the shadows near them.

Having determined that the elephants would probably water tonight at the lodge water holes, and having decided to cut across their path, he stepped out of the shadows and began to move westward.

He came up on a small herd of waterbuck, displaced in the drought, and carefully circled them. He'd been walking for some time now and was nearing the place where the elephants would come, and he didn't want them alerted by a stampeding herd of waterbuck. They watched him pass, but didn't stir as he moved silently by. An owl's wild, wavering shriek registered itself, but he disregarded the normal night sounds; instead he listened intently for the sounds of elephants.

As he passed Daka Neka Hill, he knew he was near the place they would pass, and after a short distance he heard a sharp blatting squeal; he stopped and heard a growling rumble. They were just ahead. Immediately he checked the breeze again; it was blowing full into his face and carried the scent of rich warm dung.

The elephants had stopped for the moment and were feeding on the dried branches of the bushes around them. Cautiously now, he crept up and soon saw the animals at the head of the herd. They were cows and their young.

Suddenly he stopped; the herd had begun to move forward. First one and then another left off feeding to amble on slowly, while some still browsed. They were unaware of his presence as one by one they began to resume their trek to the water. He stayed crouched beneath a bush and as they moved slowly by he unwrapped the covering of dik-dik skin from his arrowheads. The bulls must be off to the edge of the group, perhaps a little to the rear. Good. He would stay where he was and pick out his prey as they moved forward past him.

They were close, very close, and just at that moment a big cow stopped near him. As she spaced out her huge legs, a thick stream of urine hissed to the ground beneath her, while massive cannonballs of dung were pushed forth to drop wet and heavy to the ground. He remained crouched where he was, hardly breathing, and as she stepped on again, the still-warm river of urine began to trickle over his sandaled foot.

The moon was high now, and still they moved slowly past in a long strung-out procession; still they were unaware of him. He continued to watch carefully, and now he spotted a bull. He was off to the far side, a little to himself, and while his tusks were longer and much thicker than those of the cows, he was not the one. Several younger bulls passed, and he let them go as well, and still he looked about for the *mzee,* the one with the big ivory; and then he saw one at the back, behind the last of the cows and youngsters, and the moonlight gleamed softly on the dirty ivory that stretched heavy and long, to almost touch at the tips beyond the trunk.

He let the last cow pass and began to creep forward. The bull had stopped to feed on an overlooked patch of dry herbage. He didn't mind trailing the others; he preferred it, in fact, rather than be irritated by the squeals and shrieks of the calves and the nervous cows.

The wind was still with Heekuta as he crept toward the bull. He was coming up on the animal's right side and just a little behind. He began to shift to the left, and each time the bull moved or shook his great head, his ears flapping like wet sheets, the man froze and held his breath. Crossing behind the bull, he again checked the dying breeze and moved in a little, now a bit to the left. Thirty-five feet, and then a few careful steps; out to the side to bring the animal's left flank into view, but not far enough to give him his scent. Thirty feet, a few more silent steps, and stop. The bull moved, turned a little to the left, and reached for another trunkful of forage.

The man stood like an image carved in stone as the bull rumbled loudly and continued feeding. Twenty-five feet, and as he crept stealthily forward, he took one of his arrows and fitted its nocked end to the bowstring, holding it loosely in place between the three callused fingers of his right hand. He stopped and watched; the bull went on feeding. Twenty feet, and the animal's smell was in his nostrils. Slowly he came up out of his crouching position, took a step forward, and then another as he raised his arms and paused a moment before bringing his arms down and his bow into action.

Suddenly the silence was blasted by a shot. The bull's head came up; with ears extended, he wheeled to face the departing herd, and the man dropped back into a crouch. Squeals of terror and screaming trumpets of fear and rage were heard ahead, and the sounds of shots reverberated through the darkness. The bull charged forward, and Heekuta melted back into the bush.

As he dived deeper into the thick underbrush, he saw for the first time the stabbing arcs of light that shifted and played over where the main herd had been ambushed behind him. What was happening?

He stayed hidden and tense as a few of the terrified elephants thundered back past him in their escape. More than one left splashes of blood to darken the moonlit soil. Finally all was quiet except for a scream of pain and terror that repeated itself over and over until a last shot was heard; and then only silence. Not the ordinary quiet of the bush, with its minute sounds of life stirring in the darkness. This was the absolute silence of waiting fear.

The wind had shifted a little, and he could smell the scent of blood and hear the soft murmur of voices in the distance. He quietly crept out of his hiding place and began to move toward the sounds ahead. The lights were dimmed now and stationary, and as he crept closer he could see the figures of men passing before the spots of light as they went to work with the axes. Soon the dull thud of metal biting into flesh could be heard, followed by the wet crack of steel axheads' cutting into recently living bone.

As he came up, the voices became louder; they were speaking in Swahili, and he could see the indistinct shapes of two vehicles, whose headlamps illuminated the scene. Two vehicles, one of which seemed familiar, and perhaps six men; he counted five at work on the elephants, axing out the ivory, and the shadowy figure of another man who stood just at the side of one of the Toyotas, behind the lights.

Something nagged at Heekuta; the vehicle—he seemed to have seen it somewhere. And the man in the darkness—his outline was not unknown to him. Leaving his bow and arrows behind, he circled around the vehicle until the man was between him and the bright light. Yes, he'd seen that man, but where?

Creeping closer on his belly, he reached the back end of the Toyota and carefully peered around just as the man stepped away from the side of the vehicle and stood illuminated by the lights. There was no mistaking the size of the man or his bulk; nor the way he moved as he stepped forward to take the bloody tusk from the Somali who'd just finished hacking it free from the face of the big bull. As he stooped, lifted, and turned, the glare of the headlamps played golden lights over his large sweating face. Heekuta had seen him only once before, but there was no way of mistaking Jombo Maimbo.

V · THURSDAY

CHAPTER SIXTEEN

Morning

DUNCAN SHELBY FINISHED shaving his upper lip and inspected his jaw for signs of an overlooked patch of bristles. There were none. Splashing cold water over his face and neck, he wondered how some men could stand beards in this climate; he'd never understood it and had consequently remained clean-shaven, despite the periodically recurring fashion which had decreed beards or mustaches for the colonial settler during the past fifty years.

After drying his face and brushing his white hair with a pair of old-fashioned silver-backed brushes, he returned to his bedroom to dress, and then proceeded out onto the veranda. Sitting down, he poured the waiting coffee and studied the new day. It was beautiful, but already hot. The sky was a clear dark blue only lightly spotted with patches of white clouds which might later mass and form a thick cover. Even now, a line of blue-gray smudged the southwest horizon, indicating far-off cloud formations only waiting to be pushed into place by the rising breeze.

As he waited for the appearance of his breakfast he reviewed the conversation of two days ago with Warden Karanja. He relished the idea that for the first time in the estate's history, the fields might be protected from the elephants.

He knew if it was possible, Karanja would assist. He liked this young Warden; even though Karanja was a wildlife conservationist, he appeared to realize that wildlife had to coexist with the world outside and so was willing to do what he could to help. It was certainly an improvement over those who sometimes seemed to forget that people had needs which demanded fulfillment as did the wildlife.

Somehow Karanja managed to walk the thin line between the needs of his wildlife and those of the people who lived outside the park; Shelby knew that like himself, the small *shamba* farmers were listened to and their problems with elephant or buffalo dealt with immediately and as effectively as possible.

As he finished his coffee, his breakfast arrived, and he sat back to enjoy his favorite meal of the day. . . .

"Bwana Shelby."

He glanced up at the gardener who had appeared on the veranda. *"Ndiyo?"*

"Njoo," said the man, beckoning.

Shelby rose and crossed the veranda to look in the direction in which the man pointed.

As he squinted against the bright morning sunlight, he saw that the smudge on the southwest horizon had grown, and he noted and understood the meaning of the wisps of rising haze.

"Moto, Bwana."

Moto. Fire. In the far southwestern fields. He turned back to the table and picked up the telephone receiver as he cranked impatiently on the handle. When the township exchange came on, he gave the number of his field foreman's phone. He glanced at his watch. With luck, he just might catch the man before he left his house. He waited tensely as the phone's ring blatted urgently in his ear; the sound ceased with a click, and he heard the voice of his Indian foreman.

Raising his voice, he bellowed, "Ali?"

The affirmative reply came back muted. It was the normally bad connection.

"There's a fire in the southwest fields. Can you hear me?"

Ali's voice mumbled softly.

"Get all the field workers out to start beating down the flames immediately. Then collect the factory people as they come in and send them out as well. Have you got that?"

Ali's "Yes" was louder now.

"Move the tractors over as quickly as you can and start grading a firebreak ahead of the flames. I'll be out as soon as I can."

He replaced the receiver and cranked the phone. He could depend on Ali; he'd have the entire labor force out within a half-hour.

He dashed down a note to Karanja to inform him of the fire, which, once through the sisal fields, would soon threaten the park area beyond. Calling out for the cook, who was the only one of the house servants who could drive, he gave him the note and sent him out to the park Headquarters.

Glancing down, he saw his breakfast as he'd left it and decided to finish his meal before going out to the fire. He'd seen so many that he'd long ago lost the sudden feeling of adrenaline-produced panic the word "Fire" could bring.

As he finished his fruit, he idly wondered just how many fires he had fought, and realized he couldn't remember exactly. It must be a couple of hundred at least.

Either they would stop it against a firebreak; or they wouldn't. It would burn for hours; or possibly for weeks. It might consume one field; or all of them. It depended on the wind plus a few other factors, but he did know that the days when he was young and had rushed out to battle the blaze full of his own bullheaded determination were over.

In the past he'd almost welcomed the opportunity to pit his strength against a fire, and he'd marshaled his men together and led them out with shovels, wet sacks, and leafy branches of trees to smother and beat out the flames. He'd been young and strong and, most of all, impatiently sure of himself. At the first sign of fire, he'd leaped about shouting orders, wielding his shovel in a cloud of flying dirt and smoke, beating at the hungry flames, and laughing with excitement. But for every one he'd put out, three more had gained on him as they spread down the rows of quickly burning and close-packed sisal plants, and so he'd redouble or triple his efforts with a feeling of overwhelming urgency until he'd become a virtual dervish; a singed, ash-blackened figure in perpetual motion. If he'd had an early warning and could move fast enough, he could do it; give him a shovel and a minute's head start and he'd been sure he could beat the blaze single-handed.

Now, as he dipped his butter knife into the small pot of amber-colored honey, he smiled to himself. What a feisty bastard he'd been! He shook his head in fond recollection and realized that there was one really marvelous thing about growing old: now he knew he had time to finish his breakfast.

THE PARK'S MAIN GATE had been unlocked for an hour, and Mulolo stood by impatiently waiting for the battered light blue VW to come around the far bend approaching the park to deliver the newly arrived morning newspapers from Nairobi. Was it late? Or did it just seem so because he was anxious to deliver the information

Margaret had given him? Muttering in exasperation, he looked to the sun: it must be about seven, and the VW could come at any moment now.

As he paced back and forth before the gate, he congratulated himself on the manner in which he'd handled Margaret the evening before. All he had to do was suggest an interest in a subject, and she opened up and started talking in an effort to impress him with how much she knew. Sometimes, though, it was hard to keep from showing his irritation with her stupidity and his distaste for her physically, and it was all he could do to smile and call her his angel. He snorted in disgust. Still, his relationship with her was valuable.

Reminded of this, he smugly speculated on just how much he'd get for his bit of intelligence. The reporting of the Field Force daily patrols paid a flat fee each week, but this was worth an additional sum, and he considered carefully how much he should ask for. These people paid well, but they didn't throw money away either; after studying the problem, he decided that he ought to demand 1,000 shillings. It was a lot of money, but then the warning that the park was to be inspected inch by inch by ten planes was worth it. Just as he resolved the question in his mind, he heard the clattering whine of the VW approaching.

He walked quickly to the iron gates and swung them open; stepping around to the driver's window, he said, *"Nataka gazeti."*

The driver's heavy-lidded eyes betrayed no reaction to the request, which signaled that Mulolo had a note to pass. Folding one of the newspapers beside him in half, he handed it through the window as Mulolo reached into his pocket for the coins and the note folded small.

As he took the paper and gave the driver the note sandwiched between the coins, Mulolo muttered in Swahili, "This should be worth a thousand."

The driver said nothing, but his eyes darted up to Mulolo's face and then away.

He was a heavily built man, and his round black face had just one expression: indifference to everything and everyone. Mulolo had never seen him smile, and when the man spoke his voice was as flat and indifferent as his features.

Putting the car in gear and looking straight ahead, the man softly replied, *"Labda"* and drove away.

As Mulolo closed the gate, he scowled at the departing VW. "We'll see about 'maybe,' " he muttered.

For a minute he contemplated going direct to the head of the operation to discuss the money, then discarded the idea. The man would be annoyed; extremely annoyed. He'd made it plain from the beginning that Mulolo was never to approach him unless it was an emergency; unless he had information that was immediately critical and that required delivery before the VW was scheduled to return. He was not even to acknowledge by word or look that they were acquainted should they meet accidentally in town. This wasn't an emergency, and try as he could, Mulolo couldn't think of a way to get to the man without doing what he'd been told specifically not to do.

For all he knew, the driver could get the 1,000 shillings and give him only part of it and say that was all there was. As this thought occurred to him, he seized on it and wondered if any other sums had been diverted. The longer he thought about it, the angrier he became.

"Who does he think he's dealing with?" he stormed to himself.

He knew he had valuable information every week, and he knew the poaching operation depended on his eyes and ears to avoid the Field Force patrols. Yet he was treated like a child who couldn't be trusted to even talk face to face with the big man whose identity he'd learned by accident a year and a half ago.

Still, he couldn't just go to town and demand an audience; not after being warned not to. Seething with frustration, he flung the paper through the window of the gate office and stomped around the side of the gate, where he tripped over a box of wilting weeds beside the kneeling gardener who was cleaning out the flower beds.

Breaking into a string of oaths, he kicked the offending box and glared at the man in the blue coveralls of the subordinate labor force.

"*Pole, Bwana, pole,*" the man said as he scrambled out of the way.

Mulolo grunted in irritation, and continued on toward the large rock under a shade tree where he was accustomed to sit when he wasn't opening or shutting the gates, while the gardener resumed his weeding with eyes that never appeared to leave the ground.

JOMBO MAIMBO PULLED his cream-colored Datsun into the space marked out with white-painted rocks beside the old Game Department Headquarters building in Moda which had become, after the merger with Parks, another Department of Wildlife office.

As he got out, he noticed the rear end of the blue VW protruding from around the other side of the small building and knew his brother would be waiting for him inside. Passing around the back of the VW, he noticed that the rusted exhaust pipe was only inches from the ground and nudged it with his foot; it bobbled up and down erratically, and he was mildly irritated.

Neither he nor his brother drove an expensive car, like some fools he knew who couldn't wait to acquire valuable possessions with the money they acquired illegally; and Jombo had no intention of rushing out to get himself a shiny new Mercedes to drive slowly around town. That sort of stupidity only gave the C.I.D. a place to start investigating, and so he drove an older-model medium-priced car, and he saw to it that Mnyambo continued to drive the battered VW. Even so, there was no excuse for letting it fall apart; it was typical, though.

He crossed the small veranda and opened the door that led directly into his office.

"*Jambo,*" said Mnyambo without looking up from the newspaper he was reading.

"*Jambo sana,*" replied Jombo before lapsing into Taita. "Your exhaust pipe is falling off."

His brother grunted, "I know" and folded his paper.

Jombo sighed in resignation and sat down heavily behind the desk.

Mnyambo handed him a folded note. "The little jackal has news for you."

Jombo was immediately interested; unfolding the paper, he quickly scanned the contents—and swore under his breath. A game count of all rhinos and elephants; ten planes full of observers scattered over the park and the surrounding areas. A dik-dik wouldn't get by without being spotted.

He glanced up at his brother. "Did you read it?" he asked.

Mnyambo smiled thinly and nodded. "I thought it might be interesting. The little jackal thinks it's worth a thousand shillings."

Jombo's surprise showed on his face. "Is that what he asked for?" he inquired incredulously.

His brother's smile broadened as he nodded.

Jombo exploded in laughter. A thousand shillings. It was unbelievable that the man could be so stupid. He'd have paid ten times that sum to know that the park was to be covered by one plane, let alone ten planes. He waved the paper and sputtered, "A thousand shillings," and started laughing again.

Mnyambo had stopped smiling, and now he warned, "He is a fool, Jombo, and fools can be dangerous."

"That's true," conceded Maimbo. "But not this one—he's too stupid; and besides," he added, "he's afraid of me." His slow grin spread itself across his face.

Mnyambo shrugged. His brother was the elder by two years; he was the *Bwana Mkubwa*. He'd done his duty in delivering his opinion.

Jombo lit a match and burned the small slip of paper in the ashtray. As he watched the paper blacken and begin to curl, he said, "This means we'll have to cancel the hunt tomorrow. Notify the men. In fact"—he paused and thought a moment before coming to a decision—"get them out of town for two weeks, or even better, a month.

"We've been lucky so far," he continued, "and it wouldn't be a bad idea to stop operating for a while. So far Karanja hasn't any idea of his losses, thanks to the help we got in Nairobi delaying the return of his plane." He smiled and added, "That was money well spent."

"But why for a month?" asked Mnyambo indignantly. "The count will be over by Sunday and the planes will leave."

"Because we've been greedy," replied Maimbo. "The first year we were not so greedy. We took two or three here and there, and we concealed the carcasses well. We were more cautious; but during the last eight months there was no plane to concern ourselves with, and so we took anything we could get out of any area that didn't have a patrol in the immediate vicinity. And remember, we are not the only ones taking ivory out of the park. Karanja has no idea how many trophy animals are missing; but by Sunday he will know, and then we can expect him to try to do something about it."

"What will that be?"

"Obviously, an anti-poaching campaign," replied Jombo. "What else? Also, once he has planes here, he'll be sure to manage to keep at least one permanently, and he'll have the cooperation of Department Headquarters. This is one of the best of the country's national parks, and it's because of the elephant and rhino; when they discover how many are gone, they'll give Karanja all the assistance he needs; they can't afford not to."

Mnyambo frowned in concentration. "Does that mean we're finished?" he asked.

"Of course not," Maimbo replied. "It means that we take a leave from business, that's all. Look," he said as he leaned forward, "the elephant and rhino are counted Friday and Saturday, and then Karanja knows the number of missing trophy animals. So what happens? Department Headquarters sends reinforcements from the other parks and the Special Anti-Poaching Forces, and there's a big operation throughout the park, and for how long? Three weeks? Four weeks? Then it's over and they all go home again, after eliminating all our competition for us. Karanja will be back to his original force, and that's when we go back to work."

"But Karanja will have a plane," Mnyambo pointed out.

Maimbo leaned back in the swivel chair and rocked slowly for a moment. "And perhaps," he said in slow speculation, "that will be when Karanja will have another accident in that plane, just like the one we arranged for him last time. He won't walk away from the wreck again." He stood up, stretched, and turned away to look out the window.

"Where are the men?" he asked.

"At the warehouse. They've started sawing up the ivory we took last night."

Maimbo grunted and continued to think. He had the perfect operation, and he didn't intend to jeopardize it by continuing to poach when the odds had momentarily turned to favor Karanja. It wouldn't hurt to go to ground for a bit. He'd been very lucky, and he knew it: nearly two years of operating and not one arrest, thanks mainly to the information provided by the little jackal.

Also, his men were professionals; he'd selected only the best. He himself, in the course of his duties as a warden, had picked up each of them for poaching, and after a little rough treatment, followed by a lucrative business proposition, they had agreed to hunt for him rather than be charged with the offense he held them on. And why not? They got the same 100 shillings a kilo they'd get if they worked alone, but with him as the boss and buyer, they had the best semi-automatic rifles that money could buy and the increased firepower; they were told when to hunt, and where, on the basis of the information he received from Mulolo, and so their respective incomes were many times what they would be if they worked alone.

Besides, there was little, if any, chance of their being caught; if, however, there was a slip-up and one or all of them were taken, then it would be a simple matter for Maimbo to manage. Evidence had a way of disappearing, as he'd proved when they got off the first time he'd arrested them.

Now it was time they left the area. Up to now they'd been kept busy, either on safari hunting or preparing the ivory to be smuggled out of the area, so there had been little opportunity for them to sit around in the village *pombe* clubs drinking, and perhaps talking too much. He'd send them to the coast with enough of the earnings he held for them to keep them drunk and happy for a month while he held back a sufficient sum to guarantee their return. Then when Karanja's reinforcements were gone, he'd go to the coast himself and arrange to bring them back. Mnyambo's milk-and-newspaper kiosk would return to doing business only in milk and newspapers, and his own charcoal warehouse would deal in sacks of just charcoal.

"When will they be finished preparing the ivory?" he asked.

"Tomorrow."

"Get them out tonight," Maimbo ordered. "Use one of the Toyotas at the warehouse. I want them away before the count starts. You can finish whatever is left to be done."

Mnyambo looked sullenly at his brother, but said nothing.

Maimbo saw the look on his face and suppressed his irritation. "You'd better go now. I don't want you seen here more than necessary." The fact that he and Mnyambo were the sons of one man by two different wives was not generally known. They bore little resemblance to each other, and there was no reason why people should know their relationship. "See the men and tell them they're leaving tonight at midnight. That will give you enough time to get them to the coast and be back before dawn. Come to the Total Petrol Station at eight tonight; I'll give you their money then."

His brother grunted his acknowledgment and rose. Throwing the newspaper onto his chair, he nodded and left.

Maimbo stood at the window and watched his brother climb into his car and start the engine, which promptly died. After several tries he got the VW moving in a cloud of black exhaust, and he rattled away with the exhaust pipe bobbing erratically up and down.

He's getting fat and lazy, Maimbo thought. "Or rather," he muttered, "he's always been lazy, and now he's becoming fat." It wasn't Mnyambo's aversion to physical labor that irritated him so much as his indolent lack of interest in thinking. He never considered the end result of any action he took. If it were left to him, the poaching operation would fall apart within days.

There was something to be said for doing business with one's own tribe, because there was an understanding between people of the same background, and there were good reasons for doing business with your relatives, since they were more likely to be trusted. Your interests were their interests. But then sometimes one's relatives did not possess the characteristics a man would wish for in a business partner, and he knew he was going to have to look harder at some nephews and cousins to find someone who, with the proper training, could become his second-in-command. Someone who wouldn't have to be told what to do and why every minute of the day.

There was no point in explaining to his brother why he should keep his car in repair any more than he could explain why they should discontinue hunting for a while, or why the men and the ivory must be moved out and away.

Maimbo made up his mind: he'd look for someone with a little bit of sense to bring into the business and be of some real help to him. There were a couple of young relatives who worked for him in various capacities in his business dealings. Of course, they didn't know what was going on with the charcoal business and the ivory, but that would come later, when he'd watched them carefully and made a decision.

He had a good operation, and he intended to protect it as long as it lasted—which, he reflected, wouldn't be too long. The elephants and rhinos were disappearing, and in a very few years, if not a few months, they'd all be gone. There were too many people involved in poaching and smuggling for it to be otherwise. Everyone wanted a piece of the profits before there was nothing left, and there were many ways to do it besides actually getting a gun and going out into the bush.

For instance, he knew that much of the ivory confiscated from arrested poachers, or from trophy animals found dead of the drought or natural causes, never made it to the Ivory Room in Mombasa where it was supposed to be sold at auction. Some of it was siphoned off by rangers or their superiors, or it was diverted into the hands of a few corrupt officials or their families, and rumor whispered that whole planeloads took off at night from Embakasi Airport for unknown destinations and private bank accounts abroad. It had ceased to matter who took it or where; what did matter was that it was gone, and the proceeds from this so-called legitimate ivory went into private pockets instead of the Government Treasury.

It was definitely going fast, and sooner or later the Government would have to do something. By then, of course, it might be too late for the herds of elephants, but still a gesture would have to be made and a few heads would have to roll for appearance' sake. He did not intend that his should be one of them.

He smiled at himself. "Yes," he murmured, "we'll let Karanja make his stand against the poachers as we let the *Mzungu* rancher, Dan Boyd, make his. And as with Boyd, it will be the last thing Karanja does."

DAVID WAS READING HIS checklist, marking all items completed for the count: all forms were ready and assembled—check; film rolls on hand and numbered—check; 8 planes and pilots confirmed—

check; 30 observers, but no standbys—he frowned and then checked it.

The door opened to Komora Duba. "Radio messages, sir."

"*Asante.*"

David quickly read the assorted messages resulting from the 8 A.M. call-up from Nairobi. Good—the Australian film crew were postponing their filming in the park for two weeks; he glanced up at the calendar and saw with satisfaction that they'd be arriving in the middle of the anti-poaching campaign, so there would be something exciting and, most of all, positive for them to film. He made a note on his calendar and went to the next message: Department Headquarters was sending a plane and pilot from Research in Nairobi and confirming for Warden Davis at Mountain Parks, who would make it as well. David was jubilant; he had his ten planes. Turning back to his checklist, he triumphantly changed 8 to 10 planes and pilots confirmed.

After disposing of the few remaining routine messages, he returned to his checklist. Aviation fuel—he had that; and now reminded, he began to study the map designating the airfields to be used for refueling and the number of drums on hand at each one. "I just hope those lorry drivers remember to leave a hand pump at each airfield," he muttered to himself. That was just the kind of snafu that he could expect. Hastily scribbling a note to McKinney to double-check on it, he bellowed, "Lemboko!"

The door snapped open. "Yes, sir."

"Send Margaret in."

A moment later she slipped into the office and softly shut the door. When he chanced to look up he saw her standing timidly at the corner of the desk.

"Someday," he remarked, "I'm going to teach you how to slam doors."

She looked perplexed.

"Tell me, Margaret," he asked as he leaned forward, "has it ever occurred to you to walk into a room and say loudly, 'Here I am'?"

She shook her head "no," and still didn't seem to understand, but since he was smiling, she smiled too.

"It's all right," he said and added, "Sit down." No, he thought, it wasn't likely that she'd ever conquer her timidity enough to do anything but creep about, hoping not to be noticed.

He handed her the note and said, "I want you to take this to McKinney in a moment and bring me his reply, but first I want you to tell me how it went last night with Mulolo. Did you tell him about the count?"

For a minute she looked uncomfortable; then the moment passed and she said, "Yes, I told him about the planes and everything you told me to say. I said I stayed with Miss Abdi."

"Did he believe you? Did he seem to think anything was wrong?"

"He believed me. He believed everything I said."

"Are you sure?" he pressed.

Her "Yes" was definite.

"What else happened?" he asked.

The uncomfortable look returned as she squirmed about on the chair and modestly avoided his gaze.

Now it was David's turn to look bewildered as he wondered what was the matter with her.

"I need to . . ." he began, and stopped short as an explanation for her shamefaced expression occurred to him. "Oh," he said in confusion as he thought, Damnation, I didn't expect that. He couldn't think of anything to say, but it occurred to him to worry about her reliability now; yet at the same time he had second thoughts as to what he'd let her in for.

"I know," she said softly, and then looked up at him directly. "I didn't think of it either." She seemed to gain courage by bringing it out in the open. "I couldn't think of how not to, without making him wonder why, so . . ." She shrugged her shoulders. "It doesn't really matter."

He watched her carefully without saying anything. His doubt showed.

"No"—she shook her head—"it doesn't change anything, if that's what you're thinking. I still want what I wanted before."

"Which is?" he asked pointedly.

"To see him in prison," she answered simply. Her small face was set, her eyes hard. "Now, more than ever."

"I'm sorry," David said, adding, "You can stop seeing him if you want to."

"No," she said as she stood up. "When he goes to prison I want him to know that I helped to put him there." She turned and went to the door. "I'll see Assistant Warden McKinney for you now."

After she left he continued to consider the situation between them. How stupid to have overlooked the fact that with Mulolo unaware of Margaret's knowledge of his activities, he would naturally expect their relationship to continue as before. At least, it tended to prove that he was unsuspecting; but the problem was whether or not Margaret could remain trustworthy. Could she maintain a physical relationship with the man without beginning to care for him again? Would she be able to lie with him and then give him the information she knew would lead him and the others into a trap when the time came? Could a woman do that? He honestly didn't know, but he realized that his inability to judge the situation was due to the fact that he didn't understand women very well; and he'd never thought of it before, never noticed his ignorance. Men he knew well, and he understood them. But women?

A sharp tattoo at the door interrupted his thoughts, and it opened ahead of an exultant sandy-haired man who loudly announced, "I got it."

David grinned and said, "Congratulations. I figured you would; you've been out there long enough. What's it been? Two weeks?"

Patrick Owen was a well-known wildlife photographer and film-maker, and it would have been hard to find a moviegoer or television viewer who enjoyed nature films and who hadn't seen Patrick's documentary work. He'd recently become interested in the hotly disputed question of whether elephants would occasionally remove the tusks from the skulls of dead elephants and carry them off to dispose of in the bush, sometimes smashing the tusks against trees or rocks before disposal, and also of the incidences of elephants' covering fresh carcasses with brush, branches, and dirt. These accounts had usually been dismissed as amusing folklore, rather like the tales of an "elephant graveyard," but both David and Owen had believed that these behavior patterns were true, and Owen had set out to prove it by building a blind where he sat for days with his camera overlooking the Namu water hole, where the remains of a dead elephant lay on the bank.

"Tell me about it," said David as Owen sat down.

"I got it all," Owen replied, grinning. "Of course, not every animal's reaction was the same. The degree of concern varied, but not one elephant ignored that carcass. The majority just closely inspected the remains. You know, running their trunks over it, occasionally picking up or rearranging a limb, touching it, feeling it." He shook his head in wonderment. "Fantastic animals. Most species have little or no interest at all in the death or the remains of one of their kind."

David nodded. "Most of the plains game will go on grazing within a few hundred meters of where predators are consuming someone who was one of the herd just moments before."

"Not elephant," Owen responded. "It's marvelous how they'll immediately go to the aid of a fallen member."

"Unfortunately," David added, thinking of the massacred herd in the north, "the same trait leaves them vulnerable to attack. Shoot one and the others will mill about in confusion." Forcing his attention back to Owen's success, he asked, "Did you see them pick up the ivory?"

Owen beamed. "On four occasions. One just picked up a tusk and dropped it immediately, while two carried the tusks some distance before dropping them. But one elephant pulled a tusk and carried it way off into the bush. I never thought I'd find it."

"How about burying the carcass?" David asked.

"Not much good footage there," Owen replied. "Several instances of dirt and litter being thrown over the carcass, but not what I'd hoped for. I'm sure what's needed is a really fresh carcass. Then we'll see bushes uprooted, tree branches torn off, and a really obvious attempt at burial."

"When you do get it, be ready for the screams of 'Anthropomorphism!' from the boys in the lab coats," David responded, chuckling.

"The academic, scientific types ought to spend more time in fieldwork," Owen replied wryly. "Besides, who can argue with filmed and recorded behavior? I'm not speculating on 'why' they do it, only showing that it's done. But"—his eyes twinkled at David—"it makes you wonder, doesn't it?"

With that he stood up to shake David's hand. "I'm off. Got to get up to Nairobi before dark. Look for me in a couple of weeks. I'll be back with fresh film and, hopefully, a rough cut of what I've got so far. I'll radio you to let you know when I plan to arrive, and if you could have your men scouting for a fresh carcass I'd appreciate it."

"I'll see to it," David replied, and as Owen left he murmured to himself, "That's one thing we have more than enough of: carcasses."

The door opened again to frame Sergeant Lemboko's face. "A message from the sisal estate, sir."

David nodded, and the door swung open wide to admit a small, thin *mzee* who stepped over and handed him a note.

David read the note and swore. "A fire," he muttered, "in the sisal." The fiber-filled leaves guaranteed a hot, furiously burning conflagration which, once going, could set the whole boundary burning. He stood and crossed to the window. As was normal at that time of year, a strong morning wind was building out of the southeast to stir the bare branches of the trees outside and push the fire through the sisal and into the park. He studied the southwest. Daka Neka Hill was between Headquarters and the burning fields, but still he could see the rising plumes of dark smoke as they were caught by the wind and dispersed into a dark haze that floated ominously in the sky.

He turned away and said, *"Njoo."*

Leaving his office with the messenger trailing him, he entered the Radio Room and addressed Duba. "Which unit is closest to the sisal-estate fields?"

Duba checked the Field Force Report file before him. As each unit reached their assigned patrol area they checked in with Duba and confirmed their whereabouts.

"Unit One, sir. Corporal Lugumba in charge."

"Where exactly are they?"

"Ambushing a house on the east side of town, sir."

"A house?" David wondered, and then remembered the abandoned hut in a thicket where Lugumba had confirmed the presence of tracks identical to those of the hunter who'd poached the elephant cow—the poacher Heekuta Neko. He considered the situation. They'd been watching the thicket since Tuesday evening; today was Thursday and the man hadn't returned. David still wanted the man apprehended, but then the events of the past days had reduced the Waliangulu to where he was now the least of his problems.

"Call up Unit One," he directed.

Duba turned to the VHF transmitter and proceeded: "Lima eight-five, six-oh-three," he said, and then repeated himself.

When the response came, Duba requested Lugumba, and after his voice was heard, he pushed the microphone toward David.

"Lugumba?" David asked. When the corporal answered, David continued in Swahili: "Has anyone come near the house?"

"No," Lugumba's voice came back distorted.

"I want you to proceed to the fire at the sisal estate and then radio in the following information: Exactly where is it? How big is it? And how fast is it moving? See Duncan Shelby and ask him what he needs. Have you got that?"

Lugumba's reply was affirmative.

"Leave two men to cover the house and the rest of you proceed as directed."

He signed off, turned to the messenger and continued in Swahili, "Tell *Bwana* Shelby I'm sending one unit of Field Force. Ask him to tell Corporal Lugumba what he needs in the way of assistance. *Sawa-sawa?*"

The man nodded and left.

David stepped out into the corridor. "Lemboko!"

The sergeant hurried up.

"Go to the workshop and tell McKinney that we have a fire near the southwest boundary, and I want at least three graders standing by and ready to be moved out if necessary."

"Yes, sir." He turned and left immediately as David went back into his office, where he saw that Mdomo had arrived and had begun to push all the pens, pencils, and loose papers from the desk top onto the floor.

He chucked an eraser at the small bird, who fluttered out of reach and regarded him with cocked head and bright eyes while David bent down and began to gather up his things. He muttered darkly to himself, "Somehow, the day is getting away from me.

"And you," he added with a string of coarse expressions regarding the small bird's ancestry, "are about to be transported to north of the Lalaga Lana River!" Just as he reached for his last pencil under the desk, the door slammed loudly, startling him and causing him to bash his head on the underside of the desk.

He looked up, his face a thundercloud, to see Margaret standing by the closed door. "Here I am," she said with a timid smile. She'd finally understood.

CHAPTER SEVENTEEN

Afternoon

BUBU SLOWLY AND rhythmically swung the metal slasher with its curved and sharpened end from left to right in a wide arc. As the curved end passed before him, a flurry of grass clippings flew up, to follow the bright blade into the air, then, as the blade descended, the clippings began to lazily drift to earth. The blade slashed through the grass again and more clippings followed. Taking a small step forward without breaking his swing, he continued cutting a swath through the green lawn in front of Karanja's house.

As he worked, his mind was busy with the events of the night before. Following his discovery of the identity of the poachers, he'd crawled back through the bush, and after retrieving his bow and arrows he had returned home, where he'd sat alone and thought about what had happened.

It was obvious that Maimbo was the *Bwana Mkubwa*; he had been giving the orders last night while the others did the work. It was also apparent that he was the one who was responsible for the big kill in the Northern Area; the two vehicles, the rifles, and the number of men fitted. And also, Maimbo knew the park as well as anyone could. The question that bothered him was: Why?

Maimbo was a warden, and he asked himself: How could this be? Bubu thought of Karanja and compared the two. That led nowhere: they were nothing alike. Karanja guarded the elephants— Maimbo killed them. Bubu's face registered disgust as the bright honed blade slashed viciously through the grass.

His own people were not allowed to hunt, even though it was

their way of life. But Maimbo could. He could even arrest him, Heekuta, for poaching. Lock him away in a small room with bars if he was caught hunting on his own land for one of his own elephants. But Maimbo could take the Government's shillings because he worked for the Government, and then he could sneak out at night and kill the elephants and take the ivory as well. He was a thief.

Bubu reached the edge of the lawn and stopped. Wiping the sweat from his face, he looked out over the river valley below, and his eyes picked out the tall trees in the curve of the riverbed which marked the place where his house had once stood in the village at Shokoke that had been destroyed when the Waliangulu were moved out of the park.

This was our land, he said to himself, and the herds of *aruba* were ours too, but the Government took it all. His eyes narrowed against the bright, hot sun and his rage. But if it is no longer ours, then it is not his.

He turned back to the lawn and began to cut another adjoining swath through the grass, and the violent anger in him was reflected in the swift rise and fall of the blade.

He took the big bull, he thought; my bull. The one I watched for many days, the one whose ivory I need for the boy. It was mine.

But then, he decided, they are all mine. If the elephant are not to be kept and protected in the park, then they must come back to the Waliangulu. To me, and to the boy.

He stopped. His rapid and relentless slashing had left him breathless, and he decided to take a brief rest and think this new idea through. Crossing the lawn to the veranda, he sat down on the wide cement steps in the shade and picked up a metal file.

As he began to hone a sharp edge on the scythe, he slowly continued his train of thought, trying to understand what was happening in a world that seemed to have left him behind. The land and the animals had been taken from his people by the Government and given to all the people of Kenya. But Maimbo killed the big bull, my bull; he took the tusks, my tusks; and they were not his to take.

He stopped honing the blade; it was as sharp as a knife, and as he ran his callused thumb over the warm metal, he smiled.

So I will take back the tusks of the bull, he decided. If they are not to be for everyone, then they will not be for Maimbo. I will take them back. I will take them all back.

* * *

SALIM RAJAN preceded his guest from the dining room and onto the wide veranda, where they seated themselves in lounge chairs beside a low table overlooking one of the lodge water holes.

"Coffee?" inquired Salim.

"Please."

Salim turned to the hovering waiter. *"Lete kahawa mbili."*

Turning back to his guest from Mombasa, Salim took a moment to study the Arab while the man occupied himself lighting an after-lunch cigar. He was about fifty, and although the pure-white hair, worn long and brushed back in thick wings above his ears and forehead, suggested a greater age, his dark brown and nearly un-lined face appeared to be that of a man much younger.

At that moment the man's dark eyes darted up to catch Salim's gaze; he settled back comfortably in the thick-cushioned chair and said, "An excellent lunch, Salim. My compliments to your staff."

Salim nodded in acceptance of the commendation, and continued to consider the meaning of a puzzling statement made by the man just before they'd left their table. He and the Arab had had many business dealings in the past, primarily in the illegal purchase of Kenyan coffee from plantations in the highlands, and its move-ment out of the country to buyers who were willing to pay much higher prices than did the Government, which controlled the in-dustry. The Arab, however, had just mentioned something which suggested that he knew of a business deal in which he, Salim, was involved, but which made no sense to him. What was he talking about? Salim wondered.

"You never answered my question," the man murmured in his peculiar purring voice.

Salim continued to study the man's face as he searched for a clue to the Arab's meaning. Salim had many and varied interests, and he kept them separated; a man with whom he dealt in coffee was unaware of what else and with whom Salim did business in other areas. He was close-mouthed about his affairs. It was safer that way. The swarthy-complexioned, high-cheekboned face of his companion told him nothing, aside from the slightly raised eyebrow that indi-cated his inquiry. Since the man did not intend to give any clues as to his meaning, Salim decided to be honest.

"I'm sorry, my friend," he said, smiling. "I didn't answer because I don't know what you are referring to."

The Arab accepted this statement without reaction. The waiter began placing cups, coffeepot, sugar, and a small pitcher of hot milk on the low table. After the waiter left, the Arab remonstrated softly: "Come, now, Salim. I find that hard to believe."

"Believe it or not as you choose—I still don't understand."

"I said," the man recalled, "that I am grieved that you did not think to include me in your local and, I might add, very profitable industry here. I should have thought that my transportation organization would have proved helpful." He drew thumb and forefinger down the length of his nose before suggesting, "Perhaps my services were underbid?"

Salim smiled to relieve his words of any sting. "I heard what you said. My confusion results not from your words, but from your meaning. Exactly what local industry are you referring to? My hotel?"

The lean, chiseled face studied his own in disappointment for a moment, and then the dark eyes moved away to observe the water hole. "No," he said, "I don't mean the hotel."

Salim followed the man's interested gaze, and he noticed that a group of some dozen elephants were watering below the veranda.

"What then?" he inquired with an edge of boredom in his voice; he was becoming tired of the man's veiled allusions.

"I mean, of course," the Arab replied, "the ivory." He nodded slightly in the direction of the elephants.

Salim's eyebrows flicked up in surprise. "I don't deal in trophies. You know that."

The Arab's face was politely disbelieving. "No?"

"No." Salim's voice was flat and decisive. "I should think it would be obvious. You are aware that my family and I have large investments in the tourist industry." He indicated the huge, sprawling lodge with a wave of his hand. "Hotels, tour companies, and car-rental agencies, to name just a few things. And all," he stressed, "are dependent on the wildlife. No wildlife"—he spread his hands—"no tourists. So what purpose would I serve in dealing in illicit trophies? To make a small profit in ivory now, I'd be committing financial suicide. This hotel would be empty, and valueless, in a year."

The Arab watched him closely. There was doubt in the dark eyes. "The profits I'm speaking of are not small, Salim. Not at all. They are in fact quite large. Large enough to tempt a man to participate, particularly if"—he paused to emphasize his next words—"a man were to quietly unload his valuable tourist-oriented investments in order to escape the eventual death of the tourist industry itself." He sipped his coffee before adding nonchalantly, "I understand you're quietly looking for a buyer for this hotel, which you appear only to manage for your family, but yet actually own outright yourself."

Salim was surprised, and now he saw how the man's train of thought had led him to suppose that he might be dealing in ivory. It was true that he was looking for a buyer—very quietly looking, in Europe; so how did the Arab know of it? Or the fact that he was more than just the manager? The possible sale of this lodge was not, of course, because he intended to unload his tourist-industry-related investments. On the contrary, it was because he wanted to start a line of floating hotel ships to cruise along the east coast of Africa, and he needed the capital out of the lodge to launch the other, which would be a much larger and eventually more valuable investment. It would be impossible to mention this at the moment; the concept, the idea, was his own, and he didn't want anyone else to be the first to put it into operation. He intended to provide the one and only such service at first; the imitators could come later and take the smaller share of the market.

Besides, he considered the Arab's reference to "large profits in ivory." Exactly what, and how much, was large? It was the first he'd heard of it, but because the ivory was coming from this area, he was curious as to who and how. He didn't like the traffic in trophies; it was a dirty business; and besides, it threatened the continued profitability of his investments. He decided to sidestep the question of the lodge. Instead he would gently goad the other man into revealing more information about the ivory.

Smiling sardonically, Salim said, "I'm surprised at you, my friend. How could you think I would be foolish enough to contemplate such a game for the sake of a few pounds of ivory?"

The Arab leaned forward and murmured, "I am not talking about a few pounds, Salim; I'm discussing several tons."

Salim's face registered only polite interest, although he was astounded. He smiled condescendingly. "You must be mistaken," he said, and finished his coffee.

The Arab studied him a moment. He weighed what he knew of Salim, his business interests and the probable extent of his involvement in ivory. He knew they were both fencing for information and neither wished to show his hand, but one of them would have to, or the conversation would end. He was interested in only one thing: Why had Salim not cut him into this profitable venture? It seemed, though, that he would have to be direct. Salim obviously intended to pretend ignorance.

He leaned back again and slowly fingered the rough-cut-ruby cuff link at his wrist. His soft, whispering voice purred, "Between two and three tons of ivory move out of Aruba each week and find their way to Mombasa. This is a fact that has recently come to my attention, and so I asked myself"—his thin-lipped mouth suggested a small smile—"Who in this village could put together and run such a large operation? Who has considerable experience in, shall we say"—the thin smile became more pronounced—"the movement of illegally owned goods?" He paused and shrugged. "I came to the only possible conclusion: my dear Salim, of course.

"And now I shall repeat my original question," he added. "Why did you not choose to allow me to participate?"

Salim thought quickly. He did not doubt what the man was telling him. The Arab's sources of information were invariably correct. If the man wasn't actually involved in a particular smuggling operation, he at least knew of it, and usually knew who was involved and for what kind of profit. Still, the idea of such a large organization's operating so close to him and without even his suspicion surprised him. More than that: it staggered him. The ivory had to come from inside the park. There were few elephants left outside. He thought of David Karanja, and an involuntary grimace darkened his face.

He had to find out what was going on, not only for his own sake, for his investments, but for David. Two to three tons of ivory a week, he rapidly calculated. The tusks, he knew, were down to roughly thirty-five pounds a side, for seventy pounds per elephant. My God, he thought, that's somewhere between sixty and a hundred elephants a week! How long could the herds survive losses like that? How long could the park?

He glanced up at the Arab. Now was the time to lay all the cards down, face up. He had to have the man's cooperation, his sources of information. He'd never get them if the Arab continued to think that he had been deliberately overlooked in some lucrative operation.

He leaned forward and looked into the man's eyes. "You're right about my ownership of the lodge, and you're also right about my decision to sell; but," he said, "you're wrong about my reasons. I'm not unloading my tourist services. I'm selling the lodge to raise the capital to invest very heavily in another group of hotels, which will need a thriving tourist industry to survive." He observed the Arab's face and saw the man's earlier expression of doubt return.

"I am not now, nor have I ever been, involved in ivory. I don't know who is, and what you mentioned today is the first, the absolute first, that I've heard of it."

The Arab murmured in Swahili, *"Kweli?"*

"Kweli!" Salim said decisively. Yes, it was true.

The Arab's eyebrows lifted in surprise; he raised his shoulders slightly in resignation. "It is not what I expected to hear. You astonish me, Salim." He looked at him carefully before saying, with a nod, "But I believe you.

"You see," he added, "I based my opinion that you were involved on the fact that you were the only one here in this area who had such business experience. That and the rumors about the possible sale of the hotel. Still, it did not fit with what I knew of your aversion to traffic in trophies, and with the dependence of your family's investment on the tourist trade." He smiled. "I'm pleased to have been proved wrong."

"I'm glad you feel that way," replied Salim, "but the fact remains that you did seriously entertain the unkind idea that I might have overlooked a friend." His face was bland, although his voice had a hard edge to it. "That does not please me. I do not like to think," he continued coldly, "that I am not trusted by those with whom I do business."

The Arab regarded him speculatively. He didn't want to offend Salim. Had he done so? Or was it a pose? He smiled to himself. What theater business was.

His expression was one of humble contrition. "Forgive me," he murmured softly, bending slightly at the waist in a not ungraceful gesture. "How can I make amends?"

Salim accepted the apology and smiled to indicate his willingness to forgive. "It is forgotten. But . . ." He appeared to think a moment before continuing: "I would appreciate your assistance in a small matter. . . ." He paused, and the Arab waited.

"I would very much like to know who is involved in this poaching operation. Who are they? And where? It is a matter of interest to me," he added, "to know who is doing business in my area. You understand, of course."

The Arab smiled. "Of course," he said. "It will not be easy, and it will not be inexpensive information to come by, but of course, anything to make amends for my rude and unworthy suspicions. I will call you tomorrow." They both smiled in perfect understanding.

IT WAS UNBELIEVABLY HOT, and there was no chance of its beginning to cool for hours yet. Duncan Shelby squinted against the sun's glare; it was midafternoon, and he'd been out in the fields since after breakfast.

He couldn't remember a hotter day, and so dry that his smoke-filled nostrils felt as if they were about to crack open. The clouds had drifted on hours ago, and now the sky was a hard, almost metallic blue, against which the rising billows of thick black smoke floated aimlessly. At least, the wind had died to almost nothing, but while it slowed the progress of the flames, the lack of wind seemed to increase the heat of the sun, which was augmented by the burning sisal.

He turned to the new firebreak dug at the edge of the sisal field, and watched as his foreman and one unit of Karanja's Field Force supervised the field hands and the park's labor force as they beat wearily at the burning sisal with branches of thick green leaves. They were all tired, so now they were working in teams: one lot beat at the flames while the other group rested; then they changed about. The men had been at it for over eight hours, and if their luck and the wind held, they might have it halted before dark.

So far, the fire had spread itself out unevenly along a four-kilometer front, and had reached the firebreak in only one place, where it promptly died out for lack of combustible material. The rest of the fire was still creeping slowly through the thick sisal crop, and it was here that the men moved about with flailing arms waving scorched leafy branches to beat out and smother the flames. Even if they stopped the flames' advance, the fire would continue to smolder for days in the thick clumps of charred sisal and in the cannonball droppings of the elephants. Then all it would take would be a stiff breeze to fan it up and move it out again. It was going to require a lot of watching, but thank God, the wind was on their side today.

"Good Lord," Shelby murmured, "it's hot." He wiped his forehead and was surprised that he wasn't sweating. His face was very hot and dry; but then, the air was dry; as dry as a bleached bone. The heat danced over the sisal, and his vision wavered and became distorted. Closing his eyes, he became aware of a headache, and again he was irritated; like an absentminded nit, he'd run off this morning without his hat, and now his head seemed as if it had been baked.

He felt it first: a gentle pressure against the side of his face. He opened his eyes and glanced around. What was it? Suddenly the thick smoke was in his nostrils, and he realized that the wind was picking up.

He began to walk awkwardly through the prickly sisal plants to a position where he could see better. The smoke no longer rose straight up into the air; now it drifted sideways, and he could see the figures of the men becoming indistinct in the dark haze. He heard the foreman call out the resting men, and now everyone was in the sisal.

Red tongues of flames began to appear as the wind fanned smoldering heaps of blackened sisal into flaming bushes; a small spurt of red would show itself against the black, and grow until it became a spear of flame that multiplied, grew taller and, as the wind gusted, bent down to stab at the next plant, the next row.

"Blast it!" Shelby yelled in irritation and frustration. Why couldn't it have held off just a little longer? It was coming up as it often did; no wind one minute, then strong gusts the next, and they were growing in strength each moment. It could get worse, or it could immediately die out: both were equally possible. He continued through the sisal ahead of the flames and behind the line of men, whose flailing branches rose and fell in a faster rhythm than before.

"Good," he murmured to himself. His foreman was doing his job. He could see that the men were deployed well and working hard. Then he noticed an odd shape some distance ahead in the smoke, but he couldn't see what it was. Something big, and right behind the line of men who were falling back ahead of the encroaching flames, but flailing and fighting the creeping blaze and giving ground slowly and reluctantly. If they aren't holding it, at least they're slowing it down, he thought grimly; but what was that ahead? The flames were coming up on it quickly.

Then the haze cleared a fraction of a second and he saw it. "Damnation!" he roared, and began to run. Some blasted idiot had left one of his tractors parked in the sisal, instead of moving it far back on the other side of the firebreak.

He stumbled and nearly fell; caught himself and ran on through the clutching sisal plants. God, it's hot! he thought briefly, and he felt his heart pounding, his breath becoming labored beyond his exertion. His legs seemed to be made of rubber, and he felt queer and disoriented; in his confusion he wondered: where was he going? What was he doing? Oh, yes, the tractor.

He took two more long, wobbling strides and felt himself going down. The words "How strange" passed through his mind. He was unconscious before his face hit the dry red earth.

"IT'S A DEATH TRAP," Jeff muttered despondently as he surveyed the drying Ashaga Swamp. In the past, the huge swampland had been fed by the seasonal Moda River, and even during the dry seasons, when the river dried out to leave its sandy riverbed to unwind like a ribbon across the land, the subterranean water kept the marsh soaked. But now the extended drought and the falling water table had turned the swamp to a glutinous trap.

"Can we save them?" Audrey asked with a catch in her throat as she watched the elephants thrash feebly in the mud that held them fast.

"Maybe those three," Jeff replied hopefully. "But not the other two. One's dead, and the other is too far gone." He left her side to direct the Michigan tractor into position near the closest of the grounded elephants.

The call had come through to Research an hour before when Unit 7 of the Field Force had discovered the animals while on patrol. It had been twelve days since a patrol had passed that way, and there was no way of knowing how long the animals had been ensnared and suffering in the drying mud. Now patrols would have to check the area daily.

Audrey watched as Jeff and two rangers dragged a heavy cable out to the huge but weakened bull who lay on his side, and began to maneuver it under the animal. The massive head lifted apathetically as Jeff crawled through the mud and up onto the animal's side. Audrey's heart nearly stopped as the bull's heavy trunk snaked out to brush Jeff's leg as the men drew the cable up from under the bull and across his chest behind the forelegs. The heavy head drooped and lay once more in the mud as the cable was secured. He made no attempt to tusk or grab with his trunk at Jeff or the rangers. It was as if he knew that the men were trying to help.

The tractor began to pull the bull from the quagmire and onto the bank, where he was allowed to rest a moment before being lifted onto his feet by the tractor blade. One by one the three elephants were extracted and herded on shaking legs down the riverbed to where the rangers had dug a deep hole in the sand which was now slowly filling with seeping water. There were a number of trees nearby that would provide decent forage. With luck, those three would survive.

After the elephants had gone, Audrey jumped in sudden panic at the sound of a shot. She spun about, to see Jeff hand the rifle back to the unit corporal before walking away from the young cow he'd just destroyed. He hated having to put down an animal; there was something obscene about just giving up; but he never asked a subordinate to relieve him of the responsibility, even though it would eat at him for hours.

"There was nothing . . . ?" she asked hesitantly.

"No." He tried absentmindedly to scrape off the worst of the thick mud that covered him. "I'm sorry," he added with a feeble smile. "Let's go home. After a long soak and a stiff drink I promise I'll be human again."

As they drove back to Headquarters Hill, Audrey laid her head on the seat and closed her eyes. After a moment she heard Jeff murmur, "Even after all this time, the intelligence of the elephant never ceases to amaze me."

Still with her eyes closed, she asked, "Did they know?"

His reply was reflective: "I think they did."

She was nearly asleep when Jeff's roar jolted her awake: "What the hell?"

She sat up and glanced around in confusion. Then she saw the *kombi* van racing along in the bush about a quarter of a kilometer off the road. Jeff jerked the wheel, and the heavy Research vehicle left the road and tore after the *kombi* through the low scrub. As they drew nearer the still-unsuspecting van, Audrey saw what it was chasing: a cheetah with two half-grown cubs. Jeff hit the horn, and the *kombi* driver looked up and recognized the park vehicle. As the van slowed and stopped, the driver's expression was apprehensive.

The worst offenders against park regulations were usually the drivers of the safari-tour companies' *kombi* vans which operated out of Nairobi or Mombasa and whose services were contracted for by overseas visitors. The visitors couldn't be expected to know all the park's rules and regulations, although common sense should make them aware of some of the violations committed by their drivers, which usually fell into the categories of speeding, driving off the road, littering, and pestering or endangering the wildlife. This last category of pestering the animals was most often the result of visitors' wishing to photograph the animals "doing something." A photo of a pride of sleeping lions did not seem to be nearly as desirable as a photo of the same lions snarling and being generally ferocious, so visitors would play car radios loudly, shout, hammer on their car doors with their fists, clap their hands, and throw rocks in their efforts to arouse the animals. Another favorite was of the predators on a kill; the leopards, who usually hunted at night, were spared this indignity, but the cheetahs were often forced to go hungry because a *kombi* van had driven off the road and right up onto a feeding animal, thereby frightening it and causing it to flee. By the time the tourists left the area, the cheetah would often find that it had lost the carcass to a lion or hyena, and so was forced to hunt again or do without.

As Jeff pulled up in front of the van and jumped out, Audrey knew there was going to be trouble. He was in a foul mood, and selfish and inconsiderate tourists and their unscrupulous tip-grubbing drivers were one of his pet peeves.

"Out," Jeff growled at the alarmed driver, who clambered out the door. Suddenly remembering the half-dozen European tourists who were watching in confusion from the van, the driver attempted to recoup his composure by crossing his arms defiantly.

A beefy, wattle-necked man in a curio-shop Aussie bush hat stuck his head up through the *kombi*'s sun roof to wave his camera and bluster loudly in a thick accent, "Who do you think you are? Get out of here, you fool! The cat is getting away."

Jeff looked up at the man and said quietly, "I think you'd best stay out of this. Unless, of course, you want to be charged as well." The tourist withdrew from view.

Turning to the driver, Jeff said, "You know what this means. Two months in jail or a two-thousand-shilling fine. And you'll never be allowed to drive in this or any other national park. So that's the end of your job." He paused and then added, "Was it worth it?"

The driver stared at the ground and said nothing. His resentment had turned his face to stone.

Climbing back into his vehicle, Jeff motioned for the *kombi* to pull in behind and follow him back to Headquarters, where the driver would be arrested and the tourists asked to leave the park.

"Damn those people!" Jeff muttered. "If they aren't speeding on the roads and plowing into a herd of animals to kill and cripple dozens every year, then they're running them down in the bush. Meanwhile, Amboseli looks like a motocross course from the air.

"Why, dammit?" he asked of no one. "Why must they destroy it all?"

HE LAY QUIETLY. Collecting his thoughts with difficulty, he tried to place himself. Where was he? What was he doing? Through the confusion he dimly recalled the burning sun, the hot flames in the sisal fields, and the wind.

He felt the wind on his body; it was stronger now, but much cooler. He struggled to open his eyes, but they felt heavy and weighted. The smell of smoke was faint, almost imperceptible. Perhaps they'd succeeded in holding it, in spite of the gusts he felt playing over his body. He tensed. Someone was touching him; he was sure of it.

He forced his eyes open. There was a man standing over him waving a newspaper; it was his cook. Beside him was another man doing the same, and he recognized the gardener. What was going on?

He noticed that the room was his own; he was at home. How had he got here? His clothes were gone, and he was dressed only in a pair of what felt like wet shorts. Then he noticed the woman; she was down along the side of the bed he lay on, and she was bathing his legs with cold water.

He cleared his throat and with a great effort he mumbled, "What the hell are you doing, madam?"

Unperturbed gray eyes glanced up at him through thick spectacles.

"*Lete barafu zaidi,*" she ordered, and picking up her bowl of water, she moved up along the bed toward his head.

The cook stopped fanning him and put down his newspaper before leaving the room quickly to fetch the ice she requested.

"I said," he repeated louder, "what . . ." The chill wet cloth covered his face and mouth, and the rest of his words were muffled.

As she continued to bathe his face, she commanded, "Shut up."

He lay with eyes closed against the dripping cloth and seethed with indignant vexation. What was he doing here? He should be out at the fire—and who was that dreadful woman? He'd seen her somewhere, if he could only recall where; and then he remembered. The mission nurse. That did it. By God, he wasn't about to lie here nearly naked while some female missionary gave him a bath. He had things to do, and if he was dirty, he'd bathe himself later.

He began to struggle into a sitting position; he'd got his shoulders raised and his weight on his elbows when he began to feel lightheaded and his temples started to pound. Vera finished adding the fresh ice to the bowl of water and saw him attempting to get up; she reached down, took his hand and pulled gently; his elbow slid out from under him, and he fell back with a soft plop onto the pillows.

As his mouth opened to protest, she said quietly, "If you try to do that again, I'll have to have your men restrain you."

His mouth stayed open with astonishment. His men would *what?*

She sensed what he was thinking and replied, "They would, you know, if I told them to. You've already had one convulsion, so it wouldn't be the first time they've held you down today." She continued bathing him gently while the two men waved the newspapers to create a draft over his body.

Shelby studied their eyes; it was a habit he'd formed long ago when he'd discovered it was the most reliable way to tell what was going on inside a man. He knew these men—they'd been with him many years—and he could see that they were alarmed and frightened; for him. Not of him, but for him. A convulsion? How could that be? Yet when he took stock of himself, he realized that he felt terrible.

Vera left off the bathing and merely laid cold wet towels over his body. Taking up a thermometer, she checked it, shook it down, and after checking it again gently nudged his lip with it.

"Open," she commanded.

He glared at her.

"Well," she said sweetly, "I thought perhaps you'd prefer your temperature taken orally this time, since you're finally conscious, but if you prefer . . ." She left the sentence unfinished and reached for another thermometer with a thicker, rounded bulb on the business end.

Shelby eyed his men; they were obviously in the enemy camp. He grudgingly opened his mouth.

Vera began soaking more towels in the ice water, then replaced those on his body with the colder ones while he lay without resistance, thinking. Slowly he put the pieces of information together. He vaguely remembered the burning sisal fields and knew he must have passed out, since he couldn't recall being moved here. She'd said something about his finally being conscious; therefore he must have been unconscious—but for how long? His eyes traveled to the windows; by the shadows across the veranda, he could tell it was past six. He was astounded. It had been about four o'clock the last he knew.

She took the thermometer from his mouth and read it. Turning to the men, she told them to stop fanning him, removed the wet towels and covered him with a cool dry sheet.

Sitting down in the chair beside the bed, she took his wrist and checked his pulse. Finally she said, "You are a very lucky man, Mr. Shelby. I didn't think we were going to save you." She carefully laid his hand aside and picked up the rug she was hooking.

The blunt statement startled him, and he confronted the implication that he had very nearly died.

"What happened?" he mumbled with an effort.

"You had a heatstroke," she replied calmly. "You collapsed in the fields, and your men brought you home and sent a car for me. When I got here, you were unconscious and your skin was burning hot and very dry. Your temperature was up over a hundred and eight degrees, and I don't mind telling you that I was worried; you didn't seem to respond well to cooling at first."

He pondered this for a moment, and then asked, "A hundred and eight degrees?"

"Closer to a hundred and nine."

"What is it now?"

"It's down to just a hair under a hundred and two. I think you'll be all right."

He tried to understand, but didn't. "It doesn't make sense to me. Was it my heart?"

She frowned over her spectacles. "No—as near as I can tell, your heart is fine. I told you, it was the heat; too much heat."

"But that's preposterous," he blustered. "I've been here for fifty years and the heat's never bothered me."

The soft plop of her hook ceased, and she looked up at her patient. "That's one of the reasons you had a heatstroke; you have been here fifty years and you're an old man now, Mr. Shelby. You can't spend the day running about in the sun without a hat, the way you might have been able to do when you were a youngster."

Before he could protest further, she added, "Heatstroke is an immediate life-threatening condition, and even with prompt hospitalization, skilled doctoring, and the best facilities, the mortality rate is thirty-five percent." She paused to let this sink in before explaining further, believing that the best way to guarantee an adult patient's cooperation was by letting him know exactly what his condition was.

"When I got here you were unconscious and burning hot; your skin was as red as a beetroot and completely dry; you were unable to sweat to cool your body, so we pulled off your clothes and started bathing you in ice water to bring your terrible temperature down."

She peered at him for a moment. "Being you, of course, you didn't want to cooperate at first, but finally your temperature began to fall. If there were a hospital nearby I'd put you in it, but since there isn't, I'll just have to keep an eye on you myself."

He glared at her in frustration. He couldn't abide missionaries— he'd never liked them—and here he had one perched on a chair beside his bed like a vulture, and it appeared she'd settled in to stay. He had no patience with sickness, or with mealy-mouthed Godbotherers, and he wanted up and out of here. Now.

"I have work to do," he declared with an effort, and moved as if to get up.

"Where do you think you're going?" she inquired mildly.

"To the fields!" he roared.

"You'll do no such thing, and if you thrash about once more, I'll have you tied down." She continued working her rug hook.

"You'll do what?" he croaked loudly.

"I said," she replied quietly, "that I'll have you tied down.

You're not going anywhere, Mr. Shelby. You're a silly old fool who very nearly killed himself this afternoon, and you've taken up the better part of my afternoon doing it."

Peering over the top of her spectacles, she continued, "I've no intention of leaving, or allowing you to get out of that bed, so you'd best get used to the idea that you have several days of complete bed rest in store for you—and," she added, "my unwelcome company. So lie still, and go to sleep, or you'll make your temperature rise again."

His astonishment passed after a moment and left him feeling exhausted. He was too tired to argue with her, and this knowledge more than anything else made him realize that she was probably right. It seemed he wasn't well after all, and the experience was a new one. The soft plop of her rug hook continued, and the repetitious sound became a pleasant background for his growing drowsiness.

Just before he nodded off to sleep, he glanced over at her, and the last thing he thought was that at least she wasn't mealy-mouthed.

MOHAMED AGARAN finished giving his orders to the Gate Rangers at Kijiji Tai Gate, and after replacing the radio microphone he turned to his driver, who nodded his understanding. He'd heard the radio messages.

Agaran sat back and rubbed his eyes. They were inflamed from lack of sleep and the gritty dust that was thrown up from the corrugated service track they sped over. He'd had days of work to accomplish up north, and hours to do it in. But it was done now, and he'd hoped to be back at Main Headquarters in the south before dusk; he was needed, and Karanja was expecting him; but it didn't look as if he'd make it.

As the Toyota approached the cutoff to Kijiji Tai, the driver turned without question. There was a problem there that the Gate Rangers couldn't handle. The meeting at Headquarters, the count, the fire, and everything else had to wait.

After a half-hour the Toyota pulled up to the small gate station. Kijiji Tai was the least known and utilized of the park's entrances, since its only function was to provide access to the small tented camp on the Ruui River. Agaran climbed out of the vehicle as one of the four Gate Rangers ran up to salute.

"Where is she?" Agaran asked in Swahili.

The ranger gesticulated down the curved road approaching the gate. "Beyond the bend," he said. "In the bush beside the road."

"How long has she been there?" Agaran asked as he loaded the .303.

"*Sijui*," the Ranger replied, before explaining that since no visitors had arrived that day, they hadn't known of the elephant cow's presence until one of the men had left to drive the sixty kilometers to one of the small villages outside the park for supplies. She stood there now and would not allow any vehicle to pass into or out of the park entrance.

Agaran nodded, and after adjusting the .303 on his shoulder, he loaded the shotgun with cartridges. Putting a few extra in his shirt pocket, he said, "Stay here" and started down the road.

As he approached the blind curve in the road he slowed, then stopped to listen. There was no sound except for the drone of the insects. The wind was from the south—she wouldn't scent his approach; and if she was a hundred meters away, she probably wouldn't see him either: his khaki uniform would blend in with the dried-out vegetation. He edged around the near side of the curve, close to the thick bush, silently placing his feet in the thick powdered dirt at the edge of the road.

There she was. About fifty meters away. Standing broadside to him in the middle of the road.

The shotgun roared. Dirt and pebbles flew up from the roadbed in front of her. She spun about to face him, her ears extended in agitation, her trunk lifted high. The shotgun boomed again, and as Agaran quickly reloaded, she trumpeted a shrill scream of defiance and rushed several steps forward, her trunk lowered.

"Don't do it," he muttered as the sweat ran into his eyes, the .303 ready on his shoulder. The shotgun roared again; the pellets hit the ground before her and more dirt flew against her forelegs.

He took a step forward as she wavered, hesitating, not sure whether to charge or not. The shotgun blasted once more. She took a step backward, then another; again she screamed, her huge ears flapping as she tossed her head. He kept moving forward, pressing her, as he loaded his last two cartridges. The breech snapped shut. The gun came up again as the distance between them closed. The shotgun thundered once, then again for the last time. She was too close. Just as he reached for the .303, she turned and fled into the bush at the side of the road, leaving him standing alone on the dirt track. He took a deep breath; the first in several seconds.

He listened to her crashing through the bush till the silence returned, then walked on to where she'd been standing. Elephants didn't act peculiarly without cause. After a few moments of searching the thick bush at the side of the road, he found the reason for

325

her single-minded vigil on the road. A very small and emaciated female calf lay crumpled in death beside the track. The cow had been standing guard over her youngster.

The relationship between an elephant cow and her calf was an extremely close one, and some of the scenes he'd witnessed were almost heartbreaking. Dying calves standing by dead mothers who'd been the victims of poachers, or cows standing beside their dead calves, sometimes trying to urge and lift them onto their feet. In August he'd watched an older cow with the carcass of her very young calf and seen the cow kneel down beside the youngster and use her trunk to gather the calf up onto her tusks, and then with her trunk still clasping the calf, she'd stood and moved off slowly into the bush, carrying her dead youngster on her tusks.

Twice before he'd come across elephant cows standing in the sun beside the body of a dead calf, and knowing that the cow would probably stand there until she too died, or was killed by poachers, he'd decided to try to run the cow off. If he kept at it and could get her a mile or so away, he'd learned that the cow would then finally accept the inevitable and move off; but it was an exhausting exercise, which could last for hours as he attempted to use a Land-Rover like a cutting horse by getting the vehicle between the cow and her dead calf, and with horn honking and by banging his fists on the metal door he succeeded in making enough racket to get the cow moving. Invariably she would double back and make better and faster time through the bush than could the vehicle, but back he'd go to the calf, and the operation would be repeated over and over again, but each time he'd try to drive her a little farther than the last time, until finally she gave up.

If he'd known about the calf earlier, he'd have done the same today. He'd come very close to having to kill her.

After giving the Gate Rangers orders to load the dead calf into a vehicle for disposal far in the bush where the cow would never find it, he climbed back into his Toyota, pointed toward Headquarters in the south, and said to his driver, *"Twende, haraka."* Then he leaned back, stretched out his legs, and yawned. By the time the driver reached the cutoff to Main Headquarters, Assistant Warden Agaran was asleep and snoring gently.

CHAPTER EIGHTEEN

Evening

ASSISTANT WARDEN—Works Bruce McKinney reentered Headquarters after having been summoned from home and his now-cold bachelor dinner. It was just past six and he'd put in a long, rough day, but unplanned emergencies were part of the job, and had been for too many years to cause him any surprise now.

He tapped once at Karanja's office door and walked in.

David glanced up and said, "Good, you're here. I need your help."

McKinney sat down. "What's the problem? Not enough ground transport?"

"No, we've enough," David replied. "The planes have been coming in all afternoon, and the Radio Room has been sending vehicles to pick up the pilots and observers and get them over to the lodge. Later they'll be brought back to Headquarters for the meeting. No, it's the fire we've got problems with."

McKinney nodded and waited.

"I've got my hands full with the count, and Agaran has been sidetracked with elephant control at Kijiji Tai. That leaves only you, and we both know you've handled more fires than the rest of us put together."

"Age has its small rewards," McKinney said with a grin. "How bad is it?"

"It's still outside the park boundary and theoretically it's not yet our problem, but it will be once it's through the sisal. Unit One has been out there all day, and it seems that by midafternoon they nearly had it halted, but the wind came up and it began moving again. Then Shelby took sick, but Corporal Lugumba didn't know much about it other than the fact that he was taken home." David's face revealed his concern. "I sent a man over to check, and it seems Shelby's had a heatstroke and almost didn't regain consciousness."

McKinney shook his head. Poor Shelby. "How can I help?" he asked.

"I want you to go out and see what can be done, if anything. I'm putting you in charge. Shelby's unable to supervise the fire fighting, and I don't know anything about his foreman." Shrugging his shoulders, he added, "He may know what he's doing, but then again, he may not. As I said before, it's not really our problem at the moment, but if the wind is against us it could be into the park within hours. I'd like to stop it before it gets here. With Shelby out there I wasn't worried, but now that he's gone we've got to have someone who knows what he's doing to supervise the fire and get it either halted or contained."

McKinney nodded. "I'll go home and get changed and go on out. Where can I reach you later?"

"Here," answered David. "We have a meeting within the hour of all pilots and observers, so I'll be easy to find."

As McKinney shambled out, David heard the sound of aircraft coming in to land. He got up from his desk, crossed to the window and looked out to see two planes coming in.

The lead plane was that of the Senior Warden, and right behind it was his own. "Shepherd said he'd have it here today," David murmured exultantly, "and he's kept his promise. He made it!"

THE AGED Education Center bus groaned its way up the incline behind the Warden's residence toward the elephant *boma* ahead while Halima and the children's teacher held on to the overhead luggage racks and tried to maintain order among the busload of wriggly and giggling children.

"Sit down," Halima repeated in Swahili for what seemed to be the hundredth time that day. "Please sit down now."

The bus lurched, throwing the children against one another to produce another shrieking outburst of glee. Halima glanced down at the dark little head that had once more collided with her hip. The child peeped up with huge, darkly liquid eyes; a giggle bubbled up from inside to burst into a wide smile before her small hands covered her mouth to force it back in. Halima grinned back; it was impossible not to.

Such a busy day, she thought. It had been the second of a three-day visit of a group of thirty-three teen-agers from one of the Nairobi secondary schools, and they'd also had this group from one of the Taita Hills primary schools who had come for a day visit. With only one bus, she'd had to do some juggling to see that both groups were transported around for a conducted tour and game-viewing drive and now, before returning to the Center, the highlight of a day at Aruba for the younger children, a trip to the elephant *boma*.

As the bus rolled to a stop, Halima bent down to peer out of the window over the heads of the excited children. Good: the elephants were back and confined inside their pens. Threading her way down the crowded aisle, she got off and herded the children together as they descended.

After a nose count, she started off at the head of the group to restrain the more venturesome of the boys as they walked the last hundred meters, while the primary teacher brought up the rear and the bus driver followed with a basket of oranges. The children began to quiet down as they approached the huge elephants, and again Halima wondered if the people in Europe and the rest of the world realized that these children's interest in and regard for animals had to be awakened and taught them, just as in other parts of the world; perhaps even more so here, where the wildlife had been taken for granted.

"You're just in time."

Halima turned to see Audrey as she approached with two large formula bottles. "Super," she exclaimed. "I'd hoped we would be." Halima turned to the now-reserved, wide-eyed children, and addressed them in Swahili: "I want you boys and girls to meet *Mama Wanyama*." She smiled mischievously at the use of Audrey's sobriquet. "She cares for all the orphaned animals in the park."

The children shyly chorused a polite greeting as Audrey laughed. Murmuring in an undertone, she said with a grin, "I'll get even with you for that," as she opened the lion-proof fence around the *boma* before turning to the children to ask, "Wouldn't you like to see Miss Abdi feed a baby elephant?"

The children shrieked their approval and clearly enjoyed Halima's obvious discomfort.

"Oh, no . . . I couldn't," she protested as she eyed Sarah, who towered above her on the other side of the fence.

"Oh, yes, you can," Audrey chuckled, thrusting a large formula bottle into her hands. "There's nothing to it," she added as she opened Sarah's pen and propelled Halima inside, where her low-heeled shoes promptly sank in the dung.

Zimwi looked up from the other side of the pen and saw her

bottle. A shrill, blatting scream accompanied her headlong charge across the pen. Halima gasped and retreated a step, only to feel someone fumble gropingly at her backside. She spun about to confront an inquisitive Galogalo, who, used as he was to Audrey and Jeff's habit of keeping oranges in their pockets for the orphans, was checking out her bumps for concealed treats. The children screamed with laughter as Audrey rescued her.

It was several minutes before peace was restored to the elephant *boma*. The children ranged around the fence with their noses pressed to the chain-link as they watched, fascinated, while Audrey and Halima fed the baby elephant.

"Am I forgiven?" Audrey asked in amusement.

Halima laughed softly and nodded. "Actually, I've always wanted to help feed the orphans. Today was just a bit sudden." She ran her hand over Zimwi's head and smiled at the young elephant's dreamy-eyed contentment with her bottle as she lolled against her legs.

"Well, why didn't you say so?" Audrey exclaimed. "I certainly need the help. Come anytime."

"Then I'll come every evening," Halima replied. Noticing Audrey's smart tunic and skirt under her apron, she added, "By the way, why are you all dressed up?"

"There's a meeting soon at Headquarters for everyone who's participating in the count. And while I'm less than delighted about that, and I certainly wouldn't dress for the occasion, it seems that my husband has offered to take me to dinner later at the lodge. Guilty conscience, I think, but I'm not about to refuse an evening out."

"Oh, yes, the meeting," Halima said, reminded. "David mentioned it."

"Did he, now?" Audrey murmured, the interested glimmer in her eye unnoticed by Halima, intent on Zimwi's feeding.

"And when was that?" she asked nonchalantly.

"Last night . . ." Halima began, and then noticed Audrey's pleased smile.

"But . . ." Halima started to protest, but Audrey put her hand up.

"No. I don't want to hear. I'm sure it's awfully innocent, but I'd rather let my imagination run rampant."

"Really, it was nothing," Halima demurred in embarrassment. "He came to dinner and we talked."

"Darn," murmured Audrey wickedly. "And we had such high hopes, too."

"Who?" Halima asked, completely baffled.

"Jeff and I, of course," Audrey retorted. "Who do you think?

The first time I met you, I thought, Ah ha, a really super single female for David to meet, and when Jeff met you he agreed."

"But you never said a word," Halima replied.

"Of course not," Audrey exclaimed. "That would have ruined everything. I can remember when I was single and friends would say, 'I know someone you've *got* to meet.' And I always knew right away that he would be horrid. Besides, it's a ghastly way to have to meet someone. No, it's wretched and we wouldn't do it to either of you. We decided that since it's such a small world here, we'd let you 'discover' each other. But after six weeks we began to wonder. You're always immersed in the Education Center, and David is either at Headquarters or on patrol, so that's when we had that little party a month ago. . . ."

"And I got the flu," Halima interrupted.

"And then two weeks ago we invited you to dinner, and without saying anything, Jeff was supposed to bring David around for a drink."

"What happened then?" Halima asked. "I came."

With an exasperated expression, Audrey replied, "David was called out an hour before to put down a wounded rhino."

"Poor Audrey," Halima consoled her, and then began to laugh.

"And we tried so hard. Actually, it was the 'being subtle' that was difficult."

The low, murmuring comments of the children interrupted their conversation.

"*Ona! Ona!*" one little girl exclaimed softly, nudging a friend to come close and see how Zimwi nursed the bottle.

The bus driver began to hand out the oranges to the children who gathered around him to clutch an offering for the elephants, only to hesitate apprehensively when confronted with an undulating trunk. A small dark arm ventured timidly out of the knot of children; an orange trembled before Sarah, who reached out for it; with a squeal of fear the arm withdrew, dropping the fruit on the ground. Sarah retrieved it, put it in her mouth, and reached for another. Several were shyly offered in a chorus of "ooohs" and "ahhhs." A small hand was hesitantly extended to pat Sarah's trunk, and she accepted the homage of the children as she gently took the fruit.

"Well, that does it," Audrey murmured as the calves began to suck air. She stood up and added as she took the bottles, "Thanks again for helping, and you're welcome any day; but next time"— she grinned mischievously as she started down the hill—"bring an apron."

Halima smiled and began to brush the mud from her uniform

before gathering the children together to herd them down the road toward the waiting bus. The guttural whine of approaching aircraft caused her to look up to see the two small four-seaters as they turned overhead to circle the airfield before landing.

Her thoughts turned to David and she remembered his conversation the night before, his deep concern for the park and its future. She remembered how they'd talked, together, about the things that really mattered to them. Remembered the times when he'd groped for just the right word he'd needed at the moment, and how she'd supplied it. How she'd sought ineffectually to put a feeling into words, and he'd said, "I know what you mean." And he had. The evening had developed into a warm and exciting feeling of intimacy.

She remembered the feel of his mouth and how right and natural it was to be in his arms. Almost before she'd known what was happening, he'd asked, "May I come again?" And when she'd whispered, "Yes," he'd kissed her once more, and left.

Later she'd remembered how she'd worried that he might expect her to fall into bed at the drop of his beret, and she'd begun to laugh at herself. He'd left, and she hadn't wanted him to go. Then an old painful memory had returned, and she'd remembered the ache of rejection, the feeling of inadequacy, of having been tried and found lacking. And then she'd been glad he'd gone, because she couldn't bear for it to happen again.

"YOU GOT IT," said David as he shook John Shepherd's hand.

"If you mean your plane, yes. And I've got a few things more."

"Like what?"

"Reinforcements, permission for roadblocks, and a few other items we can discuss later. What I want to know is: Will we be able to start the aerial census tomorrow?"

"Six A.M. tomorrow will see ten pilots and thirty observers descending on the airfield."

"Marvelous!" exclaimed Shepherd enthusiastically. "I figured you'd do it. Besides, your airfield looks a little crowded at the moment. It reminds me of trying to find a parking place in downtown Nairobi."

"It's a problem I wish I'd had before," said David grimly, "when there wasn't even one plane down there."

"Well, now you've got ten," Shepherd replied, "and after the count when everyone goes home, you'll still have three here for at least a month to assist in aerial reconnaissance during your anti-poaching campaign. And," he added cheerfully, "I'm working on

332

acquiring the loan of another helicopter from the Police Air Wing to help move men ahead of your trackers to close in on detected poachers who are trying to run for it."

David sat on the edge of his desk and marveled, "You're a miracle worker. I can't believe it. After all this time we're finally getting the kind of assistance we need."

"No, I'm no miracle worker, David," the Senior Warden objected with a deprecating shake of his head. "And it's not hard to see why the Department is slow sometimes. They're in Nairobi, and your problems out here seem far away to them at times. Besides, every warden has a problem, or thinks he has. This one demands new road-building equipment; that one can't operate without a helicopter; and somebody else is desperate for a half-million shillings to put into his water projects. On top of that, poaching is endemic. Every park is suffering. That's why Department Headquarters doesn't jump right on every request," the Senior Warden concluded. "They have to study the request, and then look to see what everyone else wants and needs before they can establish priorities."

"And now I'm it," David ventured.

"Your park is number one," Shepherd confirmed. "You've got your aerial census and the wherewithal to do it, and the operating expenses, plus everyone's cooperation for a massive anti-poaching campaign. Besides that, the Department will give you at least two additional Field Force Units to stay here on a permanent basis after the campaign, because we realize that the Somali poachers are not going to go away anytime soon."

The Senior Warden looked thoughtful for a moment and seemed about to add something when they both heard a loud voice outside.

"Is there something else?" asked David of the Senior Warden.

Shepherd's normally cheerful expression had faded into one of gravity. He glanced up at David's exuberant face and smiled a little wryly. "No, it's nothing that won't keep awhile."

"But—" David said. The door burst open and a voice exclaimed, "There you are! I wondered where you were hiding."

Shepherd added, "We'll discuss it before I leave. It isn't important." He looked past David to the man at the doorway and said in a louder tone, "I see you finally got here."

"Did anyone doubt it for a minute?"

David recognized the voice of Warden Davis of Mountain Parks and turned to greet him. He liked the stocky, wiry-haired Kenyan whose family had come to the highlands as settlers three generations before. Davis had grown up on his father's homestead not far from where David had spent his own boyhood, but where David had been fascinated with elephants, Davis' obsession was with the mountain. He'd gone on to climb most of the world's more famous ranges and had finally returned five years before to accept an assistant wardenship with the National Parks to organize and train a mountain-climbing rescue team. Now his African Rescue Unit at Mount Kenya was one of the finest anywhere.

Shaking his hand, David grinned and asked, "How could I *not* doubt it? Yours was the last confirmation in. I'd begun to think you were lost on your own mountain."

Davis' squashed-nosed face mimed outrage. "Did you hear what he said? Me, lost? It's never happened. No, you didn't hear from me because my radio went out. I had to drive down to Nyeri in order to telephone Nairobi and have them pass on the information. Besides," he added in amusement, "you didn't exactly give me much time."

David crossed his arms. "Who needs more than two days' notice? Your wayward mountain climbers don't give you that."

"You're right," agreed Davis. "The little darlings tend to scamper off the trails and drop into the nearest crevasse without any warning at all."

Shepherd chuckled. "You haven't lost any recently, have you?"

"No," replied Davis laconically. "We find them and we bring them down, along with the ones who get mountain or altitude sickness." He shook his head and added, "You would not believe the stupidity of some people. Our latest incident wasn't a mountain climber at all, actually. It was an American girl walking in the higher montane forest near the main camp, and you'll never guess what she did when she saw an elephant. Instead of backing away quietly, she trailed it awhile before marching up to it, only to get tusked through the stomach for wanting to be friends." His expression was incredulous. "The amazing thing was that she lived. I visited her in the hospital, and she said that she thought all the animals were tame. Can you believe it?"

"I know," sighed Shepherd. "You wonder what people are using for brains sometimes. Not all of them are fools, but enough are to warrant putting up signs everywhere to tell people what common sense ought to tell them."

Davis interjected, "You learn that if you don't tell people not to, they'll carpet the ground with plastic sandwich bags and beer cans. They'll chop down a tree for firewood, or leave a fire unattended and burn the whole damn forest down. They'll run their vehicles over delicate patches of vegetation until they're destroyed, and they'll molest the animals until they get hurt in return, and then they complain that the parks are going to hell."

"Are we, or are we not," asked Jeff Forbes as he walked into the room, "going to have a meeting? Or are you gentlemen going to gossip all night?"

"Actually," David said jokingly, "we're having a summit conference on 'The Problems of Conservation in the World Today.'"

"And you've decided what?" asked Forbes in amusement.

"That there is too much time wasted in teaching range and wildlife management to young hopeful assistant wardens," replied Warden Davis, "and not enough on 'The Care and Feeding of Your Tourist,' with special emphasis on 'Tourist Control,' including guidelines for the suppression and restraining of his baser instincts; and in the case of your 'rogue,' or run-amok tourist, I'm suggesting classes on 'The Capture and Immobilization of the Naughty Visitor.'"

Jeff was about to add a caustic remark when Audrey stepped inside the door to say, "Shame on you. We sent you to find David and now you've disappeared as well."

"We'd better go, gentlemen," Forbes said in mock seriousness. "I'm already in trouble."

As they filed into the large conference room next door, Senior Warden Shepherd asked, "Now what have you done, Jeff?"

"I'll answer that," replied Audrey as she slipped her hand into the crook of Jeff's arm. "He volunteered my services as standby observer for the count, because so many were needed in such a short time, and guess what happened?"

"Someone didn't show," answered Shepherd, "and now you're on."

"How did you guess?" said Audrey, smiling in amusement at Jeff.

David moved through the room greeting the pilots and observers who were now trickling in after being brought in carloads from the lodge.

He noticed the tall, thin Luo research biologist Stephen Oyombe from Research Headquarters, and chubby, bearded Dr. Patel, the Indian veterinarian. Warden James Owens of Marsabit was deep in conversation with Warden Matthew Mbuvi from Amboseli. The hum of conversation increased as another vehicle disgorged its passengers to file in and join the laughing, talking congregation.

David glanced around the room. Everyone there was involved somehow in conservation, and were wardens, biologists, zoologists, and botanists or their assistants; they were in administration or in research; they studied plants or animals or both and were committed to their preservation. They were African, English, Dutch, Canadian, and Indian among others, and ranged in color from Mbuvi's deep black complexion to Davis' sunburned white skin.

335

Clearing his throat, he raised his voice to get their attention. "I think we'd better get started now."

As the room began to quiet and everyone found a seat, he began. "First of all, I want to thank you all for coming."

There were a few deprecative murmurs, and David added, "Particularly on such short notice." Several people smiled, and a chuckle was heard at the back.

"I'll try to make this as brief as possible," said David.

Turning to the map, he continued, "Aruba National Park is eighty-five hundred square miles in area, but our wildlife populations don't pay much attention to boundaries, so they're scattered over an ecosystem of approximately seventeen thousand square miles which are divided into twenty-seven blocks, and that"—he turned back to the group—"is what we're going to cover.

"I've made the block assignments, so if the pilots will just raise their hands when I call their names, I'll pass these out to you and we'll get started."

As the pilots' information was distributed, Jeff Forbes passed out the clipboards for all the observers, saying, "When you get your information, you'll see that you've each been assigned to a plane and pilot. I'd like you all to regroup yourselves with your pilots. Then we'll proceed."

David sat on the edge of the conference table as the observers found the pilots of their assigned planes. Soon the room was quiet again and each pilot sat with his three observers clustered about him.

"Now," David continued, "the pilots each have the Kenya Survey maps in which their assigned blocks are located. Plus a block map and data sheet for each block. The flight path of each transect has already been marked for you, so just follow the directions as indicated; your altitude will be three hundred feet; your speed one hundred twenty miles per hour.

"Your starting point is indicated, so begin there; as you cross your block, the pilot and the observer directly behind him will count and record all elephant and rhino on their side of the plane for a distance of five hundred meters, or one-half kilometer. Meanwhile, the observer seated beside the pilot and the one behind him will do the same on their side of the plane for the same distance.

"When you reach the end of your first transect across the block, fly over the block boundary before beginning to bank your turn. By the time you complete your turnaround, you should be approaching the boundary again approximately one kilometer from your first transect; make any adjustments necessary and fly straight back across the block, counting all elephant and rhino that fall within a half-kilometer on each side of the plane. In this manner, you will cross and recross your block in a parallel pattern, until every animal in the block is recorded."

He paused before asking, "Any questions?"

"Now," he continued when he saw there were none, "we'll move on to the method of counting and recording. You each have two forms for each block: one is the block map; the other is the data sheet. Write your name on each and note down the name of your pilot. When you are approaching the block to begin flying your first transect, note the time and write it down on the data sheet. When you finish the last transect, note that. And please," he pleaded in exaggerated seriousness, "synchronize your watches. It's confusing when four people in the same plane all appear to start and stop at wildly different times."

Smiles and scattered laughter greeted the request.

"All right, now you are into your block on your first transect, and the pilot and the observer behind him spot a group of six elephant on the left side of the plane. At that position you mark a 'one' on the left side of the path to indicate the first spotting on your side of the plane. Then turn to your data sheet. Under the heading 'Sighting Number,' write a 'one.' Under the heading 'Species,' write 'elephant.' Under the heading 'Number,' write 'six.'

"Now the pilot and the observer spot a rhino carcass on their side. You both note the position on the block map as 'two' to indicate the second sighting. Write 'two' on the data sheet, indicate 'rhino' under 'Species,' and move over to the heading 'Carcass Category.' Under that you'll see two classifications: 'Fresh' and 'Bone/Skin.' Decide which it is and check it."

He paused and looked around to make sure there were no questions before proceeding. "If you spot a small herd of elephants ahead which number approximately twelve or more, start taking photos as you count. Move to the far right of the form to the heading 'Photo.' Under that you see two headings. Under 'Film/ Frame' you write the code number of the roll of film you have been assigned, and then the frame numbers of the pictures.

"If," he cautioned, "you run into a large herd of perhaps three or four hundred, then the pilot will have to leave the transect flight path and circle the herd while the other spotter takes pictures. In that case, the estimation of their number is best done in the following manner: Take a small section of the herd and count quickly. Say you come up with thirty-five in that small area, and you think that represents about one-tenth of the elephant that are scattered over

337

the larger area. Multiply thirty-five by ten, for an estimated guess of three hundred fifty elephant. We decide the actual number from the enlarged photographs. Remember too that when estimating a large herd people usually estimate low.

"We'll all leave at first light," he continued, "so fly to your farthest block and work back in. The blocks are irregularly shaped and sized because of their natural landmarks and boundaries, but every plane assignment is roughly the same in area to be covered.

"A few more bits of information and then we're done," said David. "We're looking for something like thirty-five thousand elephant and twenty-five hundred rhino. But," he warned, "we're not going to find that many. We will find a lot of carcasses, and please be as accurate about that information as possible. We need to know where they are, what they are, how many, and how old. We're in the midst of a crippling drought, and our poaching problem is beyond belief. We need as much information as possible about what's happened out there. Our survival as a park depends on it."

The room was hushed, and every expression was grave. The effects of the drought were known by everyone present; the extent of the poaching was only guessed at, and feared.

David turned to the large wall map. "Here is where we are now, at Headquarters," he said as he pointed out their position. "And here," he added as he swept the areas north and east of Headquarters, "is where the drought mortalities are."

He turned back to the roomful of people. "Pay particular attention to areas near permanent water. There's where you'll spot the majority of the drought victims."

He turned to Jeff Forbes and said, "Do you have anything to add, Dr. Forbes?"

Jeff shook his head. "No, I don't think so. You've covered everything."

"Any questions?" David asked of the group.

There were a few odd inquiries, and when they had been answered, David checked his watch and said, grinning, "Eight thirty, and time to get you back to the lodge for dinner. Thank you again for your assistance, and we'll meet at five forty-five tomorrow morning at the airfield."

The murmur of conversation resumed as the chairs emptied and their occupants began to move toward the door and the waiting vehicles outside. Clutching their clipboards, gathering up their film, they stopped to talk to one another or to David. A small group formed around him to ask questions or to express hope for favorable weather and a good count, and then they drifted out in ones and twos and small groups.

David continued to sit on the edge of the conference table and listened to the buzz of talk receding as everyone left the building. The planning and preparation was over. The months of frustration he'd spent, aware of his lack of knowledge of the conditions in the far-flung areas of the park, were over. Tomorrow morning the air-field would be swamped with experienced wildlife observers armed with loaded cameras and clipboards; the planes were lined up fueled and waiting, and in forty-eight hours he'd know the answers to the questions that had tormented him for months.

He felt relief, and yet there was something else—something unpleasant that for a moment he couldn't put a name to. Ignorance, he decided at last, had one thing in its favor, and that was not knowing how bad it might be. That was the other something else he'd felt: fear of the worst.

MCKINNEY STOPPED SWEARING long enough to bellow out another order to the men working behind the firebreak. *"Hapa, hapa!"* he yelled as he indicated to the field workers another flare-up that had somehow jumped the graded area to begin winking red in the dark sisal field.

He stood back out of the way of the flailing branches and shoveled earth and looked up and down the fire-illuminated firebreak. The flames had reached the graded path intended to halt the flames' advance at several points now. He coughed again, a long series of hacking barks that left his throat raw. His eyes felt inflamed, and they watered constantly in the billowing smoke.

"If that bloody wind would only drop!" he muttered to himself in exasperation. He strode over to a parked Toyota and climbed up on the hood and then to the roof of the cab, where he observed the fire's progress farther up the break. The flames glowed through the night like a red tide which crept slowly and relentlessly toward the firebreak. The burned-out areas behind the fire were dark, with only an occasional pinpoint of red twinkling here and there where a thick clump of sisal burned and periodically flared a moment in a gust of wind. Shelby's foreman was barely visible in the glare farther up the line at another trouble spot, and McKinney could see that the man was effectively supervising the men at that point. There was no sign that the fire had jumped the break to get a hold on the other side.

He turned and looked through the darkness beyond, toward the park area. Perhaps a half-kilometer, he guessed. There the boundary was graded to provide another firebreak. "But still," he muttered to himself, "I'd rather stop it here."

He looked back toward the fire and to the other end of the firebreak, where a shift in the wind had caused the flames to start to veer sideways. Perhaps he'd better lengthen the firebreak at that end, rather than have a rising wind push the fire around the end in a flanking movement.

Another gust of wind blew smoke into his face, and as he covered his nostrils with a handkerchief, he felt something lightly strike the back of his hand. For a moment he didn't know what it was. He looked about and felt a delicate tap on his shoulder. Looking up in confusion, he felt another hit his face, and then another.

My God, he thought as the drops continued to spatter his up-turned face. It's raining.

CHAPTER NINETEEN

Night

DAVID FINISHED the last sandwich he'd fixed himself and sank back in the thick-cushioned chair to light a cigarette. He'd come home starving and found Bubu gone, but his own culinary efforts had proved satisfactory. In fact, he'd eaten too much, and now he was sleepy.

The veranda was cool, with a brisk breeze that stirred the bougainvillea leaves overhead. The *makuti* rustled as something small scampered across it, and a dark shape at the water hole lapped softly in the muted moonlight.

David glanced at the sky beyond the edge of the veranda roof. Usually the night sky was littered with stars, but tonight was heavily overcast to obliterate even the brightest of them, and the waning moon was dimmed to a cool haze.

Several more low, dark shapes had joined the one at the water hole, and David reached for the flashlight on the low veranda wall. Flicking it on, he caught the green reflection of the cats' eyes. A low, threatening growl greeted the unwelcome light, and David turned it off before the lions became irritated enough to move away, still thirsty. After a moment of silence the lapping began again, accompanied by the short churring call of a nightjar. David made out six dark shapes and watched as three left off drinking to turn and pad silently into the bush. Two more soon left, and then a short series of grunts was heard below the house, which were soon answered by a roar farther on. They were hunting now and probably moving in on the small herd of buffalo near the airfield.

As he watched, two more shadows slipped silently from the dense bush and stood watchful and waiting. After a moment they began to approach the water, and David saw they were being closely trailed by several smaller shapes. Two lionesses, he decided, each with a litter of cubs; he counted three cubs in one group, about half grown. The other litter was quite small. He leaned forward and peered intently into the darkness at the second lioness, whose offspring tumbled along in her wake. These were very small indeed, and again three, perhaps four; it was hard to tell. Obviously the drought and the availability of carrion were proving advantageous to the successful rearing of cubs. The lapping resumed for a time, and as the cats began to leave off drinking to drift toward the bush, the sound of an approaching car was heard, and the twin beams of headlamps became visible on the road below the house.

As the car turned into David's driveway and pulled up the slight incline, the lionesses melted back into the bush, their cubs running beside them.

The car engine was cut and a car door slammed. "Karanja?" a voice called out questioningly, and David remembered with a start that with the exception of the kitchen light at the back, the house was in darkness.

"Here," he replied, and started down the steps with the flashlight to meet Joseph Kiboko, the C.I.D. chief.

"What are you doing sitting in the dark?" asked Kiboko laughingly as they shook hands.

"Watching the lions at the water hole," replied David as he flashed the torchlight toward the pool some fifteen feet away. The water gleamed back brightly in the light.

"Lions?" asked the startled detective apprehensively. "Where?"

"They went into the bush when you got out of your car."

Kiboko's drawn breath was loud in the silence, and when he spoke, his voice was a little unsteady. "Let's go in the house."

David's smile was concealed in the shadowy darkness. He'd forgotten momentarily that most people, including Africans, did not particularly enjoy the idea of having lions nearby. There was little, if anything, interesting about them, and certainly no one in his right mind would sit outside his house, on an open veranda, in order to watch lions within rock-throwing distance.

"Let's go in now," Kiboko pressed urgently as he began to edge along the walk toward the veranda steps.

As they seated themselves in the now brightly lit sitting room, Karanja gently teased Kiboko: "Are you sure you wouldn't rather sit outside where it's cooler?"

"No, thank you," Kiboko emphatically answered with a decisive shake of his head. "And I don't know why you'd want to either. I think the park staff, including everyone from the Warden down to the laborers and their families, should live inside a stockaded *boma* where you would be safe. Not like this." He waved his hand to indicate the sprawling Headquarters area with its nearby houses and the staff quarters below.

"You're joking," said David in surprise.

"No, I'm not," Kiboko assured him. "Who would want to have lions in their front yard in the evening?"

"I do," replied David.

Kiboko looked at him in disbelief. Seeing that David was serious, he said, "If it doesn't bother you, fine, but not me. I wouldn't live here. It's only been a year since my mother's sister was taken by a lion. She got up during the night to go to the *choo* outside, and it must have been lying right by the door. None of the family heard a thing, although they were only a few feet away." He shuddered, then added, "All they found the next morning was a blood trail leading to what little was left of her—her right foot."

Shaking his head, he muttered again, "Not me," and drawing a folded paper from his shirt pocket, he began to read: "Your ranger, Mulolo, got off duty at six thirty yesterday evening and went directly to the quarters of your typist, Margaret Githu, where he stayed the night." He glanced up at David questioningly.

"I know," said David. "She told me."

"He left just after six this morning; went to his own quarters, where he took a shower and changed clothes; and returned to the gate to relieve the night guard just before six thirty A.M." He looked over to David for comment. There was none, and he resumed reading. "Just after seven, a light blue VW beetle approached the gate, and Mulolo bought a newspaper and paid for it, after which he opened the gate and let the car into the park area." Kiboko frowned as if perplexed by something before continuing: "The VW returned to the gate and left about twenty minutes later. Mulolo spent the rest of the day, opening and shutting the gate, taking entrance fees, answering tourists' questions, and so on. He went to the *choo* twice and went home for an hour at one o'clock. He talked to a few people on and off throughout the day who were hanging around the gate waiting for a lift into town or for the park lorry; I imagine those were park staff or their families?" He looked up at David.

"Yes," he replied. "The Main Gate is the last pickup point for staff to get a ride into town on the lorry, which makes regular runs

343

each day. None of them have cars, you see; that's why we provide the transportation to get the children back and forth to school, and to enable the women to get into the village to do their shopping."

Kiboko nodded. "Well, that's it," he said. "That's what he did and who he talked to all day today. After he got off duty he went back to this Margaret's quarters, and that's where he is now. My man stayed close to him all day, even went to the bathroom with him, and he overheard almost every word Mulolo said to everyone. Nothing suspicious—just everyday conversation." He sat back in the chair and waited for David's comment.

David sat and thought quietly. Mulolo had the information about the count last night. Tomorrow there would be ten planes covering the park, and that information would be vitally important to anyone poaching inside. He'd had to pass on the information today—but to whom? And how?

He reviewed the situation. Possibly the information was passed to one of the staff, but somehow he doubted it. There was a slight chance that the poaching ring was composed of people working for him, but the possibility was slight. There were the vehicles, for one thing. He considered those few in the park's employ who owned vehicles, and one by one he dismissed them from his mind. Besides, this organization appeared able to work day or night, and staff members couldn't be absent from their duties without arousing suspicion. It wasn't that it was impossible to corrupt one of his men into poaching and dealing in trophies: it had been done before; no, it was the difficulty of their being able to operate for long without detection in a small closed community. No, he decided, the organization was outside the park. It had to be. Momentarily dismissing the idea of an accomplice among the staff, he turned to the other possibility, the vehicles entering and leaving the park. The blue VW returned to his mind. There was something odd there; he'd been aware of a note of discord when Kiboko had read the account to him.

"You said that about seven, a VW beetle came in and Mulolo bought a newspaper," he asked Kiboko.

The C.I.D. man nodded and waited expectantly.

"Which one?" asked David speculatively.

Kiboko looked startled, as if he hadn't anticipated the question and failed to see why it mattered. Glancing at the paper he held, he said, *"The Nairobi Standard."* Then he added, "My man thought there was something strange about that. It seems Mulolo said something; it was just a few words, but he wasn't able to overhear what it was. The driver of the VW didn't appear to answer, and after the vehicle passed, Mulolo seemed to be angry about something. He threw the paper, muttered to himself, and"—again he consulted the note—"he kicked a box." He looked perplexed.

"I asked if Mulolo could have told the driver about the count, and my man said it wasn't likely, because Mulolo only said four or five words. And another thing"—he paused and looked up at David. "It seems Mulolo never picked up the paper all day. He never read it."

A smile slowly spread itself across David's face. "That's it," he said.

"What is?" asked a confused Kiboko.

"The newspaper. That's what seemed odd the minute you read it to me, but I couldn't put my finger on exactly what about it was strange." He began to laugh. "Great—I see it now." He leaned forward in his chair and explained. "That VW comes from the milk-and-newspaper kiosk in town, and each morning it drives out to deliver milk and the Nairobi newspapers to several houses, besides Headquarters and the Research and Education Centers. That's got to be how they've been receiving the information about the patrols each week. Mulolo passes it to them when he gets a newspaper. That's where the information went this morning."

"But," Kiboko objected, "there were only a few words."

David shrugged. "All it takes is 'Aerial count, Friday and Saturday.' Or," he added, "it's more likely that he could have written a note and passed it to the driver. It doesn't really matter which. What does matter is who."

Kiboko shook his head negatively. "I thought I was good when it came to understanding and seeing a lot come together in a seemingly inconsequential bit of information, but I don't see how you can know for sure that the VW is picking up the information just because Mulolo bought a newspaper. I'll admit that it's a possibility, but it's not a confirmed fact."

"It is to me," replied David. "And the reason I saw it is that I'm aware of something you aren't likely to know. For instance," he explained, "ninety-nine out of a hundred rangers can't speak English, and most can't read or write or do anything beyond the simplest addition and subtraction of money. Mulolo does, however, *speak*"—he emphasized the word—"a few words of English, and that's why he's on the Main Gate, where we need a man who can understand and reply to tourists' simple questions."

A look of understanding began to dawn on Kiboko's face. Chuckling, he said, "But he doesn't read or write English."

David grinned and nodded eagerly. "So why should he buy an English newspaper he can't possibly read?"

"So now we find out who owns the kiosk and hopefully we'll

begin to get somewhere. I'll let you know tomorrow evening. In the meantime we'll continue to keep an eye on your Gate Ranger."

After David walked the nervous, lion-shy Kiboko to his car, he returned to sit on the edge of the short veranda wall. It was still heavily overcast, and a cool breeze smelled faintly like rain nearby. Anything, he thought, was more than welcome, even a brief shower. It was the time of year for it, and they'd had a few isolated sprinkles here and there, but nothing that could even remotely be called the arrival of the rains. Mutely he prayed they wouldn't fail again.

His mind returned to the conversation with Joseph Kiboko. He knew he was right about the VW. It had to be, if for no other reason than that it was perfect. The battered old car had come every morning for years with the milk and newspapers for the senior staff. It was a common early-morning sight; consequently, no one paid any attention to it.

The C.I.D. man was good; he'd know everything there was to know about the kiosk by tomorrow night, and with any luck the information would be the beginning of a trail that would eventually lead to the head of the poaching ring.

He glanced again at the heavy moon-glazed overcast before he turned to go in; tomorrow was going to be an important day.

VI · FRIDAY

CHAPTER TWENTY

Morning

D AVID SIPPED the hot coffee from the plastic cup that served as a lid for the thermos flask and studied the huge pugmarks in the dirt beside the carcass. They were nearly as large as his hand with his fingers outspread.

The old buffalo must have put up quite a fight, though: the ground was torn and lacerated over a large area; but several lions had been involved, so the outcome had been a foregone conclusion. All that was left now was the heavy skull with its massive bossed horns, the backbone lying in the tattered remains of the buffalo's blackish hide, and the odd miscellaneous clutter of bones and a hoof lying in the shredded green of the stomach contents.

He glanced toward the east. Dawn wasn't far off now; the early gray was beginning to lighten perceptibly through the heavy overcast. He was the first one to the airfield; but then, he'd planned to be, since he wanted to check out his plane carefully. It looked good; all the damage from the earlier forced landing had been repaired, and now the four-seater Cessna 180 stood fueled and waiting by the runway's edge.

After finishing his coffee, he returned to his Land-Rover and began to transfer his maps, clipboard, and miscellaneous oddments to the plane. Just as he had everything stowed away, he saw a familiar older-model Toyota pickup bouncing along the road toward him. Bruce McKinney had a devoted affection for what must have been the very first Toyota assigned to the national park staff. Somehow he kept the relic together in one piece and running better than any of the park's newer vehicles. David had often joked that when Bruce retired, he'd manage to find a way to take the Toyota with him; to which McKinney always replied decisively, "Of course."

"I thought I'd find you here," said McKinney as he climbed out of the pickup.

As they shook hands, David noticed how tired the older man looked; the lines on his weather-beaten face seemed to cut deeper into his flesh, and the blue-tinged circles under the eyes said that this man was past the age when a night without sleep could be shrugged off.

"How's it going?" asked David.

McKinney shook his head in disgust. "Last night the wind drove the fire up to the firebreak in more than one place. A short shower slowed it down, but there wasn't enough rain to do much good. At least, the wind died, so I got a few hours' sleep in the car. This morning it's reached the firebreak at half a dozen points, and it's spreading out along the cut. But it's beginning to die down. If this holds"—he indicated the heavily overcast sky—"and the wind stays down, we should have it burned out at the firebreak by the middle of the day. If we're lucky," he added.

"Then I hope we are," said David. "The last thing we need during a game count is a bush fire. Have you heard anything about Shelby? How is he doing?"

"The estate foreman went to the house about midnight to report on the fire. Vera Batey told him Shelby was resting quietly. It seems he's going to be all right." Glancing at his watch, he added, "I'd better get back to the fire now. I only came in to have a shower and change, and to let you know how it was going."

"Thanks. Keep me posted."

"Good luck with the count," McKinney added as he turned to go. "I'm glad it's you and not me up there."

"Are you sure you won't change your mind about giving us a hand?" David asked with a smile. McKinney's aversion to flying was well known. He'd never been in a plane in his life, and he saw no reason to break his record at this late stage.

Now he just shook his head and grinned. "Not me," he said, and with his usual brief wave of the hand he turned to leave.

As the Toyota pulled away from the airfield, it passed the first of the vehicles arriving from the lodge, with the sleepy-eyed pilots and observers nursing their cups of coffee or tea. Piling out of their Land-Rovers, they began to move toward their respective planes laden with camera bags, thermos flasks, binoculars, and clipboards.

Jeff and Audrey Forbes drove up with their car full of research assistants, and after parking, Audrey began directing the young men toward their assigned planes while Jeff joined David.

"Thanks for taking Audrey in your plane, David," Jeff said. "I appreciate it."

David's blocks were many and small in size, and northwest of Headquarters, where there should be a heavy concentration of game, particularly rhinos. This concentrated population was why David had selected them for himself. He'd wanted to make sure the area was well covered and that nothing was overlooked.

"If she were with me north of the Lalaga Lana," Jeff continued, referring to his assigned blocks outside the park area where huge cattle ranches scrabbled for existence, "she'd be worn out by noon. They're the largest blocks in the ecosystem, so I'll be putting down to refuel and that's all. Otherwise I'll never finish by tomorrow night."

The last of the vehicles arrived with its load of people, plus two large cartons of box lunches, which the driver proceeded to distribute to the planes.

The pilots were busy checking out their aircraft; oil and fuel levels were examined, and water, lunches, and equipment loaded. The last of the observers and their paraphernalia were packed in, and doors began to slam shut as the first engine turned over and roared.

"What have we got?" David asked as Audrey approached with four box lunches.

Tipping the top off one, she answered, "Mmmm. Sliced beef." Checking another, she added, "And chicken." She moved off toward David's plane sampling a purloined banana.

As David turned to follow, he saw a vehicle approaching at top speed. Agaran's Land-Rover arrived in a cloud of dust, and the squeal of brakes was heard over the whine of the airplanes. Jumping out, he ran up to David. "I'm glad I caught you. I couldn't get you on your radio."

"It's off," admitted David. "I'm about to leave. What's the problem?"

"It looks like whoever hammered that herd in the Northern Area has moved south now. They got seventeen elephants behind Daka Neka Hill, southwest of here. I'm on my way out now, but I thought you'd want to know."

David's anger came up swift and tight inside him. Seventeen more gone. And south of the Lalaga Lana. It had to be the same group of poachers. He thought of Mulolo and his passing of information. He knew if the Gate Ranger were within his reach right now he'd beat him half to death, but at least he'd find out whom the information went to. Now he almost regretted holding the C.I.D. off. His anger began to settle into a hot core in his stomach, and he forced himself to admit that he couldn't do either. The moment suspicion fell on Mulolo, he'd be silenced; they'd get to him somehow, and David would be left with a dead end again.

"When were they taken?" he asked.

"Lugumba said maybe early yesterday, perhaps the night before. They'd been covered with brush again, and it's lucky we found them this soon. Unit One was on their way back to the fire area at first light, and to save time they didn't go by way of the village; they'd planned to take the old service track to Number Six bore-hole before dropping south through the bush. That's when they discovered the carcasses. Again, there were two vehicles and a lot of expended shell casings. All the ivory's been taken."

Twenty-four to thirty-six hours, David calculated. Gone again. The most he could do was put a unit on the trail and see where they disappeared. That, and make sure it was the same lot who were responsible for the massacre in the Northern Area. "Take a plaster cast of the tire tracks and compare those and the shell casings with what we found in the north," he said to Agaran. "And send a unit to find out where the tracks lead to.

"The other units are well scattered over the park," he continued. "I gave Duba new patrol assignments to hand out to the Southern Area units, and I want all units to maintain radio silence today except for emergency. The planes will be keeping close radio contact with Headquarters, so if any poachers are spotted from the air I want the nearest unit to respond immediately. The count was put together in a hurry, so the word won't be out yet. Maybe we'll pick up a few surprised poachers." But not the ones he really wanted, he thought grimly.

"What about the fire?" inquired Agaran.

"McKinney is taking care of that. He hopes to have it burned out on Shelby's firebreak this afternoon; but if he does need additional assistance, send out more of the labor force or the mechanics or anybody, but leave the Field Forces on patrol."

Agaran nodded. "I'll keep in contact on the radio, and if you want me, I'll be out with Unit One."

The roar of the starting planes was now loud enough to drown out conversation, and as Agaran left, the first plane pulled out of line and began to taxi slowly to the west end of the runway.

A Land-Rover pulled onto the runway to drive east in order to move the plains game away from the takeoff area. The flat graded airfield was a favorite resting place for herds of impalas and oryxes, among other hoofed species, because the lack of cover enabled them to see approaching predators at once. Sometimes hundreds of animals would be found milling about or resting on an airstrip, and incoming aircraft often had to buzz the field repeatedly to move the animals out before landing. It was another hazard of bush flying, since impact with an animal while taxiing at speed on a dirt road or airfield could destroy a small plane and everyone in it.

David headed for the Cessna and found everything neatly packed away. Audrey stood waiting with the Research Center's soil scientist, Philip Otieno, and Dr. Patel, the veterinarian from Headquarters Research Department. Both men were experienced; he'd picked his team carefully. Motioning the two men into the back seat and Audrey in front with him, he removed the blocks from the wheels and climbed into the plane.

After checking doors and seat belts, he put on his radio headset, and the last of his anger disappeared in his satisfaction at being back in a plane again. He forced his impatience to wait. His retaliation was only deferred; but it would come.

First the count, then the anti-poaching campaign. This latest kill must have occurred just prior to the poachers' receipt of Mulolo's information about the count. Now they were warned, it was true. They were out of the park; but they'd be back soon, as long as Mulolo appeared to be undetected, as long as his information was unsuspected.

In two days the count would be over and the planes would leave, all of them, and Mulolo would report their departure to the blue VW. What he woudn't know and couldn't report was that three of the planes would leave the Main Headquarters airfield only to land thirty kilometers away at the Mwanyani Number 2 substation, where they'd wait quietly for the poachers to return.

BUBU SAT ON THE EDGE of his bed and thought of his resolve of the day before. His decision to reclaim the ivory was only just, and toward that end he had plotted carefully. He had decided that Maimbo and his men had to have hidden the ivory somewhere in a safe place outside the park; somewhere away from Maimbo, yet close enough for him to get to in order that he might dispose of it. The ivory had no value to him hidden away. He had to sell it, and to sell it he had to move it to a buyer, which meant transport to Mombasa or south over the Tanzanian border. The ivory must be prepared somehow to ensure its movement undetected, and to do this Maimbo must go to it, and he would have to go at night. Therefore, he had decided yesterday that he would follow Maimbo each night until he led him to the ivory.

The previous afternoon, he had finished his work and hurried into town on the lorry. He'd gone to wait near the old Game Department office, and when Maimbo came out, he'd followed him the short distance to Maimbo's house. There he'd stayed hidden until after dark, when he'd followed him to the Total Petrol Station.

He'd known then that it was going to be more difficult than he had anticipated. Maimbo had a car and he was on foot. He'd managed to keep the Game Warden in sight when he'd left his office to go home because the house was nearby. But when it came to keeping up with the Datsun as it sped through the town to the petrol station, he had fallen behind and lost him. Furthermore, the sight of an old man running through the streets was too unusual not to be noted and talked about. Thankfully, few had noticed, because it was dark; but he could not do it again.

The most important thing was that he was too old to run for miles, as he had when he was young. He'd lost Maimbo, and it had been only luck that the road back to the park led past the petrol station and he'd seen Maimbo's car parked beside the refreshment stand. He'd crept up to the *makuti*-covered patio where beer and *samosas* were served, and he'd seen Maimbo finishing his first beer and ordering the second; he'd known then that Maimbo had come directly here—so he hadn't lost him after all. He'd watched and waited and had seen Maimbo joined by the man who owned the milk kiosk; he'd seen the money that changed hands, and then when the kiosk owner left, he'd remained to watch Maimbo.

The Game Warden had stayed and drunk beer with his friends until ten thirty, and then he'd left, and again Bubu had followed as best he could. Thankfully, Maimbo had returned the way he'd come, and he'd been able to keep up well enough to arrive at Maimbo's house shortly after the Game Warden had gone inside. He'd waited outside, concealed in the bushes nearby, and he'd watched until the lights went out and the house slept, and after several hours he'd decided that Maimbo was not going to the ivory that night, so he had returned home.

He was tired now, so he would sleep this morning to be fresh and ready for tonight. Later he would go to the shed out back and patch the tires on the old bicycle that Warden Nichols had left behind as not being worth the trouble to take. It would have to do; it was all he had.

DUNCAN SHELBY lay with his eyes closed, conscious of a lassitude that permeated his whole being. The bed was cool and comfortable, and he enjoyed the tired feeling that allowed him to lie quietly and enjoy it. He thought back and tried to remember when he'd lain abed during the day, and he realized that it had never happened before. The idea startled him, and yet he was pleased. What other man could say as much at his age?

He half opened his eyes and peered through his lashes toward the window across the room that overlooked the veranda outside and the view south. It was still as overcast as it had been when he had awakened some time ago, just after dawn. He'd been surprised then to discover he was alone. That feisty old battle-ax of a missionary had gone at some time or other during the night, and his cook had told him that she'd said she would return this morning.

He'd had his coffee then and a piece of toast before dozing off again. Now he was more or less awake, and his thoughts turned to the fire. McKinney had stopped by this morning to tell him that he was on the fire line and hoped to have it contained today. Shelby knew McKinney well; the two of them were both old bachelors and had spent more than one evening drinking and talking. He knew the assistant warden could handle the situation as completely as he himself could, and the last remnant of guilt over his being in bed faded away, to leave him feeling slightly bored.

He saw a shadow pass the window, and he opened his eyes wider. It's that woman, he thought dourly; but after a moment spent listening, he identified the sandal-dragging step of the old cook, who'd never adjusted to shoes well enough to pick up his feet. Soon he heard the steady sweeping sound of the broom as the man brushed it over the worn wooden floor of the veranda, and the steady soft sound slowly lulled him back to sleep.

As he began to become aware of his surroundings once again, he thought perhaps he'd dozed off for just a moment. The steady rhythm of sound continued, and at first he assumed it was the cook outside still sweeping. Gradually, though, he noticed a difference. This wasn't the brushing sound of before; it was a soft plopping noise.

Opening his eyes a little, he saw the woman sitting beside the bed plunging her rug hook into and out of the coarse backing, and he was surprised to realize that he was pleased to see her there.

She might be a missionary, but still, when he understood last night that he'd been seriously ill, he'd felt a grudging satisfaction and reassurance in her presence. He knew she was competent; her sharp, no-nonsense attitude told him that. His wasn't the first sickbed she'd sat beside with her damnable rug, and if she had the bedside manner of a wounded rhino, that was preferable to one of

355

the piously long-faced missionary women he'd had the misfortune to come across. He'd also, he admitted to himself, admired her outspoken decisiveness. It had been a long time since anyone had talked back to him, and he'd always enjoyed the unusual.

"How do you feel?" she asked quietly, never taking her eyes off her work.

He was disconcerted; he hadn't thought she'd known he was awake. He opened his eyes. "I feel tired and I have a headache," he said in a cranky tone before asking suspiciously, "How did you know I was awake?"

Her cool gray eyes came up to study him. "By your breathing," she answered simply.

Putting the rug aside, she reached for the thermometer on the bedside table and shook it down. He opened his mouth without being told to and settled the antiseptic-tasting glass bulb under his tongue. He too was curious.

As she sat quietly waiting and gazed out the window, he resumed his study of her. She was younger than he, he guessed, somewhere around fifty or sixty, and she had the stringy wiriness that some Europeans attained after living a hard, demanding life in the tropics. Unconsciously his memory brought back the picture of the small, daintily rounded woman he'd brought here forty years ago from England; now he could see that she'd not been made of the stuff of survivors. Taken out of the glasshouse of her English conservatory, she'd been unable to adapt to a new soil and a different climate, and so she'd died. But he knew the woman who sat beside him would survive anywhere. The history of her adaptation and survival in harsh conditions was written on her face and body like a chronicle.

She'd been thinned down to flesh and bone by the climate, and her skin had become weathered by the hot sun and the restless wind. Her strong, knobby hands and fingers with their closely pared nails were chapped from repeated washings. More importantly, they were quiet hands, and as he studied them lying in her lap, loosely clasped with lightly curled fingers still, he knew that their momentary inactivity was a luxury seldom indulged in.

That was the word he'd been groping for to describe her: "still." She was still, and there were other words that came to mind as well. Her calm gaze as she looked out the window. The still composure of her body as she sat waiting. Her quiet hands resting.

It took a lifetime to acquire that serenity, he thought. It took shocks recovered from, catastrophes overcome, suffering endured— and most of all, the acceptance of aloneness that turned the eyes of the soul inward. She'd fought many battles and won many wars to reach the quiet places she lived in now. He knew he never would, and for a moment he envied her, envied and admired her.

Her eyes returned to his, and she leaned forward to take the thermometer.

"What is it?" he demanded gruffly.

"One hundred degrees," she replied.

"Is that good or bad?"

"Good, because it's nearly normal," she replied. "Your temperature will fluctuate during the next few days and you may find yourself unable to sweat if you get hot, so you'll have to take care that you don't become overheated." She paused and seemed to be waiting for a belligerent outburst, but he didn't feel inclined to argue. He hadn't decided whether or not to admit, even to himself, that he might be sick.

"What else?" he asked warily.

"I'd suggest you go to your doctor in Nairobi or wherever and have a thorough examination—but I doubt if you'd do it, so I won't bother." She picked up her rug and resumed working.

He considered that a moment and made his decision. "I haven't a doctor to go to," he admitted. "Never needed one before."

She glanced up, and even though she'd been prepared for a bellow of rage rejecting his vulnerability to illness, had waited for it even, she wasn't surprised when it didn't come. Nor did she gloat over the possibility that he would do as she advised. "I'll give you the name of a good doctor in Nairobi," she said.

The soft plop of her rug hook resumed and her eyes returned to their work, and as he watched her he realized he was waiting for something. It finally occurred to him what it was that seemed odd; the thing missing that he'd unconsciously been waiting for.

"Aren't you going to pray over me?" he demanded.

The movement of the rug hook continued, and without raising her eyes she replied, "Do you need praying over?"

"Of course not."

"Then why do you ask?"

"Because you're a missionary, and I've not yet met one who wasn't itching to groan prayers over me and get their grasping hands on my soul."

"You've met one now," she retorted in a soft tone.

He was nonplussed. He'd seen her around the village on and off for years, and when unable to avoid doing so, he'd nodded to her and continued on his way. Never once had they spoken, and yet he'd somehow felt he knew her and didn't like her. He saw now that all he'd known of her was the word "missionary," and his dislike and dismissal of her as a human being had stemmed from that. He was somehow irritated with her for refusing to conform to his expectations.

"Well, if you're a missionary and you don't pray over people and try to 'save their souls,' as you call it, then you're not much of a missionary," he stabbed at her.

The motion of the hook ceased, and her hands were gently lowered with their work to her lap as her head came up. Her eyes looked into his with an emotion he'd not seen there before: it was one of pain. "I know, Mr. Shelby," she said softly. "You didn't need to tell me."

He was immediately sorry for what he'd said. Self-reproach filled him, and his face flushed in embarrassment. Blundering ass, he said to himself, and without pause he blurted out, "I'm sorry. That was an unforgivable thing to say."

She had turned and was looking out the window as before, and after a moment she said, "Unforgivable? No, Mr. Shelby. There are few times when the truth is unforgivable."

He studied her face intently; the pain was gone and the calm had returned. This too was a battle, then; in progress and not yet won; but somehow he did not doubt the outcome.

"Why did you become a missionary?" His curiosity was aroused now.

Her expression revealed her confusion, and again she answered a question with another question: "Why do you want to know, Mr. Shelby?"

"I don't really know," he admitted, "but it's important for me to understand."

After a moment she said uncertainly, "I'm not really very good at talking about myself."

"Have you ever tried?"

She thought about the question and then said simply, "No."

He waited, and after a moment she answered his question: "I suppose I became a missionary nurse because I felt the need to repay a debt."

"What kind of debt?" he asked, gently prodding her on.

Her hands sought the reassurance of the work in her lap, and she spoke with her eyes lowered. "My brother and I were foundlings," she said matter-of-factly. "We were left on the doorstep of a Protestant charity home in Birmingham, England. He was one and a half and I was four years old, and the parents who abandoned us were never located. We were found to be tubercular within a year or so. Perhaps our parents had the disease and hoped to spare us by giving us up. We don't know."

She looked up at him. "It was too late in any case. My brother died before he was four, and although I lived, I needed constant care and nursing for nearly twelve years."

"That was the debt?"

When she nodded, he asked, "But why did you want to become a missionary nurse?"

"Probably because to my mind, God and healing were very much the same," she said. "Being raised in a religious charity home gave me an early awareness of God, and being an invalid taught me the realities of pain and suffering. The decision of what to do with my life was inevitable. I wanted to give to others what I'd received."

He thought about the childhood she'd revealed so dispassionately; most people would have deliberately, or unconsciously, related the story of a pathetic childhood in such a way as to beg for sympathy or to make an excuse for failure as an adult. She'd mentioned it as one would speak of something that had happened to someone else. She had no need of pity; there was nothing to excuse.

He tried to reconstruct the reasoning of the young adolescent Vera Batey, to reach what she felt had been the logical decision, but he found he could progress to only a certain point. "I can see how you wanted to be a nurse," he said hesitantly, "but why as a missionary?"

For some moments she continued working on her rug, then replied, "I suppose because I felt I could do more as a missionary. I wanted to share the strength I'd found through Christianity as I helped to heal the sick and injured. The need seemed greater in underdeveloped countries, where poverty demanded strength to survive and medical care was almost nonexistent. And, I suppose," she said with a smile, "because missionaries were given a prominent place in church literature in those days. They were my only heroes, and so I wanted to be one too." She laughed softly to herself, and he remembered his own youthful dreams vividly. How little resemblance they'd borne to the reality that followed.

He chuckled, remembering how it had turned out for him. "When did you decide it wasn't all you imagined?"

"About two weeks after I arrived in Africa," she replied quietly, her smile gone. "I kept waiting for some mysterious feeling of satisfaction that would come from knowing that I'd somehow made the lives and living of the people better, or easier somehow. I nursed them, taught them, did everything I'd been trained to do, and still, the feeling never came. It has never come."

"Why not?" he asked, perplexed. "If you did everything you

359

were supposed to do, why weren't you satisfied with what you accomplished?"

"Because it was never enough. If I healed them of sickness or injury, I might only have postponed their inevitable suffering and death from starvation. If I spoke to them of the Kingdom of Heaven, I could do nothing about their poverty and suffering here on earth. There was never enough of anything; not of food, medicine, clothes, hours of the day, or enough people who cared.

"If I saved the life of one child with cholera, the rest of his family died of it. If I had milk and food enough for one family, another family in the village starved. If I led one to Christ, I watched as the others turned away. So you see, I never found that feeling of satisfaction with what I accomplished, as you put it. There was too little accomplished in the face of so much left to be done."

"But that's not your fault," he objected strenuously. "You couldn't do it all."

She looked up at him, and a little of the pain had somehow crept back into her gray eyes and her soft voice. "I know, Mr. Shelby. And that's why I'm not a very good missionary. My mission was to lead the people to Christ, and to heal their bodily sickness as an afterthought, but I realized years ago that I couldn't do both. It was too much. I chose to heal them, and somehow the more important message of Christianity became lost. I don't know how to teach the love of God to people who suffer unto death in dirt, poverty, sickness, and starvation. All I can do is lessen the suffering of their bodies, and pray for their souls' salvation."

"No one could do more," he replied gently.

She didn't speak, but her eyes refuted his statement.

He wondered about the life she'd lived, and before he thought, he found himself asking, "Have you always been alone here?"

"No," she replied, her quiet gray gaze fixed at a point somewhere outside the window. "There were two of us at first; the other missionary was to found our church and teach, while I established and worked in the dispensary."

"The church?" he asked in surprise. "But there is no church."

Her eyes came back to meet his own. "No, there isn't. My companion suffered terribly from the heat, and then tick fever with cardiac complications. She had to return to England within a few months."

"And there's been no one else?" he asked incredulously.

"The Mission Society promised to send a replacement. But no, no one ever came." She paused before adding, "So the church was never built."

"And you've accepted the blame for that?" he asked in wonderment.

"I should have been able to do what had to be done." Her voice was barely audible.

He thought back over his own life; he counted his accomplishments, and he remembered his failures. He appraised what he had, and remembered his grief over his losses, and in the end he knew he understood something that she had not yet learned, or accepted.

"Miss Batey."

She glanced up, and he studied her gentle eyes. "Don't you know," he asked, "that there will always be something left undone or something lost—that you can never do or have it all?"

CHAPTER TWENTY-ONE

Afternoon

Audrey fastened her seat belt; it was just after their lunch break, and David was preparing to take off. While the plane idled, she popped the last two sections of her orange into her mouth and dug out the paper napkin she had squirreled away in her shirt pocket; as she wiped her hot, perspiring face, David turned to raise his voice over the sound of the engine: "Ready?"

Nodding, her mouth full, she picked up one of the thick maps from where it was wedged between their seats and began to fan herself. It had been dreadfully hot in the plane since the heavily overcast sky had cleared before lunch. They'd put down about forty minutes ago to refuel and eat their box lunches, and there hadn't been a tree or bush over four feet tall that had leaves on it to shade them. Consequently, they'd sat out on the hard-baked red dirt of the runway under the plane's wings, and nibbled at their lunches with appetites dulled by heat and motion, and drunk the warm, flat-tasting water from the small plastic *debe* provided.

But at least under the plane there had been a breeze, Audrey thought, even if it did blow grit into your food. The plane, however, had merely sat above them and soaked up every available degree of heat through its metal pores, and now, stationary, with doors and windows secured, it felt like an oven.

As they began to slowly move forward, she scrunched down in her seat to ignore the takeoff. The sound of the engine increased, as did the speed at which they rattled and bounced over the airstrip, and then the vibrations ceased and she knew they were up. Now, looking out the window, she watched as the ground rushed past and retreated as the plane climbed higher and banked to the left.

She looked to the western horizon to see Block XVIII, which they'd covered first that morning. Through it ran a narrow flat-topped ridge called the Lafaroge Plateau which extended over three hundred kilometers from west to east and which bisected the park area. There were only a very few places in the lava-topped plateau where valleys cut through to allow primitive roads to connect the flat northern and southern sections of the Park, both of which had gradually eroded over some twelve to fifteen million years, leaving the lava-capped plateau standing six to nine hundred feet above the surrounding area.

The block containing the plateau should have been an auspicious way to start the count, because one of the park's two permanent rivers, the Ruui, which originated in the Aberdare Mountains, ran parallel to the plateau on the far side. At the southern tip of the block the Ruui joined the Oreyiet River from the slopes of Kilimanjaro, to form the huge Lalaga Lana, which stretched across the eastern section of the park to provide the only permanent water in that area. But what "should have been" an auspicious beginning and what "had been" were two different things.

The area had definitely not been a success in terms of the number of elephants and rhinos counted. Both species liked to drink every day if possible, so the permanent water running alongside the foot of the plateau should have drawn large numbers of them, particularly since the vegetation was not so badly stripped as it was far to the east where the drought was. But there had been few compared with their hopeful expectations. She glanced anxiously at her clipboard: there had been fewer than a hundred elephants, and only three rhinos.

As they drew away from the thick bush of Block XIX and headed southwest, she thought morosely that this one hadn't been much better. They'd covered the block just before lunch, and it was very different from the block farther west containing the plateau area. This was flat, waterless, and covered with dense scrub. Three poky little hills stood up in the middle of the block, which was shaped like a skinny piece of pie served by a frugal housewife. But this too should have had record numbers of rhinos and elephants. The area had once contained the largest concentration of big tuskers left in East Africa. They hadn't seen one of the heavily tusked bulls. There had been a few decently sized males, and one nice herd of some hundred and fifty, but even so, they hadn't been in the numbers anticipated.

It was entirely possible that the animals were widely scattered all over the park and its adjacent areas, and not congregated at what had been their favorite places before the drought. The long drought of ten years ago had been monitored less than successfully from the ground, so really, no one knew exactly how the big animals reacted to the effects of a continued water shortage. Perhaps they were on the move more than one would expect, and the usually dense populations of Blocks XVIII and XIX were now somewhere else.

It was too terrible, she thought, that they'd been without a plane for so many months. If it had been here, David would have been in the air every day; the dispersal of the elephants would have been seen and noted, and now they'd know where to look for them. Still, there were ten planes flying the count, and every inch of the ecosystem would be covered, so today or tomorrow they'd be located.

An unpleasant thought nagged in the back of her mind, and she tried to think what it was. Then she recalled the rhinos, and her stomach dipped. They had a home range of only a few kilometers. They wouldn't have moved.

She felt David pat her arm, and she looked up to see the Lalaga Lana River approaching ahead. She nodded her understanding and turned to the two men behind her. Dr. Patel's chubby round face with its pointy little beard leaned forward.

"We're coming up on the next block," she said, raising her voice above the sound of the engine.

He nodded and sat back to alert Philip Otieno, and Audrey turned around again and sat up straight in her seat as she reached for her clipboard.

As David began to turn and approach the first transect on the southern bank of the Lalaga Lana River, she checked her watch. It was two forty-five, and she jotted down the time on the data sheet as she calculated; David had estimated two and a half hours for this one, so they should be done about five fifteen. Good—they'd surely be the first ones in this evening, and she could get cleaned up before Jeff got home. She felt dirty, hot, and sticky, but the anticipation of a cool shower made her feel better. Only one more block to do. . . .

After getting her camera from under her seat, she sat up and turned to scan the area three hundred feet below.

Judging the approximate five-hundred-meter distance out from the plane as Jeff had taught her to do, she proceeded to search the area inside. A cock ostrich galloped clumsily below, with black-and-white plumage fluttering in irritation at the droning plane overhead, and three giraffes stood stolidly gazing with liquid brown eyes and waggling ears at the noisy apparition, before returning to placidly browse on the euphorbias.

It was still fairly thick here along the river; farther south the elephants, followed by bush fires, had opened up the scrub, but here it remained dense enough to require the observers to watch closely to see any rhino that might be concealed in a thicket.

Her eyes picked out a flash of movement ahead and out from the plane; they were elephants breaking into a run, and she began to count as she reached for the pen in her pocket. Six: three adult and three juvenile.

Feeling her arm tapped, she turned to David, who was pointing ahead and down. Leaning forward, she looked over the nose of the plane through the blurred circle of the spinning propeller and saw that they were coming up on a group of elephants who would pass directly underneath the plane's path.

Hurriedly she counted before they disappeared under the plane, as did David, who was stretched up in his seat with his lips silently moving, and she noted the second sighting as thirteen elephants before she turned back to her window.

A small herd of zebras dashed away below, and off to the side she saw a dark shape under the shade of a candelabra tree. What was that? For bulk, it had to be either an elephant or a rhino, but which? Then she noted the short legs—it was a rhino. Just into the block and already a rhino. She was exultant. Here the missing animals were: nineteen elephants and a rhino on her side of the plane alone. They had just moved south and east, that was all. They'd found them.

Quickly marking down her sightings, she turned back to study the ground below, and within a few minutes she spotted a big bull ahead with another, smaller bull beside him. They took off at the sound of the plane, and she noted their number and position on the forms before turning back to watch them. The bigger bull's ivory was immense. It was really one of the big tuskers from the northern area. She was excited; if they found one, they'd find them all.

She felt David's tap on her arm again, and she looked up to see him smiling broadly as he pointed at her camera. She glanced over the area outside her window and saw there wasn't a rhino or elephant in sight right at the moment, but David had obviously seen something. Then she remembered that as pilot he would look ahead more than the rest of them. Leaning forward and stretching, she could just make out some large reddish lumps scattered through the gray scrub.

As David began to veer away from the transect flight path to circle the herd, the scene ahead began to slide off the nose of the plane and creep around to the side window. Slowly the reddish-hued shapes began to take form. To her amazement, she saw a huge herd of elephants, all liberally covered with the red soil they had thrown over themselves to ward off the worst of the burning sun.

She knew that there were many too many to count, and a feeling of elation came up with a rush. They were spread out in a crescent-shaped pattern, and the plane was just coming up on the closest point. Snatching up the camera, she focused and began to take pictures as the herd passed below. One snap followed another as she quickly took a succession of overlapping shots, which would later be developed and laid side by side so that the animals could be counted one by one.

Marvelous, she thought as she wriggled about in her seat. She was ecstatic as she focused and snapped. Each shot captured another group of bulls, cows, juveniles, and calves; they were strung out below like beads fallen from a broken necklace. Some were in flight, with ears and tails extended in agitation; some milled about in confusion; while many of the big cows stood defensively in the midst of their offspring, rooted to the ground with ears out like sails and their trunks up to scent for the danger they sensed was near.

It was over too soon. They passed the far tip of the curving crescent of the scattered herd and left the agitated animals behind. Audrey turned in her seat to keep them in sight as long as possible, and she watched as the distance grew between them. David began to turn the plane back onto the transect flight path as she remembered individual scenes: a group of three cows backed up to a tree with their smallest calves under them and the older ones clustered near. Defiantly determined not to run, they'd stood to face the danger they couldn't see with their shortsighted eyes. They were so thin, so painfully thin. For a moment she was crushed, but then she reasoned, They're there—that's what's important. They may be thin, but they're there and they're alive.

She turned to David, and when she caught his eye, he pulled the headset away from his ear and she leaned forward to raise her voice. "How many?" she asked.

He shrugged his shoulders and held up four fingers.

She smiled and sat back in her seat to watch outside her window for the next sighting. Maybe four hundred in that one herd, she thought. It wasn't as big as the herds of seven or eight hundred that she'd heard of, and seen once or twice herself, but those hadn't been during an extended drought or when the elephants were as mercilessly hammered by poachers either, so four hundred was more than acceptable. A couple of sightings like that each day by each plane, and they'd do all right. She desperately hoped it would happen.

Glancing over at David during a long stretch of barren ground, she saw that his grim face had lightened a little. He was watching something carefully on his side of the plane, and when he began to scribble on his data sheet she leaned over to look. It read, *elephant—16*.

She sat back and looked out once again. The declining sun had made a mirror of her window, to reflect her contented smile. It was going to be all right.

THICK BILLOWS OF SMOKE blossomed ahead of the wind-driven flames which crept forward relentlessly, only pausing occasionally to flare into a bright blaze that consumed itself within minutes before falling back into its crouching advance. As men rushed about silent and sweating, flailing at the fingers of fire that reached hungrily for the crisp green sisal on the other side of the barrier, the huge marabou storks circled overhead, periodically plunging earthward to capture the mice, small rats, and snakes as they fled the encroaching smoke and heat below.

The rising wind was audible over the crackle and roar of the fire as it spread north and south along the plowed firebreak. Gathering speed as it moved out and spread like poured oil, it rushed at the northern end of the break, faltered a moment, then gathered itself into a solid wall of flame that hung poised for the next gust, which threw it forward with an exultant roar as it swept over and around the end of the firebreak to the sisal and the thick dry bush beyond.

McKinney left off exhorting the men and ran up toward the flanked end of the firebreak. "Damnation," he muttered. "It's away!" His frustration grew till he felt knotted up inside.

A panic-stricken dik-dik dashed in front of him, leaped sideways on discovering his presence, then stampeded toward the park area. Sparks and small bits of burning vegetation flew past his head like so many furious insects to land on the other side of the firebreak, where they flickered and danced among the sisal.

It was across and moving fast. "Damn it!" he roared over the crackling hiss of the fire, and he started to run back down the break through his men.

Shelby's Indian foreman ran up through the smoke. The whites of his brown eyes showed up stark and alarmed in his smoke-blackened face, and rivulets of sweat streaked light tracks down his forehead and cheeks.

"Pull the men out and back," McKinney ordered, pointing toward the park boundary less than a kilometer away. "Account for every man; and get those tractors moved back."

The Indian nodded and stumbled away, glad now to be second-in-command to McKinney and not responsible for the fact that they hadn't been able to hold the fire.

McKinney sent men up and down the break to direct the park's laborers and Shelby's field hands into the lorries. Staying till the last to make sure the men and equipment were moved back to the final barrier, he stood and wiped his face with what had been a clean white handkerchief earlier that morning. Now it was smeared and streaked with black. He coughed in the swirling mist and brought up choking, smoke-tasting phlegm. Spitting and wiping his eyes, he saw that the break was cleared of men and the last lorry was filled and ready to move out. Jumping over a streaming runnel of flame, he hopped onto the cab's running board and shouted to the driver, *"Twende."*

As the lorry pulled out, McKinney looked back through the smoke, and his jaw tightened as another gust of wind hit him in the face. When it came to swearing he had little imagination, and for all outbursts of anger or disappointment he had to be content with the satisfaction obtained from the available derivatives of one word. "Damn the wind," he muttered.

SALIM STOOD at the window towel-drying his hair after his daily swim in the hotel pool, and watched as the small Cessna tracked and retracked its way across the bushland in the distance. The view from his window was impressive; the lodge had been built on a large hill, and his own expensively furnished apartment was at the top of the sprawling complex which spread over the hill and down its side toward the water holes at the base of the rocks below. Consequently, he was nearly level with the still-distant plane as it flew back and forth over the bush below, and he wondered idly who was flying that particular block.

The phone rang to disturb his speculation. Throwing down the damp towel, he answered it. He listened to the message and after murmuring, *"Sawa-sawa, mzuri,"* he hung up.

Good, he thought: the French tourist who'd collapsed had been moved to the Park Headquarters airfield and picked up by the Flying Doctors. Now she was on her way to Nairobi, where a day or two in hospital would be a necessary, if disappointing, end to her vacation.

It was a pity, he thought as he began to dress in his bedroom, how people insisted on trying to do too much in too short a time. "Kenya in a Week" tourists, he called them—wanting to see and do it all, and get the most for their money. It wasn't the quality of travel they wanted, merely quantity, and every plane touching down at Nairobi disgorged another lot who leaped into waiting vehicles and sped off into the hinterland to visit one park after another. A park a day and hurry to the next, and on to the coast and back again; get into the lodge, gobble dinner, fall into bed, and be off at dawn to drive some more and get another picture on the roll for the folks at home.

He'd been hastily summoned from the dining room after lunch to find another one lying on the cool stone floor of the reception area where she'd collapsed on the way to the waiting *kombi* that was about to leave on an afternoon game run. Hot and worn out, exhausted by the heat and a stomach overfull with a bolted-down lunch, she'd been lying limply sprawled and shaking in a puddle of vomit. White-faced and incoherent, she'd tried to protest as Salim directed his staff to carry her to her room, where she could rest and be cleaned up while awaiting the airborne doctors. As the waiters and reception-desk clerks gently lifted her onto a stretcher, she'd turned her head to see the *kombi* pull away without her, and she'd begun to cry weakly.

"Incredible," he muttered as he loosely knotted his silk tie.

The phone rang again to interrupt his thoughts, and he answered it; advised that he had a call from Mombasa, he waited until he heard a faint click and a muffled voice.

Raising his voice, he answered, "Hello."

The Arab's soft voice could barely be heard over the humming connection from Mombasa Island.

"Do you have news for me?" Salim asked.

"Not yet, my friend. But tonight I will see a man who has the answers you want. I said I would let you know today. Unfortunately, tomorrow will have to do. It has not been easy. The information you seek is not on every man's lips. Few know, and the privilege of sharing such knowledge is expensive."

"How much?" Salim asked.

"For you?" the Arab replied. "Nothing. It will be my pleasure."

"Tomorrow?" inquired Salim.

"Tomorrow," the promise came, and the line was disconnected.

Salim slowly replaced the receiver. Usually, Old Town's Indian, Arab, and African population knew everything about everybody and literally hummed with information about those who were involved in the smuggling of various commodities. It appeared that such was not the case at the moment. Whoever was running this operation was as secretive as he was himself. No wonder the Arab had thought it was he. Still, he knew better now, and somehow he'd managed to find an informer who would, for a consideration, answer some delicate questions.

Salim had been right in his estimation of the softly spoken Arab; he knew everything involved with his profession, and if he didn't, he knew who did. It went without saying that now he was in the Arab's debt: he'd asked, and the Arab was delivering. There would be a reciprocation due. But then, he decided, it didn't matter. He'd always done business with the best professionals, and he would continue to do so.

As his mind returned to the question of who was behind the poaching organization, he glanced out the window and saw that the plane had advanced across the block and was now fairly close. He crossed the room and picked up the high-powered binoculars with which he tried to read the identification number stenciled on the plane, but it was still too far away.

DAVID FINISHED NOTING the last sighting on the final transect of Block XXVIII as the plane drew away from Aruba Dam, which marked the southern tip of the block. He looked down at what he'd just written: *elephant—carcasses—9—fresh*; then glanced over to Audrey, who sat hunched down in her seat with tears in her eyes and her handkerchief pressed tightly over her nose and mouth.

He couldn't blame her; the grisly scene below was enough to make anyone ill, and "depressed" was not nearly descriptive enough for the feeling inside. The revoltingly putrid smell of rotting carcasses filled the plane, and it was all he could do to ignore the sour taste of the nausea-induced saliva that collected under his tongue and threatened to make him sick.

He had to turn soon and pass once more over the dismal dam area for a last evaluation before returning to the Headquarters airstrip; but first he knew he had to give the air vents a chance to clear the choking odor from inside the plane and let everyone's stomach return to normal—his own included.

Opening his side window a crack, he felt the rush of clean wind rip through the plane, whipping the papers on their clipboards into a crackling flutter. After closing and securing the window again, he took off his headset and flipped on the overhead speaker to pick up the periodic chatter of the planes as they communicated with one another and the Radio Room at Headquarters. As he wiped the sweat from his forehead and eyes, he looked past Audrey to the Fafajaga Plain, which stretched to the south and east ahead of him.

During and after the rains, the plain resembled a gently rolling green sea of grass, interspersed with an occasional small bush or an even rarer tree. Now all that remained was the red soil scattered with patches of gray, withered grass that looked like dirty encrustations when seen from the air. There was nothing out here for miles; not a water hole or a mouthful of forage. What little grass remained from the last rains of nearly a year and a half ago was now dirty and dried out, without moisture or food value. The occasional bush had been consumed nearly level with the ground, and only nibbled stumps remained to show where a large shrub had once stood. The rare tree was stripped of leaves, and its branches were broken off as high as an elephant could reach; deep holes had been gouged in the trunk by the tusks of the starving elephants, and the thick, rough bark had been peeled away and eaten, to leave the tree's pale inner wood exposed and vulnerable. It was desolate, and it gave a terrible reality to the word "famine."

They'd got off to a promising start on Block XXIII after lunch. The sightings had been numerous, and even if the elephants and rhinos had been in a pitifully emaciated condition, they were at least there to be counted. But as they continued flying east along the Lalaga Lana River, the first of the carcasses had begun to appear. They were into the area hit hardest by the drought because the presence of permanent water drew the thirsty wildlife, who, after drinking, had consumed every shred of vegetation. As more came to drink and eat, more began to starve, and the very old and very young had begun to go down.

He had watched Audrey from the corner of his eye and seen her earlier excitement turn to horrified disbelief. As the live sightings increased because of the condensed populations, the numbers of carcasses rose as well, until finally in some places they had counted more dead elephants and rhinos than live.

The devastation was much worse along the river and its *luggas* than it had been in the blocks counted earlier. But as they'd slowly drawn away from the river's edge and worked their way south through the block, the numbers of carcasses had again begun to decline; and so they'd been unprepared for the final and worst horror at the extreme southern tip.

Reaching for his sunglasses, David began a slow turn over the

371

plain until he was heading back in a northwest-by-westerly direction toward the dam area. The barren, ravaged plain below sped swiftly by and explained the carnage at Aruba Dam.

As they approached, the scabs of dry grass grew fewer and farther apart, while the meandering game trails, now beaten hard as stone, multiplied and converged one upon another to point the way to water.

The sprawled and bloated carcasses of elephants began to increase in number as they approached, and the smell of putrefaction grew. Here in the vicinity of Aruba Dam, the predators and scavengers had gorged themselves to satiety; the lions had retreated to any available patch of shade, where they lay panting with distended bellies, while the glutted vultures sat on the swollen carcasses they fed on, too bloated to fly.

The abundance of carrion resulted in the majority of the carcasses' being left to lie unmolested; to swell in the hot sun till legs stuck out rigidly, and bellies inflated to grotesque proportions before exploding under pressure from the rotting flesh and noxious gases inside. They lay huddled in groups or alone; some were stretched out as if sleeping, while others had fallen to lie crumpled in a heap as if shot dead. The white bones of earlier victims were already bleaching in the hot sun under ragged strips of dried skin which stirred and drifted in the whistling wind.

Normally, the dam lake covered well over two hundred acres; now it had shrunk to only a quarter of that, and what remained was surrounded by acres of cracked and blistered mud.

As the plane came up on the dam lake, David reduced his speed and scanned the area. Perhaps a hundred seventy-five elephant carcasses in various stages of decomposition were counted in the immediate vicinity of the dam, maybe three hundred in the block. It was definitely the hardest-hit area in the park. Here and there he saw a small herd of zebras or a group of waterbuck; a few buffalo plodded toward the water ahead, and he noted the presence of the occasional ostrich or giraffe.

A group of impalas dashed away from the whine of the passing plane, and he was again aware of something he had noticed on and off all day. The wildlife, particularly the elephants, were abnormally skittish. It was true that they always distrusted the sound of low-flying aircraft and would move out when approached. But he'd never before seen them this alarmed. At the first indication of man's presence, they bolted in sheer panic. It was an indication of the degree of harassment they were under.

Just then he came up on a small group of elephants, some of the survivors who'd come miles for water before, hopefully, turning to trek a similar distance back into the bush for forage. A bull elephant stood listless and beaten in the hot sun beneath the shadeless skeleton of a dead and leafless tree; a juvenile knelt to drink the thick, soil-reddened water at the edge of the lake beside a half-submerged and rotting rhino carcass; and just beyond, a cow stood beside her collapsed calf; as David watched, she tottered and with hind legs buckling, sank to the earth. A short distance away, another rhino thrashed feebly in the thick gumbo beneath the dried-mud crust he'd fallen through, which now trapped and held him fast.

David counted one rhino trapped in mud and two elephants down, never to regain their feet. Many of the other elephants who were in an advanced stage of malnutrition managed to make the journey back to water one last time, and because death from starvation unconsciously seemed preferable to death from thirst, they refused to leave the water at the end. They stayed; reduced to wasted racks of protruding bones, hollow-faced and listless. They stayed and stood with lowering heads until the strength to stand was gone, and then they slowly sank to the ground, where they knelt with raised heads and dimming, wondering eyes until that too was an effort beyond their resources, and as their massive heads finally bowed to the inevitable, they slumped onto their sides, and eventually died.

"Six-oh-three, this is Whisky Bravo. Do you read me?"

"Whisky Bravo, six-oh-three. Roger."

"Send one unit of Field Force to the Aruba Dam area to check on two, I repeat, two, elephants who are down and unable to rise. Investigate rhino stuck in the mud. If possible, free him. Is that roger?"

"Roger, Whisky Bravo." Duba repeated the message and signed off.

David made one last circle over the area and saw more animals arriving for their evening watering. There were about a dozen species in ones and twos, small groups, and herds. Approximately sixty elephants plodded slowly past the carcasses of their kind to wade into the muddy water, and David spotted one solitary rhino. Too few, he thought grimly. There are too damn few.

He glanced up across the drought-stricken plain and saw the red parched earth stretch away to the horizon. It was empty, desolate, and blasted of every living thing, except for the trickling stream of wildlife who came with the late afternoon, for water.

Pointing the nose of the aircraft toward Headquarters Hill, he pulled away from the dam area and checked his watch. In a few minutes they'd be touching down, and it was none too soon. He couldn't stand to see any more today.

JEFF FORBES glanced over at the young man who sat beside him in the passenger seat. James Mugalu was looking very poorly indeed, and no wonder. Both times they'd set down to refuel, he'd wandered off to dispose of another airsick bag, and be ill again. However, he was beginning to look a little better; not much, but a little. By the time he was used to flying, the count would be over.

James had been desperately anxious to fly the count as an observer, even though he'd never before been in a plane, and Jeff recalled an old saying of his father's, which he should have mentioned earlier to his research assistant: "Be careful of what you want —you may get it." He chuckled to himself and turned back to his side window.

They were flying east over the southwest block of Sabaki Ranch, a million-and-a-half-acre cattle ranch northeast of the park, yet inside the Aruba ecosystem. The ranch held some twenty thousand cattle and innumerable wildlife, including elephants and rhinos. Just two years ago, one would have been sure of seeing a herd of eight hundred elephants drifting through the central blocks, plus two or three herds of four hundred or so. They hadn't been seen today. With luck they would be tomorrow, but the premonition that they might not hung heavily at the back of his mind.

Glancing down at his clipboard, he saw the notes he'd made on the last block before this one, and he had a gut feeling of impending disaster. They'd flown the huge northwest block, and he could recall to mind every animal spotted: one cock ostrich, two buffalo; and on the very last transect, they had made the first and only sighting of live elephants in the block—an emaciated string of six, huddled together in the meager shade of a candelabra tree.

The western blocks of the ranch were hard hit by the drought, the central blocks less so, and the eastern blocks hardly at all. Perhaps the elephants and rhinos had moved east toward the fertile coastal strip, along with the rest of the seemingly absent wildlife. Where, he wondered, have they got to? The numbers of carcasses noted, victims of both drought and poaching, gave him an answer he resisted.

Crossing over the long low ridge that marked the eastern boundary of the block, he began to bank his turn until he'd reversed his direction and reentered the block on the last transect, parallel with the Lalaga Lana River. After making sure of his position, he began to check the area below and ahead of him, and he spotted a group of three elephants, which he recorded carefully on his map and data sheet. Seeing nothing coming up, he glanced over toward the river, some five hundred meters away.

Dirty brown and only a fraction of its normal width, the river wound its sluggish way between sandy banks and sandbars, littered with debris washed down during former rains, toward Malindi, on the coast, and the Indian Ocean. The thick riverine vegetation was nearly demolished along this stretch. The grass and shrubs were gone; the trees stripped, ringbarked, or pushed over. Little was left of what had been—or, he reassured himself, what would be again. "All we need is rain," he muttered to himself, "and it will all come back."

Knowing it was the last transect somehow made the time it took to cross the block shorter, particularly since the number of sightings picked up. Almost before he knew it, he was coming up on Nyache Gate, which marked the end of the ranch's southwest block and the beginning of the national park land. After recording his time out, he glanced at his last notations before putting the clipboard away for the day. It didn't look too bad. Later he'd have to tabulate the sightings on each block to arrive at the final figures, but just a swift mental calculation told him that the last block looked very promising compared with the previous sections. There were a good number of carcasses, it was true, but even so, that was to be expected along the Lalaga Lana. The promise lay in the satisfactory number of live sightings of elephants, plus two rhinos.

He decided to follow the southern bank of the river to a point parallel with Headquarters before dropping south. Glancing over to James, he caught the young man's eye and raised his voice: "We're on our way home."

James's face reflected his obvious relief, and he smiled before turning to repeat the message to Dr. Lars Sorensen and Elijah Eki, the two observers in the back.

Increasing his altitude and speed, Jeff glanced casually over the landscape below, evaluating the remaining vegetation and the occasional glimpses of wildlife. Just as he began his bank to the south, his eye was caught by something that seemed out of place off to the left. He hesitated for a moment, then nosed the plane toward the incongruity. Uncertainly he wondered if he'd seen what he thought he'd seen out of the corner of his eye. Nothing seemed to be there. Flying low, he studied the thicket-choked ravine and a nearby cluster of acacia trees and saw nothing unusual; but he'd been almost sure he'd seen a running man.

As he circled around to fly over the area again, he recalled something David had said, about how at first, small aircraft had been so effective against poachers because they'd been so completely unprepared for detection from the sky; there had been something bordering on magic about it, and so when a poacher heard a plane, his first impulse had been to bolt from cover as any startled animal would do, to try to outrun the plane overhead. But not anymore; poachers had learned to remain motionless in whatever cover they could find—and most particularly, not to look up. It didn't mean, though, that they couldn't be seen; only that you had to look harder.

As he completed his circle and approached the area again, Jeff reduced his altitude and leaned forward to examine the thicket and trees. Eyes narrowed against the setting sun, he searched for the substance behind his suspicion, and the moment his probing study of each branch and twig revealed the figure of the man he sought, his hand was ready to move forward for the microphone. There the bugger was, on the eastern side of a tree, pressed against the trunk, now in heavy shadow and backlit by the declining sun. Nearly impossible to spot, unless you were sure he was there somewhere.

Banking in a wide circle, he depressed the mike switch. "Six-oh-three. This is Charlie Tango. Over."

A burst of crackling static preceded Duba's voice. "Charlie Tango. This is six-oh-three. I am reading you."

"We've spotted a poacher. Position is south of the Lalaga Lana"—Jeff glanced quickly around to get his bearings and continued: "just south and east of the Maika Faya Falls, in a ravine feeding the Hare Lugga, about one kilometer east of the road to signpost two-six-three. Is that roger?"

As Duba's affirmative reply came, Jeff glanced down to see that his circling was bringing him back over the thicket and trees, and he instinctively pulled back and began to climb back up to 350 feet as he scanned the area one last time before heading in to leave the poacher to the Field Force who would even now be responding.

A movement at the edge of the thicket alerted him, and he saw another figure dart out to watch the plane now passing overhead. Jeff leaned toward the side window and saw another and then a fourth man dash out of cover to follow the plane's progress. He saw one man pointing; another raised something, and he too pointed. As Jeff started to reach for the mike again in alarm, he wondered, What the—

He didn't hear the shot itself. He felt and heard the thundering bang as the heavy slug ripped through the cowling which housed the engine just in front of him. Thick black oil began to spray over the windscreen as he gripped the jerking stick to steady it.

"Mayday, mayday, this is Charlie Tango . . ." The engine stuttered and stalled as the plane quivered and dropped several feet, leaving his stomach behind. The ground was coming up fast. There was an explosion near his feet. James Mugalu jerked and stiffened in his seat, a look of surprise on his face.

"Poachers firing . . ." The stalling engine choked and died. The nose dipped. Flaps down for more lift. He eased back on the stick to steady the horizon, and knew he had only seconds. Three hundred feet. Fractions of seconds. He couldn't see forward.

"We're hit . . ." His motions were swift and simultaneous: close throttle, fuel off, brakes off, switches off, hot-air vents—no time.

"We're going down . . ." He reached across James and forced the door open against the wind. James's belly was saturated with blood. Something scratched and rattled along the underside of the plane's fuselage; they were gliding over the tops of trees.

"I repeat. We are going down. Do you roger?" He released his door catch and threw his weight against it. Audrey crossed his mind, and for a split second he panicked, then remembered: for once, she wasn't with him; she was with David; she was safe.

The scratching below now became a loud, crackling scrape that set him on edge like fingernails on a blackboard. The cockpit began to tilt, and he heard an unearthly shriek of terror behind him as the crashing increased. His hands groped for the instrument panel—mags off, master switch off—and the branches began to tear at the landing wheels, then the wings, then they beat on the windscreen.

He was thrown forward, and jerked back. The seat belt dug into his groin as he heard the scream of ripping metal. He closed his eyes to see flashing points of light, and felt his panic leave him. He was becoming strangely calm. He'd done what he could do. There was nothing else. . . . He murmured, "Father, forgive . . ." The world jerked sideways and exploded.

HEADQUARTERS HILL LOOMED large, and below it, where the slope evened out, the geometric pattern of the airfield slashed red against the thick gray bush. David came in low to check the wind sock: it indicated a southeasterly wind. Circling the airfield to approach from the northwest, he noticed that two planes were in ahead of them.

The radio crackled and spat, and David recognized Jeff Forbes's

377

voice and call letters raising Headquarters Radio Room. He heard the message regarding the discovery of the poacher and his position. Then Duba's alert to Units 1 and 6, who were in the area. For a moment he was tempted to respond to the call himself; he wanted to, and the road close by the ravine would provide a landing strip. Glancing up at Audrey, he decided that he'd better not. He couldn't take a woman into a confrontation with poachers, nor anywhere near it.

As he turned into his approach, he heard Agaran's reply and position related to communications, and he was satisfied. Unit 1 was south of Maika Faya Falls, only minutes from the poacher's position. They'd be on top of the man before he got half a kilometer away.

After lining up the aircraft, he pulled out the throttle to reduce his speed and synchronized the propeller pitch for maximum lift as he opened the cowling flaps to cool the engine and increase the drag. Adjusting the throttle, he prepared to touch down, and the nose lifted to obscure his forward vision as the tail descended.

Suddenly the radio came alive again, and Jeff's voice, loud but controlled, filled the plane.

"Mayday, mayday, this is Charlie Tango . . ." The voice ended abruptly in silence. . . . Then an explosion was heard.

Without hesitation David pushed the stick forward and opened the throttle as the nose dropped. Attaining takeoff speed, he eased back on the stick and began to climb.

He glanced at Audrey; she was staring blank and confused at the speaker, the color draining from her face. Quickly he adjusted the prop pitch and closed the flaps.

"Poachers firing . . ." An engine choked and coughed.

"We're hit . . ."

The pauses strained David's nerves to the breaking point, and as he banked sharply to clear Headquarters Hill and head north, he heard Audrey's voice mumbling, "Oh, God . . . oh, my God . . ." A chilling tingle of fear crept up his neck and under his scalp.

"We're going down . . ."

Audrey's scream cut through the cockpit like a knife as she tried to rise against the confining seat belt, slamming David against his door. He reached out and grabbed her hand as Dr. Patel shot forward and restrained her arms, holding her secure.

"I repeat. We are going down. Do you roger?"

David left Headquarters Hill behind and rapidly calculated the time it would take to reach Forbes: maybe eight to ten minutes. He glanced at the speed indicator: he was clocking 140 miles an hour— the maximum. His mind was numb with apprehension. Not Jeff—

good God, not Jeff. He looked over at Audrey, who lay in her seat whimpering, Dr. Patel's arms still locked around her.

David strained to hear. Jeff's radio was still transmitting.

A scraping sound grew from the background crackle of the radio static until it became a loud screech. An inhuman wail of fear was followed by sharp reports of rumbling crashes. Then silence.

Transmission was cut off.

Audrey lay quietly staring, hardly breathing. David reached out and took her hand. There was no response. He turned bleakly to her. "Soon," he said; "we'll be there soon." Something stuck in his throat.

She said nothing. Her eyes were huge, swallowing up her face, but they saw nothing. They had turned in, to stare in horror at the one loss she could not face.

THE TOYOTA SLOWED momentarily ahead of its cloud of boiling dust as it approached the 263 signpost designating the junction of the Lalaga Lana River road and the cutoff to Main Headquarters. Turning south on two wheels, the driver hit the accelerator, and the Toyota leaped forward on the sunbaked tourist-route road as pebbles and small rocks flew up from the tires to smack the underbody of the vehicle. Up a small incline and over the top, the wheels left the ground, and Agaran's head hit the roof just before the heavy bush vehicle slammed back onto the road.

He didn't complain; he didn't notice. His only interest was speed. He'd responded to Duba's call and had then left the radio-speaker volume on high, and he'd heard Forbes's plane go down. He checked his watch: it hadn't been three minutes. Hare Lugga was just ahead, maybe one kilometer. His blood pounded in his ears as his fingers stroked the barrel of the rifle he held between his knees.

A startled lesser kudu doe dashed from the bush at the side of the road, leaped sideways and, as the driver braked sharply, cleared the hood, inches from the windscreen. The rangers behind fell forward, to crash against the back of the cab, and then sprawled backward as the sandaled foot fell heavily on the accelerator again.

Into the sand at the bottom of the incline, the vehicle slewed sideways, and the driver's foot caressed the brake as he spun the wheel before hitting the accelerator once more. A ranger, hanging precariously from a brush bar, leaned forward, and his head appeared in the side window to shout and point to the left, and after a moment Agaran saw something sticking up through the dense bush. It was a white aircraft wing, pointing to the sky.

Reaching across Lugumba, he tapped the driver's arm and yelled, *"Hapa!"*

The driver hit the brakes, and as the vehicle slowed, he left the road and turned into the bush. Rangers leaped from the back to fall running, rifles ready. Agaran jerked the door open and was with them, Lugumba just behind. Motioning the men into a roughly crescent-shaped pattern, he put Lugumba at the far left as he took the far right position for himself, to cut off any who would try to slip past the advancing rangers. A shot was heard ahead, and they moved forward swiftly through the bush.

Another shot, and Agaran tried to increase his speed through the thick tangle of interlaced branches. Bent low, he scrambled on, dodging and ducking the clumps of thorn that tore at his face and body. The bush cleared a little; the white of the plane was coming clear, close. The figure of a man materialized in front of him, a little to his left. He was armed, and with his back to Agaran, he was aiming at something lying on the ground before him. An arm came up; a hand stretched toward the poacher with the rifle in supplication.

Agaran burst from the confining thicket. The poacher turned as Agaran's rifle came up, his expression one of disbelief; the shots cracked loud as he crumpled over.

Agaran ran up and kicked the man's rifle away. With his foot he rolled him onto his back. A Somali, dying or dead. He turned to the now-unconscious figure lying a few feet away. It was Elijah Eki, one of the research assistants. Agaran remembered seeing him around Headquarters and the Research Center. Blood bubbled brightly from the gaping wound that wheezed on the left side of his chest. The Somali had been shooting the survivors of the plane crash. He took a deep breath to try to control the hate welling up inside him. He knelt over the young man and saw there was nothing he could do.

More shots cracked out nearby. A nearly constant fusillade erupted somewhere to the left of him. He turned, and after snatching up the poacher's rifle, he ran toward the sound, shaking with anger. His mind reeled with profanities; reaching back into his memory, he grasped for the ancient curses of his forefathers that bordered on the edge of witchcraft, and as he drew them out, he knew they still fitted. He ran on, screaming in Turkana.

CORPORAL LUGUMBA CROUCHED beside an irregular jumble of rocks, partly screened by a scraggly bush. Cautiously he peered to watch a large rock beside a dead tree, some sixty feet away. He had a man penned in behind the scant cover, and he had no intention of letting him slip away.

Studying the area, he decided there wasn't much chance of that happening. The rock and its tree stood alone on a gentle slope; above, nothing but bare earth; behind, the ground rose sharply in full view of his own position; below, a clump of bush, perhaps forty feet away—the man wouldn't live to reach it if he tried to run.

He counted his shots taken and realized he had two bullets left in the magazine. Checking the rock again, he decided he had time to reload. Wiping the blood from his fingers, he fished his ammunition from his pocket and filled the magazine. The flesh wound high on his upper right arm throbbed dully. He'd killed the man responsible for that; they were even now.

The sharp reports of rifle fire had slowed; he was tired of waiting. The Somali hadn't shown himself or fired for several moments; perhaps he thought he could hide behind his rock all day. Resting his rifle barrel across his knee, Lugumba reached for a medium-sized stone and studied the ground ahead. A knee-high acacia thornbush stood thick and dried out, just halfway between him and his quarry.

He chucked the stone through the dry branches, and the resulting rustle brought the Somali's head up. Lugumba's rifle cracked, and the bullet struck—a fraction of an inch too low. The top edge of the rock exploded. There was a scream of pain from the Somali. Throwing his rifle out, he stood with his fingers pressed against his eyes and forehead; blood streamed down his face from the jagged wounds made by the flying slivers of rock. One hand came up in surrender as Lugumba rose and moved forward.

The Somali's other hand wrenched itself from the shattered eye it protected, and came up to hover limply over his head, his one remaining eye squinting through a film of blood. The hand dropped again to wipe the blood away, but before the torn eyelid could obscure his vision once more, he saw and recognized the meaning of Lugumba's expression.

With a cut-off howl of fear, he started to turn to run. The bullet caught him in the throat.

"Never shoot a fleeing poacher in the back," Lugumba had been warned, so he shot them before they turned.

Crossing the clearing, he approached the Somali and looked down at him briefly without expression.

FIELD FORCE RANGER Henry Mutisya crept through the bush, starting at every sound. Every pore in his body sweated fear. He ducked into a narrow hiding place between a rock and a clump of thick bush and wondered again—what was he doing here?

He was a clerk. He had a fourth-form education, but his job had become redundant and then he'd been without another for months. He'd applied for office work at the Ministry of Tourism and Wildlife and nothing had happened, until the notice came about the recruitment of men for the Field Force. He'd taken it because jobs were scarce. He hadn't known what it was like, and two months in army training school and three months' Field Force duty hadn't helped educate him.

He'd heard of gun battles with poachers, but until now he'd been lucky. Before, either he'd been on guard duty at Headquarters, or the confrontations he'd had with poachers had been with Wakamba like himself, who'd been armed with bows and arrows. Not Somali; not with automatic rifles. His hand trembled as he wiped the sweat from his eyes. He knew he'd run if he could, but he didn't know which way to go. The intermittent firing was all around him.

A crashing in the bush nearby startled him. He jumped to his feet and his rifle came up as a Somali burst into the clearing in front of him. The man saw him and immediately raised his arms in surrender, his rifle still in his hand. Blood ran from a ragged red stripe on his shoulder.

Henry Mutisya stepped out from his rock, his legs shaking. He lowered his rifle, and his dragging foot caught an exposed root, making him stumble and look down. The Somali's hands dropped, the rifle held ready. Henry tried to recover himself; his forefinger groped for the trigger, but the safety catch was on.

The bullets caught him in the stomach. Fear had become reality, and it hurt. The Somali slipped into the bush.

JEFF FORBES SLOWLY became aware of sporadic rifle fire. That first, and then his head—it hurt horribly. He was thirsty. Licking his lips, he tasted sweat and blood; it was salty. A pain was growing in his arm; after a moment it was almost unbearable. He opened his eyes with difficulty; coagulating blood had glued his eyelashes together.

He turned his head and saw that he was lying at the foot of a tree trunk, partially concealed by a thick tangle of bush. The plane was some forty feet away, on its side, one wing torn away. A man was there. Dressed in ragged shorts and a torn shirt, he crouched behind some rocks with a rifle and shot at something, or someone. Jeff tried to sit up, but the pain in his arm was excruciating, and he fell back with a groan and lost consciousness again.

It was quiet now. The sun showed red behind his closed eyelids, and then a shadow came down and blocked out the declining sun. He opened his eyes and saw Lance Corporal Dadacho leaning over him.

"*Habari?*" Dadacho asked, and Jeff nodded. A can of warm water was offered and his head was held up to drink.

Lying back, he glanced around. He looked for the man in ragged shorts who'd been by the rocks. He was still there, but now he was stretched out limply, his tattered shirt stained red, his eyes staring blankly at the sun. Jeff heard the sound of an approaching plane and looked up as the Cessna 180 began to circle high overhead.

DAVID HAD SPOTTED the plane wreckage and come in high, at five hundred feet, to circle. It appeared to be over. The two unit vehicles were off near the road. Figures were scattered around the twisted wreckage. Dropping altitude, he circled lower; the figure of Agaran detached itself from a group to wave all clear, and he knew he could take Audrey in now.

He headed north to the river road, where the bush thinned to allow him to land on the dirt surface of the vehicle track. Reaching for his mike, he radioed for Unit 1's vehicle to come and pick them up.

Minutes later he was scrambling through the bush beside Audrey, the worst of his fears allayed. Forbes wasn't dead, but he was badly hurt. Audrey's face was still drawn and white, although the terrible stunned look of impending grief had gone.

They passed two rangers carrying a dead Somali at head and foot, and then they were into the trampled area around the plane.

"Here!" Agaran shouted as he saw them.

Audrey ran stumbling over the broken ground, and as she saw Jeff's hand come up, tears began to run down her face.

Agaran stepped over to David and said, "There were nine of them. Five are dead and one was knocked out by a rifle butt. Three got away into the bush, and one of them is leaving a blood trail."

"How about the observers?"

"Forbes is hurt, but I think he'll be all right. Dr. Sorensen is cut up and his leg is broken, but that's all. James Mugalu is gut-shot and he's lost a lot of blood; I don't think he'll make it. Eki is dead." He paused, then added, "The Somali had started shooting the survivors when we arrived. Eki was the first; they didn't have time to get to the others."

David's expression hardened, and as he glanced toward the growing pile of poachers' bodies sprawled brokenly, he remembered

Jeff's question on the day they planned the count. Three hundred feet, he'd asked: wasn't that a bit low? Poachers had been known to fire at low-flying planes—probably because they thought the plane was looking for them. And he remembered his reply: "I think the chances of its happening here are one in a thousand, if that."

So they'd flown low, and Jeff had nearly paid for David's mistake with his life. He passed his hand over his eyes.

"And our men?" he asked.

"Only two are wounded, but Mutisya is dead."

David looked up and asked, "Mutisya: isn't that one of the new men?"

Agaran nodded and then added, "A Kamba. He was a clerk of some kind before."

David shook his head. It had always been his opinion that the Field Forces should be made up of the men from the northern tribes. Mutisya had been one of the first recruits taken from outside that area and background, and he'd felt it was a mistake. There might be an occasional man who would work out well, but he would be an exception, not the rule.

He turned and went to kneel beside Jeff Forbes. His friend's head was badly lacerated, and his broken arm lay twisted grotesquely; a trickle of blood seeped from the jagged wound made by a sliver of protruding bone. Audrey was washing his face with her handkerchief, her own face almost cheerful with relief.

Jeff looked up, and in a hoarse voice he croaked, "Will you look at the woman? I think she's pleased I'm busted up so that she can fuss over me." He smiled weakly.

"I think she's just pleased you're here to be fussed over," David replied, trying to smile. His face felt frozen. "I'm sorry," he added.

"For what?" Jeff asked, perplexed. And then the corners of his mouth twitched into his lopsided grin. "Oh, yes, I thought of that, just as they opened fire." A grimace of pain crossed his features as Audrey tried to move the fractured arm onto a makeshift splint fashioned from a clipboard.

"Forget it," he murmured to David, and reached out with his good arm to lay his hand on David's shoulder. "We're even now."

Agaran came up and drew David aside. "The helicopter is on its way, and vehicles have left Headquarters for the village airstrip."

"We had better get going, then," David said. "I'd rather head straight for Mombasa, but Mugalu needs immediate attention. We'll get him to the dispensary first—it might make the difference. I'll take him in my plane now, with the two wounded Rangers. Dr. Sorensen can follow with Audrey and Jeff in the 'copter. What about the wounded poacher?"

"He's just got a headache. I'll send Unit Six into town with the prisoner and the bodies of the others."

"And you?"

"Three got away," Agaran replied, his expression grim. "I'm going after them."

CHAPTER TWENTY-TWO

Evening

THE GATE SWUNG OPEN and the departing Land-Rover rattled through; its roof rack, overloaded with tents, sleeping bags, and boxes of cooking paraphernalia, barely cleared the *makuti* roof over Main Gate. Towheaded children popped tired, dirty faces out the windows to wave and chorus their "*Kwa-heri*'s," which were echoed by the sharp yap of a concealed and forbidden puppy, who was promptly shushed.

Mulolo neither heard nor consciously saw their departure. He was numb with panic. Swinging the gate shut, he returned to the small office and sat down where he could watch the small footpath to the *campini*. "For once," he implored under his breath, "let my relief be on time."

It was only luck that had led him to decide to start tallying the daily receipts early. Usually the late afternoon saw him under the big acacia tree, sitting on his favorite rock in conversation with whoever was waiting for a lift into town. But today no one had been waiting, and so in boredom he'd gone into the office just in time to hear the voice of *Daktari* Forbes on the sputtering radio. Checking the huge wall map of the park area, he'd located the poacher's reported position and frowned. Who was crazy enough to be poaching south of Lalaga Lana? he wondered. And during the daylight, as well.

Poachers were operating everywhere, it was true. But the one place avoided was the area above Headquarters, north to the Lalaga Lana River, where tourist roads and game-viewing drives abounded. The area was thick with wildlife, particularly elephants, but few were willing to risk the chance of being spotted by the frequent patrols and sight-seers. He did know of one gang, however, that operated in that area regularly at night, and he'd smiled in satisfaction, since that was because they knew when no patrol was in the area.

He knew there were a few others who ventured there, drawn by the large number of elephants in the thick bush near the river, but they were Kamba, with their silent bows and arrows, and they had the sense to do their hunting at dusk and dawn, when the tourists were safely occupied with dinner or early-morning tea in the lodge. He'd idly speculated on who it was that Forbes had spotted.

The radio had come alive then with messages; Duba's voice had started raising the units, who had been unusually silent all day. Agaran's reply came, with his position nearby. Mulolo stared at the map in confusion; something was wrong. He'd frowned in concentration as he tried to remember the patrol schedule he'd passed along days ago. It was now Friday. Where were the patrols deployed Friday? Then he'd remembered. The Northern Area units had been assigned to patrol the west and northwestern boundary; Southern Area units were to be on the Moda River/Aruba Dam, working south-southeast. So what were Units 1 and 6 doing along the Lalaga Lana? he'd wondered stupidly. Why weren't they in their assigned patrol areas? What was going on?

His pondering had been interrupted by Forbes's "Mayday," and Mulolo's attention was riveted to the radio. "Poachers firing" had caught him like a blow. Rifles—they had rifles. They weren't Kamba; so who could they be? Who had rifles?

The answer forced his mind to return to the patrol schedule which indicated that no one was patrolling south of the Lalaga Lana. *They* had rifles, and they had been told that no one was patrolling near the river. Was it possible? No, it was insane.

It couldn't be, he tried to reason. He had passed the information on about the upcoming aerial count. It had been only yesterday. They wouldn't dare. But would they? The men were the best hunters money could buy. Warned, they'd know they could listen for and hear an approaching plane, and they knew how to melt into the ground until it passed.

Another possibility had occurred to him then, an even worse one. What if they hadn't been warned? What if the men had been in the bush when he'd sent the information? Perhaps they couldn't be contacted. It had been only twenty-four hours' warning—perhaps it hadn't been enough.

The radio had continued babbling. Forbes had gone down. Mulolo had stood before the radio horrified; his hands, gripping the countertop, were wet with sweat. He pictured the flaming plane crashing, a ball of fire and black smoke, the charred bodies. Who would dare fire on the planes? He knew the answer, and his mind screamed a warning. The rangers. The rangers are right there.

He tried to be calm, to reassure himself that it wasn't possible. But it was. The longer he sat and thought, the more possible it became.

The radio hadn't shut up. He'd heard Agaran's later request for the helicopter, for vehicles to carry the dead and wounded. Was it five or six dead? He couldn't remember. "Murder" repeated itself in his mind.

He glanced up and looked hopefully up the pathway. His relief wasn't yet in sight. Where was he? Why didn't he come?

He had to get to town. He had to see the man, the *Bwana Mkubwa*. He had to find out what had happened. The C.I.D. would be all over the park. They'd never give up until everyone responsible was picked up. He thought of Margaret, the messages. He'd hang.

No, he wouldn't hang, he reassured himself. He could run—so far into the bush that no one would ever find him; run until he was across the border. But first he had to get to the man to find out.

"Jambo," the Luo Ranger's deep voice boomed through the window. Mulolo leaped startled to his feet.

"Habari?" the man said questioningly as Mulolo sped out the door toward the staff quarters without a word.

As he ran, he began to unbutton his shirt. He had only a few minutes until the last lorry left for town. Dashing into his room, he flung off the sweat-drenched khaki uniform and jerked on a pair of pants. Running out again with his shirt in his hand, he saw the lorry passing by.

"Simama!" he screamed.

The lorry slowed and halted.

VERA REMOVED THE thick glob of petroleum jelly from the child's ear, and as Adam held the small penlight steady, she pulled the outer ear until the ear canal straightened and she could see what she was looking for. Just below the eardrum a smothered tick lay on the floor of the ear canal, where he'd attached himself for a meal and caused intense discomfort to the youngster, who now sat as still as a mouse with wide, frightened eyes.

As she reached for the small forceps, Vera wondered again why it was that people who'd suffered all day with an ailment finally decided in the early evening that they couldn't make it through the night without medical attention.

Reaching into the ear canal, she grasped the fat, bloated body and gently pulled. The suffocated tick had relaxed its hold on the delicate tissue, and she was able to draw it out without damaging the membrane above. After dropping it into the kidney dish, she reached for a stopper full of warmed antibiotic eardrops to soothe and prevent infection.

"*Nimemaliza.* I have finished," Vera said to the boy after packing his ear with clean cotton. The youngster jumped up and gently prodded at the cotton which muffled her voice, and smiled in wonderment. The irritation and a maddening sensation of something rattling about in his ear had probably been intense, she realized, as was usual in the all-too-frequent cases of this sort, and her instant cure by the mere removal of the cause and an application of warm oil had amazed him. Another miracle of modern medicine, she thought wryly.

She stood stiffly, and staggered; caught herself sharply and grabbed hold of the back of a chair. The muscles of her back and legs had refused to stretch to allow her to stand. She felt Adam's hand at her elbow, felt his eyes examining her in consternation.

"*Mimi, sawa-sawa.* I'm all right," she murmured, and forced a smile to her face. Moving to her desk, she sat down, filled out a treatment slip and entered the boy's case in the dispensary case logbook for the next day. Today's cases were already counted up and closed out. It was the reason she'd still been here when the boy arrived.

The youngster hesitantly sidled up to the desk to watch her, but when she glanced up at him he looked away in confusion. Crossing to the door to retrieve the parcel he'd set there on the floor when he arrived, he returned to her desk and knelt down to unwrap the curiously clanking bundle. When next she looked up, to hand him the treatment slip, she saw that he was carefully removing beer bottles from the soiled and tattered remains of an old shirt.

There were five of them lined up when he had finished. Tusker, Pilsner, and one Whitecap; green or brown glass, and all carefully washed and dried. Each worth a 1-shilling deposit, except for the one cracked one. She glanced at the thin boy who stood staring at the floor; he was an urchin, quite dirty and very ragged, probably eleven years old or so, and Kamba, by his pronunciation of Swahili. Undoubtedly the unwanted child of one of the village prostitutes, and most likely on his own ever since he'd been kicked out by his mother at the age of six or seven. There were a dozen like him in the village.

He looked up at her uncertainly. Like the others, he lived from hand to mouth, and slept in any shelter available: an abandoned hut if he was lucky; if not—then under a bush. He got by as best he could by sweeping out *pombe* clubs, begging from tourists, and gathering wild fruits and vegetables in the bush. He had no money, and the bottles were probably pilfered, but he'd been in pain, and he wouldn't come empty-handed. His eyes met hers in mute appeal.

She smiled and murmured, *"Asante."*

His bottles were accepted. His bright childish grin flashed before he ducked his head in embarrassment.

How young he is, she thought, and how proud. Turning to the locked cupboard behind her desk, she reached for her keys and unlocked it. Opening it to reveal three shelves stacked with donated "Food for the Hungry," she began to pull out several items as she wondered how best to handle this. Begging from the *wageni,* the tourists, was one thing—that was what they were provided for by *Mungu*; they were so rich that they could easily share. But she'd lived here for years, she'd been accepted as one of them, as much as anyone of her color could be. Her sympathy had to be handled more delicately. Otherwise it could wound, and never be forgiven.

Arranging the canned milk, dried potatoes, and tinned meat before her, she forced her voice to its harshest: *"Ninataka kijana kumsaidia Adam kusafisha dispensary. Unajua mmoja anataka kazi?"**

She glared demandingly at the boy, who stood transfixed staring at the food. His pink tongue crept out to taste his full lower lip. *"Mimi, Mama."*

Handing him two of the cans, she told him to report to Adam at the second hour of the next morning. After giving Adam the rest of the food with instructions to give the boy two more cans for each morning's work, she shooed them both out of the office as she avoided Adam's eye. She'd not fooled him, and she knew it.

Alone now, she began to remove the litter of discarded needles and empty medicine bottles from the cracked deal table. She was tired again this evening. Her steps dragged and her movements were slow and weary. Finishing finally, she left the office, locked the door and began to slowly walk around the building for her early-evening stroll.

Just as she reached the corner of the dispensary, she heard the sound of a vehicle approaching and glanced up to see the first dark

---

* "I want a boy to help Adam clean the dispensary. Do you know one who wants work?"

green Land-Rover hurtling down the dirt road. Two more followed close behind.

Recognizing the park vehicles, she murmured, "Oh, dear God, not again."

Hurriedly returning to the dispensary door, she unlocked it just as two rangers approached carrying a stretcher on which lay a young man whose abdomen was covered with blood-soaked bandages.

"Adam!" she bellowed. More rangers approached carrying Jeff Forbes and another man she didn't recognize.

David was at her elbow leading a ranger whose eyes and forehead were enveloped with red-stained gauze wrapped about his head; the ranger suddenly stumbled and sagged, and David caught him in his arms.

"Here," she directed, throwing open the door to the ward with its six iron cots. She heard David's voice in her office: "Leave the dead on the veranda."

She closed her eyes for a fleeting prayer before moving to the first cot to remove the wet bandages from the stomach of the young man whose eyes registered only pain. He was obviously the worst off of the lot. Tersely giving directions to Adam over her shoulder, she set to work. A syringe, a needle, and the necessary drugs appeared at her side. Out of the corner of her eye, she saw Jeff Forbes refuse a bed and take a chair. The other man groaned and caught his breath as he was laid on a bed with what appeared to be a crushed leg and foot.

A rubber tube and a large bottle appeared beside her as she searched for a vein in the slender dark arm. She felt a hand on her shoulder and heard David's voice: "It's only an hour until dusk." There was an apology in his statement.

She nodded in understanding: it would take him an hour to fly to Mombasa.

"I'll do all I can," she said. It caught in her throat—she'd said it so many times.

She felt despair prickle her eyes. The boy's veins were collapsing.

LEANING BACK AGAINST the soft chair cushions, David sighed in relief and put his feet up on the veranda wall. He closed his eyes and tried to empty his mind of all thought and worry. But the day's events chased one another around his head and denied him peace.

Forbes would be all right. With his arm set in plaster and his lacerated head bandaged, he'd fought a losing battle demanding to leave the hospital and return by car to Aruba. Only when confronted by Audrey's threat to hit him did he back down, put on the hospital nightgown and get into bed. Dr. Sorensen's foot and leg was set and in traction; in time he would heal. But James Mugalu was critical, and the British doctor had sorrowfully shaken his head and said, "I'll do all I can, but . . ." The sentence had been left unfinished.

After a late dinner with Audrey at the small hotel where he'd obtained a room for her, he'd returned to Aruba by car, courtesy of the Senior Warden, who'd done everything he could by radio from the park—including the return of his plane by a Police Air Wing pilot first thing in the morning.

It seemed impossible that so much could have happened in one day, and still it wasn't over. There was to be one last demand on him, for as if on cue, a pair of headlamp beams showed up brightly in the darkness on the road below his house.

A few moments later Joe Kiboko ran up the veranda steps. "I was sorry to hear about what happened this afternoon," he said, shaking his hand.

David filled him in on the condition of the survivors and then asked, "Were you able to get any information out of the prisoner we took?"

Kiboko shook his head, "No, and I don't think we will."

"Why?" David asked in surprise.

"He's a half-wit."

David's expression was that of dumbfounded disbelief.

"I know," Kiboko muttered. "He had a head wound and I figured he was just knocked silly. Either that or he was acting. But we took him to Vera Batey and she examined him."

"What was her verdict?" David asked.

"Well, she said the head wound didn't help matters, but yes, she felt he was simple. With her, he opened right up and started talking. He says he was with his brother. His brother always took him hunting with him. It was his job to cook, keep the camp, get the firewood and water, and help carry the ivory. He says he's from the north, but he seems genuinely confused by a map and can't remember the name of his village.

"When I asked him if he knew how the guns were obtained, he seemed happy to be able to answer, 'Yes.'

"When I asked, 'How?' he told me his brother brought them." Kiboko threw up his hands. "There's a lot more of the same. He's childlike. He wants to answer, and tries, but doesn't give us anything useful."

"Unbelievable," David muttered in disgust. "The one prisoner we were able to take alive, and he's an *mtoto*."

"It's probably why you were able to take him," suggested Kiboko. "He didn't have a gun, so he couldn't fight back, and wouldn't know how to anyway. When the firing started, he ran and hid."

"Tell me about Mulolo," David asked in resignation. Draw a blank on one gang, try another. Somewhere, something had to break.

Kiboko took a small notebook from his pocket and began to read: "He worked the gate as usual. Nothing out of the ordinary occurred until around five thirty, when he went to the office and didn't come out for some time. Our man looked in the window a couple of times and Mulolo didn't even notice him. He seemed in a panic about something, and was listening intently to the radio transmissions about the plane crash and the shoot-out with the poachers." Joe looked up inquiringly.

David shook his head. "I don't understand either."

"When his relief came on," Kiboko continued, "he ran home, changed clothes, and caught the last lorry to town. He was in such a hurry that he nearly lost our tail. When he got to town, he hit one *pombe* club after another until it got dark. He seemed to be interested in drinking as much as he could in as short a time as possible.

"After it was dark, he left the last bar and slipped over to the milk kiosk in the square, where he knocked on the back door and was admitted."

David leaned forward in interest.

"Unfortunately," Kiboko went on, "the kiosk was closed for the night. The doors were shut and the shutters down. Only a few cracks of light showed from the place. Mulolo's tail got right up to the building, but he couldn't see inside and he could only hear a murmur of conversation; not loud enough to be able to distinguish individual voices or words. Except for one instance when it seemed an argument was going on. Someone shouted, '*Mjinga*. Fool,' and there was a short scuffle. Sounded as if someone was knocked down." He checked his notes. "Then the conversation resumed, but it was even less audible." Kiboko glanced up in apology.

"Don't worry about it." David grinned sardonically. "We couldn't expect them to invite your man inside."

Kiboko chuckled and resumed his report. "Shortly after, Mulolo came out. He left the square, and headed up the road—and here," he added, "my man was in a dilemma. He wanted to find out who was inside the kiosk, whom Mulolo had been in such a panic to see, but he couldn't let Mulolo out of sight either, and he didn't have time to get to a phone to get another man to assist."

He apologized. "I should have foreseen this, but I didn't. My man hung around as long as he could, and when no one showed signs of leaving immediately, he took off after Mulolo. By the time he could get to me by phone and I got down to the square, the kiosk was dark and padlocked. Whoever was in there had left."

"Where is Mulolo now?" David asked.

"He returned to the park and went to the staff canteen. He's drinking there now. With a rapidly swelling jaw."

David chuckled sourly. "Well, at least we know who the 'fool' was who hit the floor." He rubbed his eyes and thought in disgust, A half-wit and a fool, and somehow, by sheer numbers, they've been winning. "Who owns the milk kiosk?" he asked.

"A man by the name of Mnyambo."

"What do you have on him?"

Joe shook his head.

"No arrest record?"

"None. He has a small house, old car, one wife"—he checked his notes—"three children. He's Taita, but that's not uncommon in this area. Usual circle of friends. Nothing. But I'll keep trying. You've been sure he's the one who's getting the information from Mulolo. After tonight I think you're right." He smiled. "Starting tomorrow I'll have the kiosk watched. We'll take note of everyone who comes near Mnyambo. Perhaps tomorrow night I'll be able to give you more information.

"There's one other thing," he continued.

"What is it?"

"Mulolo appears to be very friendly with the tour-company drivers."

"Another fiddle?"

"Possibly. There are a lot of visitors coming in Main Gate at the moment. It would be a temptation to someone like Mulolo."

"Have your man count heads and vehicles tomorrow. We'll compare them with Mulolo's returns. If there's a discrepancy . . ." David let the statement hang. "Well," he added, "at this point, anything helps. We might be able to use it to put on a little pressure later."

Kiboko nodded and stood. "I'm sorry we don't have more for you. But we'll get it yet. If not today, then tomorrow or the next day."

David saw him to the car and returned to the house, to flip off the light switches on his way to bed. Tomorrow or the next day, he thought. Let's hope it isn't too late. He had a feeling it was a race now, a dash for time. Was he ahead? Or trailing just behind?

* * *

NO ONE NOTICED the old man with a drinking gourd curled up beside the wheel of a bread wagon in the village square near the milk kiosk; or if anyone did, he paid no attention. There were too many like him—old *wazee* who spent their last years peering at a strange world through blurred, rheumy eyes over the edge of a gourd of cheap but potent homemade *pombe*.

This old *mzee* wasn't drinking, though, and his gourd was empty. In the darkness he appeared to be sleeping, but his narrowed eyes never closed. He'd been watching the shuttered milk kiosk ever since Maimbo entered it just as darkness fell, and he would continue to watch it until he came out. In the meantime he observed everyone else who came near.

He'd recognized the Gate Ranger who'd approached furtively, and he'd laughed to himself. The man had crept up to the kiosk as if he hadn't wanted to be seen there, but his very actions screamed for attention as he glanced over his shoulder, then up and down the square, strolled by with a swagger, circled, peered around a pole, and then dashed around to the back door. He couldn't have been more noticeable if he'd run naked through the square at *saa sita* while beating on a drum.

Another man had soon approached. But for a long time Bubu hadn't been able to decide the meaning of this one's actions. He'd merely walked up and glanced about, checked his watch, and then leaned up against the side of the kiosk to wait. He'd lit a cigarette, moved to the front of the small tin building, and stood smoking. It wasn't until the Gate Ranger came out the back door that he indicated the reason for his presence.

When the back door opened, he'd stepped into the darker shadows under the overhanging roof and watched the ranger depart. He'd seemed undecided as to what to do at first, but when the ranger was lost to sight up the road, he took off after him.

Then Bubu guessed. The ranger worked for Warden Karanja, and for some reason the Warden must want to know where he went and what he did and so he'd set someone to spy on him. Why? Bubu didn't know, although he wondered if Karanja knew about Maimbo. Perhaps he suspected. That made it even more important that he find out where the ivory was hidden. He had to get there before the rangers.

It hadn't been long after when the kiosk lights went out and the two men stepped outside. One paused to lock the door, and then they crossed the darkened square and turned into a side street. Bubu had recognized the taller of the two men: Maimbo.

He was up immediately. He wrapped his gourd in the frayed

piece of sacking he'd worn about his shoulders, threw the bundle into the basket of the old bicycle he'd concealed behind a row of reeking garbage bins and wheeled it out.

Pedaling across the square, he saw Maimbo's headlamps flick on up the street where he'd parked away from the kiosk, and as the car pulled into the road and drove away, Bubu followed.

The car moved slowly over the deeply rutted road that wound up a hill behind the village. Bubu had no trouble following the bright beacon of Maimbo's lights as they dipped and swayed through the darkness.

In places the road arched steeply and he was forced to jump off and run beside the bicycle, pushing it up and over the broken ground, but that was a small price to pay for a situation which demanded that Maimbo drive slowly to avoid ripping open the underside of his car.

Bubu ran on, smiling in the darkness. It was all right. He had them in sight. Just ahead, the car slowed and stopped, and the lights went out.

Maimbo stood at the open window. It was hot in the old mud-walled warehouse—one of several erected by a company that had mined rubies here for years. The mine was played out now and the site abandoned, and all the structures had fallen down; all but this one.

Maimbo had seen the promise in the old building nearly three years ago. It was far enough from town to escape surveillance by neighbors, and large enough to suit his needs, so he had bought the site, repaired the old warehouse, and quietly started a small business buying and reselling charcoal.

Three days a week, an old Bedford lorry made its scheduled rounds through nearby villages in the surrounding area, picking up the jute bags of locally made charcoal, which were then brought back and stored until enough had been collected to warrant a trip to Mombasa to sell it.

As a business it was satisfactory; at least, it made enough profit to warrant its existence; but money made from the resale of the charcoal was nothing compared with the profits made from the ivory secreted inside the bags under the charred wood.

As he turned away from the window, his thoughts went back to a question that had briefly occurred to him yesterday morning when he'd received the message from the little jackal. Why had Karanja not mentioned the upcoming count to him? He'd seen him Monday afternoon, and nothing had been said about it. He'd decided it must have been arranged quickly, and he'd expected to hear from Karanja yesterday, or today at least, but there hadn't been a word.

Maimbo's expression was thoughtful as he speculated on Karanja's motives. They weren't friends; they had too little in common for that. Their relationship began and ended with the fact that they both worked for the same Government department. In the past there had always been to some degree a "hands-off" attitude between park wardens and game wardens and their areas of responsibility. But was it more than that? Did Karanja suspect anything?

After considering the question carefully, he dismissed the possibility. The park was Karanja's concern; if he wanted to count his trophy animals without his, Maimbo's, assistance, it meant only that Karanja didn't need or want his help; and that was fine with him. He didn't like flying anyway. Still, he felt better knowing his hunters were out of the area and safely away in Mombasa. Soon the ivory would be gone as well, and that would leave only one problem to deal with.

Sitting on an old chair, minus its back, he leaned against the cracked mud wall and remarked to his half-brother, "You were right."

Mnyambo glanced up from the dirty white tusk he was carefully sawing into sections. "Mulolo?"

Maimbo nodded. "He is dangerous. I thought his fear would keep him in line, but it's doing just the opposite. He almost cracked today. If anyone had noticed and started asking him questions . . ." Maimbo snorted in disgust. The stupid bastard. A band of Somali panic and open fire on a plane and his fear for his own skin did the rest. It was almost beyond belief, and he could easily have brought the C.I.D. down on their heads without warning. Maimbo had been tempted to break his neck there and then, but he'd caught himself in time. Not yet: it wasn't safe. Later.

"I told you so," Mnyambo replied glumly.

Maimbo glared at his half-brother. Did no one around him know when to keep his mouth shut? If Mnyambo wasn't careful, he'd find himself replaced as well; not as permanently of course, but still, replaced.

Shoving that consideration aside for the moment, he said, "After the count and the anti-poaching campaign are over, and after Karanja's reinforcements leave and the park routine returns to normal, I want you to arrange an accident for Mulolo."

Mnyambo ceased sawing and looked up. "What sort of accident?"

"Anything—it doesn't matter, as long as it appears an accident. Take him to town, get him drunk, and then arrange for him to be hit by a car, or have him robbed and knifed."

Mnyambo nodded and went back to work. His expression clearly said that it was about time.

"And if," Maimbo added after a moment's consideration, "anything goes wrong before then, get to Mulolo immediately. Shut him up."

Mnyambo set down his file and looked puzzled. "What do you mean, 'if anything goes wrong'? What could that be?"

"How do I know?" Maimbo shouted, his patience strained to the breaking point. "If I knew that beforehand, it wouldn't be allowed to happen." He stood up and walked back to the window. Was there no one around him but fools? He'd better spend the next month recruiting another second-in-command from among his numerous relatives. Perhaps Mwakiu, his elder sister's son. The *kijana* drove the charcoal lorry; he made the pickups around the area, and later, after the charcoal had been repacked with the ivory inside, he drove the load to Mombasa for delivery. When he returned with the money sealed in a packet, he never asked questions; nor had he ever opened the parcel, or tried to subtract a little for himself. He was a smart boy—he must know that the weight of the packet surpassed any reasonable payment for a lorry-load of charcoal. Maimbo wondered how much the boy knew, then smiled into the darkness outside; he was sure it was more than he let on about. Nodding to himself, he decided—yes, the boy might be the one. In the meantime, there was something more that his half-brother could do for him.

Turning back to Mnyambo, he said, "I doubt if you've thought of it yet, but removing one problem will create another."

Mnyambo didn't look up. He went on carefully sawing the last section of the tusk. Inside, he was simmering. He knew Maimbo was clever; he knew his older brother was better at figuring things out than he himself was, and so he'd always given way to Maimbo's judgment. But still, there was no reason for Maimbo to treat him like an idiot. As the blade broke through the ivory, he stacked the two sections aside and stood to light a cigarette. "What problem?" he asked sullenly.

"We still need his information."

Mnyambo nodded, but didn't offer a solution for Maimbo to sneer at and disregard.

"I was reading something interesting in the paper yesterday," Maimbo continued, unaware of his brother's resentment. "One of the gates at Marsabit National Reserve was robbed by Somali, and two rangers were killed. The Somali were after the guns, of course, but they took everything they could get their hands on: the cash box, clothes, blankets, even food."

Mnyambo nodded, but said nothing. He didn't see what that had to do with anything, but he'd be damned if he'd say so.

"After Mulolo's taken care of," Maimbo continued, "the same thing will happen at Aruba National Park and the motive will appear to be the same. Two of our men are Somali. Let them run around and shout a lot in Afsomali—leave one survivor who can report that later. Take everything—the guns, ammunition, cash, and most particularly—the radio."

He smiled in satisfaction. "With a park radio tuned for their VHF frequency, we can do without Mulolo. Northern Area units receive their patrols by radio transmission from Main Headquarters. The Southern Area units are handed theirs in writing; but"—he chuckled—"when the southern units arrive at their patrol destination, they check in by radio and give their position. We don't need Mulolo. In fact," he added as an afterthought, "this is even better, because if there is a last-minute change in orders or any emergency, we'll know as soon as communications knows."

Mnyambo still didn't trust himself to speak, but he had to admit that he'd never have thought of it. He had not even understood about the robbery until it had all been spelled out for him. He nodded in mute acceptance. Still, he thought, it wasn't fair. "Which gate?" he asked in resignation.

"Nyache Gate," replied Maimbo without hesitation. "It's on the far eastern boundary, and there are a lot of Somali poaching in that area. Also, a lot of tourist traffic travels by that route from the coast, so the cash take should be considerable, and I want the motive to appear to be robbery." He thought for a moment. "Make it on a Sunday night. The rangers will be tired and sleeping heavily, and the cash box will be full."

Mnyambo nodded in acquiescence once more.

Maimbo stood and stretched before looking around in disgust. The place was filthy with charcoal and littered with sections of stacked ivory. "Clean this up," he ordered in irritation. "Mwakiu will be here tomorrow with the last pickup load before he takes it all to Mombasa on Sunday morning, and I don't want him to know about the ivory yet."

After his older brother left, Mnyambo finished his cigarette and began the work of repacking the heavy jute bags with the charcoal interspersed with sections of ivory. Having laced the tops closed again, he stacked the bags against the wall as the boy had unloaded them three days before. As he swept the ivory filings and coal dust from the floor, he kicked an extra bag out of his way and discovered beneath it one last set of tusks which had not yet been sectioned. They were the biggest of the lot—the tusks from the big bull; it would take hours to file them down.

He rebelled. He wouldn't do it now—not after having done all the rest. Not after being up all night driving to Mombasa and back. Not after being told he wasn't smart; not after Maimbo was at home in bed asleep. They could wait. Tomorrow night, or the following morning, would be soon enough. Putting the two huge tusks in a corner under a pile of empty sacks, he finished sweeping, closed and latched the windows, and went outside to secure the heavy doors with a large padlock before turning to walk slowly back to his battered old VW.

Neither he nor Maimbo had noticed the darker shadow pressed to the warehouse wall, behind a shrub by the window.

VII · SATURDAY

CHAPTER TWENTY-THREE

Morning

HALIMA SAT AT THE dining-room table near the window and heard the last of the planes as they took off from the airfield nearby. She watched first one and then a second pass by below her house as they climbed in altitude and turned toward the southwest.

The steaming cup of tea brought a welcome warmth to her cold fingers, and she searched the overcast sky for a glimpse of a particular red-and-white Cessna. But it didn't appear, and the ragged growl of the departing planes faded in the distance and was gone.

She sighed and sipped the cooling tea. She tried to smile at her disappointment, but she couldn't. She knew it was silly, but she had hoped that he would come. Either last night or this morning—and so she'd waited up until very late, and then, even as tired as she was, she'd risen before dawn to wait again.

She'd heard the first of the rumors late yesterday afternoon, then anxiously pieced together the facts as they became known and circulated by stunned park personnel. Poachers had shot down Jeff Forbes's plane, and he was seriously injured; some of his observers were dead or dying, no one knew for sure. Halima's anguish for Audrey had been real, and her relief, when she learned Jeff was alive and would recover, had been overwhelming. Two units of the Field Force had clashed with the Somali poachers responsible, with many casualties on both sides, and all the while inside she was aware of a mounting feeling of panic as she demanded, "What of the Warden? What has happened to David?"

Her first reaction to the news that he was all right allowed her to breathe again, but as the evening wore on she realized that he'd escaped only physical injury. There were other wounds that this man would feel. Aruba was his park; the men who worked under him were his men, his friends, his responsibility. The downed plane, the casualties, the dead he would lay at his own door.

There was more: the rumors whispered that the count wasn't going well; pilots and observers were disappointed in the number of rhinos and elephants found, and that was even worse. She remembered his confident excitement when he'd talked about the count, his hopes, his plans for Aruba's future. What was he feeling now? How much adversity could one man take?

She'd wanted then to be with him, to make it better if she could. But more than that, and selfishly, she knew, she wanted him to come to her, to need her to talk to, to feel, himself, that she could be turned to.

It had become so important, and he hadn't come.

DAVID FINISHED explaining the count operation to Assistant Warden —Accountant Balaga, who had immediately grasped the procedure. As far as he was concerned, the data sheet was a ledger, and the elephants and rhinos were shillings; live ones were credits, each dead one a debit. It was really very simple, and much easier to cope with than a normal payday.

David looked inquiringly at his assistant warden, who nodded. David was relieved: he had not looked forward to breaking in a new observer to take Audrey's place.

As Balaga left to check on the progress of the Cessna's refueling after its arrival from Mombasa, David went over the pilot re-assignments.

Unit 6 had recovered the data collected by Forbes and his observers from the crashed plane, so at least those blocks didn't require re-counting. However, Forbes's block assignments for today would have to be redistributed, and this morning he'd been relieved when Warden Davis and three other pilots had volunteered to stay another day and finish the count for him the following morning; after checking his notes, he decided they'd all be finished and returned to Headquarters by 9:30 A.M. or so. In twenty-four hours he'd know the results of the census.

"We're ready," advised Balaga.

David looked up to see the airfield attendant rolling an empty aviation fuel drum from the plane. "Let's go," he said to Otieno and Dr. Patel.

As David secured the doors, a light shower spattered the windscreen with a sprinkling of raindrops. He glanced up hopefully at the overcast sky; it looked sullen and reluctant. The humidity was oppressive, and the air seemed charged with a threat—or was it a promise?

The sound of raindrops drumming on the metal roof of the plane grew louder as the shower continued and built in intensity, only to cease abruptly as the rain cloud moved on.

Disappointed again, David immediately turned the engine over to drown the sudden silence inside the plane. As he taxied to the end of the runway, he speculated on the possibility of another failure of the rains. The question hung like a menace and demanded an answer: Can we possibly survive another dry season if the rains don't come? He had to acknowledge that it was beginning to look as if they'd have to.

BY THE TIME darkness had fallen the night before, Assistant Warden Agaran and Unit 1 had trailed the fleeing Somali across the Lalaga Lana River and into the broken lava at the base of the Lafaroge Plateau. But then dusk had made tracking impossible, so they'd halted. After a drink of river water and a communal cigarette, his men had rolled over and gone to sleep under an overhanging ledge of rock while Agaran took the first watch.

When the stars dimmed and the dew brought a sharp, fresh smell to the morning, he called his men together and they moved out, following the trail, which came and went, doubled back, circled, and sometimes disappeared altogether.

They tracked the poachers up the side of the plateau and onto the ragged, deteriorating lava cap, interspersed with pockets of soil and scrub. The trail was faint or nonexistent, but Agaran knew. Each patch of dirt was magnified and had a story to tell, and he read it. Leather-soled sandals left no mark on the rocks, but a bent blade of grass that had gained a foothold in the porous lava did, and so did a crushed beetle; an overturned pebble; the track of a small startled animal who'd fled, hours before, from those who'd passed by.

At times there was nothing, but he plunged on, knowing. When the trail disappeared he became the men he followed, and within a kilometer or two when they picked up the trail again he found he'd been right.

VERA PARKED THE old station wagon beside the dispensary, to be greeted by The Cat's piercing yowl.

"Yes, I see you," she grumbled, "and it's not my fault you didn't get your dinner last night." The Cat had been kept in for four days while the strays in the area were rounded up and the village pets vaccinated. The incarceration he'd been subjected to hadn't been appreciated, and when he'd finally been given his freedom yesterday afternoon he'd retaliated by staying out all night.

Following her into the kitchen, he waited hopefully for his already-prepared dish of meat, and when given it, he set to and finished it rapidly. As she waited for her kettle of water to commence boiling, Vera studied him with an expression of resigned exasperation. His voracious hunger, followed by the suddenly lethargic attitude of appetites fed to satiety, told a story an elderly missionary lady might not be expected to understand. But she understood, all right, as she studied his drooping tail, and all too well.

"Shame on you," she muttered as he slumped over, stretched once, and promptly closed his eyes.

Sitting in her rocker for her midmorning elevenses before relieving Adam, she smiled in remembrance of Duncan Shelby's contentious nattering that morning. She'd been checking on him every morning and afternoon since his collapse in the fields, and he was coming along fine; not as fine as he'd wish, of course, and that made him cantankerous. There was nothing she hated worse than nursing an ailing man; five sick women or ten ill children couldn't compare with one man for fuss and bother and belligerence in a sickroom. And he was worse than most.

If she was fifteen minutes late, he sulked. And once she was there, he wanted her to entertain him with conversation about herself, and he wouldn't hear of her leaving until an hour or two had passed, even though they did more arguing than anything else. Now that he was definitely on the mend he was becoming feisty, and seemed to delight in contradicting or criticizing her. When she talked back to him, he'd crow like a delighted child, slap her on the knee, and say, "That's the way," then lie back on his pillows and add, "I like you, by God."

Yesterday evening he'd had the nerve to suggest she'd been alone too long, much too long, and when she flared out at him he'd just smiled approvingly and said, "You'll do. I like pepper."

Really, he'd got completely out of hand; and then this morning— her face flushed now, remembering.

She'd taken his pulse, and before she'd had time to withdraw her hand, he'd caught and held it for close inspection. She'd not been able to figure out what he was up to as he studied her fingers and palm before turning it over to smooth the skin on the back and murmur, "These hands have worked a lifetime; they're good hands.

They've done something to make the world a little better." Then he'd kissed her fingers.

Why, she'd nearly leaped out of her skin. When she'd jumped up and left, she heard his laughter all the way to her car.

Now she shook her head and laughed softly. "The silly old fool," she murmured fondly, as she unconsciously smoothed her hair. Then she wondered, and glanced down at her hands. What in the world did he see?

A series of rapid taps at her door ended her speculation, and she got up to open it, to find Jeff and Audrey Forbes on the step. Jeff's head was a patchwork of gauze pads and strips of adhesive tape, and his arm was encased from armpit to fingertip in a plaster cast.

"What in the world are you doing here?" she exclaimed. She hadn't expected to see Jeff Forbes out of hospital in less than a week.

"He wouldn't stay," remarked Audrey with an indignant sidewise glance at her husband. "He got up this morning, ate his breakfast, and just signed himself out. And now," she announced triumphantly, "he says his arm hurts."

"Well, come in and get out of the sun, for heaven's sake," Vera urged.

"I feel fine," Jeff declared as he sat down and awkwardly arranged his injured arm on the sofa cushions.

Vera and Audrey exchanged a look and Audrey opened her mouth to speak, but Vera shook her head mutely as if to say, "Why bother? He won't listen."

"Of course you're fine," Vera soothed as she went into the kitchen for some tablets and a glass of water. Returning, she added, "But if taking an aspirin makes Audrey feel better, what harm does it do?"

Jeff thought a moment and then conceded cheerfully, "No harm at all." Smiling benignly at his wife, he accepted the two tablets, which were considerably stronger than the aspirin Vera had mentioned, and swallowed them obediently.

Changing the subject of conversation away from Jeff's condition, Vera asked, "Have you heard anything more about the rabies, Jeff?"

He nodded. "The results of one pathological examination came in by radio. A stray shot near the village, inside the park boundary—it was definitely rabid."

"Will there be more problems? Is there something I should be doing?" she inquired.

"No, it's done. It really isn't that uncommon, you know. I was involved in such a situation years ago at Garsen. There was a flare-up of rabies in the wildlife populations of predators, and the stray domesticated animals brought it into the settlement area.

When the strays were eliminated and the village animals vaccinated, there wasn't another case of an attack on a human for years."

"So it's over?" Vera asked hopefully.

"As over as it can be in an area with a large concentration of wildlife. The seeds will always be there; periodically it will flare up and measures will have to be taken to control it. Then it's over for the time being."

"Like the bubonic-plague epidemics that occur once in a while?" suggested Vera.

"Just the same," agreed Jeff. "Particularly wet years start the plague off. The rodents breed like crazy and the disease breaks out somewhere among them, usually in the mountains. A sick rat dies, and his fleas and ticks desert him to hitch a ride on a healthy rat, but the parasites carry the infection to the new host, who eventually sickens and dies. Somewhere, a human gets bitten by a flea or a rat and it's loose among the human population as well.

"Now, of course," he added, "it's not too difficult to control. Antibiotics made the difference; but at one time the plague wiped out something like half the population of Europe." His speech was slowing almost imperceptibly; his words were a bit less crisp.

"I think it's time we went home so you can have a little rest," suggested Audrey.

"Nonsense," Jeff replied indignantly. "I'm fine."

"Of course," said Audrey innocently. "But dear," she reminded him, "Vera has to get back to work."

"Oh, yes," said Jeff in embarrassment. "Sorry, Vera, we didn't mean to interrupt...."

"That's quite all right." Vera smiled. "I'm glad to see you feeling better."

"Besides," Jeff continued as he went through the doorway, "I've got yesterday's data to tabulate today."

Audrey said nothing. Quietly accepting the small packet of tablets from Vera, who whispered, "Two every four hours," she nodded and followed her husband's slightly erratic progress toward the car.

Chuckling to herself, Vera closed the door and removed her teacup to the kitchen. As she washed and dried the delicate china cup and saucer, her thoughts returned to Duncan Shelby, and she smiled with pleasure. Catching herself, she scolded, "Good heavens, woman—you're too old for that kind of nonsense." But somewhere inside there was a hope that it wasn't true.

Adam's head popped in the door with a slightly embarrassed and anxious expression. *"Njoo, Mama, njoo."*

Sighing heavily, Vera hung up the tea towel and followed him into the dispensary. What ever is it now? she wondered, and remembering Adam's expression, she decided, A female problem. That was the only condition that reduced him to confusion. Chuckling to herself about men in general, she went back to work.

THE VINTAGE Bedford lorry struggled to the top of the hill in first gear, its forward progress slowing from thirty kilometers per hour to twenty and finally fifteen before it began its descent down the other side, banging and rattling ahead of a plume of oily exhaust.

Mwakiu rode the clutch all the way to the bottom of the decline, delighted by the illusion of speed. He loved anything on wheels, and the faster it went the better. Someday, he promised himself, I'll have a car of my own. A fast one.

It wasn't impossible, he reasoned. He'd worked for his uncle for over a year now, and he knew Maimbo was pleased with him—and why shouldn't he be? Mwakiu had seen the difference between how Maimbo and his own family lived, in a mud hut on a *shamba* high in the hills on a washed-out and eroded slope. He wanted Maimbo's kind of life, so he'd tried hard to make himself useful and therefore valuable. It might be that he'd succeeded. He'd been conscious of Maimbo's watching him for some time now.

His mother, Maimbo's elder sister, had told him that her brother was a clever man who would someday be a wealthy one. If Mwakiu worked hard for him, he too could rise in the world.

"But," his mother had cautioned with a trace of fear behind her eyes, "never give him reason not to trust you. Never take what he does not offer. Never know of things he does not explain to you. Speak of him or his concerns to no one. If you do," she warned, "he will never forgive you; he will never forget." The rest of the warning had hung in silence between them.

He'd believed her. She knew her brother well, and, like the rest of his huge family, respected and feared him. Mwakiu was her only living son; she wanted more for him than the worn-out *shamba* could offer. She'd weighed what she knew of her brother and what she wanted for her son, and then she'd gone to Maimbo to speak of her boy. The opportunity had outweighed the possible consequences.

He had followed her advice. Whatever Maimbo asked of him, he did, and he took for himself only what was given. Sometimes it was enough: an envelope with money, a cast-off but still good jacket. Sometimes it was less and he had no money at all, and it was at these times that he felt Maimbo's eyes watching him closely. But he kept his eyes on the future and did without, and he saw the regard grow in Maimbo's attitude toward him, and soon he'd been taken into Maimbo's confidence in small things. He wondered how long it would be before Maimbo told him about the ivory.

It had been the only time he'd done other than his mother advised; he'd noticed that the sacks of charcoal seemed heavier when he picked them up to take them to Mombasa than they had when he'd first collected them. Then he'd also noticed that there were more of them; he'd collect forty or fifty bags from the *shamba* people and when he went to load them for Mombasa, there might be sixty-two bags. So one day, when he was on his way to the coast, he'd stopped the lorry and opened one of them, to find the huge chunks of ivory secreted under the charcoal. He'd kept his knowledge to himself and told no one, not even his mother—and most particularly, not Maimbo. It seemed, though, that Maimbo suspected he might know. He never asked; he just smiled in approval of Mwakiu's silence.

Yes, he decided, perhaps soon he and I will talk. Perhaps there will be more work for me and more money, and someday, a car.

He laughed out loud and began to sing.

SHE SAT ON A ROCK in the shade of the thick baobab trunk which shielded her from the glare of the climbing sun; the early-morning clouds had cleared, and now the midmorning sun was fiercely blinding.

Mwale was an old woman. How old, no one knew, but she had lost the last of her teeth years ago, and her sparse hair was snow white beneath the *kitambaa* about her head. She was a tiny thing, a small woman shrunken with years and a life of hard labor. Her arms and legs were wreathed in finely wrinkled, dusty-black skin which was pierced with dozens of old scars that showed shiny and smooth against the skin's aged texture. Her gnarled hands nestled together in her lap, and her broad splayed feet, with their broken and missing nails, rested stolidly in the hot red dust. Her face, crumpled at the sunken jaw and tracked with old tribal patterns, turned to watch the road before her, and her small bright eyes peered hopefully in the direction of town.

She'd been sitting there since *saa mbili* with her two sacks of charcoal, and the arrival of the expected lorry and the payment of 30 shillings meant that she and her small family would eat again tonight. The little maize that had resulted from the last poor harvest was gone; it had been little enough to show for the weeks of hard work spent in preparing the land, sowing the seed, and then hauling the *madebe* of water from the Machaka railroad station the five kilometers to the *shamba* in order to keep alive a portion of the crop.

For weeks now they'd been surviving on the birds and small animals they could catch or trap, and twice her son-in-law had been able to bring home larger game he'd taken with his bow and arrow, but the national park was several kilometers away, and there was little game left in the areas outside.

So they had turned to making charcoal, even though all the good trees were gone. They'd had to walk for miles to find one that was only just satisfactory, and after hacking it down with their small hand axes, they'd removed the branches, stripped them of their few leaves, and sectioned the trunk; then they'd carried it all the long distance back to their *shamba*. After digging a large hole several feet deep, they'd lined it with dried grass packed between the sections of green wood. They had used the last of their paraffin to soak the wood, after which they had covered it with sand and dirt before lighting the pyre from beneath through a small opening left for the air to circulate. Then they'd watched and waited patiently for days until it stopped smoking, at which point they removed the dirt and dug out the charcoal to break into small pieces to pack into the strong jute bags.

Looking at them now, she sighed heavily. So much work, for so little. She wished the lorry would hurry; there was the food to buy yet, and then the long walk home to help as best she could in the preparation of the small *shamba* fields. It was time for the rains, and the bush had to be burned back, cleared, and hoed so that the seed could be planted the first week of the rains.

Glancing apprehensively at the bright blue sky, she wondered if perhaps the rains might not come again, and she whispered a prayer to Mungu. Not again—please, not again. They could not go on—it was too hard. Her old eyes swam with the tears of weariness.

THE GROUND SQUIRREL dashed out of the bush onto the tarmac, hesitated, tried to turn to flee, and was hit by one of the lorry's front wheels. Mwakiu hadn't had time to avoid him, nor would it have occurred to him to try if he had.

He saw the old woman by the baobab just ahead with her two bags of charcoal, and for a moment he considered not stopping; he'd had a busy morning, and between what he'd picked up today and what was waiting at the warehouse, he had a full load for Mombasa. At the last moment he hit the brakes and pulled onto the shoulder of the road. It was only two bags—he could make them fit.

Jumping down off the running board, he greeted her with the boisterousness of youth: *"Shikamuu, Mama!"*

Nodding happily, she returned the greeting in the thin cracked voice of the very old: *"Marahaba, mwanangu."*

After loading the two jute bags, Mwakiu carefully counted 30 shillings into her anxious hands and then swung himself into the cab, slammed the door, and pulled back onto the road.

She watched him until the lorry was out of sight around a curve, then looked at the money still clasped in her hand. It was so little, but it was better than nothing.

Turning, she walked a short distance back along the road and stopped to look up and down the highway. No one was coming. Crossing the hot tarmac, she bent with difficulty to pick up the dead squirrel. It wasn't very big and it was thin, but it was meat. Returning to the baobab, she picked up her worn *kikapu* and stepped into the wind-whipped bush to begin the long walk to the *duka,* and home.

SALIM STRODE QUICKLY across the stone-flagged reception area in response to the summons to the telephone and took the call at the desk.

"Hello?" There was no response other than a series of chattering clicks. Repeating himself louder, he swore under his breath about telephones in general and was rewarded with a louder clack; then the connection was through and the Arab's voice could be heard surprisingly well.

"Yes?" he replied, trying to close his ears to the babble of voices as tourists checked out at the desk.

"I have the information you requested. It was not easy to obtain. Much time was spent at certain bars with one of those who know the identity of the man you want to know of. . . ."

"Who is it?" Salim asked impatiently. The question had been at the back of his mind for days, and now the Arab's spun-out verbosity was irritating.

The reply was for once brief and to the point: "It's the Warden."

The words jolted him. He'd considered carefully every man in the area as a possible candidate, and David Karanja had been the first name discarded as an impossibility. The idea unsettled him—it was too unexpected.

"Who?" he demanded in disbelief. "Say that again."

"I said," the Arab repeated, "the poaching operation is run by the Warden."

"I don't believe it," Salim replied flatly.

"Nevertheless, it's true. I arranged to have one of my men introduced to one of his hired hunters as an ivory buyer. They spent half the night drinking and talking. It seems he and the rest of the men were sent to the coast two days ago, to be out of the way during a game count and an anti-poaching campaign. Afterward, they are to return, and more ivory is to find its way to the coast from Aruba."

Salim thought rapidly. Was it possible? Fragments of remembered conversations with David came to his mind, and he sifted through them searching for some hint of Karanja's involvement in the illegal ivory trade. But there was nothing. On the contrary, everything pointed to the opposite.

"No," he said into the receiver, "I can't believe it. I know the man. If anyone has named Karanja as being involved, then they're lying. Perhaps it's an *uhusuda*. A grudge. He's made enemies among many people in the ivory trade, and now someone's out to make trouble for him."

"I didn't say he was referred to by name," the Arab protested. "The man who runs this poaching operation is known to his men simply as 'the Warden.' Karanja's name was not mentioned. The information is correct, but there is more than one warden in Kenya. I'm afraid it's for you to discover which one it is."

After ringing off, Salim went into the office and sat down at his desk to study the possibilities. Could it be Karanja? he mused. He wouldn't be the first man to be corrupted by the availability of so much money. What did a warden make? Fifteen hundred shillings a month—about 180 dollars. How many university-educated men would accept so little for so much work, particularly when a highly lucrative income to supplement their own was there within their grasp?

He nodded in understanding. It wasn't as impossible as he'd first thought. When he'd considered it before, he'd overlooked one factor. The human one. What would I do in his position? he mused, and then he smiled ruefully. The obvious answer was not complimentary.

Returning to the possibility of Karanja, he decided that yes, it was possible, but highly improbable. "The Warden," he muttered to himself. Who else could it be? His thoughts turned to Jombo Maimbo.

CHAPTER TWENTY-FOUR

Afternoon

THE THICK BLANKET OF smoke broke up before the gusting onslaught of the wind, driven hard from the south. The rushing fire had extended its front as it overran the sisal fields and gained a foothold in the thick tinder-dry bush outside the cultivated area. Now it spread contagiously through the wide swath of scrub between the sisal estate and the park boundary. And as the wind rose and the heat intensified, trees and thickets exploded through spontaneous combustion, throwing flaming brands through the hot air to land elsewhere and be fanned by the wind into yet another blaze.

In first one and then two places, fingers of fire reached out to test the edge of the park's firebreak/boundary. A fifty-foot-wide graded path marked the outer boundary line; next came a hundred-foot-wide cleared space, followed by another fifty-foot graded area; all together, two hundred feet of bare earth greeted the encroaching fire and denied it the sustenance it needed to continue its advance.

That was where the men waited, across the barren barrier that separated them from the fire. Every field and factory hand from the sisal plantation, every park employee not engaged in the aerial count or in the Field Force Units was there; laborers, mechanics, office clerks, drivers, off-duty Gate Rangers spread out in a thin, smoke-blackened line eight kilometers long to stand armed and waiting with their shovels, water-soaked bags, or thick leafy branches.

They were tired. Some of them had been on the fire lines for forty-eight hours; but this was the last chance to stop the fire. Once it was across and into the park, five million acres and tens of thousands of animals would lie vulnerable and unprotected, and there was nowhere to halt a runaway conflagration that could burn for weeks along a hundred-mile front, until every twig and blade of grass was consumed and every living thing driven to an exhausted death before the flames.

As each stream of fire reached the boundary, it burgeoned and began to spread out, searching along the edge. And as the flames built ahead of the prodding wind, the hissing crackle of the burning bush grew louder and was interspersed with the cracking reports of exploding trees. More rivers of fire reached the graded area to spread east and west, and the waiting men faced a wall of flame whose heat scorched their faces from two hundred feet away.

As they fell back before the heat, the roaring wind hurled the first burning shreds across the cleared area, and a park plumber dashed to the left to slap at an infant blaze with a wet sack. One by one, nearly four hundred men were galvanized into a frenzied dance as more burning shreds crossed the open space into the tangle of bush inside the park.

Bruce McKinney wielded his shovel with a fury. Smoke-blackened, with pale streaks of white showing where rivulets of sweat had washed clean tracks on his face and down his arms, he pounded the hot brands as they landed, and scooped up a spadeful of dirt with which to smother yet another flare.

Pausing to catch his breath, he noticed a widening gap in the line ahead as men dashed this way and that beating at the flames. Running forward yelling, *"Hapa, hapa!"* he filled in the breach with a few men and then turned to survey the line. As far as he could see, it was holding.

Looking across the firebreak, he tried to judge how long it would take for the fire to burn itself out. If they could just hold it a little longer, the flames would die down for lack of fuel. It was burning fast—it shouldn't be long.

His eye was caught by a movement on the firebreak, and squinting against the swirling smoke, he made out the humped form of a leopard land tortoise, ponderously yet relentlessly plodding toward him. Dismissing the animal, he turned away, and then stopped. Looking back over his shoulder, he reluctantly watched the awkward tortoise struggling forward on singed feet as he sought to escape the heat that must even now be half-cooking him in his shell. Muttering under his breath, McKinney strode out onto the cleared area to scoop up the tortoise, who immediately withdrew his legs and head into the safety of his home.

Tucking him under his arm, McKinney continued on up the line checking on the men. Yelling over the roar of the wind, he directed them from place to place, exhorting them on as the smoke billowed and shifted on the rising gusts from the southeast, and the crackle and pop of the burning bush grew louder.

Just behind him, a small thicket burst into flame, but no one saw it until it had begun to spread out and reach north toward the park's interior. Men, startled by another's shout of alarm, turned, saw, and converged upon it with flailing arms. But they would be too late.

In the distance, McKinney's back could be seen as he continued on up the line, the tortoise under his arm.

DR. SILAS NDUTU straightened up from his brief examination of the elephant calf. It was dead, and had probably been so when spotted from the air yesterday by the Warden. Glancing over at the cow, whom he had ordered destroyed when they first arrived, he saw the Field Force Ranger finish cutting the last poorly placed arrowhead free of the female elephant's putrescent leg.

Comparing the last poisoned shaft with the other two cut from the cow, and the one taken from the calf, he noted that they were the same: all of Kamba design, and all thickly coated with old and nearly useless poison; not potent enough to kill, but strong enough to make the elephant suffer hell for weeks. He shook his head in disgust and turned away.

As a leading pathologist and head of the Department of Clinical Studies with the Faculty of Veterinary Medicine in Nairobi, he had often worked together with Jeff Forbes in the past, and he'd come down at Forbes's request to help with the examination of carcasses discovered by the census planes. What he was seeing was making him physically sick, and the stench in the dam area didn't help. He covered his nose again with his water-soaked handkerchief and picked up his small bag before turning to walk the short distance to the next carcass.

Just then a tractor rumbled past, forcing Ndutu to pause. He studied the recumbent form of the nearly unconscious rhino lying on the machine's blade. It was a young adult, suffering from advanced malnutrition and completely exhausted from his attempts to free himself from the thick mud gumbo at the edge of the dam. He'd been pulled out by the rangers and was now being transported to Headquarters, where he'd be fed and allowed to recover. It was a shame, he thought, that the black rhino had such a reputation for viciousness. This animal would be penned beside the elephant *boma,* and after a week or two of hand feeding and the company of humans, he'd most likely eat toffees from a child's hand and allow his head to be patted. Rhinos' poor eyesight and the constant harassment to which they were subjected were what rendered them unpredictable and made them instinctively charge anything they sensed near them.

As he approached a decomposing bull elephant, Dr. Ndutu wondered what he'd find this time. It might be hard, if not impossible, to tell. The animal was in an advanced state of disintegration, but statistically the chances were it had been poached.

He'd been at work now for several hours, ever since he'd arrived at Aruba Dam just after daylight. So far he'd examined the carcasses of thirty-two elephants and three rhinos. Of those, more than half had either arrowheads or bullets in them, or both.

Walking around the bloated belly of the bull, he noted that the elephant's tusks were missing: another indication of a poached animal, but certainly not conclusive. The rangers had told him that a number of people had been arrested in the area for the scavenging of trophies. Then too, the rangers had orders to collect any ivory found and turn it in to Headquarters, and with this number of carcasses in one place it was nearly impossible to tell later who it was that had removed the tusks.

After setting down his bag and removing his instruments, he resolutely ignored the frantic buzz of the swarming clouds of flies and the writhing masses of maggots and began to check over the animal's hide for any suspicious wounds. Twelve minutes later he had his answer, when he withdrew his forceps from the animal's skull with a misshapen bullet clutched firmly in the tips. As he stepped back, his foot slipped in the pool of gore he'd had to stand in; his hand shot out to steady himself against the animal's distended belly and it exploded under his weight, spewing up its contents of rotting flesh and noxious gases. It was too much for Dr. Ndutu. He bent over and began to retch and gag, the bullet still clutched in his hand.

TAKING OFF AFTER A late lunch, David banked to the left and headed east toward the next block scheduled on his assignment sheet. It was incredibly hot and humid—the early scattered showers had served only to increase the moisture in the air, to combine with the heat and make the day unbearable in spite of the wind that buffeted the plane.

Far to the south he saw the black haze that marked the position of the fire. He was sorely tempted to fly down and recce the area, but unfortunately he couldn't spare the time to do it. He'd always had a tendency to supervise any operation himself, and delegating responsibility came hard. But today he had no choice. He'd set down only once since takeoff, and then for only a half-hour to refuel and eat lunch. His late start would mean his flying until dusk. McKinney was in charge; he'd have to see to it.

His thoughts were interrupted: "Whisky Bravo, six-oh-three. Whisky Bravo, this is six-oh-three. Do you read me?"

Depressing the mike switch, he responded: "Six-oh-three, this is Whisky Bravo. Go ahead."

Duba's voice continued from the Park Headquarters Radio Room: "Message relayed from office of Senior Warden—Coast: 'Research Assistant James Mugalu died in hospital at eleven hundred hours. I repeat—James Mugalu died at eleven hundred hours.' Do you roger?"

David had not held much hope for the boy; his wound had been too severe. But the end of hope came hard.

"Roger, six-oh-three," he murmured, and thought: Only twenty-one, but he left a wife and three small *watoto*. David considered the young widow. He'd have to tell her tonight, and then Jeff Forbes. The boy had been Jeff's protégé. It was the part of his job he hated most, but the necessity of his having to perform it had become all too frequent during the past year.

"The bastards," he muttered to himself.

Most of his people were unarmed civil servants, working in conservation. Why would anyone want to harm them? He thought of Dan Boyd, shot to death on his own ranch; of the German tourist gunned down while on a game drive in one of the northern reserves. He thought of Agaran, still trailing the three Somali. Agaran would have heard the radio message. He'd know, and David hoped he'd be able to close in on the three fugitives and make them pay. "It's true, dammit," he murmured in disgust. "We can't take anymore. They've called the rules, and we'll have to play by them and give back as good as we get. Otherwise there'll be nothing left— Aruba will be finished."

"Whisky Bravo, this is Field Workshop One."

Recognizing Bruce McKinney's call sign from the vintage Toyota, he depressed his mike switch and replied, "Field Workshop One, this is Whisky Bravo. I'm reading you. Go ahead."

"Whisky Bravo. I'm sorry, David. It's away. It's inside. I couldn't hold it." McKinney's voice broke, riddled with static, and then repeated, "I'm sorry."

* * *

BY LATE MORNING, Agaran and the twelve men in Unit 1 had followed the trail west across the lava-strewn plateau toward Mwanyani, where the poachers had turned north and descended into the thick bush of the foothills. The Field Force moved on in an irregular advance behind the fleeing Somali, who continued to dodge and cut back on their trail in their efforts to lose their pursuers.

Steadily gaining ground on the poachers, the rangers had kept moving north behind Agaran through the thick bush until it began to thin out on the Uiini Plain, and here the trail had straightened to become a direct dash for distance, with no effort made at covering their tracks.

As the rangers broke into a long, loping run, Agaran noted the position ahead of Syiima Itatu—the three hills. And he remembered the small, well-concealed permanent water hole which nestled at the foot of the smallest of the hills. He paused for a moment to call up Unit 3, who hovered in the north near Kikuu, and gave directions for Corporal Akbalo Bagaja to rush his men south to cut off and encircle the Somali, who he now knew were heading for the water.

As they moved out again on the tracks, Agaran saw a dark spatter on a nearby rock. He knelt to inspect it closely: it was blood; the wounded poacher had begun to bleed again. Agaran smiled. The man would begin to weaken. Not by much, but enough. He led his men forward at a run.

It was midafternoon before a ranger shouted off to Agaran's left. They were in sight. His men fanned out and ran on to cover as much distance as possible before the Somali took cover to open fire.

Shots crackled ahead; Bagaja had come upon them from the north.

Agaran called up Unit 3 and yelled into the walkie-talkie, "Alive —I want them alive!"

The poachers veered off to the right in an attempt to avoid the converging units. They were just short of the three rocky outcroppings which could have afforded them the water they sought and the cover they needed.

Topping a small rise in the normally flat plain, Agaran paused just as the three men came into view ahead, slightly below and to his left.

They were running in a ragged file which broke as Bagaja's men burst from a shallow ravine to cut them off. The leading Field Force Ranger took a running shot, and the bullet hit two meters ahead of the poachers; they veered sharply toward Agaran, who took careful aim and brought the second man down with a bullet in the thigh. As he fell, the crippled Somali threw his rifle to the other, unarmed man, who caught it and turned to run as Corporal Lugumba dashed up and brought his rifle butt up into his face.

The last man crouched snarling. The rapidly converging circle of rangers approached warily, rifles aimed. As his rifle came up in defiance, six bullets smashed into him, killing him on his feet, and one ranger staggered as one of his compatriots' shots missed the poacher to graze his hip.

After seeing to the wounded ranger, Agaran approached the two poachers, who had been stripped naked, with their arms tied tightly behind their backs. The older of the two had a deep flesh wound across his shoulder which still trickled blood, and neat holes in either side of his upper thigh where the heavy slug from Agaran's rifle had passed through.

Agaran motioned for Lugumba to dress the two wounds; he didn't want the man to bleed to death—at least, not until some questions were answered. What happened to him later was beyond his concern.

Turning to the second man, he noted the smashed nose and the limp slack of the broken jaw. He wasn't going to do much talking. Agaran glared grimly at Lugumba, who studiously avoided his eye.

Agaran made himself comfortable on a rock, knowing that the interrogation was going to take time. He didn't doubt the outcome, considering the methods necessity forced him to use. The man would talk—that was understood; only the timetable was flexible.

Addressing the older man in Swahili, he said evenly, "I have some questions I want you to answer."

There was no reply. The heel of Agaran's boot came down hard on the man's instep to establish the tone of the questioning. There was no response.

"I said," Agaran repeated in a conversational voice, "I have some questions I want answered."

The man muttered in Afsomali, *"Wahan agan Afsomali."*

Agaran glanced up at the tall, slender, thin-faced Field Force Ranger who stood quietly beside him and nodded.

Suileman stepped forward and stood over the Somali, who looked up, recognized one of his kind, and glanced away to conceal the glimmer of resignation in his dark eyes.

"Wahan Afsomali," murmured the ranger, who was the product of a Somali father and a Boran mother.

Agaran asked the questions in Swahili, never taking his eyes off the Somali as Suileman translated.

"What is your name?"—no response.

"Where is your village?"—no response.

"Who is your chief?"—nothing.

Agaran sighed, crossed his legs, and nodded to Bagaja, who stood behind the Somali. As the Orma corporal began to beat the poacher about the head and shoulders with a rawhide *mchapo,* Agaran wondered why the man continued to refuse to talk. He'd watched him carefully as he was questioned, and he knew the man understood much, if not all, of the Swahili he heard. But why did he persist in his silence when Suileman translated the questions into a language he couldn't deny he understood?

Agaran shook his head. The man knew that he was in the hands of the Field Force Rangers—all northern tribesmen like himself, and all as hard as he himself was. They'd all been born and bred in the same environment, having learned the same lessons in survival. Only the strong lived, and pain and suffering was a large part of life; there was thus no hesitation when it came to using it for your own purpose. Agaran didn't doubt the nature of his own treatment if he were in the hands of a group of Somali; why should the man fail to recognize that he and the others knew this and reacted accordingly? He should know there was no question as to "whether" he talked—only "when."

"Enough," he said to Bagaja, who stepped back reluctantly, no doubt thinking that perhaps Agaran had spent too much time in *Mzungu* schools. He and the other rangers were in a nasty mood. One of their own had died because of these men.

Agaran glanced over at the younger Somali who'd been watching his companion being worked over. He was wide-eyed with fear.

Nodding at Lugumba, Agaran said, "Take him away—make him talk." It was a tactic used often before with success. Lugumba grinned. He loved games.

Jerking the young Somali to his feet, he led him several meters off, sat him on a rock, and with one finger, gently nudged the broken jaw. The man groaned in pain and began gabbling in terror. Unfortunately, little of what he said was intelligible. That left only one.

Agaran turned back to the Somali before him. The man's eyes glittered with hate, and he darted forward suddenly to spit on Agaran before Bagaja could yank him back.

Agaran glanced down at the bloodied spittle on his uniform shirt. After wiping it away, he calmly reached out to slap the man's face.

He motioned to Bagaja, who threw a dark bag over the Somali's head, completely enveloping his face and obscuring his vision. Agaran watched as the blindfolded poacher was forced to a squatting position.

"Now," he said, "how long have you been hunting in the park?" The question was translated. Again there was no reply.

"How many animals have you killed?"—nothing.

Agaran nodded to Lugumba, who began shouting at the younger man some distance away, while he harmlessly slapped him on the back with his open hand. The result was what Agaran wished for. The loud thwacks as Lugumba's hand clapped the man's sweaty flesh, the man's terrified gibbering sounds, and Lugumba's screaming all combined to bring the older man's swaddled head up, to turn and listen intently to what he could not see.

After a few minutes of this, Agaran judged the man's stubborn attitude to be wavering. His hand moved quickly: reaching forward, he grabbed the man's testicles and penis as they dangled exposed between his drawn-up and widely spaced legs, and crushed them in his fist. The man screamed out at the suddenness of the attack and the pain; he rocked forward and began to vomit.

Agaran nodded to Lugumba, who wrapped his arms tightly around the head and face of the younger man to prevent his making a sound. As another ranger drove his rifle butt rhythmically into the sand to produce an ominous thumping sound, Lugumba began to groan horribly before erupting vocally in a remarkably good simulation of an agonized and barely human shriek of pain that trailed off into a guttural moan. Then silence.

Agaran studied the man before him; he'd stopped vomiting and knelt with his head down, his shoulders heaving. It was time to impress upon him the lengths to which he was prepared to go to get the information he wanted.

Counting on his guess that the Somali understood at least a little Swahili, Agaran called out to Lugumba, "Has he talked?" as he shook his head to indicate the answer he wanted.

"No," Lugumba replied. "He's worthless."

"Can you understand him?" Agaran asked. If the man before him understood anything in Swahili, it would be that. It was the one phrase they all learned—"I don't understand."

Lugumba answered, "No."

Agaran watched the poacher before him carefully as he said laconically, "Then kill him." The man's head jerked up.

The report of the rifle was loud in the silence. The man kneeling before Agaran flinched. Lugumba still stood with his arms wrapped carefully around the younger man's head to prevent his making a sound. It wasn't necessary; he'd fainted when the rifle went off harmlessly behind him.

Putting his boot to the shoulder of the crouched Somali at his feet, Agaran shoved him back hard against Bagaja's legs.

Leaning forward, as Bagaja pressed his forefinger to the man's temple, he murmured softly, "Now, where were you taking the trophies?"

The man shuddered, his reply barely audible. "Garsen."

"Who buys them?"

The man's voice came choked and muffled from beneath the bag: "The Arab at the trading *duka*."

"Who supplies your guns and ammunition?"

The questions went on and on. They were all answered. And later that night the Special Anti-Poaching Strike Unit moved quickly and quietly into Garsen.

The Arab was rudely awakened. More questions were answered.

The Strike Unit moved on to the north and east, and lorryloads of confiscated ivory and prisoners moved slowly toward Nairobi under military escort.

The questions of angry men continued. And they were answered.

BUBU FINISHED PREPARING two more poisoned arrowheads. It was late Saturday afternoon; he had the rest of the day and all of Sunday off, and had planned just how to spend it.

After finding the location of the poached ivory and overhearing the conversation between Maimbo and Mnyambo the preceding evening, he'd come home and sat up half the night formulating his plan. He knew now where the ivory was; how it was concealed and moved; where it was going and when.

He'd reluctantly given up his idea of taking all the ivory. He didn't have enough time. Years ago, he could have called upon a dozen men in his clan who would have joined him on a raid on the warehouse and they would have been able to carry off everything; but now no one was left but him, and he couldn't do it alone. But he'd seen the man secrete the tusks of the big bull under the empty sacks in a corner, and he could take those.

If he'd had more time, he could have found a way to break into the warehouse. He could have removed the ivory from a laced sack, refilled it with more charcoal, and then replaced it. Given enough days, he'd have taken much of it without notice. But the ivory and charcoal was leaving for Mombasa the next morning; he would have time for only one trip—before dawn Sunday morning. The two tusks were for him, and he knew they would easily bring 6,000 shillings. It was enough. It had to be.

He would be there early, and when either Maimbo or the other man came to open the warehouse he'd be waiting. He had to go armed—he couldn't avoid a face-to-face confrontation—but there were few men who would face a poisoned Waliangulu arrow: it was more effective than a gun, because even a flesh wound meant a painful and certain death.

Setting his arrowheads aside, he faced the results of what he intended to do. He had to confront either one or the other of the two men. Maimbo might recognize him immediately, the other might not, but they would look for him. It meant he had to run.

He sighed as he glanced around the small house. He'd been content here in his old age. It had become home, because he had no other. The young Warden had come, his anger had gone, and he'd not been unhappy. David Karanja had become someone to look after, someone to approve of, and be with, even if some of his ways were strange. He knew he would miss the young Bwana—he'd become, in a way, a substitute for the sons he'd lost.

He considered his future. After the ivory was sold and the woman and child had gone on their way to the Tana, he'd go into hiding. He'd head north to the Lalaga Lana River. There were hiding places there that no one knew of, and would never find, not even the Field Force. And never Maimbo. He would live as he'd lived as a young hunter; he'd build a small hut, hunt a little, gather his firewood and water, and guard his fire. In time he would fail, and the predators would come, and his waiting would be over. It was not the way he'd thought it would end. But it didn't really matter. What happened for the boy was what was important.

CHAPTER TWENTY-FIVE

Evening

DUNCAN SHELBY SAT behind the wheel of his car parked on the burned-over field track and watched the flames stretching into the distance. He knew he had been foolish, but when he'd heard that the fire had jumped the boundary/firebreak and was into the park, he'd not been able to just lie in bed and picture the worst. He had to see for himself; and it was all he'd feared and more.

The front must be close to ten kilometers wide at the moment, and spreading. How in the world could they stop it now? He sighed, feeling old and tired. He started the car, turned around and headed back to the plantation house. There was nothing he could do, and the realization irritated him and made his headache worse.

As he approached the house he saw Vera's battered old car parked in the drive, and his mood lightened. He'd almost forgotten it was time for her afternoon call. He remembered that morning and how he'd startled her, and he chuckled. She didn't know it, but he had a few more surprises planned.

He pulled in behind her car and parked, and as he walked toward the house he saw her standing on the veranda waiting for him; and the picture of her there was right. He'd spent too many years wanting someone to be here to welcome him home; but it was never too late, and they suited each other: an old widower and an aging spinster. Never mind the years gone by; they had a good few left them, and much to share.

As he crossed the lawn and passed a flower bed, he picked one bloom, and when he started up the steps he eagerly anticipated her reaction to his escapade.

"*Mr.* Shelby. I told you—"

"Now, you listen to me, woman," he barked back at her: "I'll not stand your nattering at me the moment I come home to you."

For what was probably the first time in her life, Vera Batey was speechless.

Removing his hat in a courtly, old-fashioned gesture, he cleared his throat and began, "Miss Batey. Would you . . . ?" he stammered. "Don't you think we're . . ." he began again, only to fall silent before her startled gray eyes.

He glanced down at his flower, smiled, and recovered himself. Offering her the fully blown rose, he said, "This garden needs another rose. I've always loved 'em, in spite of their thorns."

For a moment she stared at the flower, a mist gathering behind her glasses. Her hand reached out, hesitated, and then gently took the flower. Her voice was soft: "So have I, Mr. Shelby."

Grinning broadly, he leaned forward to kiss her cheek, and she looked up at him, smiled shyly, and murmured, "You silly old fool."

KIBOKO HAD LITTLE TO REPORT on Mulolo's activities.

"He drank at the canteen last night until it closed and then went to his quarters; was on duty at six forty-five this morning and took an hour lunch break; relieved at seven fifteen this evening and went home, showered and changed, and went to Margaret Githu's room." Kiboko grinned and added, "Where he found your radio operator, Komora Duba, having tea with the lady."

David chuckled and observed drily, "It seems the past twenty-four hours have not been kind to Mulolo. He got knocked around last night, and now he might have a little competition for Margaret's attention. Good. It's nice to know he's not having an easy time of it. But still, I want to use him to draw these people into the park area at the proper time. I'll have to talk to Margaret and make sure she keeps him on the string."

He frowned, then added, "I don't like the look of what happened last night. Mulolo's friends turned on him for some reason. I don't know why, but it's possible that they no longer need him." He glanced at Kiboko. "What do you think?"

"Well, we know they've stopped operating for the time being. Perhaps they're not planning to go back into operation after the anti-poaching reinforcements leave. But I doubt it. People never know when to quit—that's why they get caught. No, I don't know what they plan for Mulolo either, but I think we'd better have some alternative strategy."

"Like what?" David asked.

"First of all—Mulolo. The main thing is to put these people away and get them out of circulation. At this point any charge will do. I have the figures my man tallied for the Main Gate today. Let's see how they compare with what Mulolo turned in."

David took the small paper prepared by the assistant accountant from his pocket and read, "Thirty-two vehicles—six hundred forty shillings. One hundred sixty-one visitors—three thousand two hundred twenty shillings." He looked up to see Kiboko smiling broadly.

"Thirty-two vehicles—six hundred and forty shillings checks; but my man counted a hundred and seventy visitors, which would add up to thirty-four hundred shillings." He chuckled gleefully. "We've got him. Theft by servant. That's good for a couple of years at least."

David smiled. "That's one down, anyway. I'll leave him on the gate; let him get all he can in the next couple of weeks. The more he takes, the longer he'll be out of circulation. It's worth a few hundred shillings to be rid of him."

"Now, about the others." Kiboko wore a smile from ear to ear. "We're getting somewhere. It's why I'm not too interested in this organization's plans for your Gate Ranger. If we can tie them all together"—he shrugged his shoulders—"fine. If not, it won't matter. We'll get them anyway, one by one.

"First of all I told you we didn't have anything on this Mnyambo, the owner/operator of the milk kiosk. And that still holds true. But we did find out something that's very interesting because of its possibilities." He studied David's expression before adding, "This afternoon we were able to get close to a young nephew of Mnyambo's who mentioned the name of another uncle, and we learned that Mnyambo and Jombo Maimbo are brothers."

"Brothers!" David exclaimed in surprise. "I didn't know Maimbo had a brother in the area."

"Neither did I," responded Kiboko, "and that's the point. If I had a brother living nearby, people *would* know. I'd refer to him. I'd be seen with him. I wouldn't conceal the relationship. Not unless I had a reason."

"An illegal one?"

"Possibly," Kiboko answered. "People don't do things without a motive. If Maimbo and his brother don't want anyone to know of their relationship, it's because they don't want to be linked

427

together. But why? Obviously because it's dangerous for them to be associated.

"Now, I know Jombo is a warden. He's a crack shot; he has access to guns and ammunition and four-wheel-drive vehicles. He knows the area like his own hand, and he knows the elephant.

"I know Mnyambo delivers papers and milk to the park each morning, and it appears that Mulolo is passing him information valuable to poachers. Nothing in that, really—but when I learn that the two of them are brothers, then I can see the obvious possibilities, particularly when I know there's a gang operating in the area."

David passed his hand over his eyes. His anger threatened to smother him. Maimbo's name repeated itself in his mind. The man's image came up; his own doubts and dislike of him returned. Was it possible? Of course. It was the only answer.

"I know something else," continued Kiboko. "Something I've known of for a long time, but it never occurred to me as important."

"What's that?" David muttered abstractedly. Mentally, he was ten kilometers away, beating the hell out of Maimbo.

"A couple of years ago, Jombo and I had to testify at an ivory dealer's trial, so during the noon recess we had a beer together. He was complaining about how hard it was to get by on a civil servant's salary. I suppose he thought he was being clever, but it seems it may have backfired on him."

David glanced up and studied the C.I.D. man intently.

"You see," he continued, "he went on too much about it, so the conversation stuck in my mind, and I remembered today how he'd planned to make a little extra money to supplement his salary." He watched David as he added, "By buying locally made charcoal to sell to exporters in Mombasa." He nodded at David's immediate understanding of how the ivory could be transported. "And if," Kiboko added, "he hadn't made such a point of it, I'd never have remembered." He shook his head and smiled. "People just don't know when to quit."

"Just tell me if we can get him," David demanded.

"Not yet," Kiboko warned, "but we will. I sent for two first-class men from Mombasa. They'll be here tomorrow to follow both Maimbo and his brother, and they're unknown to either of them. We've got to find out where the charcoal is, and the ivory. It's got to be close, and one or both of them will lead us to it. When we've got charcoal sacks with ivory hidden in them, we'll be able to prove the rest of the association." He nodded. "Don't worry. We'll get them. All we need is a little time to find the ivory."

After Kiboko left, David sat on the veranda wall chain-smoking and watching the dull red glow to the southwest. The fire was burning on a twelve-kilometer front, but the wind had dropped and it was moving more slowly.

An exhausted Bruce McKinney had been driven home that afternoon when the firebreak/boundary line was overrun and abandoned. But around seven thirty, when David had driven out to the fire, McKinney had returned. And he'd had lorryloads of tired fire-fighting field hands and laborers trailing behind him. Flatbed lorries were arriving from Mombasa with graders and drivers from the Ministry of Works. The owners of the Sabaki, Machaka, and Karesa ranches had sent their herders, house servants, and managers and come themselves in answer to McKinney's plea for help. Park trucks were hitting every village and settlement nearby, rounding up any and all who would help—and there were many who did. Vera Batey was going to set up a first-aid center, and the Unified African Church was establishing a kitchen for the fire fighters.

When the scrappy little Scot jumped out of his Toyota, he had greeted David with "Give up? Hell no, I didn't give up. I went home to take a nap, that's all."

After giving orders to spread out the lines along the road to Dakagudiu Gate and grade and back-burn into the approaching front, McKinney had turned and bellowed at the flames three kilometers away, "Hear that? I'll not give up. By God, I'll stop you, even if I have to grade the whole damn park to do it."

He'd turned back to David, who was standing nearby, and added with a grin, "Don't you have some animals to count?" and then he'd marched off to direct the lumbering graders.

David had left then, knowing it would be all right. McKinney would stop it; no matter how often he had to fall back, eventually he'd halt it, even if, as he said, he had to grade the whole damn park.

David stood up, stretched, and threw his cigarette butt into the darkness. He had to go to the lodge to give out the last assignments to finish the count the following morning. He had to see Shepherd. He needed his advice concerning Maimbo.

The huge dark Taita Game Warden came back into his thoughts. What was he doing now? Did he suspect they were getting close to him? David remembered his decision not to involve Maimbo in the count, or to tell him about the anti-poaching campaign. But Maimbo knew some of it, and would guess the rest. He'd suspect his motives for excluding him.

He'd had a premonition the night before—about its coming

429

down to a race for time. They had to get to the ivory or Maimbo would escape. Did he know it? Did they have the time Kiboko needed?

He drew a deep breath. It looked doubtful. Maimbo had a head start.

WHEN SALIM LEFT HIS office behind the reception area, he saw David entering the lobby to greet Warden Davis of Mountain Parks. As the two men stood talking, Salim took the opportunity to study his friend.

The conversation was serious; David was frowning, his expression solemn as he shook his head negatively. Warden Davis was earnestly describing something as David listened intently. A disjointed word or two was audible: "Too damn few," and "Finish tomorrow."

They were discussing the count, and Salim knew it wasn't going well. His short conversations with various pilots and observers the previous evening had indicated a general disappointment in the numbers of animals recorded.

If that weren't enough, the hotel buzzed with information and exaggerations regarding the downed plane and the confrontation with the Somali. Each time the story was told, the number of deaths climbed higher. The facts were bad enough; they didn't need embellishing. Add to that, one fire across the firebreaks and moving north. It was incredible, and as Salim watched Karanja and Davis, he remembered his doubts that afternoon about David. Was it possible that Karanja could have anything to do with the poaching in Aruba?

Studying him closely, he saw the troubled expression on Karanja's face; the harassed look of tension. The eyes that couldn't smile even when he forced his mouth to respond to a joke from the irrepressible Davis. Karanja cared, and his concern had drawn lines into his face which Salim hadn't noticed before.

No, Salim decided. It couldn't be David. He'd been right when he'd eliminated him from the list of possibilities. It had to be Maimbo.

Just as he started to walk toward them, Davis and Karanja separated, and as Davis headed for the bar, Karanja turned toward the stairway leading to the next floor. Catching up to him, Salim dropped his arm across his shoulders and said, "I think we'd better have a talk. Let's go up to my apartment and have a Scotch while we discuss it."

David grinned wryly and replied, "Don't tell me—it's the baboons again."

"No," said Salim. "Actually, I have some information that might be of some interest to you about Jombo Maimbo."

AFTER BRINGING SENIOR WARDEN John Shepherd up to date on the developments on the fire and the results obtained from Agaran's interrogation of the two poachers, David turned the conversation to Maimbo. He related the results of the C.I.D. investigation of the Gate Ranger, and how the trail had led to Mnyambo and his brother, the Game Warden. When he finished adding Salim's information, he asked, "What do you think of it? Is it Maimbo?"

John Shepherd sighed heavily and got up from the foot of the bed to fix himself another gin and tonic. With a fresh drink in his hand, he nodded dourly. "It's Maimbo, all right. It's not the first time he's been suspected of something—but if you can prove it?" He let the question hang.

"What do you think our chances are?"

"Not very good," replied Shepherd glumly. "You've got to have an airtight case to fire a Government employee. If you can't get one, all you can do is pass your headache on to someone else by transferring him to another post. That's how this area acquired Maimbo—because we couldn't prove his involvement in the trophy trade in the Eastern Province. We've got a few dozen problem employees bouncing from park to park like rubber balls. Eventually they're dumped at one of the northern outposts."

He took another sip of his drink and added, "My God, that must be a scene. Every drunk, moron, and weirdie in the Ministry, packed nose to tail in the desert, a million miles from nowhere." He chuckled. "At least they have each other's company; and most important, they're out of our hair."

He became serious again. "No, Maimbo's a smart man. He's already sent his hunters to Mombasa. Knowing him, the ivory is gone as well. Without it, you'll get nowhere. The most we'll be able to do is put pressure on Department Headquarters to get him transferred somewhere else. Preferably to where there's no game left to poach."

"If we can get hold of one or more of these hired hunters, we might be able to build a case," suggested David.

Shepherd shook his head. "Talking too much in a bar is one thing, testifying in court another. Besides, Maimbo's a respected warden, until proved otherwise. It'll be his word against that of a poacher, a man who probably has a record. How far are you going to get with that?"

David stood up and walked to the window. When he spoke, his

voice was tightly controlled. "I can't accept the possibility that he'll get away with it." He turned to face the Senior Warden. "No, I won't let it happen. From what I'm learning in bits and pieces, Maimbo's been taking tons"—he repeated: "tons of ivory out of this park. My park"—his voice was harsh: "and he won't get away with it. I can't let him do it.

"Damn him," he exploded. "How dare he do this to the rest of us?"

Shepherd got up and crossed the room. Putting his hand on David's shoulder, he murmured, "I know; I know what you're feeling."

It wasn't fair, Shepherd thought. In the past, all the wardens had been *Wazungu*, of white European-settler stock. Independence had brought young hopeful African assistant wardens into wildlife schools like Mweka, and in time they became wardens. Perhaps for a few, in too short a time. They hadn't the years and maturity. Some weren't quite sure of themselves, and the rumors spread—"They aren't as good, they don't care as much, they're easily corrupted. The parks are going to hell."

Shepherd looked at the man who stood beside him. He was young enough to be his son. And he was one of the finest Park Wardens and wildlife conservationists that Shepherd knew. Black or white, European or *Mwananchi*—he was good. And just one, like Maimbo, brought down all that David and those like him accomplished.

Shepherd sighed. "I'll do all I can to help. For as long as I can."

David turned to face him. "What do you mean, 'for as long as you can'?" His expression was puzzled.

"I meant to tell you before, but the game count got in the way." He smiled ruefully, withdrew his hand from David's shoulder, and added, "I'm being retired."

That too wasn't really fair, he added to himself. The process had started years ago; jobs were being Kenyanized—positions held by European expatriates were now being filled by Kenyans. In the recent past, the phrase had changed to "Africanized," and many white Kenyan citizens in various positions were being replaced or kicked upstairs by Africans, particularly in the highly visible government jobs. On the one hand, Shepherd rationalized, why not? It was their country. But on the other, he said to himself, it's my country too.

Perhaps for him it didn't matter. He was fifty-five, and the Government had made that the mandatory age for retirement. The old must make way for the young—it was the same everywhere. But was it too soon? Would it help David and those like him to know that an experienced and older Senior Warden was at hand if needed? Irrespective of his color? He thought it would. But perhaps that was only conceit; no one likes to feel unneeded, as if he had nothing left to offer. The earlier question returned to bother him—but would it be better if he could stay for a little while? Was it perhaps just a little bit too soon? He was afraid it was.

Looking up at David, he saw the perceptive look in his eyes.

"No," Shepherd denied with a wry smile. "It's just time, David, that's all. I'm over fifty-five."

"And McKinney?" David shot back.

Shepherd tossed off the remains of his drink and sighed heavily. "The first of the year."

David turned away swearing.

"They're lining up replacements now," Shepherd said conciliatorily.

With his back to Shepherd, David asked sarcastically, "When did they graduate? This year or last?"

Before Shepherd could reply, David turned to face him. "Where's McKinney?"

Without waiting for an answer, he answered himself: "He's on the fire lines. He's been there for days, with about four hours' sleep. Am I going to find that kind of dedication in a brand-new Assistant, just out of school and newly posted to a park he doesn't know or care about yet? No, I won't. He'll work from seven forty-five A.M. to four in the afternoon, with a two-hour lunch break, and if I need more—he'll tell me to see his union."

He snorted in disgust. "I've had lorries lost in the Lalaga Lana River when the rains broke in the highlands and sent a wall of water down unexpectedly. McKinney fished them out and got them on the road within days. Who's going to do that now?" He glanced at Shepherd.

"You've mentioned before," reminded the Senior Warden, "that your head mechanic is good."

"Very good," replied David evenly, "but he can't read or write."

John Shepherd looked away. There was nothing he could say.

Staring hard at the Senior Warden, David declared, "McKinney cannot be replaced"—and then he emphasized: "not by someone of equal value." He nodded his head slowly and deliberately, his eyes accusing. "And neither can you. Not yet."

He turned and went to the dresser, where he poured himself a stiff tot of Scotch.

The Senior Warden stared hard at the floor, studying the texture of the green pile carpet. What could he say? It was too close to the

433

truth. But there were extenuating circumstances that had to be acknowledged. Things were never as simple and uncomplicated as people would like them to appear.

"It takes time, David," Shepherd replied. "You can't take a people and start educating them in primary school, then secondary school, and on through university, and expect to have experienced professionals, all within fifteen years." He ran his freckled fingers through his gray hair, and added apologetically, "We should have given you more education and preparation before, when we could have, but we didn't."

David nodded in agreement and sat on the foot of the other bed to face him.

"I agree with you," David said. His voice was hard; the emotion and heat had cooled to rigid implacability. "But I'm sick of hearing about time."

The Senior Warden looked up to see David assessing him intently. "I've run out of time, Warden," David said flatly. "I've got an eighty-five-hundred-square-mile park, and all five million acres of it is being either burned up or poached out. And I don't want to hear any damned political platitudes from you," he warned, "or from Nairobi." His words came like bullets, each phrase delivered and bitten off in a sharp report. "I can't be in the air on a game count; in Headquarters supervising a big anti-poaching campaign; on the fire lines directing the back-burning; and in Nairobi demanding what I need and have to have out here."

His black eyes flashed angrily. "I have Agaran and Balaga. They're both good. The Field Force and Headquarters office administration are all right. But I need a good Assistant Warden—Works, and a Senior Warden to back me up in Nairobi. I need you and I need McKinney."

He leaned forward, his expression direct. Extending his hand, he tapped the Senior Warden's knee with his forefinger. "You're staying. You and McKinney owe it to me. And so does Nairobi. I won't take anything less."

He sat back and added inflexibly, "My park comes first. If I don't fight for it, no one will. And I'll fight you and the pencil sharpeners in the Ministry, and I'll get what I want. I didn't create the problems in this park, and I'll not be left to cope with them by myself, because one man can't do it all."

Enumerating on his fingers, he summarized: "When I'm through the drought, and the vegetation has begun to regenerate itself. When I've cleaned up the poaching in the park, and have enough forces left me to protect the survivors in the future so they can breed and restock the populations. And when the Department is rid of Maimbo and he's no longer a threat to me, or to anyone else"—he emphasized dispassionately: "even if we have to shoot the son-of-a-bitch in a thicket.

"Then"—he tapped the Senior Warden's knee again, his jaw tense with determination—"then, sir, you may go."

He stood up and replaced his empty glass on the dresser; the silence in the room was loud. Crossing the room, he opened the door and left without a word.

The Senior Warden continued to sit at the foot of the bed, his eyes on the small indentation on his knee where the material was still puckered from the younger man's finger. He nodded to himself and then chuckled. He's going to be all right, he decided. Just a few months and he won't notice my going at all. He's demanding the necessary pairs of hands to carry their share of the load, but he doesn't need anyone at all. Not even me.

It's not so bad, he realized suddenly, not being needed any longer. Not when you can know you helped to train them as good as David.

Replacing his glass beside David's, he pushed his fingers through his still-thick iron-gray hair and went down to dinner, smiling.

HALIMA WAS PUTTING away the evening's dishes when she heard the short, sharp raps at the front door. Draping the damp dish towel over the still-warm oven door to dry, she hurried through the sitting room and opened the door to find David standing there. Even as her breath caught in her throat with the realization that he'd come as she'd so hoped, she saw how the past twenty-four hours had worn him. His face was tightly drawn, his expression haggard, and the tension in his body was palpable.

His voice, when it came, was hoarse: "I thought perhaps you'd make me a cup of coffee if I asked." The self-consciousness of his smile wounded her with its need to explain his presence here.

"Come in," she said softly, hoping her voice was even as she opened the door wide. "I was just about to make some."

Leaning back in what had become his chair, he asked himself belatedly why he'd come. He'd left the Senior Warden to give out the pilot reassignments, then left the lodge for home, but instead of turning at the cutoff to his house, he'd driven straight here. He didn't know why; it seemed the necessary thing to do.

As he watched her making a pot of coffee through the kitchen doorway, he remembered the evening he'd spent here on Wednesday. It was only three nights ago, but it seemed years. He remembered how hard it had been to leave that evening; remembered the taste and the feel of her mouth under his, her softness pressed against him. But he'd gone because he'd felt it was too soon in their relationship for him to stay. Still, the remembering answered his question now, and he knew he needed to be with her.

"Two sugar and just a little milk. Have I got it right?" she asked as she set the coffee cup on the table beside him.

He nodded and drew the footstool close to his chair so that she would sit beside him.

Accepting the invitation, she sat down and curled up her legs beneath her, then rested her chin on his knee to look up into his face. The sense of familiarity that was growing between them brought a catch to his throat. Resting his hand on her head and then drawing his fingers down over her temple, around her ear, and along her chin, he thought of how comfortable she was to be with. It was rare in a beautiful woman.

"Would you like to tell me about it?" she suggested hesitantly, afraid of pressing him.

"About what?" he asked.

"About whatever it is that's worrying you."

He saw that her eyes were warm and knowing, with whatever it was that such women knew by instinct.

He told her, falteringly at first, then in a rush, of every problem weighing on his mind: the fire, the numbers of carcasses, the poachers; but mostly he spoke of the imminent retirement of McKinney and Shepherd, of Maimbo's corruption, of the occasional incompetence of his subordinates, and of what seemed at times the insensitivity of Department administrators.

As she listened, she felt she knew something she'd only barely sensed the first time they'd talked at the lodge, and that was an empathetic feeling of affinity between them. As she felt adrift between the past and the present, he was torn between two cultures: the one he was born to, and the one he was raised in. As she wondered about herself, he tried to reconcile his own impatience with the knowledge that these people were his and that he wanted them to be what they could not yet be. Both of them were in transit between the past and the future, what had been and what would be, the tribal tradition and the Westernized cultures. He was Africa's future, and she was—what? She smiled to herself as the answer became obvious: his woman, of course—and Africa's future too.

When he was finished, he glanced up to see her studying him thoughtfully; her lips curved up in sympathetic understanding. Leaning forward as her face came up to meet his, he kissed her gently and lingeringly. Drawing her up to sit on his lap, he held her in his arms and murmured against her hair, "Tell me. Say something that will help."

She kissed his forehead and after a moment said, "I'm afraid the only thing I can say is the one thing you don't want to hear."

He glanced up at her, a question in his eyes. "Tell me anyway," he said.

"*We* are your people and we need just a little more time. You mustn't be impatient with us, David."

As he shook his head, she laid her hand on his cheek and held his face to look into his eyes. His expression was one of denial. Then reflection. He looked in, and saw the truth in her judgment of him. He accepted it. The hurt was reflected in his eyes as he murmured, "I know it's too soon, but I need you. I need you now."

She kissed his forehead, and as her arms tightened about him, she said softly, "I know you do." She smiled and ran her fingers over his hair. "And it's never too soon to need."

He looked up, found her mouth again, and as his hands slipped down over her body, he murmured, "Maybe not."

VIII · SUNDAY

CHAPTER TWENTY-SIX

Morning

I<small>T WAS NIGHT WHEN HE WOKE.</small> He rose, crossed to the small window and looked out on the early morning. It was still dark, the birds still slept, but it was time to go.

Slipping his feet into his sandals and gathering up his waiting bow and arrows, he crossed the room and opened the door. Shutting it quietly, he moved with speed through the dark garden between the fruit trees and vegetables, his keen eyes picking the way between the light and dark shades of black. There was good reason for his care. He knew the young warden slept lightly near dawn; the kitchen lights that snapped on soon after a nearby lion's roar had taught him that long ago.

Opening the garden gate, he approached the carport, to find that the Land-Rover was missing. He stopped in perplexity. Where was he? Then he smiled and nodded, and moved on.

He covered the fifteen kilometers to the warehouse in an hour and a half, avoiding the roads and cutting through the bush. When he arrived, he saw that it was still dark and shuttered, with the heavy padlocks still intact. Checking the eastern horizon, he knew it was near dawn now. He hadn't long to wait.

Soon the twin beams of headlamps appeared below on the narrow dirt track that led up from town. He decided it was a car, not a lorry, and slipped into the bushes near the gate. He crouched down and waited until the car approached and stopped and Maimbo got out to open the gate. After driving through, stopping, and closing the gate, Maimbo drove to the warehouse and turned off the motor.

Heekuta carefully unwrapped the dik-dik skin from the waiting arrow and stuffed it under his worn shirt. But just as he stood to approach the warehouse, now bright with the paraffin lamps lit by Maimbo, he saw another pair of lights flare on the road below. He stiffened. Could it be the boy Maimbo spoke of with the lorry?

He studied the flashing arcs of the headlamps as they nodded and dipped slowly. Yes, a lorry. He moved close to the gate and crouched low in the underbrush. The sky was beginning to lighten in the east.

MWAKIU YAWNED. He wiped the sleep from his eyes and yawned again as he gripped the bucking steering wheel. Grumbling to himself, he wondered why it was Maimbo wanted him to leave so early for Mombasa.

Usually he arrived at the warehouse before lunch, loaded, and after a cup of *chai* with his other uncle, Mnyambo, would be on his way to the coast by noon or so; but yesterday he'd been told to be loaded by dawn and to leave immediately. It seemed unnecessary.

The lorry suddenly lurched sideways on the washed-out road; the steering wheel nearly jerked itself out of his hands. He scowled in irritation. The aged Bedford wheezed up the last incline, and Mwakiu saw the brightly lit warehouse ahead, with Maimbo's cream-colored car parked beside it in the light from the window. He was surprised. Whatever the reason for his early departure, it must be important; otherwise Maimbo would not have bothered to come himself.

Pulling up before the gate, he set the hand brake and jumped out.

AS THE YOUNG MAN reached for the loop of wire that held the gate closed, Heekuta slowly drew himself up from his crouch, his bow half drawn, the arrow in place; and as the boy saw him, Heekuta expelled his withheld breath in a drawn-out and clearly audible hiss.

The *kijana* stopped, his hand arrested in midair. His eyes grew wide in astonishment and then fear.

"*Hapana,*" the boy breathed, and took a step backward, and then another. Heekuta moved forward, his expression menacing. With a sudden grunt he drew the bowstring back. The boy gasped, stumbled, fell, then scrambled up to run in terror for town. He didn't look back.

Heekuta smiled. There were few men who would face the big bow, and no boys. Slipping between the sagging wires of the fence, he crossed to the truck, turned the key, and cut off the engine.

After throwing the key ring deep into a nearby thicket, he turned and moved into the bush to slip around the warehouse and approach it from the back.

MAIMBO STOOD AT THE window frowning. He'd heard the approaching lorry soon after his arrival as he was counting the stacked and waiting sacks of charcoal, and he'd expected the boy to walk in at any moment. Then he heard the motor cut, and he'd come to look out to find what was going on, but it was too dim to see anything. He could just make out the lorry, parked some hundred meters away. The lights were out, and he couldn't see Mwakiu. What was going on? Had the bloody thing broken down again? It looked that way. He'd have to go and help the boy or he'd never get away this morning.

Swearing under his breath, he glanced around for one of the large hand-held lights used for hunting at night; as usual, Mnyambo had not put things where they were supposed to be. Noticing the lumpy pile of bags in the corner, he strode over and prodded it with his foot. Something solid was under there. Snatching away the jute sacks on top, he uncovered the bottom sack, from under which protruded the end of a tusk. Angrily he ripped the last jute bag away, exposing the two biggest tusks from the last hunt. He exploded: "The stupid fool!"

Remembering the boy could walk in any minute, he hurriedly rammed the tusks into the sack he held. As he did so he sensed, rather than heard, a presence behind him.

He turned, a question on his lips. "What's the matter with the . . ." The words died. It wasn't Mwakiu. The early-morning wind gusted through the open window and set the paraffin lamps to flare, then flicker over the figure of the man who stood in the doorway with his feet widely spaced and his bow and arrow poised.

Maimbo stood slowly and turned to face the man, questions crowding into his mind. What is going on here? Who is this? Where's Mwakiu?

The man stepped closer and made an abrupt sweeping motion with the bow and arrow, warning him back and away from the corner. Maimbo stepped back reluctantly, and as the man moved forward into the glare of the lamps, Maimbo felt his memory prod him. He knew that face; he'd seen this old man somewhere. The dark, leathery features with their ritual scars; the black, tightly curled hair sprinkled with white; the wood-plugged earlobes were familiar. But from where?

"What do you want?" he demanded in Swahili.

443

The old man said nothing. He merely smiled and motioned again for Maimbo to move back. Maimbo studied the now brightly illuminated bow and arrow. It was one of the Waliangulu big bows—he hadn't seen one in years; and the foreshaft below the barbed arrowhead appeared liberally covered with tarlike black poison that gleamed slick and shiny in the lamplight.

A flicker of fear chilled his spine as beads of sweat broke out on his forehead. He stepped back quickly until his foot hit something solid. Never taking his eyes off the arrow tip, he reached backward and felt the bulk of the tightly packed sack of charcoal behind him, and on top, one of the heavy metal files used to section the ivory. For once he blessed his brother's lazy stupidity. As he closed his large hand, now damp with the perspiration of fear, over the file, he demanded loudly, "Who are you? What do you want here?"

The *mzee* said nothing as he glided forward to stand facing Maimbo, the sack containing the ivory just behind him by his right foot. The silence was eerie. Then it hit Maimbo. The silence. The mute, the *bubu*. It was the old man who worked for Karanja. Anger flooded over him. What was this insanity? Then he stopped and calculated quickly. Karanja must know something which the old man had overheard. Otherwise how would the *mzee* know of the ivory? Karanja had suspected after all, and must soon be ready to move in on him, but the old man had got here first to get a little something for himself. The old fool must have stolen the bow and arrow from the Headquarters armory to frighten him with, since the Waliangulu were all gone.

He had to get rid of him; had to get the ivory out of here. It never occurred to him to wonder why the old man had not taken Karanja's more accessible rifle from his house.

Heekuta had seen the recognition flash briefly in Maimbo's face before the huge, dark Taita froze his features into their normally guarded expression. He'd been recognized, and Heekuta felt a twinge of sadness; he'd almost hoped he wouldn't have to run. He'd seen something else, too: when Maimbo realized who he was, his fear had left him.

Heekuta gave Maimbo the opportunity he waited for. As he held the bow securely in his left hand with his forefinger cocked tightly over the arrow shaft, he withdrew his right hand and slowly reached back toward the sack as he crouched, perfectly poised and balanced on his widely spaced feet, and he watched Maimbo for the first flicker of tensing muscles that presaged action. Men were no different from the animals he'd hunted all his life.

Maimbo saw the hand move away from the lightly drawn bow;

six inches away, a foot. Less than eight meters—maybe twenty-five feet—lay between them. The hand touched the sack; it was two feet from the bow. As Maimbo jerked his hand back to fling the heavy file at the *mzee*'s head, the old man's fingertips were already back at the bowstring; his body jerked to the right when the file left the Game Warden's hand, and as it sailed past his head, he rose, the arrow pointing to the roof; his arms came down in a fluid motion, the left arm thrust rigidly forward, the right jerking back, its thin muscles bulging.

Maimbo had never seen anything move so quickly in his life; before the file left his hand, he knew he was too late. The Waliangulu were not all gone. The bowstring thrummed; the arrow moved too quickly for conscious sight. The blow knocked him backward, off his feet, into the piled sacks of charcoal behind. The pain was instant and horrible.

Heekuta knelt quickly and grasped the open end of the sack containing the tusks of the big bull; he lashed it closed with the strip of dik-dik skin, swung it over his shoulder, and scooped up his bow. At the doorway, he glanced at Maimbo.

The Game Warden was staring stupidly with bulging eyes at the hole high on the left side of his abdomen, just below the ribs, from which streamed a persistent trickle of blood. Heekuta smiled; he always took his prey on the left side, with the difficult spleen shot, at twenty to twenty-five feet.

Ducking through the wire fence, he looked down the deeply rutted road that led to town. Several vehicles were winding slowly up the hill in the distance; the flashing blue lights on their roofs told him where the boy had run to and that now the police were on their way. Slipping off his sandals and breaking a thin branch from a small tree, he began to back into and through the thick bush, obliterating his trail as he went.

Maimbo didn't see him go. His shaking hands came up to pluck at the hole in his stomach. He had to get it out. It was poisoned; it was going to kill him. His trembling fingertips found the end of the wooden foreshaft, but he couldn't grasp it. It was too deep. As he breathed in deep, shuddering gasps, he could feel the barbed head scraping the ribs in his back. Sweat poured off him in spite of the cool breeze through the open doorway. His mouth was dry; a sickening nausea was joined by a sudden pain in his chest. The poison was already at work.

He began to scream. His hand stretched out to claw at a bulging sack of charcoal as he tried to drag himself to his feet. A hospital; he had to get to the hospital. His legs trembled and shook; his body quivered violently. He fell sideways, knocking over a sack, which burst open, spewing its charcoal and ivory over his body.

As he reached a heavily traveled footpath, Heekuta looked up to see a boy driving a herd of goats, and he was relieved. The police were poor trackers at best, but with his tracks overrun with those of a herd of goats, they'd never find his trail. He stopped and looked back toward the road. The police were nearly at the gate. The screams from the warehouse stopped, and Heekuta nodded speculatively. Two hours for a bull elephant, seconds for an antelope, minutes for a man.

Heekuta smiled broadly in the knowledge that now he didn't have to run after all. As he turned back onto the well-beaten footpath, the sun came up red between the horizon and the thick, sullen overcast, to wash the land from the predawn gray to pink.

SENIOR WARDEN JOHN SHEPHERD'S THICK, blunt fingers painstakingly tapped out digits on the pocket calculator as he added up the live sightings on each of the blocks he'd flown during the past two days. The tabulation of the carcasses reported and their condition would be evaluated by the Research Center during the following week, prior to the scheduled anti-poaching campaign. Today, only one question wanted an immediate answer, and that was: How many elephants and rhinos remained alive?

Passing the calculator back to Jeff Forbes, so that he might continue adding up the data-sheet information now coming in from the returning pilots who'd taken Forbes's blocks, John Shepherd studied the total number of recorded sightings of each of his three observers and himself. The total figures looked small—much less than he would have expected; but then, his assigned area was south and east of the park. No one had expected much in that section. Still, he wasn't pleased. With any luck the other teams had better results.

David read his sightings on Block XVIII to Audrey, who pecked them out on an adding machine; then Philip Otieno read his. The total figures concurred. Comparing Audrey's figure with Dr. Patel's, they found they also agreed. The totals for the two sides of the plane were added, wondered at, worried over; and then they passed on expectantly to the next block.

Warden Davis ambled in and took a seat beside Jeff Forbes. The two of them rapidly added up the sightings Davis and his observers had just recorded out on the Sabaki Ranch. Their muted exchange added to the hum of conversation, interspersed with the click and grind of the adding machines.

Throwing down his pencil and rubbing his eyes, David sighed and glanced around. The conference room was crowded with pilots and observers intent on their calculations. One by one, the totals were reached, and people set aside their machines and glanced up to check on the progress of others.

Noticing that the room was dim, David got up and flipped on the overhead lights before crossing to the window. The heavy overcast hadn't lifted. In fact, it seemed worse, and the sun, which had come up like a red ball of fire earlier that morning, was invisible behind the banks of dingy gray clouds. Thinking of the sun's brief appearance recalled the fire to his mind.

McKinney's last radio communication at nine thirty had indicated that the morning wind was still up and the fire had almost reached the Dakagudiu Gate road. Studying the wind-whipped tree branches flailing the air outside, David saw that instead of blowing itself out as it often did, the wind was increasing. If it got much worse, the departing pilots would have a rough time taking off. He hesitated even to speculate on the effect it would have on McKinney's new firebreak along the road.

Turning back to the crowded conference room, he saw that all the pilots and observers had apparently finished their tabulations and were now watching him expectantly.

Smiling ruefully, he said, "Are we ready?"

The nodding assent of the group obtained, David turned to Audrey and said, "Will you add the totals with me, Audrey? To check my figures?" She nodded.

He sat down at the head of the conference table, pulled a small computer toward himself and called out, "Block One?"

A man with a shock of red hair slashed with gray stood up, and Warden James Owens of Marsabit answered, "Elephant—four hundred eighty-one. Rhino—four." He sat down again as David wrote the number on a tally sheet and punched out the correct keys on two small computers, while Audrey's adding machine clicked.

"Block Two?"

The Kamba Warden of Amboseli, Matthew Mbuvi, answered, "Elephant—one hundred eighty-nine. Rhino—two."

HALIMA ROLLED UP THE huge wall map of Kenya, and as she put away the materials she'd used for her lecture, she observed the group of sixteen- and seventeen-year-olds as they filed out the door on their way to the bus waiting outside to take them for a game drive.

They were fourth-form students from an expensive and private

447

Nairobi school, and undoubtedly one of the most ill-mannered groups with which she'd had to contend. Approximately half were *Wazungu*, the children of European or American professional people, who lived and worked in Kenya for a contracted period of time; the remaining half of the class was composed of the offspring of affluent Indian and African business and professional people and politicians.

The almost total lack of discipline in each individual, and therefore the group, had resulted in dissension and disorderly confrontations between her irritated Education Center staff and the students from the moment of their arrival. Once they became interested in an outing or discussion they were all right, if a bit boisterous, but it was ridiculous that young people their age had to be distracted as if they were teething infants. It was a peculiarity she'd often seen among the upper-middle classes, and was such an unfavorable comparison with the poorer African *shamba* children from the Harambee schools, who were models of quiet attention. She wondered why it was.

What caused this difference? She doubted if it was racial or cultural. All three races and all three cultures in this group were equally rude. But who taught whom? Was it perhaps the result of affluence? As if the acquisition of material possessions elevated some individuals above the heads of the less fortunate, and exempted them from polite behavior. She felt this might be the answer.

She smiled at herself. Her habit of asking questions and finding the answers had probably been the reason she'd become a teacher; that, and the desire to share her knowledge. This group would leave after lunch, and she would be largely forgotten tomorrow; but she would remember them, and wonder about them for days.

As she deposited her lecture notes in a cupboard, she heard the guttural whine of an approaching plane. The last of the planes sent out to cover the remaining three blocks was coming in; she heard the pilot cut the throttle preparatory to his runway approach, and realized that soon the final results of the count would be known.

She remembered last night, when she'd first awakened feeling strange because she was not alone. David had been lying quietly beside her, staring at the ceiling in the dark, and as soon as she'd realized he was awake, her earlier fear that he too might be disappointed in her returned to make her afraid. Sensing that she also was awake, he'd reached out to her, and just as she asked fearfully, "Was I . . . ?" he murmured, "Perfect," before his mouth closed over hers. "Absolutely perfect," he murmured against her lips. Then she'd known that he hadn't expected her to be anything other than what she was, and that she hadn't asked for too much at all.

"Then what is it?" she'd asked gently as she turned to him and felt his arms tighten around her body.

"Tomorrow," he'd said. "I'm thinking of tomorrow."

She'd known what to do then, and as her hand slipped down his chest and over his hard flat stomach, she'd whispered, "Not yet. Tomorrow isn't now." And again she'd made his tension fade away.

Now, as she watched the small plane begin its runway approach, she wanted to be with him, because as she'd known last night, she knew he needed her now, in a different way.

Leaving the lecture hall, she saw that the bus had left, and the *kombi* was gone as well; there was no transportation to Headquarters. It was just a kilometer and a half: certainly not too far to walk; but small groups of *wazee* buffalo and the occasional elephant often meandered between the islands of human population in the Education, Research, and Headquarters complexes. So she could stay and wait for the *kombi,* or she could walk and risk running into a grumpy bull elephant. Then she smiled and decided that she'd best get used to it. He would expect it of her. Slipping off her high-heeled shoes, she began the walk up the dusty road.

"BLOCK TWENTY-SIX?"

Forbes looked up from the scrap of paper he held in his hand. His face reflected his disappointment. He, like a few others in the crowded room, had been adding the block results, but he alone knew the totals of the last two blocks on the Sabaki. "Two hundred nine elephant, and two rhino," he said softly.

David carefully recorded the figures on the block tally, his pencil gripped tightly in unfeeling fingers, and then pecked out the additions on the calculators as Audrey totaled the elephants on the adding machine and added the rhinos on another slip of paper.

The room was unnaturally quiet; no one spoke, moved, coughed, or audibly breathed as David asked, "Block Twenty-seven?"

Forbes glanced up, and his eyes reflected his anguish and his apology: "Elephant—six. Rhino—zero." His voice was muted.

David chewed his underlip as he willed himself to ignore the sinking feeling in his chest, and the mechanical numbers as they flashed on the upper right-hand corner of the small computers, until he'd added the figures for the last block and the machine had computed the total.

Finally he could postpone knowing the worst no longer. He studied the bright red electric numbers before him and disbelieved for a fraction of a second—and then accepted that which he'd been afraid of.

449

"The total . . ." His voice was almost inaudible. He stopped, cleared his throat, and began again: "The total elephant population is recorded at eight thousand three hundred sixty-nine." He heard the sharp intake of someone's breath, a muttered oath. Somewhere a muffled voice said, "Oh, no." Another groaned and swore audibly.

The pitifully small number staggered his imagination. There were only eight thousand left, out of thirty-five thousand. Twenty-seven thousand elephants were gone.

"And rhino?" asked the Senior Warden despondently.

David glanced at the second computer, then looked in disbelief at Audrey. She nodded, and mouthed the number with tears in her eyes.

David looked to John Shepherd and said, "We have only thirty-eight left."

Senior Warden Shepherd closed his eyes, shook his head as if to deny the possibility, and muttered, "Good God."

The meeting broke up soon. There was nothing anyone could say. They'd all come to do a job, and they'd done it, but no one could count what wasn't there.

David tried to smile as he passed among them, offering his thanks for their help, and accepting their sympathy.

"If there's anything I can do," muttered a for-once solemn Warden Davis, "just call—I'll come."

And Warden Mbuvi of Amboseli: "I have a unit I can spare you. Of course, they're not quite as capable as your units from the north, but—"

"I'll take them," David said, forcing down a catch in his throat. "And thank you."

Gradually the room emptied, as he'd wanted it to since the totals had come in. He wanted, and needed, to be alone; to accept what had to be accepted and find the way to go on from there.

Feeling a presence at his arm, he turned to see John Shepherd standing beside him, looking ten years older than he'd looked the night before.

"I'll stay. As long as you feel you can use my help, I'll stay." He pushed his fingers through his gray hair in what was becoming a familiar gesture, and added with a good imitation of a smile, "We'll go up to Nairobi this week and let them know about your change in their plans."

David nodded. "Thank you, sir. It won't be for long."

"I know," replied Shepherd in understanding. "That's why I won't mind going in the end."

After the Senior Warden left, Jeff Forbes came to sit beside him.

"I'm sorry," he said. "I should have seen it earlier. Perhaps we could have done something if we'd known sooner."

"No," David said mechanically. "It wouldn't have helped. It was happening too quickly. By the time we saw we were in serious trouble, it was too late to make much difference in the outcome."

He sighed heavily and looked up to ask, "What's going to happen now? What can I expect to occur as a direct result of this big a drop in our elephant population?"

"Well," Forbes considered. "The bush will begin to regenerate. The small seedlings that were previously uprooted or trampled in the past will get a chance to take hold and grow rapidly. Some of your grassland will go, but not too much, because fire will help keep it down. In ten years you'll still have a combination of grass and bushland."

"And the elephant?" inquired David heavily.

"They'll come back, David," Forbes replied with a hopeful expresssion, the first of the day. "Given complete protection, they'll recover. When the rains come again and the vegetation regenerates, there will be more than enough forage and water for the survivors. If you can just protect what's left, they'll respond and step up their rate of reproduction. The age of puberty will occur sooner in the juveniles, and the interval between calves will shorten in the breeding females. You'll soon realize a five-percent increase in your herds each year. I'm sure we missed a few, and some have most likely left the fringe areas of the ecosystem. They'll come back when the rains do, and we'll find we have a population of perhaps ten thousand. That's not a bad start for a breeding-stock herd."

David sat and tried to curb his impatience. What had happened had happened quickly; the recovery, if it came, would take years. "What will that increase mean in numbers? How many will I have in five years? In ten?"

Forbes calculated rapidly. "In five years, you'll have around thirteen thousand. In ten, sixteen thousand elephant." He smiled ruefully. "I know it isn't anything like what we had two years ago, but it's something. It's a place to start all over again."

And how many chances, David wondered, will we have to start over again?

Over a thousand elephants had been taken each month for two years. The rest could be gone within six months, unless he could eliminate the poaching immediately.

"And the rhino?" he asked despondently.

Forbes shook his head sadly. After a moment in which he tried to think of something hopeful to say, he gave up and told David what he feared was the truth: "Perhaps for them, the only answer will ultimately be in zoological gardens. With so few left . . . and rhino horn at over three thousand shillings a kilo? No," he answered his speculation, "the park is too big to protect so few. If they're given total protection, then perhaps their numbers will stabilize; but we'll never know them in thousands again.

"I'm sorry," Forbes muttered. He stood slowly and adjusted his heavy cast in its sling. David glanced up and met his eyes.

"Well, hell, man, we can't just give up," Forbes muttered in a thick voice. David's calculating glance and raised eyebrows voiced his disagreement.

After Forbes had left, David continued to sit and stare at the huge map on the wall as he considered Jeff's parting words. Why not? he wondered. At what point does a man cease being conscientious, and begin being a fool?

His speculation was interrupted by the sound of heavy, unfamiliar footsteps in the corridor, and Joe Kiboko came in, a smile on his face. He carefully laid a newsprint-wrapped article on the table before him and answered the question in David's face by saying, "Open it. But be careful," he amended.

Gingerly unfolding the paper, David saw a poisoned arrowhead inside, smeared with bloodstains. "Where did you get this?" he asked in a puzzled tone.

"Out of Jombo Maimbo. He was murdered this morning at dawn in a warehouse chock-full of charcoal sacks and ivory." Kiboko grinned. "We got it all, and we've arrested both his nephew and his brother Mnyambo. I telephoned the coast earlier, and the C.I.D. in Mombasa has just confirmed that they've picked up six of his hunters." He chuckled. "That's one gang that's out of operation."

"Maimbo murdered!" David exclaimed. "What happened?"

"It seems the nephew arrived to pick up the charcoal to take to Mombasa and somebody popped out of the bush and threatened him with a bow and arrow. The boy was scared half to death, and he took off to get the police. I'm afraid that we don't have a good description of the man, since it was still pretty dark. When we arrived a half-hour later Maimbo was still alive, but just barely. Only his eyes moved; the rest of him just quivered all over. He died soon after." Kiboko shuddered. "What a way to die! I didn't like him, and I'd have done anything to put him in prison—forever, if I could. But just then I felt sorry for him."

After a few more words, the C.I.D. man left to pick up Mulolo. Mnyambo had implicated him. The Gate Ranger had several counts to answer for.

David studied the arrowhead, left behind for comparison with the park's specimens of confiscated weapons, and on impulse he took out his pocketknife. Scraping off the remains of the thick poison, he found the two spiral patterns which met to form a series of X's along the wooden foreshaft, and he nodded. When the X centered between two slash marks was revealed, he was sure.

He remembered the day, less than a week ago, when he'd last seen such an arrowhead, and recalled a thought he'd had about the reason behind the hunter's identification marks: that their purpose had been to provide proof of ownership of the animal slain; that hunters rarely appropriated another's kill, since the penalty, if you were caught, was high, and there were pleasanter ways to die.

He knew then that somehow Maimbo had taken one of the Waliangulu poacher's elephants, and he nodded silently at the appropriateness of his execution. He'd died by the rules he had lived by, and no man could ask for more justice than that.

A sudden gust of wind came in through the open window, to scatter papers everywhere and bring a fresh smell of something only half-remembered.

As he got up to cross the room to the window, the first clap of thunder hit, to reverberate like an explosion throughout the building and cause the lights in the conference room to flicker.

It was strangely still; the turbulent gusts of wind that had kept the tree branches thrashing just an hour ago were over. He heard a plane take off, and looking to the nearby airfield, he saw the black thunderheads moving in from the east beyond. The sky was a smudged gray, and thick banks of slate-colored clouds roiled and billowed westward, bringing the fertile smell of rain.

The low growl of the thunder began to rumble in the distance and grow in intensity, until it broke overhead in another deafening boom.

The first drops of rain fell in the red dust as the guttural grumbling of the rains grew louder, overlaid with a sharp, staccato crackling.

The lightning flicked and splashed in the distance as the pounding of the rain intensified. The outlines of the mountains and the distant horizon on the plains began to fade, and were finally obliterated as the rain began to pour down in torrents.

The lightning drew closer still, until suddenly it flashed to wash the world in a trembling rose light that quivered and died. The thunderclap accompanying it roared immediately and threatened to bring the building down. The lights went out, but he didn't notice; he didn't see.

His sight had turned inward to grasp at the thoughts that raced one another in his mind:

Only eight thousand remaining—twenty-seven thousand gone.

Given complete protection—they'll come back. . . .

Given time—people will learn, but . . .

"We'll never know them in thousands again. . . ."

There's no way we can win in the end.

He realized that his face was wet; the dying remnants of the earlier wind were blowing sheets of rain in through the window where he stood; but was it only the rain? He passed his hand over his eyes, wiping his face, and when he looked up, it was to see a woman materialize out of the mist-shrouded trees; and in bare muddied feet, carrying her shoes, she ran toward him laughing.

He caught her at the door, and remembered other words from what seemed a long time ago . . . "But we must none of us give up in despair." And when he found her mouth, he found the truth in those words. Now he knew he'd found the way to go on: Take one step at a time, and don't walk alone.

HISTORICAL AFTERWORD

THIS BOOK TOOK MORE THAN FIVE YEARS to research, write, edit, and produce, and while the story reflects as accurate a representation as possible of the situation in Kenya as it was in late 1977, some circumstances have changed, and so I feel that an epilogue of sorts is in order.

During the sixties the average wholesale prices of ivory and rhino horn remained relatively stable, but in the early to middle seventies they began to rise, and then soar. The rhino population in Kenya at the beginning of 1970 was estimated at between 16,000 and 20,000, and the average wholesale price for rhino horn was $23.55 per kilo; by 1979 the price had risen as high as $800 per kilo, and the rhino population had fallen to 1,500 to 2,000 animals. The number of elephants in Kenya declined from a reported 167,000 in the early seventies to a maximum of 65,000 in 1979 as the wholesale price of ivory rocketed from $7.25 to a high of $100 per kilo. Predation by man has been the major cause of the decline in the rhino and elephant populations and was inevitable under the circumstances when one considers the prices paid for trophies in a country where the annual per capita income was only $245.

What happened happened quickly, and while the Department of Wildlife and the various wildlife organizations responded as best they could, it wasn't enough, soon enough. It takes time, and money, to train and equip park rangers and anti-poaching units for the field; to educate wardens, ecologists, scientists, and management staff; and most important, to educate a population.

In March 1978, the late President Jomo Kenyatta banned the trophy trade in Kenya, and the tide began to turn. New anti-poaching units were fielded, and the international wildlife organizations assisted with equipment and funds for operating expenses of anti-poaching units, as well as continuing their support of wildlife studies, research, and education. The guardianship of Kenya's wildlife passed to President Daniel arap Moi. With his intensified support the situation has stabilized, and the poaching in Kenya is considered to be contained at the moment. The discovery of a rhino or elephant fatality due to poaching has become a rare occurrence today, but immense damage has already been done. The Kenya Rangeland Ecological Monitoring Unit (KREMU) reports that "The rhino population is at a dangerously low level with the groups so small and scattered that productivity will undoubtedly be subnormal. In many areas their numbers may be below the 'threshold for survival' . . . unless the sparse population is augmented by an introduction of animals from elsewhere." The World Wildlife Fund (WWF) and the International Union for Conservation of Nature and Natural Resources (IUCN) consider that "Though the elephant is not endangered . . . the declines have been dramatic in many countries. Poaching constitutes a major danger to many of the surviving populations. Unless it is constantly combated, poaching could lead to the extinction or near-extinction of elephants in a number of countries where they now exist."

Kenya has just managed to forestall the destruction of its herds of elephants, and efforts are being made to translocate the remaining rhinos from easily accessible areas into parks with maximum security where they can more readily find each other and breed. But the problem has not disappeared—it has merely moved elsewhere, and the slaughter continues at a tremendous rate in other countries. Tanzania is especially hard-hit at the moment, and Uganda's wildlife is devastated as a result of war. Poaching has spread from East Africa to Central and West Africa, and the reality of the loss of 90 percent of East Africa's rhinos within ten years is being repeated elsewhere.

However, poaching is not the only threat to Africa's elephants and rhinos. The destruction of habitat and the relentless encroachment of an exploding human population will ultimately deal the final blow to the wildlife and the parks that protect them. Whether or not they survive will depend largely on the rest of the world.

In 1948, Kenya's population was approximately 5 million. Thirty years later there were 15 million, with the highest population growth rate in the world. Should the growth rate rise to 4.5 percent as the population increases, Kenya's wildlife will be competing for existence with 60 million people, more than 250 per square mile, just thirty years from now. Kenya has few important natural resources besides her wildlife, and while the country's economy depends largely on agriculture, only 20 to 25 percent of the land can be successfully farmed or used for grazing livestock. Still, the human desire to own and occupy a piece of land, however marginal, is universal, and the national parks are already under heavy pressure from the landless.

In 1977 there were thirty-three national parks and reserves, comprising more than 6 percent of the land; today there are thirty-seven, which total 7.5 percent of the country, and five more parks are in the planning stages. The Government and its leaders are deeply committed to the preservation of the country's wildlife, but the benefits of these living resources must continue to be experienced in real terms by the people of Kenya.

The most important contribution to the country's cash income is the tourist trade that is attracted to the national parks and the animals they contain. These parks need the support of the rest of the world if they are to remain inviolate. Within a few years, if not months, there will be no wildlife in existence outside these sanctuaries. They are the last remaining vestiges of what was once the wild and beautiful "dark continent." Visit them, and they will survive. Pass them by, and they will soon pass away.

The international conservation organizations need help in order to help. They can and do provide scientific and technical experts to study and survey wildlife populations in order to produce action plans for their survival. They fund research and study projects; purchase equipment, ranging from planes and vehicles to two-way radios, for use in national parks; provide books, film projectors, and educational materials for Africa's children; and pay for the training of African wardens, ecologists, and rangers. They also make representations to the heads of state and governments of Africa seeking their personal commitment to wildlife conservation, and actively promote the strengthening of the Convention on International Trade in Endangered Species of Wild Fauna and Flora (CITES). Perhaps most important of all, as international organizations they can assist in coordinating the conservation efforts of neighboring African countries whose wildlife cross borders, thereby easing conflict and eliminating patchwork efforts. The support they receive, financial and otherwise, will eventually benefit Africa's remaining wildlife:

International Union for Conservation of Nature and Natural
  Resources (IUCN)
World Wildlife Fund (WWF)
African Wildlife Leadership Foundation (AWLF)
East African Wildlife Society
New York Zoological Society
Frankfurt Zoological Society
David Sheldrick Memorial Appeal
Elsa Wild Animal Trust

457

ACKNOWLEDGMENTS

THIS IS A WORK of fiction in that the principal locale and the characters are the creations of this author's imagination. There is no Aruba National Park in Kenya, or anywhere else that the author knows of, and the men and women who people the novel are invented, with no reference to actual persons, living or dead, intended. It is, however, faithful to the spirit of the handful of dedicated people who work in wildlife conservation, and the incidents and situations concerning the wildlife are true.

My own interest in wildlife conservation led to nearly three years of research in Kenya's national parks and reserves, and it would be impossible to overestimate the assistance given me by the Government of Kenya. When I first approached Mr. Yuda Komora, then Permanent Secretary, Ministry of Tourism and Wildlife, in February 1977 and requested permission to gather material for a novel dealing with the state of Africa's rapidly declining wildlife populations, and the efforts being made to save them, he responded with his wholehearted cooperation and assistance. I was made a research fellow with the Ministry's Department of Wildlife Conservation and Management, authorized to visit and observe all of Kenya's then thirty-three parks and reserves, and given access to the parks' Warden's Reports and records for the past thirty years. A small banda was placed at my disposal in Tsavo East National Park, and I spent the next two and a half years on patrol with the park's Field Units, flying recce and game counts with the wardens, working in the Headquarters, Research, and Education Centers, and writing.

Space does not permit the acknowledgment by name of all the Gate Rangers, Field Force personnel, herdsmen, and Headquarters staff who assisted me during this time. All those I met and worked with treated me with invariable courtesy and shared freely with me their years of experience, their stories, and their hopes and fears for the wildlife they care for. I am grateful to all of them, but to the following I am particularly indebted:

Mr. Yuda Komora, whose enthusiasm and sponsorship made this book not only a possibility, but a reality; Mr. F. A. Njiri, then Deputy Director of the Department of Wildlife Conservation and Management, who arranged my passes, permits, and authorizations and who enlisted the cooperation of the Department's senior wardens and wardens. Park

Wardens Gideon Leitipan, Bob Oguya, and Phil Snyder were most helpful, as were Assistant Wardens E. Gow and M. S. Mbithi; but I owe a special thank-you to Warden Ted Goss, now head of the Department's Anti-poaching Unit, for his suggestions and information; to Senior Warden Bill Woodley, for his knowledge of the Waliangulu and for his proofing those sections which relate to them; and to Warden Joseph Kioko and his wife, Christine, who gave me invaluable advice and criticism, besides reading many sections for error; and who, in the case of Christine, not only became a good friend but also volunteered to type the manuscript's entire 1,200-page first draft.

The Education Center's Wardens Rosalie Osborn and Wilson Mulli were most informative, as were their assistants, James Muthamia and John Ndome, and I greatly appreciate the hours they spent translating for me during my long conversations with the elder Waliangulu. Research Center Warden Joseph Ayieko was a special friend, and I am grateful for the months he and his research assistants, Felix Nderitu, Robert Chebei, and Oliver Mnyambo, spent with me in the field and at the Research Center—their instruction in all aspects of biology and the Research Project reports and studies they placed at my disposal were critical to the accuracy of the story. Willem van Wijngaarden, research geologist, introduced me to geology and generously explained to me his findings relating to the soils and vegetation he studied and their relationship to range management.

There were also many people in addition to Department personnel who were of great help, but none more so than Daphne Sheldrick, who graciously shared with me her years of experience and knowledge of the care and feeding of young animals, and who was kind enough to read and check for error those parts of the manuscript relating to orphans. Professor E. Gleeson, Dr. Susan Hird, and Dr. Susan Mbugua of the University of Nairobi, Faculty of Veterinary Medicine, gave me much valuable information regarding both the wildlife and the effects of *Acocanthera* poisoning, as did Mr. Elias Monk. Rita Mount, missionary nurse with the Independent Faith Mission, was most helpful, as was Dr. I. S. Batey, who kindly proofed all the medical information.

The National Museum was of great help, particularly the African Studies Department; Alexander Mackay, Curator of Herpetology; Issa Aggundey, Mammalogy and Osteology; Dr. G. R. Van Someren, Ornithology; and M. Clifton, Entomology. Mika Mukoko of the Wildlife Clubs of Kenya, Perez Olindo and the East African Wildlife Society, and the McMillan Memorial Library were all equally cooperative and helpful.

For the preparation of the Afterword, as well as for their help in the past, I would like to thank the following for their information and assistance: Sandra Price, Director of African Operations, African Wildlife Leadership Foundation; Dr. Kes Hillman, Chairman, IUCN/SSC African Rhino Group; Dr. Iain Douglas-Hamilton, Chairman, IUCN/SSC Specialist Group on African Elephant, and his wife, Oria; and Dr. J. W. Thorsell, Resource Planner, Ministry of Environment and Natural Resources, Wildlife Planning Unit.

Last, but by no means least, I owe a special debt of gratitude to Simon and Laila Trevor, who not only made me feel a part of their lovely family, but also provided me with a wealth of information from the years they've spent living in the bush, and from Simon's considerable experience as a former park warden and one of Africa's foremost wildlife cinematographers. His expertise was invaluable, and I thank him for taking time from his busy schedule to read several sections of the manuscript for error.

* * *

Many people consented to read those parts of the manuscript which dealt with their areas of specialization. I asked for their opinions and criticism and appreciated their suggestions. When in error I made corrections. To any that remain, the author pleads *Mea culpa*.

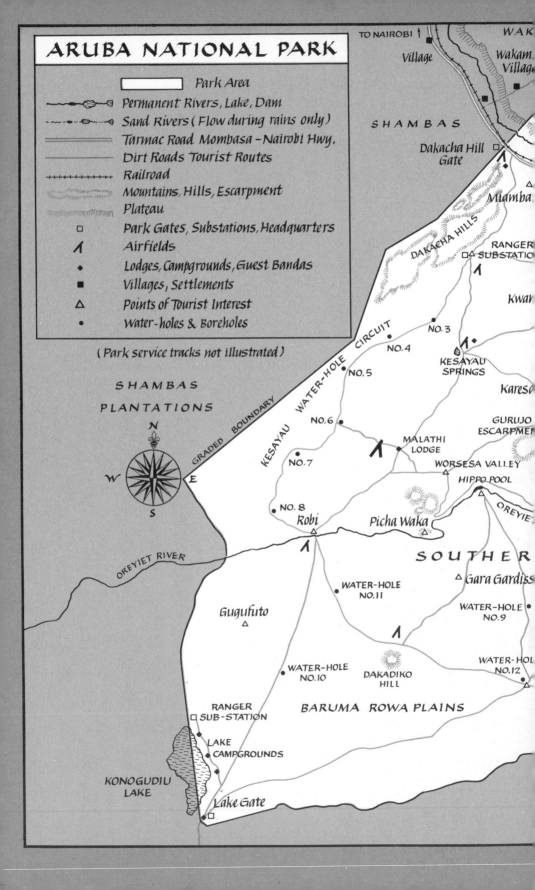